The Headsman
Or, The Abbaye Des Vignerons

by

James Fenimore Cooper

The Headsman
Or, The Abbaye Des Vignerons
by James Fenimore Cooper

Copyright © 2024

All Rights reserved.

No part of this publication may be reproduced, stored in a retrieval system, or transmitted in any form or by any means, electronic, mechanical, photocopying or Otherwise, without the written permission of the publisher.
The author/editor asserts the moral right to be identified as the author/editor of this work.

ISBN: 978-93-62764-68-3

Published by

DOUBLE 9 BOOKS
2/13-B, Ansari Road
Daryaganj, New Delhi – 110002
info@double9books.com
www.double9books.com
Tel. 011-40042856

This book is under public domain

ABOUT THE AUTHOR

James Fenimore Cooper was born on September 15, 1789, was an American author. He wrote authentic romantic stories portraying colonist and Native characters from the seventeenth to the nineteenth centuries. His most popular work is The Last of the Mohicans, often regarded as a masterpiece. James Fenimore Cooper was the 11th offspring of William Cooper and Elizabeth (Fenimore) Cooper. He wedded Susan Augusta de Lancey at Mamaroneck, Westchester Area, New York on January 1, 1811. The Coopers had seven children, but only five of them live to adulthood. The Last of the Mohicans (1826) was written in New York City where Cooper and his family resided. It became one of the most-read American books of the nineteenth century. The series includes the racial friendship of Natty Bumppo with the Delaware Indians. In 1826, Cooper moved his family to Europe to acquire more income from his books. He became friends with painters Samuel Morse and Gilbert du Motier and Marquis de Lafayette. In 1832, he entered the list as a political writer in a series of letters to Le National.

CONTENTS

Introduction 7
Chapter I 11
Chapter II 22
Chapter III 33
Chapter IV 44
Chapter V 57
Chapter VI 72
Chapter VII 87
Chapter VIII 100
Chapter IX 113
Chapter X 128
Chapter XI 139
Chapter XII 149
Chapter XIII 158
Chapter XIV 165
Chapter XV 175
Chapter XVI 186
Chapter XVII 196
Chapter XVIII 205
Chapter XIX 220
Chapter XX 233
Chapter XXI 243

Chapter XXII 253

Chapter XXIII 264

Chapter XXIV 274

Chapter XXV 285

Chapter XXVI 297

Chapter XXVII 307

Chapter XXVIII 318

Chapter XXIX 329

Chapter XXX 340

Chapter XXXI 352

Introduction

Early in October 1832, a travelling-carriage stopped on the summit of that long descent where the road pitches from the elevated plain of Moudon in Switzerland to the level of the lake of Geneva, immediately above the little city of Vévey. The postilion had dismounted to chain a wheel, and the halt enabled those he conducted to catch a glimpse of the lovely scenery of that remarkable view.

The travellers were an American family, which had long been wandering about Europe, and which was now destined it knew not whither, having just traversed a thousand miles of Germany in its devious course. Four years before, the same family had halted on the same spot, nearly on the same day of the month of October, and for precisely the same object. It was then journeying to Italy, and as its members hung over the view of the Leman, with its accessories of Chillon, Châtelard, Blonay, Meillerie, the peaks of Savoy, and the wild ranges of the Alps, they had felt regret that the fairy scene was so soon to pass away. The case was now different, and yielding to the charm of a nature so noble and yet so soft, within a few hours, the carriage was in remise, a house was taken, the baggage unpacked, and the household gods of the travellers were erected, for the twentieth time, in a strange land.

Our American (for the family had its head) was familiar with the ocean, and the sight of water awoke old and pleasant recollections. He was hardly established in Vévey as a housekeeper, before he sought a boat. Chance brought him to a certain Jean Descloux (we give the spelling at hazard,) with whom he soon struck up a bargain, and they launched forth in company upon the lake.

This casual meeting was the commencement of an agreeable and friendly intercourse. Jean Descloux, besides being a very good boatman, was a respectable philosopher in his way; possessing a tolerable stock of general information. His knowledge of America, in particular, might be deemed a little remarkable. He knew it was a continent, which lay west of his own quarter of the world; that it had a place in it called New Vévey; that all the whites who had gone there were not yet black, and that there were plausible hopes it might one day be civilized. Finding Jean so enlightened on a subject under which most of the eastern savans break down, the American thought it well enough to prick him closely on other matters. The worthy boatman turned out to be a man of singularly just discrimination. He was a reasonably-good judge of the weather; had divers marvels to relate concerning the doings of the lake; thought the city very wrong for not making a port in the great square; always maintained that the wine of St. Saphorin was very savory drinking for those who could get no better; laughed at the idea of their being sufficient cordage in the world to reach the bottom of the Genfer See; was of opinion that the trout was a better fish than the fêrà; spoke with singular moderation of his ancient masters, the bourgeoïsie of Berne, which, however, he always affirmed kept singularly bad roads In Vaud, while those around its own city were the best in Europe, and otherwise showed himself to be a discreet and observant man. In short, honest Jean Descloux was a fair sample of that homebred, upright common-sense which seems to form the instinct of the mass, and which it is greatly the fashion to deride in those circles in which mystification passes for profound thinking, bold assumption for evidence, a simper for wit, particular personal advantages for liberty, and in which it is deemed a mortal offence against good manners to hint that Adam and Eve were the common parents of mankind.

"Monsieur has chosen a good time to visit Vévey," observed Jean Descloux, one evening, that they were drifting in front of the town, the whole scenery resembling a fairy picture rather than a portion of this much-abused earth; "it blows sometimes at this end of the lake in a way to frighten the gulls out of it. We shall see no more of the steam-boat after the last of the month."

The American cast a glance at the mountain, drew upon his memory for sundry squalls and gales which he had seen himself, and thought the boatman's figure of speech less extravagant than it had at first seemed.

"If your lake craft were better constructed, they would make better weather," he quietly observed.

Monsieur Descloux had no wish to quarrel with a customer who employed him every evening, and who preferred floating with the current to being rowed with a crooked oar. He manifested his prudence, therefore, by making a reserved reply.

"No doubt, monsieur," he said, "that the people who live on the sea make better vessels, and know how to sail them more skilfully. We had a proof of that here at Vévey," (he pronounced the word like v-*vais*, agreeably to the sounds of the French vowels,) "last summer, which you might like to hear. An English gentleman--they say he was a captain in the marine--had a vessel built at Nice, and dragged over the mountains to our lake. He took a run across to Meillerie one fine morning, and no duck ever skimmed along lighter or swifter! He was not a man to take advice from a Swiss boatman, for he had crossed the line, and seen water spouts and whales! Well, he was on his way back in the dark, and it came on to blow here from off the mountains, and he stood on boldly towards our shore, heaving the lead as he drew near the land, as if he had been beating into Spithead in a fog,"--Jean chuckled at the idea of sounding in the Leman--"while he flew along like a bold mariner, as no doubt he was!"

"Landing, I suppose," said the American, "among the lumber in the great square?"

"Monsieur is mistaken. He broke his boat's nose against that wall; and the next day, a piece of her, big enough to make a thole-pin, was not to be found. He might as well have sounded the heavens!"

"The lake has a bottom, notwithstanding?"

"Your pardon, monsieur. The lake has no bottom. The sea may have a bottom, but we have no bottom here."

There was little use in disputing the point.

Monsieur Descloux then spoke of the revolutions he had seen. He remembered the time when Vaud was a province of Berne. His observations on this subject were rational, and were well seasoned with wholesome common sense. His doctrine was simply this. "If one man rule, he will rule for his own benefit, and that of his parasites; if a minority rule, we have many masters instead of one," (honest Jean had got hold here of a cant saying of the privileged, which he very ingeniously converted against themselves,) "all of whom must be fed and served; and if the majority rule, and ruled wrongfully, why the minimum of harm is done." He admitted, that the people might be deceived to their own injury, but then, he did not think it was quite as likely to happen, as that they should be oppressed when they were governed without any agency of their own. On these points, the American and the Vaudois were absolutely of the same mind.

From politics the transition to poetry was natural, for a common ingredient in both would seem to be fiction. On the subject of his mountains, Monsieur Descloux was a thorough Swiss. He expatiated on their grandeur, their storms, their height, and their glaciers, with eloquence. The worthy boatman had some such opinions of the superiority of his own country, as all are apt to form who have never seen any other. He dwelt on the glories of an Abbaye des Vignerons, too, with the gusto of a Vévaisan, and seemed to think it would be a high stroke of state policy, to get up a new, *fête* of this kind as speedily as possible. In short, the world and its interests were pretty generally discussed between these two philosophers during an intercourse that extended to a month.

Our American was not a man to let instruction of this nature easily escape him. He lay hours at a time on the seats of Jean Descloux's boat, looking up at the mountains, or watching some lazy sail on the lake, and speculating on the wisdom of which he was so accidentally made the repository. His view on one side was limited by the glacier of Mont Vélan, a near neighbor of the celebrated col of St. Bernard; and on the other, his eye could range to the smiling fields that surround Geneva. Within this setting is contained one of the most magnificent pictures that Nature ever drew, and he bethought him of the human actions, passions, and interests of which it might have been the scene. By a connexion that was natural enough to the situation, he imagined a fragment of life passed between these grand limits, and the manner in which men could listen to the never-wearied promptings of their impulses in the immediate presence of the majesty of the Creator. He bethought him of the analogies that exist between inanimate nature and our own wayward inequalities; of the fearful admixture of good and evil of which we are composed; of the manner in which the best betray their submission to the devils, and in which the worst have gleams of that eternal principle of right, by which they have been endowed by God; of those tempests which sometimes lie dormant in our systems, like the slumbering lake in the calm, but which excited, equal its fury when lashed by the winds; of the strength of prejudices; of the worthlessness and changeable character of the most cherished of our opinions, and of that strange, incomprehensible, and yet winning *mélange* of contradictions, of fallacies, of truths, and of wrongs, which make up the sum of our existence.

The following pages are the result of this dreaming. The reader is left to his own intelligence for the moral.

A respectable English writer observed:--"All pages of human life are worth reading; the wise instruct; the gay divert us; the imprudent teach us what to shun; the absurd cure the spleen."

Chapter I

Day glimmered and I went, a gentle breeze
Ruffling the Leman lake.

Rogers.

The year was in its fall, according to a poetical expression of our own, and the morning bright, as the fairest and swiftest bark that navigated the Leman lay at the quay of the ancient and historical town of Geneva, ready to depart for the country of Vaud. This vessel was called the Winkelried, in commemoration of Arnold of that name, who had so generously sacrificed life and hopes to the good of his country, and who deservedly ranks among the truest of those heroes of whom we have well-authenticated legends. She had been launched at the commencement of the summer, and still bore at the fore-top-mast-head a bunch of evergreens, profusely ornamented with knots and streamers of riband, the offerings of the patron's female friends, and the fancied gage of success. The use of steam, and the presence of unemployed seamen of various nations, in this idle season of the warlike, are slowly leading to innovations and improvements in the navigation of the lakes of Italy and Switzerland, it is true; but time, even at this hour, has done little towards changing the habits and opinions of those who ply on these inland waters for a subsistence. The Winkelried had the two low, diverging masts; the attenuated and picturesquely-poised latine yards; the light, triangular sails; the sweeping and projecting gangways; the receding and falling stern; the high and peaked prow, with, in general, the classical and quaint air of those vessels that are seen in the older paintings and engravings. A gilded ball glittered on the summit of each mast, for no canvass was set higher than the slender and well-balanced yards, and it was above one of these that the wilted bush, with its gay appendages, trembled and fluttered in a fresh western wind. The hull was worthy of so much goodly apparel, being spacious, commodious, and, according to the wants of the navigation, of approved mould. The freight, which was sufficiently obvious, much the greatest part being piled on the ample deck, consisted of what our own watermen would term an assorted cargo. It was, however, chiefly composed of those foreign luxuries, as they were then called, though use has now rendered them nearly indispensable to domestic economy, which were consumed, in singular moderation, by the more affluent of those who dwelt deeper among the mountains, and of the two principal products of the dairy; the latter being destined to a market in the less verdant countries of the south. To these must be added the personal effects of an unusual number of passengers, which were stowed on the top of the heavier part of the cargo, with an order and care that their value would scarcely seem to require. The arrangement, however, was necessary to the convenience and even to the security of the bark, having been made by the patron with a view to posting each individual by his particular wallet, in a manner to prevent confusion in the crowd, and to leave the crew space and opportunity to discharge the necessary duties of the navigation.

With a vessel stowed, sails ready to drop, the wind fair, and the day drawing on apace, the patron of the Winkelried, who was also her owner, felt a very natural wish to depart. But an unlooked-for obstacle had just presented itself at the water-gate, where the officer charged with the duty of looking into the characters of all who went and came was posted, and around whom some fifty representatives of half as many nations were now clustered in a clamorous throng, filling the air with a confusion of tongues that had some probable affinity to the noises which deranged the workmen of Babel. It appeared, by parts of sentences and broken remonstrances, equally addressed to the patron, whose name was Baptiste, and to the guardian of the Genevese laws, a rumor was rife among these truculent travellers, that Balthazar, the headsman, or executioner, of the powerful and aristocratical canton of Berne, was about to be smuggled into their company by the cupidity of the former, contrary, not only to what was due to the feelings and rights of men of more creditable callings, but, as it was vehemently and plausibly insisted, to the very safety of those who were about to trust their fortunes to the vicissitudes of the elements.

Chance and the ingenuity of Baptiste had collected, on this occasion, as party-colored and heterogeneous an assemblage of human passions, interests, dialects, wishes, and opinions, as any admirer of diversity of character could desire. There were several small traders, some returning from adventures in Germany and France, and some bound southward, with their scanty stock of wares; a few poor scholars, bent on a literary pilgrimage to Rome; an artist or two, better provided with enthusiasm than with either knowledge or taste, journeying with poetical longings towards skies and tints of Italy; a *troupe* of street jugglers, who had been turning their Neapolitan buffoonery to account among the duller and less sophisticated inhabitants of Swabia; divers lacqueys out of place; some six or eight capitalists who lived on their wits, and a nameless herd of that set which the French call bad "subjects;" a title that is just now, oddly enough, disputed between the dregs of society and a class that would fain become its exclusive leaders and lords.

These with some slight qualifications that it is not yet necessary to particularise, composed that essential requisite of all fair representation--the majority. Those who remained were of a different caste. Near the noisy crowd of tossing heads and brandished arms, in and around the gate, was a party containing the venerable and still fine figure of a man in the travelling dress of one of superior condition, and who did not need the testimony of the two or three liveried menials that stood near his person, to give an assurance of his belonging to the more fortunate of his fellow-creatures, as good and evil are usually estimated in calculating the chances of life. On his arm leaned a female, so young, and yet so lovely, as to cause regret in all who observed her fading color, the sweet but melancholy smile that occasionally lighted her mild and pleasing features, at some of the more marked exuberances of folly among the crowd, and a form which, notwithstanding her lessened bloom, was nearly perfect. If these symptoms of delicate health, did not prevent this fair girl from being amused at the volubility and arguments of the different orators, she oftener manifested apprehension at finding herself the companion of creatures so untrained, so violent, so exacting, and so grossly ignorant. A young man, wearing the roquelaure and other similar appendages of a Swiss in foreign military service, a character to excite neither observation nor comment in that age, stood at her elbow, answering the questions that from time to time were addressed to him by the others, in a manner to show he was an intimate acquaintance, though there were signs about his travelling equipage to prove he was not exactly of their ordinary society. Of all who were not immediately engaged in the boisterous discussion at the gate, this young soldier, who was commonly addressed by those near him as Monsieur Sigismund, was much the most interested in its progress. Though of herculean frame, and evidently of unusual physical force, he was singularly agitated. His cheek, which had not yet lost the freshness due to the mountain air, would, at times, become pale as that of the wilting flower near him; while at others, the blood rushed across his brow in a torrent that seemed to threaten a rupture of the starting vessels in which it so tumultuously flowed. Unless addressed, however, he said nothing; his distress gradually subsiding, until it was merely betrayed by the convulsive writhings of his fingers, which unconsciously grasped the hilt of his sword.

The uproar had now continued for some time: throats were getting sore, tongues clammy, voices hoarse, and words incoherent, when a sudden check was given to the useless clamor by an incident quite in unison with the disturbance itself. Two enormous dogs were in attendance hard by, apparently awaiting the movements of their respective masters, who were lost to view in the mass of heads and bodies that stopped the passage of the gate. One of these animals was covered with a short, thick coating of hair, whose prevailing color was a dingy yellow, but whose throat and legs, with most of the inferior parts of the body, were of a dull white. Nature, on the other hand, had given a dusky, brownish, shaggy dress to his rival, though his general hue was relieved by a few shades of a more decided black. As respects weight and force of body, the difference between the brutes was not very obvious, though perhaps it slightly inclined in favor of the former, who in length, if not in strength, of limb, however, had more manifestly the advantage.

It would much exceed the intelligence we have brought to this task to explain how far the instincts of the dogs sympathised in the savage passions of the human beings around them, or whether they were conscious that their masters had espoused opposite sides in the quarrel, and that it became them, as faithful esquires, to tilt together by way of supporting the honor of those they followed; but, after measuring each other for the usual period with the eye, they came violently together, body to body, in the manner of their species. The collision was fearful, and the struggle, being between two creatures of so great size and strength, of the fiercest kind. The roar resembled that of lions, effectually drowning the clamor of human voices. Every tongue was mute, and each head was turned in the direction of the combatants. The trembling girl recoiled with averted face, while the young man stepped eagerly forward to protect her, for the conflict was near the place they occupied; but powerful and active as was his frame, he hesitated about mingling in an affray so ferocious. At this critical moment, when it seemed that the furious brutes were on the point of tearing each other in pieces, the crowd was pushed violently open, and two men burst, side by side, out of the mass. One wore the black robes, the conical, Asiatic-looking, tufted cap, and the white belt of an Augustine monk, and the other had the attire of a man addicted to the seas, without, however, being so decidedly maritime as to leave his character a matter that was quite beyond dispute. The former was fair, ruddy, with an oval, happy face, of which internal peace and good-will to his fellows were the principal characteristics, while the latter had the swarthy hue, bold lineaments, and glittering eye, of an Italian.

"Uberto!" said the monk reproachfully, affecting the sort of offended manner that one would be apt to show to a more intelligent creature, willing, but at the same time afraid, to trust his person nearer to the furious conflict, "shame on thee, old Uberto! Hast forgotten thy schooling--hast no respect for thine own good name?"

On the other hand, the Italian did not stop to expostulate; but throwing himself with reckless hardihood on the dogs, by dint of kicks and blows, of which much the heaviest portion fell on the follower of the Augustine, he succeeded in separating the combatants.

"Ha, Nettuno!" he exclaimed, with the severity of one accustomed to exercise a stern and absolute authority, so soon as this daring exploit was achieved, and he had recovered a little of the breath lost in the violent exertion--"what dost mean? Canst find no better amusement than quarrelling with a dog of San Bernardo! Fie upon thee, foolish Nettuno! I am ashamed of thee, dog: thou, that hast discreetly navigated so many seas, to lose thy temper on a bit of fresh water!"

The dog, which was in truth no other than a noble animal of the well-known Newfoundland breed, hung his head, and made signs of contrition, by drawing nearer to his master with a tail that swept the ground, while his late adversary quietly seated himself with a species of monastic dignity, looking from the speaker to his foe, as if endeavoring to comprehend the rebuke which his powerful and gallant antagonist took so meekly.

"Father," said the Italian, "our dogs are both too useful, in their several ways, and both of too good character to be enemies. I know Ubarto of old, for the paths of St. Bernard and I are no strangers, and, if report does the animal no more than justice, he hath not been an idle cur among the snows."

"He hath been the instrument of saving seven Christians from death." answered the monk, beginning again to regard his mastiff with friendly looks, for at first there had been keen reproach and severe displeasure in his manner--"not to speak of the bodies that have been found by his activity, after the vital spark had fled."

"As for the latter, father, we can count little more in favor of the dog than a good intention. Valuing services on this scale, I might ere this have been the holy father himself, or at least a cardinal; but seven lives saved, for their owners to die quietly in their beds, and with opportunity to make their peace with heaven, is no bad recommendation for a dog. Nettuno, here, is every way worthy to be the friend of old Uberto, for thirteen drowning men have I myself seen him draw from the greedy jaws of sharks and other monsters of deep water. What dost thou say, father; shall we make peace between the brutes?"

The Augustine expressed his readiness, as well as his desire, to aid in an effort so laudable, and by dint of commands and persuasion, the dogs, who were predisposed to peace from having had a mutual taste of the bitterness of war, and who now felt for each other the respect which courage and force are apt to create, were soon on the usual terms of animals of their kind that have no particular grounds for contention.

The guardian of the city improved the calm produced by this little incident, to regain a portion of his lost authority. Beating back the crowd with his cane, he cleared a space around the gate into which but one of the travellers could enter at a time, while he professed himself not only ready but determined to proceed with his duty, without further procrastination. Baptiste, the patron, who beheld the precious moments wasting, and who, in the delay, foresaw a loss of wind, which, to one of his pursuits, was loss of money, now earnestly pressed the travellers to comply with the necessary forms, and to take their stations in his bark with all convenient speed.

"Of what matter is it," continued the calculating waterman, who was rather conspicuously known for the love of thrift that is usually attributed to most of the inhabitants of that region, "whether there be one headsman or twenty in the bark, so long as the good vessel can float and steer? Our Leman winds are fickle friends, and the wise take them while in the humor. Give me the breeze at west, and I will load the Winkelried to the water's edge with executioners, or any other pernicious creatures thou wilt, and thou mayest take the lightest bark that ever swam in the *bise*, and let us see who will first make the haven of Vévey!"

The loudest, and in a sense that is very important in all such discussions, the principal, speaker in the dispute, was the leader of the Neapolitan *troupe*, who, in virtue of good lungs, an agility that had no competitor in any present, and a certain mixture of superstition and bravado, that formed nearly equal ingredients in his character, was a man likely to gain great influence with those who, from their ignorance and habits, had an inherent love of the marvellous, and a profound respect for all who possessed, in acting, more audacity, and, in believing, more credulity than themselves. The vulgar like an excess, even if it be of folly; for, in their eyes, the abundance of any particular quality is very apt to be taken as the standard of its excellence.

"This is well for him who receives, but it may be death to him that pays," cried the son of the south, gaining not a little among his auditors by the distinction, for the argument was sufficiently wily, as between the buyer and the seller. "Thou wilt get thy silver for the risk, and we may get watery graves for our weakness. Nought but mishaps can come of wicked company, and accursed will they be, in the evil hour, that are found in brotherly communion, with one whose trade is hurrying Christians into eternity, before the time that has been lent by nature is fairly up. Santa Madre! I would not be the fellow-traveller of such a wretch, across this wild and changeable lake, for the honor of leaping and showing my poor powers in the presence of the Holy Father, and the whole of the learned conclave!"

This solemn declaration, which was made with suitable gesticulation, and an action of the countenance that was well adapted to prove the speaker's sincerity, produced a corresponding effect on most of the listeners, who murmured their applause in a manner sufficiently significant to convince the patron he was not about to dispose of the difficulty, simply by virtue of fair words. In this dilemma he bethought him of a plan of overcoming the scruples of all present, in which he was warmly seconded by the agent of the police, and to which, after the usual number of cavilling objections that were generated by distrust, heated blood, and the obstinacy of disputation, the other parties were finally induced to give their consent. It was agreed that the examination should no longer be delayed, but that a species of deputation from the crowd might take their stand within the gate where all who passed would necessarily be subject to their scrutiny, and, in the event of their vigilance detecting the abhorred and proscribed Balthazar, that the patron should return his money to the headsman, and preclude him from forming one of a party that was so scrupulous of its association, and, apparently, with so little reason. The Neapolitan, whose name was Pippo; one of the indigent scholars, for a century since learning was rather the auxiliary than the foe of superstition, and a certain Nicklaus Wagner, a fat Bernese, who was the owner of most of the cheeses in the bark, were the chosen of the multitude on this occasion. The first owed his election to his vehemence and volubility, qualities that the ignoble vulgar are very apt to mistake for conviction and knowledge; the second to his silence and a demureness of air which pass with another class for the stillness of deep water; and the last to his substance, as a man of known wealth, an advantage which, in spite of all that alarmists predict on one side and enthusiasts affirm on the other, will always carry greater weight with those who are less fortunate in this respect, than is either reasonable or morally healthful, provided it is not abused by arrogance or by the assumption of very extravagant and oppressive privileges. As a matter of course, these deputed guardians of the common rights were first obliged to submit their own papers to the eye of the Genevese.[1]

> [Footnote 1: As we have so often alluded to this examination, it may be well to explain, that the present system of gend'armerie and passports did not then prevail in Europe; taking their rise nearly a century later than that in which the events of this tale had place. But Geneva was a small and exposed state, and the regulation to which there is reference here, was one of the provisions which were resorted to, from time to time in order to protect those liberties and that independence, of which its citizens were so unceasingly and so wisely jealous.]

The Neapolitan, than whom an archer knave, or one that had committed more petty wrongs, did not present himself that day at the water-gate, was regularly fortified by every precaution that the long experience of a vagabond could suggest, and he was permitted to pass forthwith. The poor Westphalian student presented an instrument fairly written out in scholastic Latin, and escaped further trouble by the vanity of the unlettered agent of the police, who hastily affirmed it was a pleasure to encounter documents so perfectly in form. But the Bernese was about to take his station by the side of the other two, appearing to think inquiry, in his case, unnecessary. While moving through the passage in stately silence, Nicklaus Wagner was occupied in securing the strings of a well filled purse, which he had just lightened of a small copper coin, to reward the varlet of the hostelry in which he had passed the night, and who had been obliged to follow him to the port to obtain even this scanty boon; and the Genevese was fain to believe that, in the urgency of this important concern, he had overlooked those forms which all were, just then, obliged to respect, on quitting the town.

"Thou hast a name and character?" observed the latter, with official brevity.

"God help thee, friend!--I did not think Geneva had been so particular with a Swiss;--and a Swiss who is so favorably known on the Aar, and indeed over the whole of the great canton! I am Nicklaus Wagner, a name of little account, perhaps, but which is well esteemed among men of substance, and which has a right even to the Bürgerschaft--Nicklaus Wagner of Berne--thou wilt scarce need more?"

"Naught but proof of its truth. Thou wilt remember this is Geneva; the laws of a small and exposed state need be particular in affairs of this nature."

"I never questioned thy state being Geneva; I only wonder thou shouldst doubt my being Nicklaus Wagner! I can journey the darkest night that ever threw a shadow from the mountains, any where between the Jura and the Oberland, and none, shall say my word is to be disputed. Look 'ee, there is the patron, Baptiste, who will tell thee, that if he were to land the freight which is shipped in my name, his bark would float greatly the lighter."

All this time Nicklaus was nothing loth to show his papers, which were quite in rule. He even held them, with a thumb and finger separating the folds, ready to be presented to his questioner. The hesitation came from a feeling of wounded vanity, which would gladly show that one of his local importance and known substance was to be exempt from the exactions required from men of smaller means. The officer, who had great practice in this species of collision with his fellow-creatures, understood the character with which he had to deal, and, seeing no good reason for refusing to gratify a feeling which was innocent, though sufficiently silly, he yielded to the Bernese pride.

"Thou canst proceed," he said, turning the indulgence to account, with a ready knowledge of his duty; "and when thou gettest again among thy burghers, do us of Geneva the grace to say^ we treat our allies fairly."

"I thought thy question hasty!" exclaimed the wealthy peasant, swelling like one who gets justice, though tardily. "Now let us to this knotty affair of the headsman."

Taking his place with the Neapolitan and the Westphalian, Nicklaus assumed the grave air of a judge, and an austerity of manner which proved that he entered on his duty with a firm resolution to do justice.

"Thou 'art well known here, pilgrim," observed the officer, with some severity of tone, to the next that came to the gate.

"St. Francis to speed, master, it were else wonderful! I should be so, for the seasons scarce come and go more regularly."

"There must be a sore conscience somewhere, that Rome and thou should need each other so often?"

The pilgrim, who was enveloped in a tattered coat, sprinkled with cockle-shells, who wore his beard, and was altogether a disgusting picture of human depravity, rendered still more revolting by an ill-concealed hypocrisy, laughed openly and recklessly at the remark.

"Thou art a follower of Calvin, master," he replied, "or thou would'st not have said this. My own failings give me little trouble. I am engaged by certain parishes of Germany to take upon my poor person their physical pains, and it is not easy to name another that hath done as many messages of this kind as myself, with better proofs of fidelity. If thou hast any little offering to make, thou shalt see fair papers to prove what I say;--papers that would pass at St. Peter's itself!"

The officer perceived that he had to do with one of those unequivocal hypocrites--if such a word can properly be applied to him who scarcely thought deception necessary--who then made a traffic of expiations of this nature; a pursuit that was common enough at the close of the seventeenth and in the commencement of the eighteenth centuries, and which has not even yet entirely disappeared from Europe. He threw the pass with unconcealed aversion towards the profligate, who, recovering his document, assumed unasked his station by the side of the three who had been selected to decide on the fitness of those who were to be allowed to embark.

"Go to!" cried the officer, as he permitted this ebullition of disgust to escape him; "thou hast well said that we are followers of Calvin. Geneva has little in common with her of the scarlet mantle, and thou wilt do well to remember this, in thy next pilgrimage, lest the beadle make acquaintance with thy back,--Hold! who art thou?"

"A heretic, hopelessly damned by anticipation, if that of yonder travelling prayer-monger be the true faith;" answered one who was pressing past, with a quiet assurance that had near carried its point without incurring the risks of the usual investigation into his name and character. It was the owner of Nettuno, whose aquatic air and perfect self-possession now caused the officer to doubt whether he had not stopped a waterman of the lake--a class privileged to come and go at will.

"Thou knowest our usages," said the half-satisfied Genevese.

"I were a fool else! Even the ass that often travels the same path comes in time to tell its turns and windings. Art not satisfied with touching the pride of the worthy Nicklaus Wagner, by putting the well-warmed burgher to his proofs, but thou would'st e'en question me! Come hither, Nettuno; thou shalt answer for both, being a dog of discretion. We are no go-betweens of heaven and earth, thou knowest, but creatures that come part of the water and part of the land!"

The Italian spoke loud and confidently, and to the manner of one who addressed himself more to the humors of those near than to the understanding of the Genevese. He laughed, and looked about him in a manner to extract an echo from the crowd, though not one among them all could probably have given a sufficient reason why he had so readily taken part with the stranger against the authorities of the town, unless it might have been from the instinct of opposition to the law.

"Thou hast a name?" continued the half-yielding, half-doubting guardian of the port.

"Dost take me to be worse off than the bark of Baptiste, there? I have papers, too, if thou wilt that I go to the vessel in order to seek them. This dog is Nettuno, a brute from a far country, where brutes swim like fishes, and my name is Maso, though wicked-minded men call me oftener Il Maledetto than by any other title."

All in the throng, who understood the signification of what the Italian said, laughed aloud, and apparently with great glee, for, to the grossly vulgar, extreme audacity has an irresistible charm. The officer felt that the merriment was against him, though he scarce knew why; and ignorant of the language in which the other had given his extraordinary appellation, he yielded to the contagion, and laughed with the others, like one who understood the joke to the bottom. The Italian profited by this advantage, nodded familiarly with a good-natured and knowing smile, and proceeded. Whistling the dog to his side, he walked leisurely to the bark, into which he was the first that entered, always preserving the deliberation and calm of a man who felt himself privileged, and safe from farther molestation. This cool audacity effected its purpose, though one long and closely hunted by the law evaded the authorities of the town, when this singular being took his seat by the little package which contained his scanty wardrobe.

Chapter II

"My nobiel liege! all my request
Ys for a nobile knyghte,
Who, tho' mayhap he has done wronge,
Hee thoughte ytt stylle was righte."

Chatterton.

While this impudent evasion of vigilance was successfully practised by so old an offender, the trio of sentinels, with their volunteer assistant the pilgrim, manifested the greatest anxiety to prevent the contamination of admitting the highest executioner of the law to form one of the strangely assorted company. No sooner did the Genevese permit a traveller to pass, than they commenced their private and particular examination, which was sufficiently fierce, for more than once had they threatened to turn back the trembling, ignorant applicant on mere suspicion. The cunning Baptiste lent himself to their feelings with the skill of a demagogue, affecting a zeal equal to their own, while, at the same time, he took care most to excite their suspicions where there was the smallest danger of their being rewarded with success. Through this fiery ordeal one passed after another, until most of the nameless vagabonds had been found innocent, and the throng around the gate was so far lessened as to allow a freer circulation in the thoroughfare. The opening permitted the venerable noble, who has already been presented to the reader, to advance to the gate, accompanied by the female, and closely followed by the menials. The servitor of the police saluted the stranger with deference, for his calm exterior and imposing presence were in singular contrast with the noisy declamation and rude deportment of the rabble that had preceded.

"I am Melchior de Willading, of Berne," said the traveller, quietly offering the proofs of what he said, with the ease of one sure of his impunity; "this is my child--my only child," the old man repeated the latter words with melancholy emphasis, "and these, that wear my livery, are old and faithful followers of my house. We go by the St. Bernard, to change the ruder side of our Alps for that which is more grateful to the weak--to see if there be a sun in Italy that hath warmth enough to revive this drooping flower, and to cause it once more to raise its head joyously, as until lately, it did ever in its native halls."

The officer smiled and repeated his reverences, always declining to receive the offered papers; for the aged father indulged the overflowing of his feelings in a manner that would have awakened even duller sympathies.

"The lady has youth and a tender parent of her side," he said; "these are much when health fails us."

"She is indeed too young to sink so early!" returned the father, who had apparently forgotten his immediate business, and was gazing with a tearful eye at the faded but still eminently attractive features of the young female, who rewarded his solicitude with a look of love; "but thou hast not seen I am the man I represent myself to be."

"It is not necessary, noble baron; the city knows of your presence, and I have it, in especial charge, to do all that may be grateful to render the passage through Geneva, of one so honored among our allies, agreeable to his recollections."

"Thy city's courtesy is of known repute," said the Baron de Willading, replacing his papers in their usual envelope, and receiving the grace like one accustomed to honors of this sort:--"art thou a father?"

"Heaven has not been niggardly of gifts of this nature: my table feeds eleven, besides those who gave them being."

"Eleven!--The will of God is a fearful mystery! And this thou seest is the sole hope of my line;--the only heir that is left to the name and lands of Willading! Art thou at ease in thy condition?"

"There are those in our town who are less so, with many thanks for the friendliness of the question."

A slight color suffused the face of Adelheid de Willading, for so was the daughter of the Bernese called, and she advanced a step nearer to the officer.

"They who have so few at their own board, need think of those who have so many," she said, dropping a piece of gold into the hand of the Genevese: then she added, in a voice scarce louder than a whisper--"If the young and innocent of thy household can offer a prayer in the behalf of a poor girl who has much need of aid, 'twill be remembered of God, and it may serve to lighten the grief of one who has the dread of being childless."

"God bless thee, lady!" said the officer, little used to deal with such spirits, and touched by the mild resignation and piety of the speaker, whose simple but winning manner moved him nearly to tears; "all of my family, old as well as young, shall bethink them of thee and thine."

Adelheid's cheek resumed its paleness, and she quietly accompanied her father, as he slowly proceeded towards the bark. A scene of this nature did not fail to shake the pertinacity of those who stood at watch near the gate. Of course they had nothing to say to any of the rank of Melchior de Willading, who went into the bark without a question. The influence of beauty and station united to so much simple grace as that shown by the fair actor in the little incident we have just related, was much too strong for the ill-trained feelings of the Neapolitan and his companions. They not only let all the menials pass unquestioned also, but it was some little time before their vigilance resumed its former truculence. The two or three travellers that succeeded had the benefit of this fortunate change of disposition.

The next who came to the gate was the young soldier, whom the Baron de Willading had so often addressed as Monsieur Sigismund. His papers were regular, and no obstacle was offered to his departure. It may be doubted how far this young man would have been disposed to submit to these extra-official inquiries of the three deputies of the crowd, had there been a desire to urge them, for he went towards the quay, with an eye that expressed any other sensation than that of amity or compliance. Respect, or a more equivocal feeling, proved his protection; for none but the pilgrim, who displayed ultra-zeal in the pursuit of his object, ventured so far as to hazard even a smothered remark as he passed.

"There goes an arm and a sword that might well shorten a Christian's days," said the dissolute and shameless dealer in the church's abuses, "and, yet no one asks his name or calling!"

"Thou hadst better put the question thyself," returned the sneering Pippo, "since penitence is thy trade. For myself, I am content with whirling round at my own bidding, without taking a hint from that young giant's arm."

The poor scholar and the burgher of Berne appeared to acquiesce in this opinion, and no more said in the matter. In the mean while there was another at the gate. The new applicant had little in his exterior to renew the vigilance of the superstitious trio. A quiet, meek-looking man, seemingly of a middle condition in life, and of an air altogether calm and unpretending, had submitted his passport to the faithful guardian of the city. The latter read the document, cast a quick and inquiring glance at its owner, and returned the paper in a way to show haste, and a desire to be rid of him.

"It is well," he said; "thou canst, go thy way."

"How now!" cried the Neapolitan, to whom buffoonery was a congenial employment, as much by natural disposition as by practice; "How now!--have we Balthazar at last, in this bloody-minded and fierce-looking traveller?" As the speaker had expected, this sally was rewarded by a general laugh, and he was accordingly encouraged to proceed. "Thou knowest our office, friend," added the unfeeling mountebank, "and must show us thy hands. None pass who bear the stain of blood!"

The traveller appeared staggered, for he was plainly a man of retired and peaceable habits, who had been thrown, by the chances of the road, in contact with one only too practised in this unfeeling species of wit. He showed his open palm, however, with a direct and confiding simplicity, that drew a shout of merriment from all the by-standers.

"This will not do; soap, and ashes, and the tears of victims, may have washed out the marks of his work from Balthazar himself. The spots we seek are on the soul, man, and we must look into that, ere thou art permitted to make one in this goodly company."

"Thou didst not question yonder young soldier thus," returned the stranger, whose eye kindled, as even the meek repel unprovoked outrage, though his frame trembled violently at being subject to open insults from men so rude and unprincipled; "thou didst not dare to question yonder young soldier thus!"

"By the prayers of San Gennaro! which are known to stop running and melted lava, I would rather thou should'st undertake that office than I. Yonder young soldier is an honorable decapitator, and it is a pleasure to be his companion on a journey; for, no doubt, some six or eight of the saints are speaking in his behalf daily. But he we seek is the outcast of all, good or bad, whether in heaven or on earth, or in that other hot abode to which he will surely be sent when his time shall come."

"And yet he does no more than execute the law!"

"What is law to opinion, friend? But go thy way; none suspect thee to be the redoubtable enemy of our heads. Go thy way, for Heaven's sake, and mutter thy prayers to be delivered from Balthazar's axe."

The countenance of the stranger worked, as if he would have answered; then suddenly changing his purpose, he passed on, and instantly disappeared in the bark. The monk of St. Bernard came next. Both the Augustine and his dog were old acquaintances of the officer, who did not require any evidence of his character or errand from the former.

"We are the protectors of life and not its foes," observed the monk, as, leaving the more regular watchman of the place, he drew near to those, whose claims to the office would have admitted of dispute: "we live among the snows, that Christians may not die without the church's comfort."

"Honor, holy Augustine, to thee and thy office!" said the Neapolitan, who, reckless and abandoned as he was, possessed that instinct of respect for those who deny their natures for the good of others which is common to all, however tainted by cupidity themselves. "Thou and thy dog, old Uberto, can freely pass, with our best good wishes for both."

There no longer remained any to examine, and, after a short consultation among the more superstitious of the travellers, they came to the very natural opinion that, intimidated by their just remonstrances, the offensive headsman had shrunk, unperceived, from the crowd, and that they were at length happily relieved from his presence. The annunciation of the welcome tidings drew much self-felicitation from the different members of the motley company, and all eagerly embarked, for Baptiste now loudly and vehemently declared that a single moment of further delay was entirely out of the question.

"Of what are you thinking, men!" he exclaimed with well-acted heat; "are the Leman winds liveried lackeys, to come and go as may suit your fancies; now to blow west, and now east, as shall be most wanted, to help you on your journeys? Take example of the noble Melchior de Willading, who has long been in his place, and pray the saints, if you will, in your several fashions, that this fair western wind do not quit us in punishment of our neglect."

"Yonder come others, in haste, to be of the party!" interrupted the cunning Italian; "loosen thy fasts quickly, Master Baptiste, or, by San Gennaro! we shall still be detained!"

The Patron suddenly checked himself, and hurried back to the gate, in order to ascertain what he might expect from this unlooked-for turn of fortune.

Two travellers, in the attire of men familiar with the road, accompanied by a menial, and followed by a porter staggering under the burthen of their luggage, were fast approaching the water-gate, as if conscious the least delay might cause their being left. This party was led by one considerably past the meridian of life, and who evidently was enabled to maintain his post more by the deference of his companions than by his physical force. A cloak was thrown across one arm, while in the hand of the other he carried the rapier, which all of gentle blood then considered a necessary appendage of their rank.

"You were near losing the last bark that sails for the Abbaye des Vignerons, Signori," said the Genevese, recognizing the country of the strangers at a glance, "if, as I judge from your direction and haste, these festivities are in your minds."

"Such is our aim," returned the elder of the travellers, "and, as thou sayest, we are, of a certainty, tardy. A hasty departure and bad roads have been the cause--but as, happily, we are yet in time to profit by this bark, wilt do us the favor to look into our authority to pass?"

The officer perused the offered document with the customary care, turning it from side to side, as if all were not right, though in a way to show that he regretted the informality.

"Signore, your pass is quite in rule as touches Savoy and the country of Nice, but it wants the city's forms."

"By San Francesco! more's the pity. We are honest gentlemen of Genoa, hurrying to witness the revels at Vévey, of which rumor gives an enticing report, and our sole desire is to come and go peaceably. As thou seest, we are late; for hearing at the post, on alighting, that a bark was about to spread its sails for the other extremity of the lake, we had no time to consult all the observances that thy city's rules may deem necessary. So many turn their faces the same way, to witness these ancient games, that we had not thought out quick passage through the town of sufficient importance to give thy authorities the trouble to look into our proofs."

"Therein, Signore, you have judged amiss. It is my sworn duty to stay all who want the republic's permission to proceed."

"This is unfortunate, to say no more. Art thou the patron of the bark, friend?"

"And her owner, Signore," answered Baptiste, who listened to the discourse with longings equal to his doubts. "I should be a great deal too happy to count such honorable travellers among my passengers."

"Thou wilt then delay thy departure until this gentleman shall see the authorities of the town, and obtain the required permission to quit it? Thy compliance shall not go unrewarded."

As the Genoese concluded, he dropped into a palm that was well practised in bribes a sequin of the celebrated republic of which he was a citizen. Baptiste had long cultivated an aptitude to suffer himself to be influenced by gold, and it was with unfeigned reluctance that he admitted the necessity of refusing, in this instance, to profit by his own good dispositions. Still retaining the money, however, for he did not well know how to overcome his reluctance to part with it, he answered in a manner sufficiently embarrassed, to show the other that he had at least gained a material advantage by his liberality.

"His Excellency knows not what he asks," said the patron, fumbling the coin between a finger and thumb; "our Genevese citizens love to keep house till the sun is up, lest they should break their necks by walking about the uneven streets in the dark, and it will be two long hours before a single bureau will open its windows in the town. Besides, your man of the police is not like us of the lake, happy to get a morsel when the weather and occasion permit; but he is a regular feeder, that must have his grapes and his wine before he will use his wits for the benefit of his employers. The Winkelried would weary of doing nothing, with this fresh western breeze humming between her masts, while the poor gentleman was swearing before the town-house gate at the laziness of the officers. I know the rogues better than your Excellency, and would advise some other expedient."

Baptiste looked, with a certain expression, at the guardian of the water-gate, and in a manner to make his meaning sufficiently clear to the travellers. The latter studied the countenance of the Genevese a moment, and, better practised than the patron, or a more enlightened judge of character, he fortunately refused to commit himself by offering to purchase the officer's good-will. If there are too many who love to be tempted to forget their trusts, by a well-managed venality, there are a few who find a greater satisfaction in being thought beyond its influence. The watchman of the gate happened to be one of the latter class, and, by one of the many unaccountable workings of human feeling, the very vanity which had induced him to suffer Il Maledetto to go through unquestioned, rather than expose his own ignorance, now led him to wish he might make some return for the stranger's good opinion of his honesty.

"Will you let me look again at the pass, Signore?" asked the Genevese, as if he thought a sufficient legal warranty for that which he now strongly desired to do might yet be found in the instrument itself.

The inquiry was useless, unless it was to show that the elder Genoese was called the Signer Grimaldi and that his companion went by the name of Marcelli. Shaking his head he returned the paper in the manner of a disappointed man.

"Thou canst not have read half of what the paper contains," said Baptiste peevishly; "your reading and writing are not such easy matters, that a squint of the eye is all-sufficient. Look at it again, and thou mayest yet find all in rule. It is unreasonable to suppose Signori of their rank would journey like vagabonds, with papers to be suspected."

"Nothing is wanting but our city signatures, without which my duty will let none go by, that are truly travellers."

"This comes, Signore, of the accursed art of writing, which is much pushed and greatly abused of late. I have heard the aged watermen of the Leman praise the good old time, when boxes and bales went and came, and no ink touched paper between him that sent and him that carried; and yet it has now reached the pass that a christian may not transport himself on his own legs without calling on the scriveners for permission!"

"We lose the moments in words, when it were far better to be doing," returned the Signore Grimaldi. "The pass is luckily in the language of the country, and needs but a glance to get the approval of the authorities. Thou wilt do well to say thou canst remain the time necessary to see this little done."

"Were your excellency to offer me the Doge's crown as a bribe, this could not be. Our Leman winds will not wait for king or noble, bishop or priest, and duty to those I have in the bark commands me to quit the port as soon as possible."

"Thou art truly well charged with living freight already," said the Genoese, regarding the deeply loaded bark with a half-distrustful eye 'I hope thou hast not overdone thy vessel's powers in receiving so many?"

"I could gladly reduce the number a little, excellent Signore, for all that you see piled among the boxes and tubs are no better than so many knaves, fit only to give trouble and raise questions touching the embarkation of those who are willing to pay better than themselves. The noble Swiss, whom you see seated near the stern, with his daughter and people, the worthy Melchior de Willading, gives a more liberal reward for his passage to Vévey than all those nameless rogues together."

The Genoese made a hasty movement towards the patron, with an earnestness of eye and air that betrayed a sudden and singular interest in what he heard.

"Did'st thou say de Willading?" he exclaimed, eager as one of much fewer years would have been at the unexpected announcement of some pleasurable event. "Melchior, too, of that honorable name?"

"Signore, the same. None other bears the title now, for the old line, they say, is drawing to an end. I remember this same baron, when he was as ready to launch his boat into a troubled lake, as any in Switzerland--"

"Fortune hath truly favored me, good Marcelli!" interrupted the other, grasping the hand of his companion, with strong feeling. "Go thou to the bark, master patron, and advise thy passenger that--what shall we say to Melchior? Shall we tell him at once, who waits him here, or shall we practise a little on his failing memory? By San Francesco! we will do this, Enrico, that we may try his powers! 'Twill be pleasant to see him wonder and guess--my life on it, however, that he knows me at a glance. I am truly little changed for one that hath seen so much."

The Signor Marcelli lowered his eyes respectfully at this opinion of his friend, but he did not see fit to discourage a belief which was merely a sudden ebullition, produced by the recollection of younger days. Baptiste was instantly dispatched with a request that the baron would do a stranger of rank the favor to come to the water-gate.

"Tell him 'tis a traveller disappointed in the wish to be of his company," repeated the Genoese. "That will suffice. I know him courteous, and he is not my Melchior, honest Marcelli, if he delay an instant:--thou seest! he is already quitting the bark, for never did I know him refuse an act of friendliness--dear, dear Melchior--thou art the same at seventy as thou wast at thirty!"

Here the agitation of the Genoese got the better of him, and he walked aside, under a sense of shame, lest he might betray unmanly weakness. In the mean time, the Baron de Willading advanced from the water-side, without suspecting that his presence was required for more than an act of simple courtesy.

"Baptiste tells me that gentlemen of Genoa are here, who are desirous of hastening to the games of Vévey," said the latter, raising his beaver, "and that my presence may be of use in obtaining the pleasure of their company."

"I will not unmask till we are fairly and decently embarked, Enrico," whispered the Signor Grimaldi; "nay--by the mass! not till we are fairly disembarked! The laugh against him will never be forgotten. Signore," addressing the Bernese with affected composure, endeavoring to assume the manner of a stranger, though his voice trembled with eagerness at each syllable, "we are indeed of Genoa, and most anxious to be of the party in your bark--but--he little suspects who speaks to him, Marcelli!--but, Signore, there has been some small oversight touching the city signatures, and we have need of friendly assistance, either to pass the gate, or to detain the bark until the forms of the place shall have been respected.'

"Signore, the city of Geneva hath need to be watchful, for it is an exposed and weak state, and I have little hope that my influence can cause this trusty watchman to dispense with his duty. Touching the bark, a small gratuity will do much with honest Baptiste, should there not be a question of the stability of the breeze, in which case he might be somewhat of a loser."

"You say the truth, noble Melchior," put in the patron; "were the wind ahead, or were it two hours earlier in the morning, the little delay should not cost the strangers a batz--that is to say, nothing unreasonable; but as it is, I have not twenty minutes more to lose, evep were all the city magistrates cloaking to be of the party, in their proper and worshipful persons."

"I greatly regret, Sigriore, it should be so," resumed the baron, turning to the applicant with the consideration of one accustomed to season his refusals by a gracious manner; "but these watermen have their secret signs, by which, it would seem, they know the latest moment they may with prudence delay."

"By the mass! Marcelli, I will try him a little--should have known him in a carnival dress. Signor Barone, we are but poor Italian gentlemen, it is true, of Genoa. You have heard of our republic, beyond question--the poor state of Genoa?"

"Though of no great pretensions to letters, Signore," answered Melchior, smiling, "I am not quite ignorant that such a state exists. You could not have named a city on the shores of your Mediterranean that would sooner warm my heart than this very town of which you speak. Many of my happiest hours were passed within its walls, and often, even at this late day, do I live over again my life to recall the pleasures of that merry period. Were there leisure, I could repeat a list of honorable and much esteemed names that are familiar to your ears, in proof of what I say."

"Name them, Signor Barone;--for the love of the saints, and the blessed virgin, name them, I beseech you!"

A little amazed at the eagerness of the other. Melchior de Willading earnestly regarded his furrowed face; and, for an instant, an expression like incertitude crossed his own features.

"Nothing would be easier, Signore, than to name many. The first in my memory, as he has always been the first in my love, is Gaetano Grimaldi, of whom, I doubt not, both of you have often heard?"

"We have, we have! That is--yes, I think we may say, Marcelli, that we have often heard of him, and not unfavorably. Well, what of this Grimaldi?"

"Signore, the desire to converse of your noble townsman is natural, but were I to yield to my wishes to speak of Gaetano, I fear the honest Baptiste might have reason to complain."

"To the devil with Baptiste and his bark! Melchior,--my good Melchior!--dearest, dearest Melchior! hast thou indeed forgotten me?"

Here the Genoese opened wide his arms, and stood ready to receive the embrace of his friend. The Baron de Willading was troubled, but he was still so far from suspecting the real fact, that he could not have easily told the reason why. He gazed wistfully at the working features of the fine old man who stood before him, and though memory seemed to flit around the truth, it was in gleams so transient as completely to baffle his wishes.

"Dost thou deny me, de Willading?--dost thou refuse to own the friend of thy youth--the companion of thy pleasures--the sharer of thy sorrows---thy comrade in the wars--nay, more--thy confidant in a dearer tie?"

"None but Gaetano Grimaldi himself can claim these titles!" burst from the lips of the trembling baron.

"Am I aught else?--am I not this Gaetano?--that Gaetano--thy Gaetano,--old and very dear friend?"

"Thou Gaetano!" exclaimed the Bernois, recoiling a step, instead of advancing to meet the eager embrace of the Genoese, whose impetuous feelings were little cooled by time--"thou, the gallant, active, daring, blooming Grimaldi! Signore, you trifle with an old man's affections."

"By the holy mass, I do not deceive thee! Ha, Marcelli, he is slow to believe as ever, but fast and certain as the vow of a churchman when convinced. If we are to distrust each other for a few wrinkles, thou wilt find objections rising against thine own identity as well as against mine, friend Melchior. I am none other than Gaetano--the Gaetano of thy youth--the friend thou hast not seen these many long and weary years."

Recognition was slow in making its way in the mind of the Bernese. Lineament after lineament, however, became successively known to him, and most of all, the voice served to awaken long dormant recollections. But, as heavy natures are said to have the least self-command when fairly excited, so did the baron betray the most ungovernable emotion of the two, when conviction came at last to confirm the words of his friend. He threw himself on the neck of the Genoese, and the old man wept in a manner that caused him to withdraw aside, in order to conceal the tears which had so suddenly and profusely broken from fountains that he had long thought nearly dried.

Chapter III

Ha, cousin Silence, that thou hadst seen
That, that this knight and I have seen!

King Henry IV.

The calculating patron of the Winkelried had patiently watched the progress of the foregoing scene with great inward satisfaction, but now that the strangers seemed to be assured of support powerful as that of Melchior de Willading, he was disposed to turn it to account without farther delay. The old men were still standing with their hands grasping each other, after another warm and still closer embrace, and with tears rolling down the furrowed face of each, when Baptiste advanced to put in his raven-like remonstrance.

"Noble gentlemen," he said, "if the felicitations of one humble as I can add to the pleasure of this happy meeting, I beg you to accept them; but the wind has no heart for friendships nor any thought for the gains or losses of us watermen. I feel it my duty, as patron of the bark, to recall to your honors that many poor travellers, far from their homes and pining families, are waiting our leisure, not to speak of foot-sore pilgrims and other worthy adventurers, who are impatient in their hearts, though respect for their superiors keeps them tongue-tied, while we are losing the best of the breeze."

"By San Francesco! the varlet is right;" said the Genoese, hurriedly erasing the marks of his recent weakness from his cheeks. "We are forgetful of all these worthy people while joy at our meeting is so strong, and it is time that we thought of others. Canst thou aid me in dispensing with the city's signatures?"

The Baron de Willading paused; for well-disposed at first to assist any gentlemen who found themselves in an unpleasant embarrassment, it will be readily imagined that the case lost none of its interest, when he found that his oldest and most tried friend was the party in want of his influence. Still it was much easier to admit the force of this new and unexpected appeal than to devise the means of success. The officer was, to use a phrase which most men seem to think supplies a substitute for reason and principle, too openly committed to render it probable he would easily yield. It was necessary, however, to make the trial, and the baron, therefore, addressed the keeper of the water-gate more urgently than he had yet done in behalf of the strangers.

"It is beyond my functions; there is not one of our Syndics whom I would more gladly oblige than yourself, noble baron," answered the officer; "but the duty of the watchman is to adhere strictly to the commands of those who have placed him at his post."

"Gaetano, we are not the men to complain of this! We have stood together too long in the same trench, and have too often slept soundly, in situations where failure in this doctrine might have cost us our lives, to quarrel with the honest Genevese for his watchfulness. To be frank, 'twere little use to tamper with the fidelity of a Swiss or with that of his ally."

"With the Swiss that is well paid to be vigilant!" answered the Genoese, laughing in a way to show that he had only revived one of those standing but biting jests, that they who love each other best are perhaps most accustomed to practice.

The Baron de Willading took the facetiousness of his friend in good part, returning the mirth of the other in a manner to show that the allusion recalled days when their hours had idly passed in the indulgence of spontaneous outbreakings of animal spirits.

"Were this thy Italy, Gaetano, a sequin would not only supply the place of a dozen signatures, but, by the name of thy favorite, San Francesco! it would give the honest gate-keeper that gift of second-sight on which the Scottish seers are said to pride themselves."

"Well, the two sides of the Alps will keep their characters, even though we quarrel about their virtues--but we shall never see again the days that we have known! Neither the games of Vévey, nor the use of old jokes, will make us the youths we have been, dear de Willading!"

"Signore, a million of pardons," interrupted Baptiste, "but this western wind is more inconstant even than the spirits of the young."

"The rogue is again right, and we forget yonder cargo of honest travellers, who are wishing us both in Abraham's bosom, for keeping the impatient bark in idleness at the quay. Good Marcelli, hast thou aught to suggest in this strait?"

"Signore, you forget that we have another document that may be found sufficient"--the person questioned, who appeared to fill a middle station between that of a servant and that of a companion, rather hinted than observed:

"Thou sayest true--and yet I would gladly avoid producing it--but anything is better than the loss of thy company, Melchior."

"Name it not! We shall not separate, though the Winkelried rot where she lies. 'Twere easier to separate our faithful cantons than two such friends."

"Nay, noble baron, you forget the wearied pilgrims and the many anxious travellers in the bark."

"If twenty crowns will purchase thy consent, honest Baptiste, we will have no further discussion."

"It is scarce in human will to withstand you, noble Sir!--Well, the pilgrims have weary feet, and rest will only fit them the better for the passage of the mountains; and as for the others, why let them quit the bark if they dislike the conditions. I am not a man to force my commerce on any."

"Nay, nay, I will have none of this. Keep thy gold, Melchior, and let the honest Baptiste keep his passengers, to say nothing of his conscience."

"I beseech your excellency," interrupted Baptiste, "not to distress yourself in tenderness for me. I am ready to do far more disagreeable things to oblige so noble a gentleman."

"I will none of it! Signor officer, wilt thou do me the favor to cast a glance at this?"

As the Genoese concluded, he placed in the hands of the watchman at the gate, a paper different from that which he had first shown. The officer perused the new instrument with deep attention, and, when half through its contents, his eyes left the page to become rivetted in respectful attention on the face of the expectant Italian. He then read the passport to the end. Raising his cap ceremoniously, the keeper of the gate left the passage free, bowing with deep deference to the strangers.

"Had I sooner known this," he said, "there would have been no delay. I hope your excellency will consider my ignorance--?"

"Name it not, friend. Thou hast done well; in proof of which I beg thy acceptance of a small token of esteem."

The Genoese dropped a sequin into the hand of the officer, passing him, at the same time, on his way to the waterside. As the reluctance of the other to receive gold came rather from a love of duty than from any particular aversion to the metal itself, this second offering met with a more favorable reception than the first. The Baron de Willading was not without surprise at the sudden success of his friend, though he was far too prudent and well-bred to let his wonder be seen.

Every obstacle to the departure of the Winkelried was now removed, and Baptiste and his crew were soon actively engaged in loosening the sails and in casting off the fasts. The movement of the bark was at first slow and heavy, for the wind was intercepted by the buildings of the town; but, as she receded from the shore, the canvass began to flap and belly, and ere long it filled outward with a report like that of a musket; after which the motion of the travellers began to bear some relation to their nearly exhausted patience.

Soon after the party which had been so long detained at the water-gate were embarked, Adelheid first learned the reason of the delay. She had long known, from the mouth of her father, the name and early history of the Signor Grimaldi, a Genoese of illustrious family, who had been the sworn friend and the comrade of Melchior de Willading, when the latter pursued his career in arms in the wars of Italy. These circumstances having passed long before her own birth, and even before the marriage of her parents, and she being the youngest and the only survivor of a numerous family of children, they were, as respected herself, events that already began to assume the hue of history. She received the old man frankly and even with affection, though in his yielding but still fine form, she had quite as much difficulty as her father in recognizing the young, gay, gallant, brilliant, and handsome Gaetano Grimaldi that her imagination had conceived from the verbal descriptions she had so often heard, and from her fancy was still wont to draw as he was painted in the affectionate descriptions of her father. When he suddenly and affectionately offered a kiss, the color flushed her face, for no man but he to whom she owed her being had ever before taken that liberty; but, after an instant of virgin embarrassment, she laughed, and blushingly presented her cheek to receive the salute.

"The last tidings I had of thee, Melchior," said the Italian, "was the letter sent by the Swiss Ambassador, who took our city in his way as he traveled south, and which was written on the occasion of the birth of this very girl."

"Not of this, dear friend, but of an elder sister, who is, long since, a cherub in heaven. Thou seest the ninth precious gift that God bestowed, and thou seest all that is now left of his bounty."

The countenance of the Signor Grimaldi lost its joyousness, and a deep pause in the discourse succeeded. They lived in an age when communications between friends that were separated by distance, and by the frontiers of different states, were rare and uncertain. The fresh and novel affections of marriage had first broken an intercourse that was continued, under such disadvantages as marked the period, long after their duties called them different ways; and time, with its changes and the embarrassments of wars, had finally destroyed nearly every link in the chain of their correspondence.

Each had, therefore, much of a near and interesting character to communicate to the other, and each dreaded to speak, lest he might cause some wound, that was not perfectly healed, to bleed anew. The volume of matter conveyed in the few words uttered by the Baron de Willading, showed both in how many ways they might inflict pain without intention, and how necessary it was to be guarded in their discourse during the first days of their renewed intercourse.

"This girl at least is a treasure of itself, of which I must envy thee the possession," the Signor Grimaldi at length rejoined.

The Swiss made one of those quick movements which betray surprise, and it was very apparent, that, just at the moment, he was more affected by some interest of his friend, than by the apprehensions which usually beset him when any very direct allusion was made to his surviving child.

"Gaetano, thou hast a son!"

"He is lost--hopelessly--irretrievably lost--at least, to me!"

These were brief but painful glimpses into each other's concerns, and another melancholy and embarrassed pause followed. As the Baron de Willading witnessed the sorrow that deeply shadowed the face of the Genoese, he almost felt that Providence, in summoning his own boys to early graves, might have spared him the still bitterer grief of mourning over the unworthiness of a living son.

"These are God's decrees, Melchior," the Italian continued of his own accord, "and we, as soldiers, as men, and more than either, as Christians, should know how to submit. The letter, of which I spoke, contained the last direct tidings that I received of thy welfare, though different travellers have mentioned thee as among the honored and trusted of thy country, without descending to the particulars of thy private life."

"The retirement of our mountains, and the little intercourse of strangers with the Swiss, have denied me even this meagre satisfaction as respects thee and thy fortunes. Since the especial courier sent, according to our ancient agreement, to announce--"

The baron hesitated, for he felt he was again touching on forbidden ground.

"To announce the birth of my unhappy boy," continued the Signor Grimaldi, firmly.

"To announce that much-wished-for event, I have not had news of thee, except in a way so vague, as to whet the desire to know more rather than to appease the longings of love."

"These doubts are the penalties that friendship pays to separation. We enlist the affections in youth with the recklessness of hope, and, when called different ways by duties or interest, we first begin to perceive that the world is not the heaven we thought it, but that each enjoyment has its price, as each grief has its solace. Thou hast carried arms since we were soldiers in company?"

"As a Swiss only."

The answer drew a gleam of habitual humor from, the keen eye of the Italian, whose countenance was apt to change as rapidly as his thoughts.

"In what service?"

"Nay, a truce to thy old pleasantries, good Grimaldi--and yet I should scarce love thee, as I do, wert thou other than thou art! I believe we come at last to prize even the foibles of those we truly esteem!"

"It must be so, young lady, or boyish follies would long since have weaned thy father from me. I have never spared him on the subjects of snows and money, and yet he beareth with me marvellously. Well, strong love endureth much. Hath the baron often spoken to thee of old Grimaldi--young Grimaldi, I should say--and of the many freaks of our thoughtless days?"

"So much, Signore," returned Adelheid, who had wept and smiled by turns during the interrupted dialogue of her father and his friend, "that I can repeat most of your youthful histories. The castle of Willading is deep among the mountains, and it is rare indeed for the foot of stranger to enter its gates. During the long evenings of our severe winters, I have listened as a daughter would be apt to listen to the recital of most of your common adventures, and in listening, I have not only learned to know, but to esteem, one that is justly so dear to my parent."

"I make no doubt, now, thou hast the history of the plunge into the canal, by over-stooping to see the Venetian beauty, at thy finger's ends?"

"I do remember some such act of humid gallantry," returned Adelheid, laughing.

"Did thy father tell thee, child, of the manner in which he bore me off in a noble rescue from a deadly charge of the Imperial cavalry?"

"I have heard some light allusion to such an event, too," returned Adelheid, evidently trying to recall the history of the affair, to her mind "but--"

"Light does he call it, and of small account? I wish never to see another as heavy! This is the impartiality of thy narratives, good Melchior, in which a life preserved, wounds received, and a charge to make the German quail, are set down as matters to be touched with a light hand!".

"If I did thee this service, it was more than deserved by the manner in which, before Milan----"

"Well, let it all pass together. We are old fools, young lady, and should we get garrulous in each other's praise, thou mightest mistake us for braggarts; a character that, in truth, neither wholly merits. Didst thou ever tell the girl, Melchior, of our mad excursion into the forests of the Apennines, in search of a Spanish lady that had fallen into the hands of banditti; and how we passed weeks on a foolish enterprise of errantry, that had become useless, by the timely application of a few sequins on the part of the husband, even before we started on the chivalrous, not to say silly excursion?"

"Say chivalrous, but not silly," answered Adelheid, with the simplicity of a young and sincere mind. "Of this adventure I have heard; but to me it has never seemed ridiculous. A generous motive might well excuse an undertaking of less favorable auspices."

"'Tis fortunate," returned the Signor Grimaldi, thoughtfully, "that, if youth and exaggerated opinions lead us to commit mad pranks under the name of spirit and generosity, there are other youthful and generous minds to reflect our sentiments and to smile upon our folly."

"This is more like the wary grey-headed ex-pounder of wisdom than like the hot-headed Gaetano Grimaldi of old!" exclaimed the baron, though he laughed while uttering the words, as if he felt, at least a portion of the other's indifference to those exaggerated feelings that had entered much into the characters of both in youth. "The time has been when the words, policy and calculation, would have cost a companion thy favor!"

"'Tis said that the prodigal of twenty makes? the miser of seventy. It is certain that even our southern sun does not warm the blood of threescore as suddenly as it heats that of one. But we will not darken thy daughter's views of the future by a picture too faithfully drawn, lest she become wise before her time. I have often questioned, Melchior, which is the most precious gift of nature, a worm fancy, or the colder powers of reason. But if I must say which I most love, the point becomes less difficult of decision. I would prefer each in its season, or rather the two united, with a gradual change in their influence. Let the youth commence with the first in the ascendant, and close with the last. He who begins life too cold a reasoner may end it a calculating egotist; and he who is ruled solely by his imagination is in danger of having his mind so ripened as to bring forth the fruits of a visionary. Had it pleased heaven to have left me the dear son I possessed for so short a period, I would rather have seen him leaning to the side of exaggeration in his estimate of men, before experience came to chill his hopes, than to see him scan his fellows with a too philosophical eye in boyhood. 'Tis said we are but clay at the best, but the ground, before it has been well tilled, sends forth the plants that are most congenial to its soil, and though it be of no great value, give me the spontaneous and generous growth of the weed, which proves the depth of the loam, rather than a stinted imitation of that which cultivation may, no doubt, render more useful if not more grateful."

The allusion to his lost son caused another cloud to pass athwart the brow of the Genoese.

"Thou seest, Adelheid," he continued, after a pause--"for Adelheid will I call thee, in virtue of a second father's rights--that we are making our folly respectable, at least to ourselves--Master Patron, thou hast a well-charged bark!"

"Thanks to your two honors;" answered Baptiste, who stood at the helm, near the group of principal passengers. "These windfalls come rarely to the poor, and we must make much of such as offer. The games at Vévey have called every craft on the Leman to the upper end of the lake, and a little mother-wit led me to trust to the last turn of the wheel, which, as you see, Signore has not come up a blank."

"Have many strangers passed by your city on their way to these sports?"

"Many hundreds, noble gentleman; and report speaks of thousands that are collecting at Vévey and in the neighboring villages. The country of Vaud has not had a richer harvest from her games this many a year."

"It is fortunate, Melchior, that the desire to witness these revels should have arisen in us at the same moment. The hope of at last obtaining certain tidings of thy welfare was the chief inducement that caused me to steal from Genoa, whither I am compelled to return forthwith. There is truly something providential in this meeting!"

"I so esteem it," returned the Baron de Willading; "though the hope of soon embracing thee was strongly alive in me. Thou art mistaken in fancying that curiosity, or a wish to mingle with the multitude at Vévey, has drawn me from my castle. Italy was in my eye, as it has long been in my heart." "How!--Italy?"

"Nothing less. This fragile plant of the mountains has drooped of late in her native air, and skilful advisers have counselled the sunny side of the Alps as a shelter to revive her animation. I have promised Roger de Blonay to pass a night or two within his ancient walls, and then we are destined to seek the hospitality of the monks of St. Bernard. Like thee, I had hoped this unusual sortie from my hold might lead to intelligence touching the fortunes of one I have never ceased to love."

The Signor Grimaldi turned a more scrutinizing took towards the face of their female companion. Her gentle and winning beauty gave him pleasure; but, with his attention quickened by what had just fallen from her father, he traced, in silent pain, the signs of that early fading which threatened to include this last hope of his friend in the common fate of the family. Disease had not, however, set its seal on the sweet face of Adelheid, in a manner to attract the notice of a common observer. The lessening of the bloom, the mournful character of a dove-like eye, and a look of thoughtfulness, on a brow that he had ever known devoid of care and open as day with youthful ingenuousness, were the symptoms that first gave the alarm to her father, whose previous losses, and whose solitariness, as respects the ties of the world, had rendered him keenly alive to impressions of such a nature. The reflections excited by this examination brought painful recollections to all, and it was long before the discourse was renewed.

In the mean time, the Winkelried was not idle. As the vessel receded from the cover of the buildings and the hills, the force of the breeze was felt, and her speed became quickened in proportion; though the watermen of her crew often studied the manner in which she dragged her way through the element with a shake of the head, that was intended to express their consciousness that too much had been required of the craft. The cupidity of Baptiste had indeed charged his good bark to the uttermost. The water was nearly on a line with the low stern, and when the bark had reached a part of the lake where the waves were rolling with some force, it was found that the vast weight was too much to be lifted by the feeble and broken efforts of these miniature seas. The consequences were, however, more vexatious than alarming. A few wet feet among the less quiet of the passengers, with an occasional slapping of a sheet of water against the gangways, and a consequent drift of spray across the pile of human heads in the centre of the bark, were all the immediate personal inconveniencies. Still unjustifiable greediness of gain, had tempted the patron to commit the unseaman-like fault of overloading his vessel. The decrease of speed was another and a graver consequence of his cupidity, since it might prevent their arrival in port before the breeze had expended itself.

The lake of Geneva lies nearly in the form of a crescent, stretching from the south-west towards the north-east. Its northern, or the Swiss shore, is chiefly what is called, in the language of the country, a *côte*, or a declivity that admits of cultivation; and, with few exceptions, it has been, since the earliest periods of history, planted with the generous vine. Here the Romans had many stations and posts, vestiges of which are still visible. The confusion and the mixture of interests that succeeded the fall of the empire, gave rise, in the middle ages, to various baronial castles, ecclesiastical towns, and towers of defence, which still stand on the margin of this beautiful sheet of water, or ornament the eminences a little inland. At the time of which we write, the whole coast of the Leman, if so imposing a word may be applied to the shores of so small a body of water, was in the possession of the three several states of Geneva, Savoy, and Berne. The first consisted of a mere fragment of territory at the western, or lower horn of the crescent; the second occupied nearly the whole of the southern side of the sheet, or the cavity of the half-moon; while the latter was mistress of the whole of the convex border, and of the eastern horn. The shores of Savoy are composed, with immaterial exceptions, of advanced spurs of the high Alps, among which towers Mont Blanc, like a sovereign seated in majesty in the midst of a brilliant court, the rocks frequently rising from the water's edge in perpendicular masses. None of the lakes of this remarkable region possess a greater variety of scenery than that of Geneva, which changes from the smiling aspect of fertility and cultivation, at its lower extremity, to the sublimity of a savage and sublime nature at its upper. Vévey, the haven for which the Winkelried was bound, lies at the distance of three leagues from the head of the lake, or the point where it receives the Rhone; and Geneva, the port from which the reader has just seen her take her departure, is divided by that river as it glances out of the blue basin of the Leman again, to traverse the fertile fields of France, on its hurried course towards the distant Mediterranean.

    It is well known that the currents of air, on all bodies of water that lie amid high and broken mountains, are uncertain both as to their direction and their force. This was the difficulty which had most disturbed Baptiste during the delay of the bark, for the experienced waterman well knew it required the first and the freest effort of the wind to "drive the breeze home," as it is called by seamen, against the opposing currents that frequently descend from the mountains which surrounded his port. In addition to this difficulty, the shape of the lake was another reason why the winds rarely blow in the same direction over the whole of its surface at the same time. Strong and continued gales commonly force themselves down into the deep basin, and push their way, against all resistance, into every crevice of the rocks; but a power less than this, rarely succeeds in favoring the bark with the same breeze, from the entrance to the outlet of the Rhone.

    As a consequence of these peculiarities, the passengers of the Winkelried had early evidence that they had trifled too long with the fickle air. The breeze carried them up abreast of Lausanne in good season, but here the influence of the mountains began to impair its force, and, by the time the sun had a little fallen towards the long, dark, even line of the Jura, the good vessel was driven to the usual expedients of jibing and hauling-in of sheets.

Baptiste had only to blame his own cupidity for this disappointment; and the consciousness that, had he complied with the engagement, made on the previous evening with the mass of his passengers, to depart with the dawn, he should now have been in a situation to profit by any turn of fortune that was likely to arise from the multitude of strangers who were in Vévey, rendered him moody. As is usual with the headstrong and selfish when they possess the power, others were made to pay for the fault that he alone had committed. His men were vexed with contradictory and useless orders; the inferior passengers were accused of constant neglect of his instructions, a fault which he did not hesitate to affirm had caused the bark to sail less swiftly than usual, and he no longer even answered the occasional question of those for whom he felt habitual deference, with his former respect and readiness.

Chapter IV

> Thrice to thine, and thrice to mine,
> And thrice again, to make up nine
>
> Macbeth.

Baffling and light airs kept the Winkelried a long time nearly stationary, and it was only by paying the greatest attention to trimming the sails and to all the little minutiæ of the waterman's art that the vessel was worked into the eastern horn of the crescent, as the sun touched the hazy line of the Jura. Here the wind failed entirely, the surface of the lake becoming as glassy and smooth as a mirror, and further motion, for the time at least, was quite out of the question. The crew, perceiving the hopelessness of their exertions, and fatigued with the previous toil, threw themselves among the boxes and bales, and endeavored to catch a little sleep, in anticipation of the north breeze, which, at this season of the year, usually blew from the shores of Vaud within an hour or two of the disappearance of the sun.

The deck of the bark was now left to the undisputed possession of her passengers. The day had latterly been sultry, for the season, the even water having cast back the hot rays in fierce reflection, and, as evening drew on, a refreshing coolness came to relieve the densely packed and scorching travellers. The effect of such a change was like that which would have been observed among a flock of heavily fleeced sheep, which, after gasping for breath beneath trees and hedges, during the time of the sun's power, are seen scattering over their pastures to feed, or to play their antics, as a grateful shade succeeds to cool their panting sides.

Baptiste, as is but too apt to be the case with men possessed of brief authority, during the day had mercilessly played the tyrant with all the passengers that were beneath the privileged degrees, more than once threatening to come to extremities with several, who had betrayed restlessness under the restraint and suffering of their unaccustomed situation. Perhaps there is no man who feels less for the complaints of the novice than your weather-beaten and hardened mariner; for, familiarized to the suffering and confinement of a vessel, and at liberty himself to seek relief in his duties and avocations, he can scarcely enter into the privations and embarrassments of those to whom all is so new and painful. But, in the patron of the Winkelried, there existed a natural in difference to the grievances of others, and a narrow selfishness of disposition, in aid of the opinions which had been formed by a life of hardship and exposure. He considered the vulgar passenger as so much troublesome freight, which, while it brought the advantage of a higher remuneration than the same cubic measurement of inanimate matter, had the unpleasant drawback of volition and motion. With this general tendency to bully and intimidate, the wary patron had, however, made a silent exception in favor of the Italian, who has introduced himself to the reader by the ill-omened name of Il Maledetto, or the accursed. This formidable personage had enjoyed a perfect immunity from the effects of Baptiste's tyranny, which he had been able to establish by a very simple and quiet process. Instead of cowering at the fierce glance, or recoiling at the rude remonstrances of the churlish patron, he had chosen his time, when the latter was in one of his hottest ebullitions of anger, and when maledictions and menaces flowed out of his mouth in torrents, coolly to place himself on the very spot that the other had proscribed, where he maintained his ground with a quietness and composure which it might have been difficult to say was more to be imputed to extreme ignorance, or to immeasurable contempt. At least so reasoned the spectators; some thinking that the stranger meant to bring affairs to a speedy issue by braving the patron's fury, and others charitably inferring that he knew no better. But thus did not Baptiste reason himself. He saw by the calm eye and resolute demeanor of his passenger that he himself, his pretended professional difficulties, his captiousness, and his threats, were alike despised; and he shrank from collision with such a spirit, precisely on the principle that the intimidated among the rest of the travellers shrunk from a contest with his own. From this moment Il Maledetto, or, as he was called by Baptiste him self, who it would appear had some knowledge of his person, Maso, became as completely the master of his own movements, as if he had been one of the more honored in the stern of the bark, or even her patron. He did not abuse his advantage, however, rarely quitting the indicated station near his own effects, where he had been mainly content to repose in listless indolence, like the others, dozing away the minutes.

But the scene was now altogether changed. The instant the wrangling, discontented, and unhappy, because disappointed, patron, confessed his inability to reach his port before the coming of the expected night-breeze, and threw himself on a bale, to conceal his dissatisfaction in sleep, head arose after head from among the pile of freight, and body after body followed the nobler member, until the whole mass was alive with human beings. The invigorating coolness, the tranquil hour, the prospect of a safe if not a speedy arrival, and the relief from excessive weariness, produced a sudden and agreeable re-action in the feelings of all. Even the Baron de Willading and his friends, who had shared in none of the especial privations just named, joined in the general exhibition of satisfaction and good-will, rather aiding by their smiles and affability than restraining by their presence the whims and jokes of the different individuals among the motley group of their nameless companions.

The aspect and position of the bark, as well as the prospects of those on board as they were connected with their arrival, now deserve to be more particularly mentioned. The manner in which the vessel was loaded to the water's edge has already been more than once alluded to. The whole of the centre of the broad deck, a portion of the Winkelried which, owing to the over-hanging gangways, possessed, in common with all the similar craft of the Leman, a greater width than is usual in vessels of the same tonnage elsewhere, was so cumbered with freight as barely to leave a passage to the crew, forward and aft, by stepping among the boxes and bales that were piled much higher than their own heads. A little vacant space was left near the stern, in which it was possible for the party who occupied that part of the deck to move, though in sufficiently straitened limits, while the huge tiller played in its semicircle behind. At the other extremity, as is absolutely necessary in all navigation, the forecastle was reasonably clear, though even this important part of the deck was bristling with the flukes of no less than nine anchors that lay in a row across its breadth, the wild roadsteads of this end of the lake rendering such a provision of ground-tackle absolutely indispensable to the safety of every craft that ventured into its eastern horn. The effect of the whole, seen as it was in a state of absolute rest, was to give to the Winkelried the appearance of a small mound in the midst of the water, that was crowded with human beings, and seemingly so incorporated with the element oh which it floated as to grow out of its bosom; an image that the fancy was not slow to form, aided as it was by the reflection of the mass that the unruffled lake threw back from its mirror-like face, as perfectly formed, as unwieldy, and nearly as distinct, as the original. To this picture of a motionless rock, or island, the spars, sails, and high, pointed beak, however, formed especial exceptions. The yards hung, as seamen term it, a cockbill, or in such negligent and picturesque positions as an artist would most love to draw, while the drapery of the canvass was suspended in graceful and spotless festoons, as it had fallen by chance, or been cast carelessly from the hands of the boatmen. The beak, or prow, rose in its sharp gallant stem, resembling the stately neck of a swan, slightly swerving from its direction, or inclining in a nearly imperceptible sweep, as the hull yielded to the secret influence of the varying currents.

When the teeming pile of freight, therefore, began so freely to bring forth, and traveller after traveller left his wallet, there was no great space found in which they could stretch their wearied limbs, or seek the change they needed. But suffering is a good preparative for pleasure, and there is no sweetner of liberty like previous confinement. Baptiste was no sooner heard to snore, than the whole hummock of cargo was garnished with upright bodies and stretching arms and legs, as mice are known to steal from their holes during the slumbers of their mortal enemy, the cat.

The reader has been made sufficiently acquainted with the moral composition of the Winkelried's living freight, in the opening chapter. As it had undergone no other alteration than that produced by lassitude, he is already prepared, therefore, to renew his communications with its different members, all of whom were well disposed to show off in their respective characters, the moment they were favored with an opportunity. The mercurial Pippo, as he had been the most difficult to restrain during the day, was the first to steal from his lair, now that the Argus-like eyes of Baptiste permitted the freedom, and the exhilarating, coolness of the sunset invited action. His success emboldened others, and, ere long, the buffoon had an admiring audience around him, that was well-disposed to laugh at his witticisms, and to applaud all his practical jokes. Gaining courage as he proceeded, the buffoon gradually went from liberty to liberty, until he was at length triumphantly established on what might be termed an advanced spur of the mountain formed by the tubs of Nicklaus Wagner, in the regular exercise of his art; while a crowd of amused and gaping spectators clustered about him, peopling every eminence of the height, and even invading the more privileged deck in their eagerness to see and to admire.

Though frequently reduced by adverse fortune to the lowest shifts of his calling, such as the horse-play of Policinello, and the imitation of uncouth sounds, that resembled nothing either in heaven or earth, Pippo was a clever knave in his way, and was quite equal to a display of the higher branches of his art, whenever chance gave him an audience capable of estimating his qualities. On the present occasion he was obliged to address himself both to the polished and to the unpolished; for the proximity of their position, as well as a good-natured readiness to lend themselves to fooleries that were so agreeable to most around them, had brought the more gentle portion of the passengers within the influence of his wit.

"And now, illustrissimi signori," continued the wily juggler, after having drawn a burst of applause by one of his happiest hits in a sleight-of-hand exhibition, "I come to the most imposing and the most mysterious part of my knowledge--that of looking into the future, and of foretelling events. If there are any among you who would wish to know how long they are to eat the bread of toil, let them come to me; if there is a youth that wishes to learn whether the heart of his mistress is made of flesh or of stone--a maiden that would see into a youth's faith and constancy, while her long eyelashes cover her sight like a modest silken veil--or a noble, that would fain have an insight into the movements of his rivals at court or council, let them all put their questions to Pippo, who has an answer ready for each, and an answer so real, that the most expert among the listeners will be ready to swear that a lie from his mouth is worth more than truth from that of another man."

"He that would gain credit for knowledge of the future," gravely observed the Signor Grimaldi, who had listened to his countryman's voluble eulogium on his own merits with a good-natured laugh, "had best commence by showing his familiarity with the past. Who and what is he that speaks to thee, as a specimen of thy skill in sooth-saying?"

"His eccellenza is more than he seems, less than he deserves to be, and as much as any present. He hath an old and a prized friend at his elbow; hath come because it was his pleasure, to witness the games at Vévey--will depart for the same reason, when they are over, and will seek his home at his leisure--not like a fox stealing into his hole, but as the stately ship sails, gallantly, and by the light of the sun, into her haven."

"This will never do, Pippo," returned the good-humoured old noble; "at need I might equal this myself. Thou shouldst relate that which is less probable, while it is more true."

"Signore, we prophets like to sleep in whole skins. If it be your eccellenza's pleasure and that of your noble company to listen to the truly wonderful, I will tell some of these honest people matters touching their own interests that they do not know themselves, and yet it shall be as clear to every body else as the sun in the heavens at noon-day."

"Thou wilt, probably, tell them their faults?"

"Your eccellenza has a right to my place, for no prophet could have better divined my intention;" answered the laughing knave. "Come nearer, friend," he added, beckoning to the Bernois; "thou art Nicklaus Wagner, a fat peasant of the great canton, and a warm husbandman, that fancies he has a title to the respect of all he meets because some one among his fathers bought a right in the bürgerschaft. Thou hast a large stake in the Winkelried, and art at this moment thinking what punishment is good enough for an impudent soothsayer who dares dive so unceremoniously into the secrets of so warm a citizen, while all around thee wish thy cheeses had never left the dairy, to the discomfort of our limbs and to the great detriment of the bark's speed."

This sally at the expense of Nicklaus drew a burst of merriment from the listeners; for the selfish spirit he had manifested throughout the day had won little favor with a majority of his fellow travellers, who had all the generous propensities that are usually so abundant among those who have little or nothing to bestow, and who were by this time so well disposed to be merry that much less would have served to stimulate their mirth.

"Wert thou the owner of this good freight friend, thou might find its presence less uncomfortable than thou now appearest to think," returned the literal peasant, who had no humour for raillery, and to whom a jest on the subject of property had that sort of irreverend character that popular opinion and holy sayings have attached to waste. "The cheeses are well enough where they find themselves; if thou dislikest their company thou hast the alternative of the water."

"A truce between us, worshipful burgher! and let our skirmish end in something that may be useful to both. Thou hast that which would be acceptable to me, and I have that which no owner of cheeses would refuse, did he know the means by which it might be come at honestly."

Nicklaus growled a few words of distrust and indifference, but it was plain that the ambiguous language of the juggler, as usual, had succeeded in awakening interest. With the affectation of a mind secretly conscious of its own infirmity, he pretended to be indifferent to what the other professed a readiness to reveal, while with the rapacity of a grasping spirit he betrayed a longing to know more.

"First I will tell thee," said Pippo, with a parade of good-nature, "that thou deservest to remain in ignorance, as a punishment of thy pride and want of faith; but it is the failing of your prophet to let that be known which he ought to conceal. Thou flatterest thyself this is the fattest cargo of cheeses that will cross the Swiss waters this season, on their way to an Italian market? Shake not thy head.--'Tis useless to deny it to a man of my learning!"

"Nay, I know there are others as heavy, and, it may be, as good; but this has the advantage of being the first, a circumstance that is certain to command a price."

"Such is the blindness of one that nature sent on earth to deal in cheeses!"--The Herr Von Willading and his friends smiled among themselves at the cool impudence of the mountebank--"Thou fanciest it is so; and at this moment, a heavily laden bark is driving before a favorable gale, near the upper end of the lake of the four cantons, while a long line of mules is waiting at Flüellen, to bear its freight by the paths of the St. Gothard, to Milano and other rich markets of the south. In virtue of my secret power, I see that, in despite of all thy cravings, it will arrive before thine."

Nicklaus fidgeted, for the graphic particularity of Pippo almost led him to believe the augury might be true.

"Had this bark sailed according to our covenant," he said, with a simplicity that betrayed his uneasiness, "the beasts bespoken by me would now be loading at Villeneuve; and, if there be justice in Vaud, I shall hold Baptiste responsible for any disadvantage that may come of the neglect."

"Luckily, the generous Baptiste is asleep," returned Pippo, "or we might hear objections to this scheme. But, Signiori, I see you are satisfied with this insight into the character of the warm peasant of Berne, who, to say truth, has not much to conceal from us, and I will turn my searching looks into the soul of this pious pilgrim, the reverend Conrado, whose unction may well go near to be a leaven sufficient to lighten all in the bark of their burthens of backslidings. Thou earnest the penitence and prayers of many sinners, besides some merchandise of this nature of thine own."

"I am bound to Loretto, with the mental offerings of certain Christians, who are too much occupied with their daily concerns to make the journey in person," answered the pilgrim, who never absolutely threw aside his professional character, though he cared in general so little about his hypocrisy being known. "I am poor, and humble of appearance, but I have seen miracles in my day!"

"If any trust valuable offerings to thy keeping, thou art a living miracle in thine own person! I can foresee that thou wilt bear nought else beside aves."

"Nay, I pretend to deal in little more. The rich and great, they that send vessels of gold and rich dresses to Our Lady, employ their own favorite messengers; I am but the bearer of prayer and the substitute for the penitent. The sufferings that I undergo in the flesh are passed to the credit of my employers, who get the benefit of my aches and pains. I pretend to be no more than their go-between, as yonder manner has so lately called me."

Pippo turned suddenly, following the direction of the other's eye, and cast a glance at the self-styled Il Maledetto. This individual, of all the common herd, had alone forborne to join the gaping and amused crowd near the juggler. His forbearance, or want of curiosity, had left him in the quiet possession of the little platform that was made by the stowage of the boxes, and he now stood on the summit of the pile, conspicuous by his situation and mein, the latter being remarkable for its unmoved calmness, heightened by the understanding manner that is so peculiar to a seaman when afloat."

"Wilt thou have the history of thy coming perils, friend mariner?" cried the mercurial mountebank: "A journal of thy future risks and tempests to amuse you in this calm? Such a picture of sea-monsters and of coral that grows in the ocean's caverns, where mariners sleep, that shall give thee the night-mare for months, and cause thee to dream of wrecks and bleached bones for the rest of thy life? Thou hast only to wish it, to have the adventures of thy next voyage laid before thee, like a map."

"Thou would'st gain more credit with me, as one cunning in thy art, by giving the history of the last."

"The request is reasonable, and thou shalt have it: for I love the bold adventurer that trusts himself hardily upon the great deep;" answered the unabashed Pippo. "My first lessons in necromancy were received on the mole of Napoli, amid burly Inglesi, straight-nosed Greeks, swarthy Sicilians, and Maltese with spirits as fine as the gold of their own chains. This was the school in which I learned to know my art, and an apt scholar I proved in all that touches the philosophy and humanity of my craft. Signore, thy palm?"

Maso spread his sinewy hand in the direction of the juggler, without descending from his elevation, and in a way to show that, while he would not balk the common humor, he was superior to the gaping wonder and childish credulity of most of those who watched the result. Pippo affected to stretch out his neck, in order to study the hard and dark lines, and then he resumed his revelations, like one perfectly satisfied with what he had discovered.

"The hand is masculine, and has been familiar with many friends in its time. It hath dealt with steel, and cordage, and saltpetre, and most of all with gold. Signori, the true seat of a man's digestion lies in the palm of his hand; if that is free to give and to receive, he will never have a costive conscience, for of all damnable inconveniences that afflict mortals, that of a conscience that will neither give up nor take is the heaviest curse. Let a man have as much sagacity as shall make him a cardinal, if it get entangled in the meshes of one of your unyielding consciences, ye shall see him a mendicant brother to his dying day; let him be born a prince with a close-ribbed opinion of this sort, and he had better have been born a beggar, for his reign will be like a river from which the current sets outward, without any return. No, my friends, a palm like this of Maso's is a favorable sign, since it hinges on a pliant will, that will open and shut like a well-formed eye, or the jacket of a shell-fish, at its owner's pleasure. Thou hast drawn near to many a port before this of Vévey, after the sun has fallen low, Signor Maso!"

"In that I have taken a seaman's chances, which depend more on the winds than on his own wishes."

"Thou esteemest the bottom of the craft in which thou art required to sail, as far more important than her ancient. Thou hast an eye for a keel, but none for color; unless, indeed, as it may happen to be convenient to seem that thou art not."

"Nay, Master Soothsayer, I suspect thee to be an officer of some of the Holy Brotherhoods, sent in this guise to question us poor travellers to our ruin!" answered Maso. "I am, what thou seest, but a poor mariner that hath no better bark under him than this of Baptiste, and on a sea no larger than a Swiss lake."

"Shrewdly observed," said Pippo, winking to those near him, though he so little liked the eye and bearing of the other that he was not sorry to turn to some new subject. "But what matters it, Signori, to be speaking of the qualities of men! We are all alike, honorable, merciful, more disposed to help others than to help ourselves, and so little given to selfishness, that nature has been obliged to supply every mother's son of us with a sort of goad, that shall be constantly pricking us on to look after our own interests. Here are animals whose dispositions are less understood, and we will bestow a useful minute in examining their qualities. Reverend Augustine, this mastiff of thine is named Uberto?"

"He is known by that appellation throughout the cantons and their allies. The fame of the dog reaches even to Turin and to most of the towns in the plain of Lombardy."

"Now, Signori, you perceive that this is but a secondary creature in the scale of animals. Do him good and he will be grateful; do him harm, and he will forgive. Feed him, and he is satisfied. He will travel the paths of the St. Bernard, night and day, to do credit to his training, and when the toil is ended, all he asks is just as much meat as will keep the breath within his ribs. Had heaven given Uberto a conscience and greater wit, the first might have shown him the impiety of working for travellers on holy days and festas, while the latter would be apt to say he was a fool for troubling himself about the safety of others at all."

"And yet his masters, the good Augustines themselves, do not hold so selfish a creed!" observed Adelheid.

"Ah! they have heaven in view! I cry the reverend Augustine's pardon-- but, lady, the difference is in the length of the calculation. Woe's me, brethren; I would that my parents had educated me for a bishop, or a viceroy, or some other modest employment, that this learned craft of mine might have fallen into better hands! Ye would lose in instruction, but I should be removed from the giddy heights of ambition, and die at last with some hopes of being a saint. Fair lady, thou travellest on a bootless errand, if I know the reason that tempts thee to cross the Alps at this late season of the year."

This sudden address caused both Adelheid and her father to start, for, in despite of pride and the force of reason, it is seldom that we can completely redeem our opinions from the shackles of superstition, and that dread of the unseen future which appears to have been entailed upon our nature, as a ceaseless monitor of the eternal state of being to which all are hastening, with steps so noiseless and yet so sure. The countenance of the maiden changed, and she turned a quick, involuntary glance at her anxious parent, as if to note the effect of this rude announcement on him before she answered.

"I go in quest of the blessing, health," she said, "and I should be sorry to think thy prognostic likely to be realized. With youth, a good constitution, and tender friends of my side, there is reason to think thou mayest, in this at least, prove a false prophet."

"Lady, hast thou hope?"

Pippo ventured this question as he had adventured his opinion; that is to say, recklessly, pretendingly, and with great indifference to any effect it might have, except as it was likely to establish his reputation with the crowd. Still, it would seem, that by one of those singular coincidences that are hourly occurring in real life, he had unwittingly touched a sensitive chord in the system of his fair fellow-traveller. Her eyes sank to the deck at this abrupt question, the color again stole to her polished temples, and the least practised in the emotions of the sex might have detected painful embarrassment in her mein. She was, however, spared the awkwardness of a reply, by the unexpected and prompt interference of Maso.

"Hope is the last of our friends to prove recreant," said this mariner, "else would the cases of many in company be bad enough, thine own included, Pippo; for, judging by the outward signs, the Swabian campaign has not been rich in spoils."

"Providence has ordered the harvests of wit much as it has ordered the harvests of the field," returned the juggler, who felt the sarcasm of the other's remark with all the poignancy that it could derive from truth; since, to expose his real situation, he was absolutely indebted to an extraordinary access of generosity in Baptiste, for his very passage across the Leman. "One year, thou shall find the vineyard dripping liquors precious as diamonds, while, the next, barrenness shall make it its seat. To-day the peasant will complain that poverty prevents him from building the covering necessary to house his crops, while to-morrow he will be heard groaning over empty garners. Abundance and famine travel the earth hard upon each other's heels, and it is not surprising that he who lives by his wits should sometimes fail of his harvest, as well as he who lives by his hands."

"If constant custom can secure success, the pious Conrad should be prosperous," answered Maso, "for, of all machinery, that of sin is the least seldom idle. His trade at least can never fail for want of employers."

"Thou hast it, Signor Maso; and it is for this especial reason that I wish my parents had educated me for a bishoprick. He that is charged with reproving his fellow creatures for their vices need never know an idle hour."

"Thou dost not understand what thou sayest," put in Conrad; "love for the saints has much fallen away since my youth, and where there is one Christian ready now to bestow his silver, in order to get the blessing of some favorite shrine, there were then ten. I have heard the elders of us pilgrims say, that, fifty years since, 'twas a pleasure to bear the sins of a whole parish, for ours is a business in which the load does not so much depend on the amount as the quality; and, in their time there were willing offerings, frank confessions, and generous consideration for those who undertook the toil."

"In such a trade, the less thou hast to answer for, in behalf of others, the more will pass to thy credit on the score of thine own backslidings," pithily remarked Nicklaus Wagner, who was a sturdy Protestant, and apt enough at levelling these side-hits at those who professed a faith, obnoxious to the attacks of all who dissented from the opinions and the spiritual domination of Rome.

But Conrad was a rare specimen of what may be effected by training and well-rooted prejudices. In presenting this man to the mind of the reader, we have no intention to impugn the doctrines of the particular church to which he belonged, but simply to show, as the truth will fully warrant, to what a pass of flagrant and impudent pretension the qualities of man, unbridled by the wholesome corrective of a sound and healthful opinion, was capable of conducting abuses on the most solemn and gravest subjects. In that age usages prevailed, and were so familial to the minds of the actors as to excite neither reflection nor comment, which would now lead to revolutions, and a general rising in defence of principles which are held to be clear as the air we breathe. Though we entertain no doubt of the existence of that truth which pervades the universe, and to which all things tend, we think the world, in its practices, its theories, and its conventional standards of right and wrong, is in a condition of constant change, which it should be the business of the wise and good to favor, so long as care is had that the advantage is not bought by a re-action of evil, that shall more than prove its counterpoise. Conrad was one of the lowest class of those fungi that grow out of the decayed parts of the moral, as their more material types prove the rottenness of the vegetable, world; and the probability of the truth of the portraiture is not to be loosely denied, without mature reflection on the similar anomalies that are yet to be found on every side of us, or without studying the history of the abuses which then disgraced Christianity, and which, in truth, became so intolerable in their character, and so hideous in their features, as to be the chief influencing cause to bring about their own annihilation.

Pippo, who had that useful tact which enables a man to measure his own estimation with others, was not slow to perceive that the more enlightened part of his audience began to tire of this pretending buffoonery. Resorting to a happy subterfuge, by means of one of his sleight-of-hand expedients, he succeeded in transferring the whole of that portion of the spectators who still found amusement in his jugglery, to the other end of the vessel, where they established themselves among the anchors, ready as ever to swallow an aliment, that seems to find an unextinguishable appetite for its reception among the vulgar. Here he continued his exhibition, now moralizing in the quaint and often in the pithy manner, which renders the southern buffoon so much superior to his duller competitor of the north, and uttering a wild jumble of wholesome truths, loose morality, and witty inuendoes, the latter of which never failed to extort roars of laughter from all but those who happened to be their luckless subjects.

Once or twice Baptiste raised his head, and stared about him with drowsy eyes, but, satisfied there was nothing to be done in the way of forcing the vessel ahead, he resumed his nap, without interfering in the pastime of those whom he had hitherto seemed to take pleasure in annoying. Left entirely to themselves, therefore, the crowd on the forecastle represented one of those every-day but profitable pictures of life, which abound under our eyes, but which, though they are pregnant with instruction, are treated with the indifference that would seem to be the inevitable consequence of familiarity.

The crowded and overloaded bark might have been compared to the vessel of human life, which floats at all times subject to the thousand accidents of a delicate and complicated machinery: the lake, so smooth and alluring in its present tranquillity, but so capable of lashing its iron-bound coasts with fury, to a treacherous world, whose smile is almost always as dangerous as its frown; and, to complete the picture, the idle, laughing, thoughtless, and yet inflammable group that surrounded the buffoon, to the unaccountable medley of human sympathies, of sudden and fierce passions, of fun and frolic, so inexplicably mingled with the grossest egotism that enters into the heart of man: in a word, to so much that is beautiful and divine, with so much that would seem to be derived directly from the demons, a compound which composes this mysterious and dread state of being, and which we are taught, by reason and revelation, is only a preparation for another still more incomprehensible and wonderful.

Chapter V

"How like a fawning publican he looks!"

Shylock.

The change of the juggler's scene of action left the party in the stern of the barge, in quiet possession of their portion of the vessel. Baptiste and his boatmen still slept among the boxes; Maso continued to pace his elevated platform above their heads; and the meek-looking stranger, whose entrance into the barge had drawn so many witticisms from Pippo, sate a little apart, silent, furtively observant, and retiring, in the identical spot he had occupied throughout the day. With these exceptions, the whole of the rest of the travellers were crowding around the person of the mountebank. Perhaps we have not done well, however, in classing either of the two just named with the more common herd, for there were strong points of difference to distinguish both from most of their companions.

The exterior and the personal appointments of the unknown traveller, who had shrunk so sensitively before the hits of the Neapolitan, was greatly superior to those of any other in the bark beneath the degree of the gentle, not even excepting those of the warm peasant Nicklaus Wagner, the owner of so large a portion of the freight. There was a decency of air that commanded more respect than it was then usual to yield to the nameless, a quietness of demeanor that denoted reflection and the habit of self-study and self-correction, together with a deference to others that was well adapted to gain friends. In the midst of the noisy, clamorous merriment of all around him, his restrained and rebuked manner had won upon the favor of the more privileged, who had unavoidably noticed the difference, and had prepared the way to a more frank communication between the party of the noble, and one who, if not their equal in the usual points of worldly distinction, was greatly superior to those among whom he had been accidentally cast by the chances of his journey. Not so with Maso; he, apparently, had little in common with the unobtruding and silent being that sat so near his path, in the short turns he was making to and fro across the pile of freight. The mariner was thirty, while the head of the unknown traveller was already beginning to be sprinkled with gray. The walk, attitudes, and gestures, of the former, were also those of a man confident of himself, a little addicted to be indifferent to others, and far more disposed to lead than to follow. These are qualities that it may be thought his present situation was scarcely suited to discover, but they had been made sufficiently apparent, by the cool, calculating looks he threw, from time to time, at the manoeuvres commanded by Baptiste, the expressive sneer with which he criticised his decisions, and a few biting remarks which had escaped him in the course of the day, and which had conveyed any thing but compliments to the nautical skill of the patron and his fresh-water followers. Still there were signs of better stuff in this suspicious-looking person than are usually seen about men, whose attire, pursuits and situation, are so indicative of the world's pressing hard upon their principles, as happened to be the fact with this poor and unknown seaman. Though ill clad, and wearing about him the general tokens of a vagrant life, and that loose connexion with society that is usually taken as sufficient evidence of one's demerits, his countenance occasionally denoted thought, and, during the day, his eye had frequently wandered towards the group of his more intelligent fellow-passengers, as if he found subjects of greater interest in their discourse, than in the rude pleasantries and practical jokes of those nearer his person.

The high-bred are always courteous, except in cases in which presumption repels civility; for they who are accustomed to the privileges of station, think far less of their immunities, than they, who by being excluded from the fancied advantages, are apt to exaggerate a superiority that a short experience would show becomes of very questionable value in the possession. Without this equitable provision of Providence, the laws of civilized society would become truly intolerable, for, if peace of mind, pleasure, and what is usually termed happiness, were the exclusive enjoyment of those who are rich and honoured, there would, indeed, be so crying an injustice in their present ordinances as could not long withstand the united assaults of reason and justice. But, happily for the relief of the less gifted and the peace of the world, the fact is very different. Wealth has its peculiar woes; honors and privileges pall in the use; and, perhaps, as a rule, there is less of that regulated contentment, which forms the nearest approach to the condition of the blessed of which this unquiet state of being is susceptible, among those who are usually the most envied by their fellow-creatures, than in any other of the numerous gradations into which the social scale has been divided. He who reads our present legend with the eyes that we could wish, will find in its moral the illustration of this truth; for, if it is our intention to delineate some of the wrongs that spring from the abuses of the privileged and powerful, we hope equally to show how completely they fall short of their object, by failing to confer that exclusive happiness which is the goal that all struggle to attain.

Neither the Baron de Willading, nor his noble friend, the Genoese, though educated in the opinions of their caste, and necessarily under the influence of the prejudices of the age, was addicted to the insolence of vulgar pride. Their habits had revolted at the coarseness of the majority of the travellers, and they were glad to be rid of them by the expedient of Pippo; but no sooner did the modest, decent air of the stranger who remained, make itself apparent, than they felt a desire to compensate him for the privations he had already undergone, by showing the civilities that their own rank rendered so easy and usually so grateful. With this view, then, as soon as the noisy *troupe* had departed, the Signor Grimaldi raised his beaver with that discreet and imposing politeness which equally attracts and repels, and, addressing the solitary stranger, he invited him to descend, and stretch his legs on the part of the deck which had hitherto been considered exclusively devoted to the use of his own party. The other started, reddened, and looked like one who doubted whether he had heard aright.

"These noble gentlemen would be glad if you would come down, and take advantage of this opportunity to relieve your limbs;" said the young Sigismund, raising his own athletic arm towards the stranger, to offer its assistance in helping him to reach the deck.

Still the unknown traveller hesitated, in the manner of one who fears he might overstep discretion, by obtruding beyond the limits imposed by modesty. He glanced furtively upwards at the place where Maso bad posted himself, and muttered something of an intention to profit by its present nakedness.

"It has an occupant who does not seem disposed to admit another," said Sigismund, smiling; "your mariner has a self-possession when afloat, that usually gives him the same superiority that the well-armed swasher has among the timid in the street. You would do well, then, to accept the offer of the noble Genoese."

The stranger, who had once or twice been called rather ostentatiously by Baptiste the Herr Müller, during the day, as if the patron were disposed to let his hearers know that he had those who at least bore creditable names, even among his ordinary passengers, no longer delayed. He came down from his seat, and moved about the deck in his usual, quiet, subdued manner, but in a way to show that he found a very sensible and grateful relief in being permitted to make the change. Sigismund was rewarded for this act of good-nature by a smile from Adelheid, who thought his warm interference in behalf of one, seemingly so much his inferior, did no discredit to his rank. It is possible that the youthful soldier had some secret sentiment of the advantage he derived from his kind interest in the stranger, for his brow flushed, and he looked more satisfied with himself, after this little office of humanity had been performed.

"You are better among us here," the baron kindly observed, when the Herr Müller was fairly established in his new situation, "than among the freight of the honest Nicklaus Wagner, who, Heaven help the worthy peasant! has loaded us fairly to the water's edge, with the notable industry of his dairy people. I like to witness the prosperity of our burghers, but it would have been better for us travellers, at least, had there been less of the wealth of honest Nicklaus in our company. Are you of Berne, or of Zurich?"

"Of Berne, Herr Baron."

"I might have guessed that by finding you on the Genfer See, instead of the Wallenstätter. There are many of the Müllers in the Emmen Thal?"

"The Herr is right; the name is frequent, both in that valley, and in Entlibuch."

"It is a frequent appellation among us of the Teutonick stock. I had many Müllers in my company, Gaetano, when we lay before Mantua, I remember that two of the brave fellows were buried in the marshes of that low country; for the fever helped the enemy as much as the sword, in the life-wasting campaign of the year we besieged the place."

The more observant Italian saw that the stranger was distressed by the personal nature of the conversation, and, while he quietly assented to his friend's remark, he took occasion to give it a new direction.

"You travel, like ourselves, Signore, to get a look at these far-famed revels of the Vévasians?"

"That, and affairs, have brought me into this honorable company;" answered the Herr Müller, whom no kindness of tone, however, could win from his timid and subdued manner of speaking.

"And thou, father," turning to the Augustine, "art journeying towards thy mountain residence, after a visit of love to the valleys and their people?"

The monk of St. Bernard assented to the truth of this remark, explaining the manner in which his community were accustomed annually to appeal to the liberality of the generous in Switzerland, in behalf of an institution that was founded in the interest of humanity, without reference to distinction of faith.

"'Tis a blessed brotherhood," answered the Genoese, crossing himself, perhaps as much from habit as from devotion, "and the traveller need wish it well. I have never shared of your hospitality, but all report speaks fairly of it, and the title of a brother of San Bernardo, should prove a passport to the favor of every Christian."

"Signore," said Maso, stopping suddenly, and taking his part uninvited in the discourse, and yet in a way to avoid the appearance of an impertinent interference, "none know this better than I! A wanderer these many years, I have often seen the stony roof of the hospice with as much pleasure as I have ever beheld the entrance of my haven, when an adverse gale was pressing against my canvass. Honor and a rich *quête* to the clavier of the convent, therefore, for it is bringing succor to the poor and rest to the weary!"

As he uttered this opinion, Maso decorously raised his cap, and pursued his straitened walk with the industry of a caged tiger. It was so unusual for one of his condition to obtrude on the discourse of the fair and noble, that the party exchanged looks of surprise; but, the Signor Grirnaldi, more accustomed than most of his friends to the frank deportment and bold speech of mariners, from having dwelt long on the coast of the Mediterranean, felt disposed rather to humor than to repulse this disposition to talk.

"Thou art a Genoese, by thy dialect," he said, assuming as a matter of course the right to question one of years so much fewer, and of a condition so much inferior to his own.

"Signore," returned Maso, uncovering himself again, though his manner betrayed profound personal respect rather than the deference of the vulgar, "I was born in the city of palaces, though it was my fortune first to see the light beneath a humble roof. The poorest of us are proud of the splendor of Genova la Superba, even if its glory has come from our own groans."

The Signor Grimaldi frowned. But, ashamed to permit himself to be disturbed by an allusion so vague, and perhaps so unpremeditated, and more especially coming as it did from so insignificant a source, his brow regained its expression of habitual composure.

An instant of reflection, told him it would be in better taste to continue the conversation, than churlishly to cut it short for so light a cause.

"Thou art too young to have had much connexion, either in advantage or in suffering," he rejoined, "with the erection of the gorgeous dwellings to which thou alludest."

"This is true, Signore; except as one is the better or worse for those who have gone before him. I am what I seem, more by the acts of others than by any faults of my own. I envy not the rich or great, however; for one that has seen as much of life as I, knows the difference between the gay colors of the garment, and that of the shrivelled and diseased skin it conceals. We make our feluccas glittering and fine with paint, when their timbers work the most, and when the treacherous planks are ready to let in the sea to drown us."

"Thou hast the philosophy of it, young man, and hast uttered a biting truth, for those who waste their prime in chasing a phantom. Thou hast well bethought thee of these matters, for, if content with thy lot, no palace of our city would make thee happier."

"If, Signore, is a meaning word!--Content is like the north-star--we seamen steer for it, while none can ever reach it!"

"Am I then deceived in thee, after all? Is thy seeming moderation only affected; and would'st thou be the patron of the bark in which fortune hath made thee only a passenger?"

"And a bad fortune it hath proved," returned Maso, laughing. "We appear fated to pass the night in it, for, so far from seeing any signs of this land-breeze of which Baptiste has so confidently spoken, the air seems to have gone to sleep as well as the crew. Thou art accustomed to this climate, reverend Augustine; is it usual to see so deep a calm on the Leman at this late season?"

A question like this was well adapted to effect the speaker's wish to change the discourse, for it very naturally directed the attention of all present from a subject that was rather tolerated from idleness than interesting in itself, to the different natural phenomena by which they were surrounded. The sunset had now fairly passed, and the travellers were at the witching moment that precedes the final disappearance of the day. A calm so deep rested on the limpid lake, that it was not easy to distinguish the line which separated the two elements, in those places where the blue of the land was confounded with the well-known and peculiar color of the Leman.

The precise position of the Winkelried was near mid-way between the shores of Vaud and those of Savoy, though nearer to the first than to the last. Not another sail was visible on the whole of the watery expanse, with the exception of one that hung lazily from its yard, in a small bark that was pulling towards St. Gingoulph, bearing Savoyards returning to their homes from the other side of the lake, and which, in that delusive landscape, appeared to the eye to be within a stone's throw of the base of the mountain, though, in truth, still a weary row from the land.

Nature has spread her work on a scale so magnificent in this sublime region that ocular deceptions of this character abound, and it requires time and practice to judge of those measurements which have been rendered familiar in other scenes. In like manner to the bark under the rocks of Savoy, there lay another, a heavy-moulded boat, nearly in a line with Villeneuve, which seemed to float in the air instead of its proper element, and whose oars were seen to rise and fall beneath a high mound, that was rendered shapeless by refraction. This was a craft, bearing hay from the meadows at the mouth of the Rhone to their proprietors in the villages of the Swiss coast. A few light boats were pulling about in front of the town of Vévey, and a forest of low masts and latine yards, seen in the hundred picturesque attitudes peculiar to the rig, crowded the wild anchorage that is termed its port.

An air-line drawn from St. Saphorin to Meillerie, would have passed between the spars of the Winkelried, her distance from her haven, consequently, a little exceeded a marine league. This space might readily have been conquered in an hour or two by means of the sweeps, but for the lumbered condition of the decks, which would have rendered their use difficult, and the unusual draught of the bark, which would have caused the exertion to be painful. As it has been seen, Baptiste preferred waiting for the arrival of the night breeze to having recourse to an expedient so toil some and slow.

We have already said, that the point just described was at the place where the Leman fairly enters its eastern horn, and where its shores possess their boldest and finest faces. On the side of Savoy, the coast was a sublime wall of rocks, here and there clothed with chestnuts, or indented with ravines and dark glens, and naked and wild along the whole line of their giddy summits. The villages so frequently mentioned, and which have become celebrated in these later times by the touch of genius, clung to the uneven declivities, their lower dwellings laved by the lake, and their upper confounded with the rugged faces of the mountains. Beyond the limits of the Leman, the Alps shot up into still higher pinnacles, occasionally showing one of those naked excrescences of granite, which rise for a thousand feet above the rest of the range--a trifle in the stupendous scale of the vast piles--and which, in the language of the country are not inaptly termed Dents, from some fancied and plausible resemblance to human teeth. The verdant meadows of Noville, Aigle and Bex. spread for leagues between these snow-capped barriers, so dwindled to the eye, however, that the spectator believed that to be a mere bottom, which was, in truth, a broad and fertile plain. Beyond these again, came the celebrated pass of St. Maurice, where the foaming Rhone dashed between two abutments of rock, as if anxious to effect its exit before the superincumbent mountains could come together, and shut it out for ever from the inviting basin to which it was hurrying with a never-ceasing din. Behind this gorge, so celebrated as the key of the Valais, and even of the Alps in the time of the conquerors of the world, the background took a character of holy mystery. The shades of evening lay thick in that enormous glen, which was sufficiently large to contain a sovereign state, and the dark piles of mountains beyond were seen in a hazy, confused array. The setting was a grey boundary of rocks, on which fleecy clouds rested, as if tired with their long and high flight, and on which the parting day still lingered soft and lucid. One cone of dazzling white towered over all. It resembled a bright stepping-stone between heaven and earth, the heat of the hot sun falling innocuously against its sides, like the cold and pure breast of a virgin repelling those treacherous sentiments which prove the ruin of a shining and glorious innocence. Across the summit of this brilliant and cloud-like peak, which formed the most distant object in the view, ran the imaginary line that divided Italy from the regions of the north. Drawing nearer, and holding its course on the opposite shore, the eye embraced the range of rampart-like rocks that beetle over Villeneuve and Chillon, the latter a snow-white pile that seemed to rest partly on the land and partly, on the water. On the vast débris of the mountains clustered the hamlets of Clarens, Montreux, Châtelard, and all those other places, since rendered so familiar to the reader of fiction by the vivid pen of Rousseau. Above the latter village the whole of the savage and rocky range receded, leaving the lake-shore to vine-clad côtes that stretch away far to the west.

This scene; at all times alluring and grand, was now beheld under its most favorable auspices. The glare of day had deserted all that belonged to what might be termed the lower world, leaving in its stead the mild hues, the pleasing shadows, and the varying tints of twilight. It is true that a hundred châlets dotted the Alps, or those mountain pasturages which spread themselves a thousand fathoms above the Leman, on the foundation of rock that lay like a wall behind Montreux, shining still with the brightness of a bland even, but all below was fast catching the more sombre colors of the hour.

As the transition from day to night grew more palpable, the hamlets of Savoy became gray and hazy, the shades thickened around the bases of the mountains in a manner to render their forms indistinct and massive, and the milder glory of the scene was transferred to their summits. Seen by sun-light, these noble heights appear a long range of naked granite, piled on a foundation of chestnut-covered hills, and buttressed by a few such salient spurs as are perhaps necessary to give variety and agreeable shadows to their acclivities. Their outlines were now drawn in those waving lines that the pencil of Raphael would have loved to sketch, dark, distinct, and appearing to be carved by art. The inflected and capricious edges of the rocks stood out in high relief against the back-ground of pearly sky, resembling so much ebony wrought into every fantastic curvature that a wild and vivid fancy could conceive. Of all the wonderful and imposing sights of this extraordinary region, there is perhaps none in which there is so exquisite an admixture of the noble, the beautiful, and the bewitching, as in this view of these natural arabesques of Savoy, seen at the solemn hour of twilight.

The Baron de Willading and his friends stood uncovered, in reverence of the sublime picture, which could only come from the hands of the Creator, and with unalloyed enjoyment of the bland tranquillity of the hour. Exclamations of pleasure had escaped them, as the exhibition advanced; for the view, like the shifting of scenes, was in a constant state of transition under the waning and changing light, and each had eagerly pointed out to the others some peculiar charm of the view. The sight was, in sooth, of a nature to preclude selfishness, no one catching a glimpse that he did not wish to be shared by all. Vévey, their journey, the fleeting minutes, and their disappointment, were all forgotten in the delight of witnessing this evening landscape, and the silence was broken only to express those feelings of delight which had long been uppermost in every bosom.

"I doff my beaver to thy Switzerland, friend Melchior," cried the Signor Grimaldi, after directing the attention of Adelheid to one of the peaks of Savoy, of which he had just remarked that it seemed a spot where an angel might love to light in his visits to the earth; "if thou hast much of this, we of Italy must look to it, or--by the shades of our fathers! we shall lose our reputation for natural beauty. How is it young lady; hast thou many of these sun-sets at Willading? or, is this, after all, but an exception to what thou seest in common--as much a matter of astonishment to thyself, as--by San Francesco! good Marcelli, we must even own, it is to thee and me!"

Adelheid laughed at the old noble's good-humored rhapsody, but, much as she loved her native land, she could not pervert the truth by pretending that the sight was one to be often met with.

"If we have not this, however, we have our glaciers, our lakes, our cottages, our châlets, our Oberland, and such glens as have an eternal twilight of their own."

"Ay, my true-hearted and pretty Swiss, this is well for thee who wilt affirm that a drop of thy snow-water is worth a thousand limpid springs, or thou art not the true child of old Melchior de Willading; but it is lost on the cooler head of one who has seen other lands. Father Xavier, thou art a neutral, for thy dwelling is on the dividing ridge between the two countries, and I appeal to thee to know if these Helvetians have much of this quality of evening?"

The worthy monk met the question in the spirit with which it was asked, for the elasticity of the air, and the heavenly tranquillity and bewitching loveliness of the hour, well disposed him to be joyous.

"To maintain my character as an impartial judge," he answered, "I will say that each region has its own advantages. If Switzerland is the most wonderful and imposing, Italy is the most winning. The latter leaves more durable impressions and is more fondly cherished. One strikes the senses, but the other slowly winds its way into the affections; and he who has freely vented his admiration in exclamations and epithets in one, will, in the end, want language to express all the secret longings, the fond recollections, the deep repinings, that he retains for the other."

"Fairly reasoned, friend Melchior, and like an able umpire, leaving to each his share of consolation and vanity. Herr Müller, dost thou agree in a decision that gives thy much vaunted Switzerland so formidable a rival?"

"Signore," answered the meek traveller, "I see enough to admire and love in both, as is always the fact with that which God hath formed. This is a glorious world for the happy, and most might be so, could they summon courage to be innocent."

"The good Augustine will tell thee that this bears hard on certain points of theology, in which our common nature is treated with but indifferent respect. He that would continue innocent must struggle hard with his propensities."

The stranger was thoughtful, and Sigismund; whose eye had been earnestly riveted on his face, thought that it denoted more of peace then usual.

"Signore," rejoined the Herr Müller, when time had been given for reflection, "I believe it is good for us to know unhappiness. He that is permitted too much of his own will gets to be headstrong, and, like the overfed bullock, difficult to be managed; whereas, he who lives under the displeasure of his fellow-creatures is driven to look closely into himself, and comes, at last, to chasten his spirit by detecting its faults."

"Art thou a follower of Calvin?" demanded the Augustine suddenly, surprised to hear opinions so healthful in the mouth of a dissenter from the true church.

"Father, I belong neither to Rome nor to the religion of Geneva. I am a humble worshipper of God, and a believer in the blessed mediation of his holy Son."

"How!--Where dost thou find such sentiments out of the pale of the church?"

"In mine own heart. This is my temple, holy Augustine, and I never enter it without adoration for its Almighty founder. A cloud was over the roof of my father at my birth, and I have not been permitted to mingle much with men; but the solitude of my life has driven me to study my own nature, which I hope has become none the worse for the examination. I know I am an unworthy and sinful man, and I hope others are as much better than I as their opinions of themselves would give reason to think."

The words of the Herr Müller, which lost none of their weight by his unaffected and quiet manner, excited curiosity. At first, most of the listeners were disposed to believe him one of those exaggerated spirits who exalt themselves by a pretended self-abasement, but his natural, quiet, and thoughtful deportment soon produced a more favorable opinion. There was a habit of reflection, a retreating inward look about his eye, that revealed the character of one long and truly accustomed to look more at himself than at others, and which wrought singularly in his behalf.

"We may not all have these flattering opinions of ourselves that thy words would seem to imply Signor Müller," observed the Genoese, his tone changing to one better suited to soothe the feelings of the person addressed, while a shade insensibly stole over his own venerable features; "neither are all at peace that so seem. If it will be any consolation to thee to know that others are probably no more happy than thyself, I will add that I have known much pain, and that, too, amid circumstances which most would deem fortunate, and which, I fear, a great majority of mankind might be disposed to envy."

"I should be base indeed to seek consolation in such a source! I do not complain, Signore, though my whole life has so passed that I can hardly say that I enjoy it. It is not easy to smile when we know that all frown upon us; else could I be content. As it is, I rather feel than repine."

"This is a most singular condition of the mind;" whispered Adelheid to young Sigismund; for both had been deeply attentive listeners to the calm but strong language of the Herr Müller. The young man did not answer, and his fair companion saw with surprise, that he was pale, and with difficulty noticed her remark with a smile.

"The frowns of men, my son," observed the monk, "are usually reserved for those who offend its ordinances. The latter may not be always just, but there is a common sentiment which refuses to visit innocence, even in the narrow sense in which we understand the word, with undeserved displeasure."

The Herr Müller looked earnestly at the Augustine, and he seemed about to answer; but, checking the impulse, he bowed in submission. At the same time, a wild, painful smile gleamed on his face.

"I agree with thee, good canon," rejoined the simple-minded baron: "we are much addicted to quarrelling with the world, but, after all, when we look closely into the matter, it will commonly be found that the cause of our grievances exists in ourselves."

"Is there no Providence, father?" exclaimed Adelheid, a little reproachfully for one of her respectful habits and great filial tenderness. "Can we recall the dead to life, or keep those quick whom God is pleased to destroy?"

"Thou hast me, girl!--there is a truth in this that no bereaved parent can deny!"

This remark produced an embarrassed pause, during which the Herr Müller gazed furtively about him, looking from the face of one to that of another, as if seeking for some countenance on which he could rely. But he turned away to the view of those hills which had been so curiously wrought by the finger of the Almighty, and seemed to lose himself in their contemplation.

"This is some spirit that has been bruised by early indiscretion," said the Signor Grimaldi, in a low voice, "and whose repentance is strangely mixed with resignation. I know not whether such a man is most to be envied or pitied. There is a fearful mixture of resignation and of suffering in his air."

"He has not the mien of a stabber or a knave," answered the baron. "If he comes truly of the Müllers of the Emmen Thal, or even of those of Entlibuch, I should know something of his history. They are warm burghers, and mostly of fair name. It is true, that in my youth one of the family got out of favor with the councils, on account of some concealment of their lawful claims in the way of revenue, but the man made an atonement that was deemed sufficient in amount, and the matter was forgotten. It is not usual, Herr Müller, to meet citizens in our canton who go for neither Rome nor Calvin."

"It is not usual, mein Herr, to meet men placed as I am. Neither Rome nor Calvin is sufficient for me;--I have need of God!"

"I fear thou hast taken life?"

The stranger bowed, and his face grew livid, seemingly with the intensity of his own thoughts. Melchior de Willading so disliked the expression, that he turned away his eyes in uneasiness. The other glanced frequently at the forward part of the bark, and he seemed struggling hard to speak, but, for some strong reason, unable to effect his purpose. Uncovering himself, at length, he said steadily, as if superior to shame, while he fully felt the import of his communication, but in a voice that was cautiously suppressed--

"I am Balthazar, of your canton, Herr Baron, and I pray your powerful succor, should those untamed spirits on the forecastle come to discover the truth. My blood hath been made to curdle to-day whilst listening to their heartless threats and terrible maledictions. Without this fear, I should have kept my secret,--for God knows I am not proud of my office!"

The general and sudden surprise, accompanied as it was by a common movement of aversion, induced the Signor Grimaldi to demand the reason.

"Thy name is not in much favour apparently, Herr Müller, or Herr Balthazar, whichever it is thy pleasure to be called," observed the Genoese, casting a quick glance around the circle. "There is some mystery in it, that to me needs explanation."

"Signore, I am the headsman of Berne."

Though long schooled in the polished habits of his high condition, which taught him ordinarily to repress strong emotions, the Signor Grimaldi could not conceal the start which this unexpected announcement produced, for he had not escaped the usual prejudices of men.

"Truly, we have been fortunate in our associate, Melchior," he said drily, turning without ceremony from the man whose modest, quiet mien had lately interested him so much, but whose manner he now took to be assumed,--few pausing to investigate the motives of those who are condemned of opinion:--"here has been much excellent and useful morality thrown away upon a very unworthy subject!"

The baron received the intelligence of the real name of their travelling companion with less feeling. He had been greatly puzzled to account for the singular language he had heard, and he found relief in so brief a solution of the difficulty.

"The pretended name, after all, then, is only a cloak to conceal the truth! I knew the Müllers of the Emmen Thal so well, that I had great difficulty in fitting the character which the honest man gave of himself fairly upon any one of them all. But it is now clear enough, and doubtless Balthazar has no great reason to be proud of the turn which Fortune has played his family in making them executioners."

"Is the office hereditary?" demanded the Genoese, quickly.

"It is. Thou knowest that we of Berne have great respect for ancient usages. He that is born to the Bürgerschaft will die in the exercise of his rights, and he that is born out of its venerable pale must be satisfied to live out of it, unless he has gold or favor. Our institutions are a hint from nature, which leaves men as they are created, preserving the order and harmony of society by venerable and well-defined laws, as is wise and necessary. In nature, he that is born strong remains strong, and he that has little force must be content with his feebleness."

The Signor Grimaldi looked like one who felt contrition.

"Art thou, in truth, an hereditary executioner?" he asked, addressing Balthazar himself.

"Signore, I am: else would hand of mine have never taken life. 'Tis a hard duty to perform, even under the obligations and penalties of the law;--otherwise, it were accursed!"

"Thy fathers deemed it a privilege!"

"We suffer for their error: Signore, the sins of the fathers, in our case, have indeed been visited on the children to the latest generations."

The countenance of the Genoese grew brighter and his voice resumed the polished tones in which he usually spoke.

"Here has been some injustice of a certainty," he said, "or one of thy appearance would not be found in this cruel position. Depend on our authority to protect thee, should the danger thou seemest to apprehend really occur. Still the laws must be respected, though not always of the rigid impartiality that we might wish. Thou hast owned the imperfection of human nature, and it is not wonderful that its work should have flaws."

"I complain not now of the usage, which to me has become habit, but I dread the untamed fury of these ignorant and credulous men, who have taken a wild fancy that my presence might bring a curse upon the bark."

There are accidental situations which contain more healthful morals than can be drawn from a thousand ingenious and plausible homilies, and in which facts, in their naked simplicity, are far more eloquent than any meaning that can be conveyed by words. Such was the case with this meek and unexpected appeal of Balthazar. All who heard him saw his situation under very different colors from those in which it would have been regarded had the subject presented itself under ordinary circumstances. A common and painful sentiment attested strongly against the oppression that had given birth to his wrongs, and the good Melchior de Willading himself wondered how a case of this striking injustice could have arisen under the laws of Berne.

Chapter VI

*Methought I saw a thousand fearful wrecks,
A thousand men that fishes gnawed upon;
Wedges of gold, great anchors, heaps of pearl,
Inestimable stones, unvalued jewels,
All scattered in the bottom of the sea.*

Richard III.

The flitting twilight was now on the wane, and the shades of evening were gathering fast over the deep basin of the lake. The figure of Maso, as he continued to pace his elevated platform, was drawn dark and distinct against the southern sky, in which some of the last rays of the sun still lingered, but objects on both shores were getting to be confounded with the shapeless masses of the mountains. Here and there a pale star peeped out, though most of the vault that stretched across the confined horizon was shut in by dusky clouds. A streak of dull, unnatural light was seen in the quarter which lay above the meadows of the Rhone, and nearly in a direction with the peak of Mont Blanc, which, though not visible from this portion of the Leman, was known to lie behind the ramparts of Savoy, like a monarch of the hills entrenched in his citadel of rocks and ice.

The change, the lateness of the hour, and the unpleasant reflections left by the short dialogue with Balthazar, produced a strong and common desire to see the end of a navigation that was beginning to be irksome. Those objects which had lately yielded so much and so pure a delight were now getting to be black and menacing, and the very sublimity of the scale on which Nature had here thrown together her elements was an additional source of uncertainty and alarm. Those fairy-like, softly-delineated, natural arabesques, which had so lately been dwelt upon with rapture were now converted into dreary crags that seemed to beetle above the helpless bark, giving unpleasant admonitions of the savage and inhospitable properties of their iron-bound bases, which were known to prove destructive to all who were cast against them while the elements were in disorder.

These changes in the character of the scene, which in some respects began to take the aspect of omens, were uneasily witnessed by all in the stern of the bark, though the careless laughter, the rude joke, and the noisy cries, which from time to time arose on the forecastle, sufficiently showed that the careless spirits it held were still indulging in the coarse enjoyments most suited to their habits. One individual, however, was seen stealing from the crowd, and establishing himself on the pile of freight, as if he had a mind more addicted to reflection, and less disposed to unmeaning revelry, than most of those whom he had just abandoned. This was the Westphalian student, who, wearied with amusements that were below the level of his acquirements, and suddenly struck with the imposing aspect of the lake and the mountains, had stolen apart to muse on his distant home and the beings most dear to him, under an excitement that suited those morbid sensibilities which he had long encouraged by a very subtle metaphysical system of philosophy. Until now, Maso had paced his lofty post with his eye fixed chiefly on the heavens in the direction of Mont Blanc, occasionally turning it, however, over the motionless bulk of the bark, but when the student placed himself across his path, he stopped and smiled at the abstracted air and riveted regard with which the youth gazed at a star.

"Art thou an astronomer, that thou lookest so closely at yonder shining world?" demanded Il Maledetto, with the superiority that the mariner afloat is wont successfully to assume over the unhappy wight of a landsman, who is very liable to admit his own impotency on the novel and dangerous element:--"the astrologer himself would not study it more deeply."

"This is the hour agreed upon between me and one that I love to bring the unseen principle of our spirits together, by communing through its medium."

"I have heard of such means of intercourse. Dost see more than others by reason of such an assistant?"

"I see the object which is gazed upon, at this moment, by kind blue eyes that have often looked upon me in affection. When we are in a strange land, and in a fearful situation, such a communion has its pleasures!"

Maso laid his hand upon the shoulder of the student, which he pressed with the force of a vice.

"Thou art right," he said, moodily; "make the most of thy friendships, and, if there are any that love thee, tighten the knot by all the means thou hast. None know the curse of being deserted in this selfish and cruel battle of interest better than I! Be not ashamed of thy star, but gaze at it till thy eye-strings crack. See the bright eyes of her that loves thee in its twinkling, her constancy in its lustre, and her melancholy in its sadness; lose not the happy moments, for there will soon be a dark curtain to shut out its view."

The Westphalian was struck with the singular energy as well as with the poetry of the mariner, and he distrusted the obvious allusion to the clouds, which were, in fact, fast covering the vault above their heads.

"Dost thou like the night?" he demanded, turning from his star in doubt.

"It might be fairer. This is a wild region, and your cold Swiss lakes sometimes become too hot for the stoutest seaman's heart. Gaze at thy star young man, while thou mayest, and bethink thee of the maiden thou lovest and of all her kindness; we are on a crazy water, and pleasant thoughts should not be lightly thrown away."

Maso walked away, leaving the student alarmed, uneasy at he knew not what, and yet bent with childish eagerness on regarding the little luminary that occasionally was still seen wading among volumes of vapor. At this instant, a shout of unmeaning, clamorous merriment arose on the forecastle.

Il Maledetto did not remain any longer on the pile, but abandoning it to the new occupant, he descended among the silent, thoughtful party who were in possession of the cleared space near the stern. It was now so dark that some little attention was necessary to distinguish faces, even at trifling distances. But, by means of moving among these privileged persons with great coolness and seeming indifference, he soon succeeded in placing himself near the Genoese and the Augustine.

"Signore," he said, in Italian, raising his cap to the former with the same marked respect as before, though it was evidently no easy matter to impress him with the deference that the obscure usually feel for the great--"this is likely to prove an unfortunate end to a voyage that began with so fair appearances. I could wish that your eccellenza, with all this noble and fair company, was safely landed in the town of Vévey."

"Dost thou mean that we have cause to fear more than delay?"

"Signore, the mariner's life is one of unequal chances: now he floats in a lazy calm, and presently he is tossed between heaven and earth, in a way to make the stoutest heart sick. My knowledge of these waters is not great, but there are signs making themselves seen in the sky, here above the peak that lies in the direction of Mont Blanc, that would trouble me, were this our own clue but treacherous Mediterranean."

"What thinkest thou of this, father; a long residence in the Alps must have given thee some insight into their storms?"

The Augustine had been grave and thoughtful from the moment that he ceased to converse with Balthazar. He, too, had been struck with the omens, and, long used to study the changes of the weather, in a region where the elements sometimes work their will on a scale commensurate with the grandeur of the mountains, his thoughts had been anxiously recurring to the comforts and security of some of those hospitable roofs in the city to which they were bound, and which were always ready to receive the clavier of St. Bernard, in return for the services and self-denial of his brotherhood.

"With Maso, I could wish we were safely landed," answered the good canon; "the intense heat that a day like this creates in our valleys and on the lakes so weakens the sub-strata, or foundations of air, that the cold masses which collect around the glaciers sometimes descend like avalanches from their heights, to fill the vacuum. The shock is fearful, even to those who meet it in the glens and among the rocks, but the plunge of such a column of air upon one of the lakes is certain to be terrible."

"And thou thinkest there is danger of one of these phenomena at present?"

"I know not; but I would we were housed! That unnatural light above, and this deep tranquillity below, which surpasses an ordinary cairn have already driven me to my aves."

"The reverend Augustine speaks like a book man, and one who has passed his time, up in his mountain-convent, in study and reflection," rejoined Maso; "whereas the reasons I have to offer savor more of the seaman's practice. A calm like this, will be followed, sooner or later, by a commotion in the atmosphere. I like not the absence of the breeze from the land, on which Baptiste counted so surely, and, taking that symptom with the signs of yonder hot sky, I look soon to see this extraordinary quiet displaced by some violent struggle among the winds. Nettuno, too, my faithful dog, has given notice, by the manner in which he snuffs the air, that we are not to pass the night in this motionless condition."

"I had hoped ere this to be quietly in our haven. What means yonder bright light? Is it a star in the heavens, or does it merely lie against the side of the huge mountain?"

"There shines old Roger de Blonay!" cried the baron, heartily; "he knows of our being in the bark, and he has fired his beacon that we may steer by its light."

The conjecture seemed probable, for, while the day remained, the castle of Blonay, seated on the bosom of the mountain that shelters Vévey to the north-east, had been plainly visible. It had been much admired, a pleasing object in a view that was so richly studded with hamlets and castles, and Adelheid had pointed it out to Sigismund as the immediate goal of her journey. The lord of Blonay being apprized of the intended visit nothing was more probable than that he, an old and tried friend of Melchior de Willading's should show this sign of impatience; partly in compliment to those whom he expected, and partly as a signal that might be really useful to those who navigated the Leman, in a night that threatened so much murky obscurity.

The Signor Grimaldi rightly deemed the circumstances grave, and, calling to him his friend and Sigismund, he communicated the apprehensions of the monk and Maso. A braver man than Melchior de Willading did not dwell in all Switzerland, but he did not hear the gloomy predictions of the Genoese without shaking in every limb.

"My poor enfeebled Adelheid!" he said, yielding to a father's tenderness: "what will become of this frail plant, if exposed to a tempest in an unsheltered bark?"

"She will be with her father, and with her father's friend," answered the maiden herself; for the narrow limits to which they were necessarily confined, and the sudden burst of feeling in the parent, which had rendered him incautious in pitching his voice, made her the mistress of the cause of alarm. "I have heard enough of what the good Father Xavier and this mariner have said, to know that we are in a situation that might be better; but am I not with tried friends? I know already what the Herr Sigismund can do in behalf of my life, and come what may, we have all a beneficent guardian in One, who will not leave any of us to perish without remembering we are his children."

"This girl shames us all," said the Signor Grimaldi; "but it is often thus with these fragile beings, who rise the firmest and noblest in moments when prouder man begins to despair. They put their trust in God, who is a prop to sustain even those who are feebler than our gentle Adel held. But we will not exaggerate the causes of apprehension, which, after all, may pass away like many other threatening dangers, and leave us hours of felicitation and laughter in return for a few minutes of fright."

"Say, rather of thanksgiving," observed the clavier, "for the aspect of the heavens is getting to be fearfully solemn. Thou, who art a mariner--hast thou nothing to suggest?"

"We have the simple expedient of our sweeps, father; but, after neglecting their use so long, it is now too late to have recourse to them. We could not reach Vévey by such means, with this bark loaded to the water's edge, before the night would change, and, the water once fairly in motion, they could not be used at all."

"But we have our sails," put in the Genoese; "they at least may do us good service when the wind shall come."

Maso shook his head, but he made no answer. After a brief pause, in which he seemed to study the heavens still more closely, he went to the spot where the patron yet lay lost in sleep, and shook him rudely.--"Ho! Baptiste! awake! there is need here of thy counsel and of thy commands."

The drowsy owner of the bark rubbed his eyes, and slowly regained the use of his faculties.

"There is not a breath of wind," he muttered; "why didst awake me, Maso?--One that hath led thy life should know that sleep is sweet to those who toil."

"Ay, 'tis their advantage over the pampered and idle. Look at the heavens, man, and let us know what thou thinkest of their appearance. Is there the stuff in thy Winkelried to ride out a storm like this we may have to encounter?"

"Thou talkest like a foolish quean that has been frightened by the fluttering of her own poultry. The lake was never more calm, or the bark in greater safety."

"Dost see yonder bright light; here, over the tower of thy Vévey church?"

"Ay, 'tis a gallant star! and a fair sign for the mariner."

"Fool, 'tis a hot flame in Roger de Blonay's beacon. They begin to see that we are in danger on the shore, and they cast out their signals to give us notice to be active. They think us be-stirring ourselves like stout men, and those used to the water, while, in truth, we are as undisturbed as if the bark were a rock that might laugh at the Leman and its waves. The man is benumbed," continued Maso, turning away towards the anxious listeners; "he will not see that which is getting to be but too plain to all the others in his vessel."

Another idle and general laugh from the forecastle came to contradict this opinion of Maso's, and to prove how easy it is for the ignorant to exist in security, even on the brink of destruction. This was the moment, when nature gave the first of those signals that were "intelligible to vulgar capacities. The whole vault of the heavens was now veiled, with the exception of the spot so often named, which lay nearly above the brawling torrents of the Rhone. This fiery opening resembled a window admitting of fearful glimpses into the dreadful preparations that were making up among the higher peaks of the Alps. A flash of red quivering light was emitted, and a distant, rumbling rush, that was not thunder but rather resembled the wheelings of a thousand squadrons into line, followed the flash. The forecastle was deserted to a man, and the hillock of freight was again darkly seen peopled with crouching human forms. Just then the bark which had so long lain in a state of complete rest slowly and heavily raised its bows, as if laboring under its great and unusual burthen, while a sluggish swell passed beneath its entire length, lifting the whole mass, foot by foot, and passing away by the stern, to cast itself on the shores of Vaud.

"'Tis madness to waste the precious moments longer!" said Maso hurriedly, on whom this plain and intelligent hint was not lost. "Signori, we must be bold and prompt, or we shall be overtaken by the tempest unprepared. I speak not for myself, since, by the aid of this faithful dog, and favored by my own arms, I have always the shore for a hope. But there is one in the bark I would wish to save, even at some hazard to myself. Baptiste is unnerved by fear, and we must act for our selves or perish!"

"What wouldest thou?" demanded the Signor Grimaldi; "he that can proclaim the danger should have some expedient to divert it?"

"More timely exertion would have given us the resource of ordinary means; but, like those who die in their sins, we have foolishly wasted most precious minutes. We must lighten the bark, though it cost the whole of her freight."

A cry from Nicklaus Wagner announced that the spirit of avarice was still active as ever in his bosom. Even Baptiste, who had lost all his dogmatism and his disposition to command, under the imposing omens which had now made themselves apparent even to him, loudly joined in the protest against this waste of property. It is rare that any sudden and extreme proposal, like this of Maso's, meets with a quick echo in the judgments of those to whom the necessity is unexpectedly presented. The danger did not seem sufficiently imminent to have recourse to an expedient so decided; and, though startled and aroused, the untamed spirits of those who crowded the, menaced pile were rather in a state of uneasiness, than of that fierce excitement to which they were so capable of being wrought, and which was in some degree necessary to induce even them, thriftless and destitute as they were, to be the agents of effecting so great a destruction of properly. The project of the cool and calculating Maso would therefore have failed entirely, but for another wheeling of those airy squadrons, and a second wave which lifted the groaning bark until the loosened yards swung creaking above their heads. The canvass flapped, too, in the darkness, like some huge bird of prey fluttering its feathers previously to taking wing.

"Holy and just Ruler of the land and the sea!" exclaimed the Augustine, "remember thy repentant children, and have us, at this awful moment, in thy omnipotent protection!"

"The winds are come down, and even the dumb lake sends us the signal to be ready!" shouted Maso. "Overboard with the freight, if ye would live!"

A sudden heavy plunge into the water, proved that the mariner was in earnest. Notwithstanding the imposing and awful signs with which they were surrounded, every individual of the nameless herd bethought him of the puck that contained his own scanty worldly effects, and there was a general and quick movement, with a view to secure them. As each man succeeded in effecting his own object, he was led away by that community of feeling which rules a multitude. The common rush was believed to be with a view to succor Maso, though each man secretly knew the falsity of the impression as respected his own particular case; and box after box began to tumble into the water, as new and eager recruits lent themselves to the task. The impulse was quickly imparted from one to another, until even young Sigismund was active in the work. On these slight accidents do the most important results depend, when the hot impulses that govern the mass obtain the ascendant.

It is not to be supposed that either Baptiste, or Nicklaus Wagner, witnessed the waste of their joint effects with total indifference. So far from this, each used every exertion in his power to prevent it, not only by his voice, but with his hands. One menaced the law--the other threatened Maso with condign punishment for his interference with a patron's rights and duties; but their remonstrances were uttered to inattentive ears. Maso knew himself to be irresponsible by situation, for it was not an easy matter to bring him within the grasp of the authorities; and as for the others, most of them were far too insignificant to feel much apprehension for a reparation that would be most likely, if it fell at all, to fall on those who were more able to bear it. Sigismund alone exerted himself under a sense of his liabilities; but he worked for one that was far dearer to him than gold, and little did he bethink him of any other consequences than those which might befall the precious life of Adelheid de Willading.

The meagre packages of the common passengers had been thrown in a place of safety, with the sort of unreflecting instinct with which we take care of our limbs when in danger. This timely precaution permitted each to work with a zeal that found no drawback in personal interest, and the effect was in proportion. A hundred hands were busy, and nearly as many throbbing hearts lent their impulses to the accomplishment of the one important object.

Baptiste and his people, aided by laborers of the port, had passed an entire day in heaping that pile on the deck of the Winkelried, which was now crumbling to pieces with a rapidity that seemed allied to magic. The patron and Nicklaus Wagner bawled themselves hoarse, with uttering useless threats and deprecations, for by this time the laborers in the work of destruction had received some such impetus as the rolling stone acquires by the increased momentum of its descent. Packages, boxes, bales, and everything that came to hand, were hurled into the water frantically, and without other thought than of the necessity of lightening the groaning bark of its burthen. The agitation of the lake, too, was regularly increasing, wave following wave, in a manner to cause the vessel to pitch heavily, as it rose upon the coming, or sunk with the receding swell. At length, a shout announced that, in one portion of the pile, the deck was attained!

The work now proceeded with greater security to those engaged, for, hitherto the motion of the bark, and the unequal footing, frequently rendered their situations, in the darkness and confusion, to the last degree hazardous. Maso now abandoned his own active agency in the toil, for no sooner did he see the others fairly and zealously enlisted in the undertaking, than he ceased his personal efforts to give those directions which, coming from one accustomed to the occupation, were far more valuable than any service that could be derived from a single arm.

"Thou art known to me, Signor Maso," said Baptiste, hoarse with his impotent efforts to restrain the torrent, "and thou shalt answer for this, as well as for other of thy crimes, so soon as we reach the haven of Vévey!"

"Dotard! thou would'st carry thyself and all with thee, by thy narrowness of spirit, to a port from which, when it is once entered, none ever sail again."

"It lieth between ye both," rejoined Nicklaus Wagner; "thou art not less to blame than these madmen, Baptiste. Hadst thou left the town at the hour named in our conditions, this danger could not have overtaken us."

"Am I a god to command the winds! I would that I had never seen thee or thy cheeses, or that thou wouldst relieve me of thy presence, and go after them into the lake."

"This comes of sleeping on duty; nay, I know not but that a proper use of the oars would still bring us in, in safety, and without necessary harm to the property of any. Noble Baron de Willading, here may be occasion for your testimony, and, as a citizen of Berne, I pray you to heed well the circumstances."

Baptiste was not in a humor to bear these merited reproaches, and he rejoined upon the aggrieved Nicklaus in a manner that would speedily have brought their ill-timed wrangle to an issue, had not Maso passed rudely between them, shoving them asunder with the sinews of a giant. This repulse served to keep the peace for the moment, but the wordy war continued with so much acrimony, and with so many unmeasured terms, that Adelheid and her maids, pale and terror-struck by the surrounding scene as they were, gladly shut their ears, to exclude epithets of such bitterness and menace that they curdled the blood. Maso passed on among the workmen, when he had interposed between the disputants. He gave his orders with perfect self-possession, though his understanding eye perceived that, instead of magnifying the danger, he had himself not fully anticipated its extent. The rolling of the waves was now incessant, and the quick, washing rush of the water, a sound familiar to the seaman, announced that they had become so large that their summits broke, sending their lighter foam ahead. There were symptoms, too, which proved that their situation was understood by those on the land. Lights were flashing along the strand near Vévey, and it was not difficult to detect, even at the distance at which they lay, the evidences of a strong feeling among the people of the town.

"I doubt not that we have been seen," said Melchior de Willading, "and that our friends are busy in devising means to aid us. Roger de Blonay is not a man to see us perish without an effort, nor would the worthy bailiff, Peter Hofmeister, be idle, knowing that a brother of the bürgerschaft, and old school associate, hath need of his assistance."

"None can come to us, without running an equal risk with ourselves," answered the Genoese. "It were better that we should be left to our own exertions. I like the coolness of this unknown mariner, and I put my faith in God!"

A new shout proclaimed that the deck had been gained, on the other side of the bark. Much the greater part of the deck-load had now irretrievably disappeared, and the movements of the relieved vessel were more lively and sane. Maso called to him one or two of the regular crew, and together they rolled up the canvass, in a manner peculiar to the latine rig; for a breath of hot air, the first of any sort that had been felt for many hours passed athwart the bark. This duty was performed, as canvass is known to be furled at need, but it was done securely. Maso then went among the laborers again, encouraging them with his voice, and directing their efforts with his counsel.

"Thou art not equal to thy task," he said, addressing one who was vainly endeavoring to roll a bale to the side of the vessel, a little apart from the rest of the busy crowd; "thou wilt do better to assist the others, than to waste thy force here."

"I feel the strength to remove a mountain! Do we not work for our lives?"

The mariner bent forward, and looked into the other's face. These frantic and ill-directed efforts came from the Westphalian student.

"Thy star has disappeared," he rejoined, smiling--for Maso had smiled in scenes far more imposing, than even that with which he was now surrounded.

"She gazes at it still; she thinks of one that loves her, who is journeying far from the fatherland."

"Hold! Since thou wilt have it so, I will help thee to cast this bale into the water. Place thine arm thus; an ounce of well-directed force is worth a pound that acts against itself."

Stooping together, their united strength did that which had baffled the single efforts of the scholar. The package rolled to the gangway, and the German, frenzied with excitement, shouted aloud! The bark lurched, and the bale went over the side, as if the lifeless mass were suddenly possessed with the desire to perform the evolution which its inert weight had so long resisted. Maso recovered his footing, which had been deranged by the unexpected movement, with a seaman's dexterity, but his companion was no longer at his side. Kneeling on the gangway, he perceived the dark bale disappearing in the element, with the feet of the Westphalian dragging after. He bent forward to grasp the rising body, but it never returned to the surface, being entangled in the cords, or, what was equally probable, retained by the frantic grasp of the student, whose mind had yielded to the awful character of the night.

The life of Il Maledetto had been one of great vicissitudes and peril. He had often seen men pass suddenly into the other state of existence, and had been calm himself amid the cries, the groans, and what is far more appalling, the execrations of the dying, but never before had he witnessed so brief and silent an end. For more than a minute, he hung suspended over the dark and working water, expecting to see the student return; and, when hope was reluctantly abandoned, he arose to his feet, a startled and admonished man. Still discretion did not desert him. He saw the uselessness, and even the danger, of distracting the attention of the workmen, and the ill-fated scholar was permitted to pass away without a word of regret or a comment on his fate. None knew of his loss but the wary mariner, nor was his person missed by any of those who had spent the day in his company. But she to whom he hud plighted his faith on the banks of the Elbe long gazed at that pale star, and wept in bitterness that her feminine constancy met with no return. Her true affections long outlived their object, for his image was deeply enshrined in a warm female heart. Days, weeks, months, and years passed for her in the wasting cheerlessness of hope deferred, but the dark Leman never gave up its secret, and he to whom her lover's fate alone was known little bethought him of an accident which, if not forgotten, was but one of many similar frightful incidents in his eventful career.

Maso re-appeared among the crowd, with the forced composure of one who well knew that authority was most efficient when most calm. The command of the vessel was now virtually with him, Baptiste, enervated by the extraordinary crisis, and choking with passion, being utterly incapable of giving a distinct or a useful order. It was fortunate for those in the bark that the substitute was so good, for more fearful signs never impended over the Leman than those which darkened the hour.

We have necessarily consumed much time in relating these events, the pen not equalling the activity of the thoughts. Twenty minutes, however, had not passed since the tranquillity of the lake was first disturbed, and so great had been the exertions of those in the Winkelried, that the time appeared to be shorter. But, though it had been so well employed, neither had the powers of the air been idle. The unnatural opening in the heavens was shut, and, at short intervals, those fearful wheelings of the aërial squadrons were drawing nearer. Thrice had fitful breathings of warm air passed over the bark, and occasionally, as she plunged into a sea that was heavier than common, the faces of those on board were cooled, as it might be with some huge fan. These were no more, however, than sudden changes in the atmosphere, of which veins were displaced by the distant struggle between the heated air of the lake and that which had been chilled on the glaciers, or, they were the still more simple result of the violent agitation of the vessel.

The deep darkness which shut in the vault, giving to the embedded Leman the appearance of a gloomy, liquid glen, contributed to the awful sublimity of the night. The ramparts of Savoy were barely distinguishable from the flying clouds, having the appearance of black walls, seemingly within reach of the hand; while the more varied and softer côtes of Vaud lay an indefinable and sombre mass, less menacing, it is true, but equally confused and unattainable.

Still the beacon blazed in the grate of old Roger de Blonay, and flaring torches glided along the strand. The shore seemed alive with human beings, able as themselves to appreciate and to feel for their situation.

The deck was now cleared, and the travellers were collected in a group between the masts. Pippo had lost all his pleasantry under the dread signs of the hour, and Conrad, trembling with superstition and terror, was free from hypocrisy. They, and those with them, discoursed on their chances, on the nature of the risks they ran, and on its probable causes.

"I see no image of Maria, nor even a pitiful lamp to any of the blessed, in this accursed bark!" said the juggler, after several had hazarded their quaint and peculiar opinions. "Let the patron come forth, and answer for his negligence."

The passengers were about equally divided between those who dissented from and those who worshipped with Rome. This proposal, therefore, met with a mixed reception. The latter protested against the neglect, while the former, equally under the influence of abject fear, were loud in declaring that the idolatry itself might cost them all their lives.

"The curse of heaven alight on the evil tongue that first uttered the thought!" muttered the trembling Pippo between his teeth, too prudent to fly openly in the face of so strong an opposition, and yet too credulous not to feel the omission in every nerve--"Hast nothing by thee, pious Conrad, that may avail a Christian?"

The pilgrim reached forth his hand with a rosary and cross. The sacred emblem passed from mouth to mouth, among the believers, with a zeal little short of that they had manifested in unloading the deck. Encouraged by this sacrifice, they called loudly upon Baptiste to present himself. Confronted with these unnurtured spirits, the patron shook in every limb, for, between anger and abject fear, his self-command had by this time absolutely deserted him. To the repeated appeals to procure a light, that it might be placed before a picture of the mother of God which Conrad produced, he objected his Protestant faith, the impossibility of maintaining the flame while the bark pitched so violently, and the divided opinions of the passengers. The Catholics bethought them of the country and influence of Maso, and they loudly called upon him, for the love of God! to come and enforce their requests. But the mariner was occupied on the forecastle, lowering one anchor after another into the water, passively assisted by the people of the bark, who wondered at a precaution so useless, since no rope could reach the bottom, even while they did not dare deny his orders. Something was now said of the curse that had alighted on the vessel, in consequence of its patron's intention to embark the headsman. Baptiste trembled to the skin of his crown, and his blood crept with a superstitious awe.

"Dost think there can really be aught in this!" he asked, with parched lips and a faltering tongue.

All distinction of faith was lost in the general ridicule. Now the Westphalian was gone, there was not a man among them to doubt that a navigation, so accompanied, would be cursed. Baptiste stammered, muttered many incoherent sentences, and finally, in his impotency, he permitted the dangerous secret to escape him.

The intelligence that Balthazar was among them produced a solemn and deep silence. The fact, however, furnished as conclusive evidence of the cause of their peril to the minds of these untutored beings, as a mathematician could have received from the happiest of his demonstrations. New light broke in upon them, and the ominous stillness was followed by a general demand for the patron to point out the man. Obeying this order, partly under the influence of a terror that was allied to his moral weakness, and partly in bodily fear, he shoved the headsman forward, substituting the person of the proscribed man for his own, and, profiting by the occasion, he stole out of the crowd.

When the Herr Müller, or as he was now known and called, Balthazar, was rudely pushed into the hands of these ferocious agents of superstition, the apparent magnitude of the discovery induced a general and breathless pause. Like the treacherous calm that had so long reigned upon the lake, it was a precursor of a fearful and violent explosion. Little was said, for the occasion was too ominous for a display of vulgar feeling, but Conrad, Pippo, and one or two more, silently raised the fancied offender in their arms, and bore him desperately towards the side of the bark.

"Call on Maria, for the good of thy soul!" whispered the Neapolitan, with a strange mixture of Christian zeal, in the midst of all his ferocity.

The sound of words like these usually conveys the idea of charity and love, but, notwithstanding this gleam of hope, Balthazar still found himself borne towards his fate.

On quitting the throng that clustered together in a dense body between the masts, Baptiste encountered his old antagonist, Nicklaus Wagner. The fury which had so long been pent in his breast suddenly found vent, and, in the madness of the moment, he struck him. The stout Bernese grappled his assailant, and the struggle became fierce as that of brutes. Scandalized by such a spectacle, offended by the disrespect, and ignorant of what else was passing near--for the crowd had uttered its resolutions in the suppressed voices of men determined--the Baron de Willading and the Signor Grimaldi advanced with dignity and firmness to prevent the shameful strife. At this critical moment the voice of Balthazar was heard above the roar of the coming wind, not calling on Maria, as he had been admonished, but appealing to the two old nobles to save him. Sigismund sprang forward like a lion, at the cry, but too late to reach those who were about to cast the headsman from the gangway, he was just in time to catch the body, by its garments, when actually sailing in the air. By a vast effort of strength its direction was diverted. Instead of alighting in the water, Balthazar encountered the angry combatants, who, driven back on the two nobles, forced the whole four over the side of the bark into the water.

The struggle between the two bodies of air ceased, that on the surface of the lake yielding to the avalanche from above, and the tempest came howling upon the bark.

Chapter VII

---and now the glee
Of the loud hills shakes with their mountain-mirth.

Byron.

It is necessary to recapitulate a little, in order to connect events. The signs of the hour had been gradually but progressively increasing. While the lake was unruffled, a stillness so profound prevailed, that sounds from the distant port, such as the heavy fall of an oar, or a laugh from the waterman, had reached the ears of those in the Winkelried, bringing with them the feeling of security, and the strong charm of a calm at even. To these succeeded the gathering in the heavens, and the roaring of the winds, as they came rushing down the sides of the Alps, in their first descent into the basin of the Leman. As the sight grew useless, except as it might study the dark omens of the impending vault, the sense of hearing became doubly acute, and it had been a powerful agent in heightening the vague but acute apprehensions of the travellers. The rushes of the wind, which at first were broken, at intervals resembling the roar of a chimney-top in a gale, had soon reached the fearful grandeur of those aërial wheelings of squadrons, to which we have more than once alluded, passing off in dread mutterings, that, in the deep quiet of all other things, bore a close affinity to the rumbling of a surf upon the sea-shore. The surface of the lake was first broken after one of these symptoms, and it was this infallible sign of a gale which had assured Maso there was no time to lose. This movement of the element in a calm is a common phenomenon on waters that are much environed with elevated and irregular head-lands, and it is a certain proof that wind is on some distant portion of the sheet. It occurs frequently on the ocean, too, where the mariner is accustomed to find a heavy sea setting in one direction, the effects of some distant storm, while the breeze around him is blowing in its opposite. It had been succeeded by the single rolling swell, like the outer circle of waves produced by dropping a stone into the water, and the regular and increasing agitation of the lake, until the element broke as in a tempest, and that seemingly of its own volition, since not a breath of air was stirring. This last and formidable symptom of the force of the coming gust, however, had now become so unequivocal, that, at the moment when the three travellers and the patron fell from her gangway, the Winkelried, to use a seaman's phrase, was literally wallowing in the troughs of the seas.

A dull unnatural light preceded the winds, and notwithstanding the previous darkness, the nature of the accident was fully apparent to all. Even the untamed spirits that had just been bent upon so fierce a sacrifice to their superstitious dread, uttered cries of horror, while the piercing shriek of Adelheid sounded, in that fearful moment, as if beings of super-human attributes were riding in the gale. The name of Sigismund was heard, too, in one of those wild appeals that the frantic suffer to escape them, in their despair. But the interval between the plunge into the water and the swoop of the tempest was so short, that, to the senses of the travellers, the whole seemed the occurrence of the same teeming moment.

Maso had completed his work on the forecasts, had seen that other provisions which he had ordered were duly made, and had reached the tiller, just in time to witness and to understand all that occurred. Adelheid and her female attendants were already lashed to the principal masts, and ropes were given to the others around her, as indispensable precautions; for the deck of the bark, now cleared of every particle of its freight, was as exposed and as defenceless against the power of the wind, as a naked heath. Such was the situation of the Winkelried, when the omens of the night changed to their dread reality.

Instinct, in cases of sudden and unusual danger must do the office of reason. There was no necessity to warn the unthinking but panic-struck crowd to provide for their own safety, for every man in the centre of the barge threw his body flaon the deck, and grasped the cords that Maso had taken care to provide for that purpose, with the tenacity with which all who possess life cling to the means of existence. The dogs gave beautiful proofs of the secret and wonderful means that nature has imparted, to answer the ends of their creation. Old Uberto crouched, cowering, and oppressed with a sense of helplessness, at the side of his master, while the Newfoundland follower of the mariner went leaping from gangway to gangway, snuffing the heated air, and barking wildly, as if he would challenge the elements to close for the strife.

A vast body of warm air had passed unheeded athwart the bark, during the minute that preceded the intended sacrifice of Balthazar. It was the forerunner of the hurricane, which had chased it from the bed where it had been sleeping, since the warm and happy noon-tide. Ten thousand chariots at their speed could not have equalled the rumbling that succeeded, when the winds came booming over the lake. As if too eager to permit anything within their fangs to escape, they brought with them a wild, dull light, which filled while it clouded the atmosphere, and which, it was scarcely fanciful to imagine, had been hurried down, in their vortex, from those chill glaciers, where they had so long been condensing their forces for the present descent. The waves were not increased, but depressed by the pressure of this atmospheric column, though it took up hogshead, of water from their crests, scattering it in fine penetrating spray, till the entire space between the heavens and the earth seemed saturated with its particles.

The Winkelried received the shock at a moment when the lee-side of her broad deck was wallowing in the trough, and its weather was protruded on the summit of a swell. The wind howled when it struck the pent limits, as if angered at being thwarted, and there was a roar under the wide gangways, resembling that of lions. The reeling vessel was raised in a manner to cause those or board to believe it about to be lifted bodily from the water, but the ceaseless rolling of the element restored the balance. Maso afterwards affirmed that nothing but this accidental position, which formed a sort of lee, prevented all in the bark from being swept from the deck, before the first gust of the hurricane.

Sigismund had heard the heart-rending appeal of Adelheid, and, notwithstanding the awful strife of the elements and the fearful character of the night, he alone breasted the shock on his feet. Though aided by a rope, and bowed like a reed, his herculean frame trembled under the shock, in a way to render even his ability to resist seriously doubtful. But, the first blast expended, he sprang to the gangway, and leaped into the cauldron of the lake unhesitatingly, and yet in the possession of all his faculties. He was desperately bent on saving a life so dear to Adelheid, or on dying in the attempt.

Maso had watched the crisis with a seaman's eye, a seaman's resources, and a seaman's coolness. He had not refused to quit his feet, but kneeling on one knee, he pressed the tiller down, lashed it, and clinging to the massive timber, faced the tempest with the steadiness of a water-god. There was sublimity in the intelligence, deliberation, and calculating skill, with which this solitary, unknown, and nearly hopeless, mariner obeyed his professional instinct, in that fearful concussion of the elements, which, loosened from every restraint, now appeared abandoned to their own wild and fierce will. He threw aside his cap, pushed forward his thick but streaming locks, as veils to protect his eyes, and watched the first encounter of the wind, as the wary but sullen lion keeps his gaze on the hostile elephant. A grim smile stole across his features, when he felt the vessel settle again into its watery bed, after that breathless moment in which there had been reason to fear it might actually be lifted from its proper element. Then the precaution, which had seemed so useless and incomprehensible to others, came in play. The bark made a fearful whirl from the spot where it had so long lain, yielding to the touch of the gust like a vane turning on its pivot, while the water gurgled several streaks on deck. But the cables were no sooner taut than the numerous anchors resisted, and brought the bark head to wind. Maso felt the yielding of the vessel's stern, as she swung furiously round, and he cheered aloud. The trembling of the timbers, the dashing against the pointed beak, and that high jet of water, which shot up over the bows and fell heavily on the forecastle, washing aft in a flood, were so many evidences that the cables were true. Advancing from his post, with some such dignity as a master of fence displays in the exercise of his art, he shouted for his dog.

"Nettuno!--Nettuno!--where art thou, brave Nettuno?"

The faithful animal was whining near him, unheard in that war of the elements. He waited only for this encouragement to act. No sooner was his master's voice heard, than, barking bravely, he snuffed the gale, dashed to the side of the vessel, and leaped into the boiling lake.

When Melchior de Willading and his friend returned to the surface, after their plunge, it was like men making their appearance in a world abandoned to the infernal humors of the fiends of darkness. The reader will understand it was at the instant of the swoop of the winds, that has just been detailed, for what we have taken so many pages to describe in words, scarce needed a minute of time in the accomplishment.

Maso knelt on the verge of the gangway, sustaining himself by passing an arm around a shroud, and, bending forward, he gazed into the cauldron of the lake with aching eyes. Once or twice, he thought he heard the stifled breathing of one who struggled with the raging water; but, in that roar of the winds, it was easy to be deceived. He shouted encouragement to his dog, however, and gathering a small rope rapidly, he made a heaving coil of one of its ends. This he cast far from him, with a peculiar swing and dexterity, hauling-in, and repeating the experiments, steadily and with unwearied industry. The rope was necessarily thrown at hazard, for the misty light prevented more than it aided vision; and the howling of the powers of the air filled his ears with sounds that resembled the laugh of devils.

In the cultivation of the youthful manly exercises, neither of the old nobles had neglected the useful skill of being able to buffet with the waves. But both possessed what was far better, in such a strait, than the knowledge of a swimmer, in that self-command and coolness in emergencies which they are apt to acquire, who pass their time in encountering the hazards and in overcoming the difficulties of war. Each retained a sufficiency of recollection, therefore, on coming to the surface, to understand his situation, and not to increase the danger by the ill-directed and frantic efforts that usually drown the frightened. The case was sufficiently desperate, at the best, without the additional risk of distraction, for the bark had already drifted to some unseen spot, that, as respects them, was quite unattainable. In this uncertainty, it would have been madness to steer amid the waste of waters, as likely to go wrong as right, and they limited their efforts to mutual support and encouragement, placing their trust in God.

Not so with Sigismund. To him the roaring tempest was mute, the boiling and hissing lake had no horrors, and he had plunged into the fathomless Leman as recklessly as he could have leaped to land. The shriek, the "Sigismund! oh, Sigismund!" of Adelheid, was in his ears, and her cry of anguish thrilled on every nerve. The athletic young Swiss was a practised and expert swimmer, or it is improbable that even these strong impulses could have overcome the instinct of self-preservation. In a tranquil basin, it would have been no extraordinary or unusual feat for him to conquer the distance between the Winkelried and the shores of Vaud; but, like all the others, on casting himself into the water, he was obliged to shape his course at random, and this, too, amid such a driving spray as rendered even respiration difficult. As has been said, the waves were compressed into their bed rather than augmented by the wind; but, had it been otherwise, the mere heaving and settling of the element, while it obstructs his speed, offers a support rather than an obstacle to the practised swimmer.

Notwithstanding all these advantages, the strength of his impulses, and the numberless occasions on which he had breasted the surges of the Mediterranean, Sigismund, on recovering from his plunge, felt the fearful chances of the risk he ran, as the stern soldier meets the hazards of battle, in which he knows if there is victory there is also death. He dashed the troubled water aside, though he swam blindly, and each stroke urged him farther from the bark, his only hope of safety. He was between dark rolling mounds, and, on rising to their summits, a hurricane of mist made him glad to sink again within a similar shelter. The breaking crests of the waves, which were glancing off in foam, also gave him great annoyance, for such was their force, that, more than once, he was hurled helpless as a log before them. Still he swam boldly, and with strength; nature having gifted him with more than the usual physical energy of man. But, uncertain in his course, unable to see the length of his own body, and pressed hard upon by the wind, even the spirit of Sigismund Steinbach could not long withstand so many adverse circumstances. He had already turned, wavering in purpose, thinking to catch a glimpse of the bark in the direction he had come, when a dark mass floated immediately before his eyes, and he felt the cold clammy nose of the dog, scenting about his face. The admirable instinct, or we might better say, the excellent training of Nettuno, told him that his services were not needed here, and, barking with wild delight, as if in mockery of the infernal din of the tempest, he sheered aside, and swam swiftly on. A thought flashed like lightning on the brain of Sigismund. His best hope was in the inexplicable faculties of this animal. Throwing forward an arm, he seized the bushy tail of the dog, and suffered himself to be dragged ahead, he knew not whither, though he seconded the movement with his own exertions. Another bark proclaimed that the experiment was successful, and voices, rising as it were from the water, close at hand, announced the proximity of human beings. The brunt of the hurricane was past, and the washing of the waves, which had been stilled by the roar and the revelry of the winds, again became audible.

The strength of the two struggling old men was sinking fast. The Signor Grimaldi had, thus far, generously sustained his friend, who was less expert than himself in the water, and he continued to cheer him with a hope he did not feel himself, nobly refusing to the last to separate their fortunes.

"How dost find thyself, old Melchior?" he asked. "Cheer thee, friend--I think there is succor at hand."

The water gurgled at the mouth of the baron, who was near the gasp.

"'Tis late--bless thee, dearest Gaetano--God be with my child--my Adelheid--poor Adelheid!"

The utterance of this precious name, under a father's agony of spirit, most probably saved his life. The sinewy arm of Sigismund, directed by the words, grasped his dress, and he felt at once that a new and preserving power had interposed between him and the caverns of the lake. It was time, for the water had covered the face of the failing baron, ere the muscular arm of the youth came to perform its charitable office.

"Yield thee to the dog, Signore," said Sigismund, clearing his mouth of water to speak calmly, once assured of his own burthen; "trust to his sagacity, and,--God keep us in mind!--all may yet be well!"

The Signor Grimaldi retained sufficient presence of mind to follow this advice, and it was probably quite as fortunate that his friend had so far lost his consciousness, as to become an unresisting burthen in the hands of Sigismund.

"Nettuno!--gallant Nettuno!"--swept past them on the gale for the first time, the partial hushing of the winds permitting the clear call of Maso to reach so far. The sound directed the efforts of Sigismund, though the dog had swum steadily away the moment he had the Genoese in his gripe, and with a certainty of manner that showed he was at no loss for a direction.

But Sigismund had taxed his powers too far. He, who could have buffeted an ordinary sea for hours, was now completely exhausted by the unwonted exertions, the deadening influence of the tempest, and the log-like weight of his burthen He would not desert the father of Adelheid, and yet each fainting and useless stroke told him to despair. The dog had already disappeared in the darkness, and he was even uncertain again of the true position of the bark. He prayed in agony for a single glimpse of the rocking masts and yards, or to catch one syllable of the cheering voice of Maso. But in both his wishes were vain. In place of the former, he had naught but the veiled misty light, that had come on with the hurricane; and, instead of the latter, his ears were filled with the washing of the waves and the roars of the gusts. The blasts now descended to the surface of the lake, and now went whirling and swelling upward, in a way to lead the listener to fancy that the viewless winds might, for once, be seen. For a single painful instant, in one of those disheartening moments of despair that will come over the stoutest, his hand was about to relinquish its hold of the baron, and to make the last natural struggle for life; but that fair and modest picture of maiden loveliness and truth, which had so long haunted his waking hours and adorned his night-dreams, interposed to prevent the act. After this brief and fleeting weakness, the young man seemed endowed with new energy. He swam stronger, and with greater apparent advantage, than before.

"Nettuno--gallant Nettuno!"--again drove over him, bringing with it the chilling certainty, that turned from his course by the rolling of the water he had thrown away these desperate efforts, by taking a direction which led him from the bark. While there was the smallest appearance of success no difficulties, of whatever magnitude, could entirely extinguish hope; but when the dire conviction that he had been actually aiding, instead of diminishing the danger, pressed upon Sigismund, he abandoned his efforts. The most he endeavored or hoped to achieve, was to keep his own head and that of his companion above the fatal element, while he answered the cry of Maso with a shout of despair.

"Nettuno!--gallant Nettuno!"--again flew past on the gale.

This cry might have been an answer, or it might merely be the Italian encouraging his dog to bear on the body, with which it was already loaded Sigismund uttered a shout, which he felt must be the last. He struggled desperately, but in vain the world and its allurements were vanishing from his thoughts, when a dark line whirled over him, and fell thrashing upon the very wave which covered his face. An instinctive grasp caught it, and the young soldier felt himself impelled ahead. He had seized the rope which the mariner had not ceased to throw, as the fisherman casts his line, and he was at the side of the bark, before his confused faculties enabled him to understand the means employed for his rescue.

Maso took a hasty turn with the rope, and, stooping forward, favored by a roll of the vessel, he drew the Baron de Willading upon deck. Watching his time, he repeated the experiment, always with admirable coolness and dexterity, placing Sigismund also in safety. The former was immediately dragged senseless to the centre of the bark, where he received those attentions that had just been eagerly offered to the Signior Grimaldi, and with the same happy results. But Sigismund motioned all away from himself, knowing that their cares were needed elsewhere. He staggered forward a few paces, and then, yielding to a complete exhaustion of his power, he fell at full length on the wet planks. He long lay panting, speechless, and unable to move, with a sense of death on his frame.

"Nettuno! gallant, gallant Nettuno!"--shouted the indefatigable Maso, still at his post on the gangway, whence he cast his rope with unchanging perseverance. The fitful winds, which had already played so many fierce antics that eventful night, sensibly lulled, and, giving one or two sighs, as if regretting that they were about to be curbed again by that almighty Master, from whose benevolent hands they had so furtively escaped, as suddenly ceased blowing. The yards creaked, swinging loosely, above the crowded deck, and the dull washing of water filled the ear. To these diminished sounds were to be added the barking of the dog, who was still abroad in the darkness, and a struggling noise like the broken and smothered attempts of human voices. Although the time appeared an age to all who awaited the result, scarcely five minutes had elapsed since the accident occurred and the hurricane had reached them. There was still hope, therefore, for those who yet remained in the water. Maso felt the eagerness of one who had already been successful beyond his hopes, and, in his desire to catch some guiding signal, he leaned forward, till the rolling lake washed into his face.

"Ha! gallant--gallant Nettuno!"

Men certainly spoke, and that near him. But the sounds resembled words uttered beneath a cover. The wind whistled, too, though but for a moment, and then it seemed to sail upward into the dark vault of the heavens. Nettuno barked audibly, and his master answered with another shout, for the sympathy of man in his kind is inextinguishable.

"My brave, my noble Nettuno!"

The stillness was now imposing, and Maso heard the dog growl. This ill-omened signal was undeniably followed by smothered voices. The latter became clearer, as if the mocking winds were willing that a sad exhibition of human frailty should be known, or, what is more probable, violent passion had awakened stronger powers of speech. This much the mariner understood.

"Loosen thy grasp, accursed Baptiste!"

"Wretch, loosen thine own!"

"Is God naught with thee?"

"Why dost throttle so, infernal Nicklaus?"

"Thou wilt die damned!"

"Thou chokest--villain--pardon!--pardon!"

He heard no more. The merciful elements interposed to drown the appalling strife. Once or twice the dog howled, but the tempest came across the Leman again in its might, as if the short pause had been made merely to take breath. The winds took a new direction; and the bark, still held by its anchors, swung wide off from its former position, tending in towards the mountains of Savoy. During the first burst of this new blast, even Maso was glad to crouch to the deck, for millions of infinitely fine particles were lifted from the lake, and driven on with the atmosphere with a violence to take away his breath. The danger of being swept before the furious tide of the driving element was also an accident not impossible. When the lull returned, no exertion of his faculties could catch a single sound foreign to the proper character of the scene, such as the plash of the water, and the creaking of the long, swinging yards.

The mariner now felt a deep concern for his dog. He called to him until he grew hoarse, but fruitlessly. The change of position, with the constant and varying drift of the vessel, had carried them beyond the reach of the human voice. More time was expended in summoning "Nettuno! gallant Nettuno!" than had been consumed in the passage of all the events which it has been necessary to our object to relate so minutely, and always with the same want of success. The mind of Maso was pitched to a degree far above the opinions and habits of those with whom his life brought him ordinarily in contact, but as even fine gold will become tarnished by exposure to impure air, he had not entirely escaped the habitual weaknesses of the Italians of his class. When he found that no cry could recall his faithful companion, he threw himself upon the deck in a paroxysm of passion, tore his hair, and wept audibly.

"Nettuno! my brave, my faithful Nettuno!" he said. "What are all these to me, without thee! Thou alone lovedst me--thou alone hast passed with me through fair and foul--through good and evil, without change, or wish for another master! When the pretended friend has been false, thou hast remained faithful! When others were sycophants thou wert never a flatterer!"

Struck with this singular exhibition of sorrow, the good Augustine, who, until now, like all the others, had been looking to his own safety, or employed in restoring the exhausted, took advantage of the favorable change in the weather, and advanced with the language of consolation.

"Thou hast saved all our lives, bold mariner," he said; "and there are those in the bark who will know how to reward thy courage and skill, Forget, then, thy dog, and indulge in a grateful heart to Maria and the saints, that they have been our friends and thine in this exceeding jeopardy."

"Father, I have eaten with the animal--slept with the animal--fought, swum, and made merry with him, and I could now drown with him! What are thy nobles and their gold to me, without my dog? The gallant brute will die the death of despair, swimming about in search of the bark in the midst of the darkness, until even one of his high breed and courage must suffer his heart to burst."

"Christians have been called into the dread presence, unconfessed and unshrived, to-night; and we should bethink us of their souls, rather than indulge in this grief in behalf of one that, however faithful, ends but an unreasoning and irresponsible existence."

All this was thrown away upon Maso, who crossed himself habitually at the allusion to the drowned, but who did not the less bewail the loss of his dog, whom he seemed to love, like the affection that David bore for Jonathan, with a love surpassing that of women. Perceiving that his counsel was useless, the good Augustine turned away, to knee and offer up his own orisons of gratitude, and to bethink him of the dead.

"Nettuno! *povera, carissima bestia!*" continued Maso, "whither art thou swimming, in this infernal quarrel between the air and water? Would I were with thee, dog! No mortal shall ever share the love I bore thee, *povero Nettuno!*--I will never take another to my heart, like thee!"

The outbreaking of Maso's grief was sudden, and it was brief in its duration. In this respect it might be likened to the hurricane that had just passed. Excessive violence, in both cases, appeared to bring its own remedy, for the irregular fitful gusts from the mountains had already ceased, and were succeeded by a strong but steady gale from the north; and the sorrow of Maso soon ended its characteristic plaints, to take a more continued and even character.

During the whole of the foregoing scenes, the Common passengers had crouched to the deck, partly in stupor, partly in superstitious dread, and much of the time, from a positive inability to move without incurring the risk of being driven from the defenceless vessel into the lake. But, as the wind diminished in force, and the motion of the bark became more regular, they rallied their senses, like men who had been in a trance, and one by one they rose to their feet. About this time Adelheid heard the sound of her father's voice, blessing her care, and consoling her sorrow. The north wind blew away the canopy of clouds, and the stars shone upon the angry Leman, bringing with them some such promise of divine aid as the pillar of fire afforded to the Israelites in their passage of the Red Sea. Such an evidence of returning peace brought renewed confidence. All in the bark, passengers as well as crew, took courage at the benignant signs, while Adelheid wept, in gratitude and joy, over the gray hairs of her father.

Maso had now obtained complete command of the Winkelried, as much by the necessity of the case, as by the unrivalled skill and courage he had manifested during the fearful minutes of their extreme jeopardy. No sooner did he succeed in staying his own grief, than he called the people about him, and issued his orders for the new measures that had become necessary.

All who have ever been subject to their influence know that there is nothing more uncertain than the winds. Their fickleness has passed into a proverb; but their inconstancy, as well as their power, from the fanning air to the destructive tornado, are to be traced to causes that are sufficiently clear, though hid in their nature from the calculations of our forethought. The tempest of the night was owing to the simple fact, that a condensed and chilled column of the mountains had pressed upon the heated substratum of the lake, and the latter, after a long resistance, suddenly finding vent for its escape, had been obliged to let in the cataract from above. As in all extraordinary efforts, whether physical or moral, reaction would seem to be a consequence of excessive action, the currents of air, pushed beyond their proper limits, were now setting back again, like a tide on its reflux. This cause produced the northern gale that succeeded the hurricane.

The wind that came from off the shores of Vaud was steady and fresh. The barks of the Leman are not constructed for beating to windward, and it might even have been questioned, whether the Winkelried would have borne her canvass against so heavy a breeze. Maso, however, appeared to understand himself thoroughly, and as he had acquired the influence which hardihood and skill are sure to obtain over doubt and timidity in situations of hazard, he was obeyed by all on board with submission, if not with zeal.

No more was heard of the headsman or of his supposed agency in the storm; and, as he prudently kept himself in the back-ground, so as not to endanger a revival of the superstition of his enemies, he seemed entirely forgotten.

The business of getting the anchors occupied a considerable time, for Maso refused, now there existed no necessity for the sacrifice, to permit a yarn to be cut; but, released from this hold on the water, the bark whirled away, and was soon driving before the wind. The mariner was at the helm, and, causing the head-sail to be loosened, he steered directly for the rocks of Savoy. This manoeuvre excited disagreeable suspicions in the minds of several on board, for the lawless character of their pilot had been more than suspected in the course of their short acquaintance, and the coast towards which they were furiously rushing known to be iron-bound, and, in such a gale fatal to all who came rudely upon its rocks. Half-an-hour removed their apprehensions. When near enough to the mountains to feel their deadening influence on the gale, the natural effect of the eddies, formed by their resistance to the currents, he luffed-to and set his main-sail. Relieved by this wise precaution, the Winkelried now wore her canvass gallantly, and she dashed along the shore of Savoy with a foaming beak, shooting past ravine, valley, glen, and hamlet, as if sailing in air.

In less than an hour, St. Gingoulph, or the village through which the dividing line between the territories of Switzerland and those of the King of Sardinia passes, was abeam, and the excellent calculations of the sagacious Maso became still more apparent. He had foreseen another shift of wind, as the consequence of all this poise and counterpoise, and he was here met by the true breeze of the night. The last current came out of the gorge of the Valais, sullen, strong, and hoarse, bringing him, however, fairly to windward of his port. The Winkelried was cast in season, and, when the gale struck her anew, her canvass drew fairly, and she walked out from beneath the mountains into the broad lake, like a swan obeying its instinct.

The passage across the width of the Leman, in that horn of the crescent and in such a breeze, required rather more than an hour. This time was occupied among the common herd in self-felicitations, and in those vain boastings that distinguish the vulgar who have escaped an imminent danger without any particular merit of their own. Among those whose spirits were better trained and more rebuked, there were attentions to the sufferers and deep thanksgivings with the touching intercourse of the grateful and happy. The late scenes, and the fearful fate of the patron and Nicholaus Wagner, cast a shade upon their joy, but all inwardly felt that they had been snatched from the jaws of death.

Maso shaped his course by the beacon that still blazed in the grate of old Roger de Blonay. With his eye riveted on the luff of his sail, his hip bearing hard against the tiller, and a heart that relieved itself, from time to time, with bitter sighs, he ruled the bark like a presiding spirit.

At length the black mass of the côtes of Vaud took more distinct and regular forms. Here and there, a tower or a tree betrayed its outlines against the sky, and then the objects on the margin of the lake began to stand out in gloomy relief from the land. Lights flared along the strand, and cries reached them, from the shore. A dark shapeless pile stood directly athwart their watery path, and, at the next moment, it took the aspect of a ruined castle-like edifice. The canvass flapped and was handed, the Winkelried rose and set more slowly and with a gentler movement, and glided into the little, secure, artificial haven of La Tour de Peil. A forest of latine yards and low masts lay before them, but, by giving the bark a rank sheer, Maso brought her to her berth, by the side of another lake craft, with a gentleness of collision that, as the mariners have it, would not have broken an egg.

A hundred voices greeted the travellers; for their approach had been seen and watched with intense anxiety. Fifty eager Vévaisans poured upon her deck, in a noisy crowd, the instant it was possible. Among others, a dark shaggy object bounded foremost. It leaped wildly forward, and Maso found himself in the embraces of Nettuno. A little later, when delight and a more tempered feeling permitted examination, a lock of human hair was discovered entangled in the teeth of the dog, and the following week the bodies of Baptiste and the peasant of Berne were found still clenched in the desperate death-gripe, washed upon the shores of Vaud.

Chapter VIII

> The moon is up; by Heaven a lovely eve!
> Long streams of light, o'er glancing waves expand,
> Now lads on shore may sigh and maids believe:
> Such be our fate when we return to land!
>
> Byron.

The approach of the Winkelried had been seen from Vévey throughout the afternoon and evening. The arrival of the Baron de Willading and his daughter was expected by many in the town, the rank and influence of the former in the great canton rendering him an object of interest to more than those who felt affection for his person and respect for his upright qualities. Roger de Blonay had not been his only youthful friend, for the place contained another, with whom he was intimate by habit, if not from a community of those principles which are the best cement of friendships.

The officer charged with the especial supervision of the districts or circles, into which Berne had caused its dependent territory of Vaud to be divided, was termed a *bailli*, a title that our word bailiff will scarcely render, except as it may strictly mean a substitute for the exercise of authority that is the property of another, but which, for the want of a better term, we may be compelled occasionally to use. The bailli, or bailiff, of Vévey was Peter Hofmeister, a member of one of those families of the bürgerschaft, or the municipal aristocracy of the canton, which found its institutions venerable, just, and, and if one might judge from their language, almost sacred, simply because it had been in possession of certain exclusive privileges under their authority, that were not only comfortable in their exercise but fecund in other worldly advantages. This Peter Hofmeister was, in the main, a hearty, well-meaning, and somewhat benevolent person, but, living as he did under the secret consciousness that all was not as it should be, he pushed his opinions on the subject of vested interests, and on the stability of temporal matters, a little into extremes, pretty much on the same principle as that on which the engineer expends the largest portion of his art in fortifying the weakest point of the citadel, taking care that there shall be a constant flight of shot, great and small, across the most accessible of its approaches. By one of the exclusive ordinances of those times, in which men were glad to get relief from the violence and rapacity of the baron and the satellite of the prince, ordinances that it was the fashion of the day to term liberty, the family of Hofmeister had come into the exercise of a certain charge, or monopoly, that, in truth, had always constituted its wealth and importance, but of which it was accustomed to speak as forming its principal claim to the gratitude of the public, for duties that had been performed not only so well, but for so long a period, by an unbroken succession of patriots descended from the same stock. They who judged of the value attached to the possession of this charge, by the animation with which all attempts to relieve them of the burthen were repelled, must have been in error; for, to hear their friends descant on the difficulties of the duties, of the utter impossibility that they should be properly discharged by any family that had not been in their exercise just one hundred and seventy-two years and a half, the precise period of the hard servitude of the Hofmeisters, and the rare merit of their self-devotion to the common good, it would seem that they were so many modern Curtii, anxious to leap into the chasm of uncertain and endless toil, to save the Republic from the ignorance and peculations of certain interested and selfish knaves, who wished to enjoy the same high trusts, for a motive so unworthy as that of their own particular advantage. This subject apart, however, and with a strong reservation in favor of the supremacy of Berne, on whom his importance depended, a better or a more philanthropic man than Peter Hofmeister would not have been easily found. He was a hearty laugher, a hard drinker, a common and peculiar failing of the age, a great respecter of the law, as was meet in one so situated, and a bachelor of sixty-eight, a time of life that, by referring his education to a period more remote by half a century, than that in which the incidents of our legend took place, was not at all in favor of any very romantic predilection in behalf of the rest of the human race. In short, the Herr Hofmeister was a bailiff, much as Balthazar was a headsman, on account of some particular merit or demerit, (it might now be difficult to say which,) of one of his ancestors, by the laws of the canton, and by the opinions of men. The only material difference between them was in the fact, that the one greatly enjoyed his station, while the other had but an indifferent relish for his trust.

When Roger de Blonay, by the aid of a good glass, had assured himself that the bark which lay off St. Saphorin, in the even tide, with yards a-cock-bill, and sails pendent in their picturesque drapery, contained a party of gentle travellers who occupied the stern, and saw by the plumes and robes that a female of condition was among them, he gave an order to prepare the beacon-fire, and descended to the port, in order to be in readiness to receive his friend. Here he found the bailiff, pacing the public promenade, which is washed by the limpid water of the lake, with the air of a man who had more on his mind than the daily cares of office. Although the Baron de Blonay was a Vaudois, and looked upon all the functionaries of his country's conquerors with a species of hereditary dislike, he was by nature a man of mild and courteous qualities, and the meeting was, as usual, friendly in the externals, and of seeming cordiality. Great care was had by both to speak in the second person; on the part of the Vaudois, that it might be seen he valued himself as, at least, the equal of the representative of Berne, and, on that of the bailiff, in order to show that his office made him as good as the head of the oldest house in all that region.

"Thou expectest to see friends from Genf in yonder bark?" said the Herr Hofmeister, abruptly.

"And thou?"

"A friend, and one more than a friend;" answered the bailiff, evasively. "My advices tell me that Melchior de Willading will sojourn among us during the festival of the Abbaye, and secret notice has been sent that there will be another here, who wishes to see our merry-making, without pretension to the honors that he might fairly claim."

"It is not rare for nobles of mark, and even princes, to visit us on these occasions, under feigned names and without the *éclat* of their rank, for the great, when they descend to follies, seldom like to bring their high condition within their influence."

"The wiser they. I have my own troubles with these accursed fooleries, for--it may be a weakness, but it is one that is official--I cannot help imagining that a bailiff cuts but a shabby figure before the people, in the presence of so many gods and goddesses. To own to thee the truth, I rejoice that he who cometh, cometh as he doth.--Hast letters of late date from Berne?"

"None; though report says that there is like to be a change among some of those who fill the public trusts."

"So much the worse!" growled the bailiff. "Is it to be expected that men who never did an hour's duty in a charge can acquit themselves like those who have, it might be said, sucked in practice with their mother's milk?"

"Ay; this is well enough for thee; but others say that even the Erlachs had a beginning."

"Himmel! Am I a heathen to deny this? As many beginnings as thou wilt, good Roger, but I like not thy ends. No doubt an Erlach is mortal, like all of us, and even a created being; but a man is not a charge. Let the clay die, if thou wilt, but, if thou wouldst have faithful or skilful servants look to the true successor. But we will have none of this to-day.--Hast many guests at Blonay?"

"Not one. I look for the company of Melchior de Willading and his daughter--and yet I like not the time! There are evil signs playing about the high peaks and in the neighborhood of the Dents since the sun has set!"

"Thou art ever in a storm up in thy castle there! The Leman was never more peaceable, and I should take it truly in evil part, were the rebellious lake to get into one of its fits of sudden anger with so precious a freight on its bosom."

"I do not think the Genfer See will regard even a bailiff's displeasure!" rejoined the Baron de Blonay, laughing. "I repeat it; the signs are suspicious. Let us consult the watermen, for it may be well to send a light-pulling boat to bring the travellers to land."

Roger de Blonay and the bailiff walked towards the little earthen mole, that partially protects the roadstead of Vévey, and which is for ever forming and for ever washing away before the storms of winter, in order to consult some of those who were believed to be expert in detecting the symptoms that precede any important changes of the atmosphere. The opinions were various. Most believed there would be a gust; but, as the Winkelried was known to be a new and well-built bark, and none could tell how much beyond her powers she had been loaded by the cupidity of Baptiste, and as it was generally thought the wind would be as likely to bring her up to her haven as to be against her, there appeared no sufficient reason for sending off the boat; especially as it was believed the bark would be not only drier but safer than a smaller craft, should they be overtaken by the wind. This indecision, so common in cases of uncertainty, was the means of exposing Adelheid and her father to all those fearful risks they had just run.

When the night came on, the people of the town began to understand that the tempest would be grave for those who were obliged to encounter it, even in the best bark on the Leman. The darkness added to the danger, for vessels had often run against the land by miscalculating their distances; and the lights were shown along the strand, by order of the bailiff, who manifested an interest so unusual in those on board the Winkelried, as to draw about them more than the sympathy that would ordinarily be felt for travellers in distress. Every exertion that the case admitted was made in their behalf, and, the moment the state of the lake allowed, boats were sent off, in every probable direction, to their succor. But the Winkelried was running along the coast of Savoy, ere any ventured forth, and the search proved fruitless. When the rumor spread, however, that a sail was to be discerned coming out from under the wide shadow of the opposite mountains, and that it was steering for La Tour de Peil, a village with a far safer harbor than that of Vévey, and but an arrow's flight from the latter town, crowds rushed to the spot. The instant it was known that the missing party was in her, the travellers were received with cheers of delight and cries of hearty greeting.

The bailiff and Roger de Blonay hastened forward to receive the Baron de Willading and his friends, who were carried in a tumultuous and joyful manner into the old castle that adjoins the port, and from which, in truth, the latter derives its name. The Bernois noble was too much affected with the scenes through which he had so lately passed, and with the strong and ungovernable tenderness of Adelheid, who had wept over him as a mother sobs over her recovered child, to exchange greetings with him of Vaud, in the hearty, cordial manner that ordinarily characterized their meetings. Still their peculiar habits shone through the restraint.

"Thou seest me just rescued from the fishes of thy Leman, dear de Blonay," he said, squeezing the other's hand with emotion, as, leaning on his shoulder, they went into the château. "But for yonder brave youth, and as honest a mariner as ever floated on water, fresh or salt, all that is left of old Melchior de Willading would, at this moment, be of less value than the meanest férà in thy lake!"

"God be praised that thou art as we see thee! We feared for thee, and boats are out at this moment in search of thy bark: but it has been wiser ordered. This brave young man, who, I see, is both a Swiss and a soldier, is doubly welcome among us,--in the two characters just named, and as one that hath done thee and us so great a service."

Sigismund received the compliments which he so well merited with modesty. The bailiff, however, not content with making the usual felicitations, whispered in his ear that a service like this, rendered to one of its most esteemed nobles, would not be forgotten by the Councils on a proper occasion.

"Thou art happily arrived, Herr Melchior," he then added, aloud; "come as thou wilt, floating or sailing in air. We have thee among us none the worse for the accident, and we thank God, as Roger de Blonay has just so well observed. Our Abbaye is like to be a gallant ceremony, for divers gentlemen of name are in the town, and I hear of more that are pricking forward among the mountains from countries beyond the Rhine. Hadst thou no other companions in the bark but these I see around us?"

"There is another, and I wonder that he is not here! 'Tis a noble Genoese, that thou hast often heard me name, Sire de Blonay, as one that I love.

Gaetano Grimaldi is a name familiar to thee, or the words of friendship have been uttered in an idle ear."

"I have heard so much of the Italian that I can almost fancy him an old and tried acquaintance. When thou first returnedst from the Italian wars, thy tongue was never weary of recounting his praises: it was Gaetano said this--Gaetano thought thus--Gaetano did that! Surely he is not of thy company?"

"He, and no other! A lucky meeting on the quay of Genf brought us together again after a separation of full thirty years, and, as if Heaven had reserved its trials for the occasion, we have been made to go through the late danger in company. I had him in my arms in that fearful moment, Roger, when the sky, and the mountains, and all of earth, even to that dear girl, were fading, as I thought for ever, from my sight,--he, that had already been my partner in so many risks, who had bled for me, watched for me, ridden for me, and did all other things that love could prompt for me, was brought by Providence to be my companion in the awful strait through which I have just passed!"

While the Baron was still speaking, his friend entered with the quiet and dignified mien he always maintained, when it was not his pleasure to throw aside the reserve of high station, or when he yielded to the torrents of feeling that sometimes poured through his southern temperament, in a way to unsettle the deportment of mere convention. He was presented to Roger de Blonay and the bailiff, as the person just alluded to, and as the oldest and most tried of the friends of his introducer. His reception by the former was natural and warm, while the Herr Hofmeister was so particular in his professions of pleasure and respect as to excite not only notice but surprise.

"Thanks, thanks, good Peterchen," said the Baron de Willading, for such was the familiar diminutive by which the bustling bailiff was usually addressed by those who could take the liberty; thanks, honest Peterchen; thy kindness to Gaetano is so much love shown to myself."

"I honor thy friends as thyself, Herr von Willading," returned the bailiff; "for thou hast a claim to the esteem of the bürgerschaft and all its servants; but the homage paid to the Signor Grimaldi is due on his own account. We are but poor Swiss, that dwell in the midst of wild mountains, little favored by the sun if ye will, and less known to the world;--but we have our manners! A man that hath been intrusted with authority as long as I were unfit for his trust, did he not tell, as it might be by instinct, when he has those in his presence that are to be honored. Signore, the loss of Melchior von Willading before our haven, would have made the lake unpleasant to us all, for months, not to say years; but, had so great a calamity arrived as that of your death by means of our waters, I could have prayed that the mountains might fall into the basin, and bury the offending Leman under their rocks!"

Melchior de Willading and old Roger de Blonay laughed heartily at Peterchen's hyperbolical compliments; though it was quite plain that the worthy bailiff himself fancied he had said a clever thing.

"I thank you, Signore, no less than my friend de Willading," returned the Genoese, a gleam of humor lighting his eye. "This courteous reception quite outdoes us of Italy; for I doubt if there be a man south of the Alps, who would be willing to condemn either of our seas to so overwhelming a punishment, for a fault so venial, or at least so natural. I beg, however, that the lake may be pardoned; since, at the worst, it was but a secondary agent in the affair, and, I doubt not, it would have treated us as it treats all travellers, had we kept out of its embraces. The crime must be imputed to the winds, and as they are the offspring of the hills, I fear it will be found that these very mountains, to which you look for retribution, will be convicted at last as the true devisers and abettors of the plot against our lives."

The bailiff chuckled and simpered, like a man pleased equally with his own wit and with that he had excited in others, and the discourse changed; though, throughout the night, as indeed was the fact on all other occasions during his visit, the Signor Grimaldi received from him so marked and particular attentions, as to create a strong sentiment in favor of the Italian among those who had been chiefly accustomed to see Peterchen enact the busy, important, dignified, local functionary.

Attention was now paid to the first wants of the travellers, who had great need of refreshments after the fatigues and exposure of the day. To obtain the latter, Roger de Blonay insisted that they should ascend to his castle, in whose grate the welcoming beacon still blazed. By means of *chars-à-banc*, the peculiar vehicle of the country, the short distance was soon overcome, the bailiff, not a little to the surprise of the owner of the house, insisting on seeing the strangers safely housed within its walls. At the gate of Blonay, however, Peterchen took his leave, making a hundred apologies for his absence, on the ground of the extensive duties that had devolved on his shoulders in consequence of the approaching fête.

"We shall have a mild winter, for I have never known the Herr Hofmeister so courteous;" observed Roger de Blonay, while showing his guests into the castle. "Thy Bernese authorities, Melchior, are little apt to be lavish of their compliments to us poor nobles of Vaud."

"Signore, you forget the interest of our friend;" observed the laughing Genoese. "There are other and better bailiwicks, beyond a question, in the gifts of the Councils, and the Signor de Willading has a loud voice in their disposal. Have I found a solution for this zeal?"

"Thou hast not," returned the baron, "for Peterchen hath little hope beyond that of dying where he has lived, the deputed ruler of a small district. The worthy man should have more credit for a good heart, his own, no doubt, being touched at seeing those who are, as it may be, redeemed from the grave. I owe him grace for the kindness, and should a better thing really offer, and could my poor voice be of account, why, I do not say it should be silent; it is serving the public well, to put men of these kind feelings into places of trust."

This opinion appeared very natural to the listeners, all of whom, with the exception of the Signor Grimaldi, joined in echoing the sentiment. The latter, more experienced in the windings of the human heart, or possessing some reasons known only to himself, merely smiled at the remarks that he heard, as if he thoroughly understood the difference between the homage that is paid to station, and that which a generous and noble nature is compelled to yield to its own impulses.

An hour later, the light repast was ended, and Roger de Blonay informed his guests that they would be well repaid for walking a short distance, by a look at the loveliness of the night. In sooth, the change was already so great, that it was not easy for the imagination to convert the soft and smiling scene that lay beneath and above the towers of Blonay, into the dark vault and the angry lake from which they had so lately escaped.

Every cloud had already sailed far away towards the plains of Germany, and the moon had climbed so high above the ragged Dent de Jaman as to its rays to stream into, the basin of the Leman. A thousand pensive stars spangled the vauk images of the benign omnipotence which unceasingly pervades and governs the universe, whatever may be the local derangements or accidental struggles of the inferior agents. The foaming and rushing waves had gone down nearly as fast as they had arisen, and, in their stead, remained myriads of curling ridges along which the glittering moonbeams danced, rioting with mild impunity on the surface of the placid sheet. Boats were out again, pulling for Savoy or the neighboring villages: and the whole view betokened the renewed confidence of those who trusted habitually to the fickle and blustering elements.

"There is a strong and fearful resemblance between the human passions and these hot and angry gusts of nature;" observed the Signor Grimaldi, after they had stood silently regarding the scene for several musing minutes-

-"alike quick to be aroused and to be appeased; equally ungovernable while in the ascendant, and admitting the influence of a wholesome reaction, that brings a more sober tranquillity, when the fit is over. Your northern phlegm may render the analogy less apparent, but it is to be found as well among the cooler temperaments of the Teutonic stock, as among us of warmer blood. Do not this placid hill-side, yon lake, and the starry heavens, look as if they regretted their late unseemly violence, and wished to cheat the beholder into forgetfulness of their attack on our safety, as an impetuous but generous nature would repent it of the blow given in anger, or of the cutting speech that had escaped in a moment of spleen? What hast thou to say to my opinion, Signor Sigismund, for none know better than thou the quality of the tempest we have encountered?"

"Signore," answered the young soldier, modestly, "you forget this brave mariner, without whose coolness and forethought all would have been lost. He has come up to Blonay, at our own request, but, until now, he has been overlooked."

Maso came forward at a signal from Sigismund, and stood before the party to whom he had rendered so signal aid, with a composure that was not easily disturbed.

"I have come up to the castle, Signore, at your commands," he said, addressing the Genoese; "but, having my own affairs on hand, must now beg to know your pleasure?"

"We have, in sooth, been negligent of thy merit. On landing, my first thought was of thee, as thou knowest: but other things had caused me to forget thee. Thou art, like myself, an Italian?"

"Signore, I am."

"Of what country?"

"Of your own, Signore; a Genoese, as I have said before."

The other remembered the circumstance, though it did not seem to please him. He looked around, as if to detect what others thought, and then continued his questions.

"A Genoese!" he repeated, slowly: "if this be so, we should know something of each other. Hast ever heard of me, in thy frequent visits to the port?"

Maso smiled; at first, he appeared disposed to be facetious; but a dark cloud passed over his swarthy lineaments, and he lost his pleasantry, in an air of thoughtfulness that struck his interrogator as singular.

"Signore," he said, after a pause, "most that follow my manner of life know something of your eccellenza; if it is only to be questioned of this that I am here, I pray leave to be permitted to go my way."

"No, by San Francesco! thou quittest us not so unceremoniously. I am wrong to assume the manner of a superior with one to whom I owe my life, and am well answered. But there is a heavy account to be settled between us, and I will do something towards wiping out the balance, which is so greatly against me, now; leaving thee to apply for a further statement, when we shall both be again in our own Genoa."

The Signor Grimaldi had reached forth an arm, while speaking, and received a well-filled purse from his countryman and companion, Marcelli. This was soon emptied of its contents, a fair show of sequins, all of which were offered to the mariner, without reservation. Maso looked coldly at the glittering pile, and, by his hesitation, left a doubt whether he did not think the reward insufficient.

"I tell thee it is but the present gage of further payment. At Genoa our account shall be fairly settled; but this is all that a traveller can prudently spare. Thou wilt come to me in our own town, and we will look to all thy interests."

"Signore, you offer that for which men do all acts, whether of good or of evil. They jeopard their souls for this very metal; mock at God's laws; overlook the right; trifle with justice, and become devils incarnate to possess it; and yet, though nearly penniless, I am so placed as to be compelled to refuse what you offer."

"I tell thee, Maso, that it shall be increased hereafter--or--we are not so poor as to go a-begging! Good Marcelli, empty thy hoards, and I will have, recourse to Melchior de Willading's purse for our wants, until we can get nearer to our own supplies."

"And is Melchior de Willading to pass for nothing, in all this!" exclaimed the Baron; "put up thy gold, Gaetano, and leave me to satisfy the honest mariner for the present. At a later day, he can come to thee, in Italy: but here, on my own ground, I claim the right to be his banker."

"Signore," returned Maso, earnestly and with more of gentle feeling than he was accustomed to betray, "you are both liberal beyond my desires, and but too well disposed for my poor wants. I have come up to the castle at your order, and to do you pleasure, but not in the hope to get money. I am poor; that it would be useless to deny, for appearances are against me--" here he laughed, his auditors thought in a manner that was forced--"but poverty and meanness are not always inseparable. You have more than suspected to-day that my life is free, and I admit it; but it is a mistake to believe that, because men quit the high-road which some call honesty, in any particular practice, they are without human feeling. I have been useful in saving your lives, Signori, and there is more pleasure in the reflection, than I should find in having the means to earn twice the gold ye offer. Here is the Signor Capitano," he added, taking Sigismund by the arm, and dragging him forward, "lavish your favors on him, for no practice of mine could have been of use without his bravery. If ye give him all in your treasuries, even to its richest pearl, ye will do no more than reason."

As Maso ceased, he cast a glance towards the attentive, breathless Adelheid, that continued to utter his meaning even after the tongue was silent The bright suffusion that covered the maiden's face was visible even by the pale moonlight, and Sigismund shrunk back from his rude grasp in the manner in which the guilty retire from notice.

"These opinions are creditable to thee, Maso," returned the Genoese, affecting not to understand his more particular meaning, "and they excite a stronger wish to be thy friend. I will say no more on the subject at present, for I see thy humor. Thou wilt let me see thee at Genoa?"

The expression of Maso's countenance was inexplicable, but he retained his usual indifference of manner.

"Signor Gaetano," he said, using a mariner's freedom in the address, "there are nobles in Genoa that might better knock at the door of your palace than I; and there are those, too, in the city that would gossip, were it known that you received such guests."

"This is tying thyself too closely to an evil and a dangerous trade. I suspect thee to be of the contraband, but surely it is not a pursuit so free from danger, of so much repute, or, judging by thy attire, of so much profit even, that thou needest be wedded to it for life. Means can be found to relieve thee from its odium, by giving thee a place in those customs with which thou hast so often trifled."

Maso laughed outright.

"So it is, Signore, in this moral world of ours. He who would run a fair course, in any particular trust has only to make himself dangerous to be bought up. Your thief-takers are desperate rogues out of business; your tide-waiter has got his art by cheating the revenue; and I have been in lands where it was said, that all they who most fleeced the people began their calling as suffering patriots. The rule is firmly enough established without the help of my poor name, and, by your leave, I will remain as I am; one that hath his pleasure in living amid risks, and who takes his revenge of the authorities by railing at them when defeated, and in laughing at them when in success."

"Young man, thou hast in thee the materials of a better life!"

"Signore, this may be true," answered Maso, whose countenance again grew dark; "we boast of being the lords of the creation, but the bark of poor Baptista was not less master of its movements, in the late gust, than we are masters of our fortunes. Signor Grimaldi, I have in me the materials that make a man; but the laws, and the opinions, and the accursed strife of men, have left me what I am. For the first fifteen years of my career, the church was to be my stepping-stone to a cardinal's hat or a fat priory; but the briny sea-water washed out the necessary unction."

"Thou art better born than thou seemest--thou hast friends who should be grieved at this?"

The eye of Maso flashed, but he bent it aside, as if bearing down, by the force of an indomitable will, some sudden and fierce impulse.

"I was born of woman!" he said, with singular emphasis.

"And thy mother--is she not pained at thy present course--does she know of thy career?"

The haggard smile to which this question gave birth induced the Genoese to regret that he had put it. Maso evidently struggled to subdue some feeling which harrowed his very soul, and his success was owing to such a command of himself as men rarely obtain.

"She is dead," he answered, huskily; "she is a saint with the angels. Had she lived, I should never have been a mariner, and--and--" laying his hand on his throat, as if to keep down the sense of suffocation, he smiled, and added, laughingly,--"ay, and the good Winkelried would have been a wreck."

"Maso, thou must come to me at Genoa. I must see more of thee, and question thee further of thy fortunes. A fair spirit has been perverted in thy fall, and the friendly aid of one who is not without influence may still restore its tone."

The Signor Grimaldi spoke warmly, like one who sincerely felt regret, and his voice had all the melancholy and earnestness of such a sentiment. The truculent nature of Maso was touched by this show of interest, and a multitude of fierce passions were at once subdued. He approached the noble Genoese, and respectfully took his hand.

"Pardon the freedom, Signore," he said more mildly, intently regarding the wrinkled and attenuated fingers, with the map-like tracery of veins, that he held in his own brown and hard palm; "this is not the first time that our flesh has touched each other, though it is the first time that our hands have joined. Let it now be in amity. A humor has come over me, and I would crave your pardon, venerable noble, for the freedom. Signore, you are aged, and honored, and stand high, doubtless, in Heaven's favor, as in that of man--grant me, then, your blessing, ere I go my way."

As Maso preferred this extraordinary request, he knelt with an air of so much reverence and sincerity as to leave little choice as to granting it. The Genoese was surprised, but not disconcerted. With perfect dignity and self-possession, and with a degree of feeling that was not unsuited to the occasion, the fruit of emotions so powerfully awakened, he pronounced the benediction. The mariner arose, kissed the hand which he still held, made a hurried sign of salutation to all, leaped down the declivity on which they stood, and vanished among the shadows of a copse.

Sigismund, who had witnessed this unusual scene with surprise, watched him to the last, and he saw, by the manner in which he dashed his hand across his eyes, that his fierce nature had been singularly shaken. On recovering his thoughts, the Signor Grimaldi, too, felt certain there had been no mockery in the conduct of their inexplicable preserver, for a hot tear had fallen on his hand ere it was liberated. He was himself strongly agitated by what had passed, and, leaning on his friend, he slowly re-entered the gates of Blonay.

"This extraordinary demand of Maso's has brought up the sad image of my own poor son, dear Melchior," he said; "would to Heaven that he could have received this blessing, and that it might have been of use to him, in the sight of God! Nay, he may yet hear of it--for, canst thou believe it, I have thought that Maso may be one of his lawless associates, and that some wild desire to communicate this scene has prompted the strange request I granted."

The discourse continued, but it became secret, and of the most confidential kind. The rest of the party soon sought their beds, though lamps were burning in the chambers of the two old nobles to a late hour of the night.

Chapter IX

Where are my Switzers? Let them guard the door:
What is the matter?

Hamlet.

The American autumn, or fall, as we poetically and affectionately term this generous and mellow season among ourselves, is thought to be unsurpassed, in its warm and genial lustre, its bland and exhilarating airs, and its admirable constancy, by the decline of the year in nearly every other portion of the earth. Whether attachment to our own fair and generous land, has led us to over-estimate its advantages or not, and bright and cheerful as our autumnal days certainly are, a fairer morning never dawned upon the Alleghanies, than that which illumined the Alps, on the reappearance of the sun after the gust of the night which has been so lately described. As the day advanced, the scene grew gradually more lovely, until warm and glowing Italy itself could scarce present a landscape more winning, or one possessing a fairer admixture of the grand and the soft, than that which greeted the eye of Adelheid de Willading, as, leaning on the arm of her father, she issued from the gate of Blonay, upon its elevated and gravelled terrace.

It has already been said that this ancient and historical building stood against the bosom of the mountains, at the distance of a short league behind the town of Vévey. All the elevations of this region are so many spurs of the same vast pile, and that on which Blonay has now been seated from the earliest period of the middle ages belongs to that particular line of rocky ramparts, which separates the Valais from the centre cantons of the confederation of Switzerland, and which is commonly known as the range of the Oberland Alps. This line of snow-crowned rocks terminates in perpendicular precipices on the very margin of the Leman, and forms, on the side of the lake, a part of that magnificent setting which renders the south-eastern horn of its crescent so wonderfully beautiful. The upright natural wall that overhangs Villeneuve and Chillon stretches along the verge of the water, barely leaving room for a carriage-road, with here and there a cottage at its base, for the distance of two leagues, when it diverges from the course of the lake, and, withdrawing inland, it is finally lost among the minor eminences of Fribourg. Every one has observed those sloping declivities, composed of the washings of torrents, the *débris* of precipices, and what may be termed the constant drippings of perpendicular eminencies and which lie like broad buttresses at their feet, forming a sort of foundation or basement for the superincumbent mass. Among the Alps, where nature has acted on so sublime a scale, and where all the proportions are duly observed, these *débris* of the high mountains frequently contain villages and towns, or form vast fields, vineyards, and pasturages, according to their elevation or their exposure towards the sun. It may be questioned, in strict geology, whether the variegated acclivity that surrounds Vévey, rich in villages and vines, hamlets and castles, has been thus formed, or whether the natural convulsions which expelled the upper rocks from the crust of the earth left their bases in the present broken and beautiful forms; but the fact is not important to the effect, which is that just named, and which gives to these vast ranges of rock secondary and fertile bases, that, in other regions, would be termed mountains of themselves.

The castle and family of Blonay, for both still exist, are among the oldest of Vaud. A square, rude tower, based upon a foundation of rock, one of those ragged masses that thrust their naked heads occasionally through the soil of the declivity, was the commencement of the hold. Other edifices have been reared around this nucleus in different ages, until the whole presents one of those peculiar and picturesque piles, that ornament so many both of the savage and of the softer sites of Switzerland.

The terrace towards which Adelheid and her father advanced was an irregular walk, shaded by venerable trees that had been raised near the principal or the carriage gate of the castle, on a ledge of those rocks that form the foundation of the buildings themselves. It had its parapet walls, its seats, its artificial soil, and its gravelled *allées*, as is usual with these antiquated ornaments; but it also had, what is better than these, one of the most sublime and lovely views that ever greeted human eyes. Beneath it lay the undulating and teeming declivity, rich in vines, and carpeted with sward, here dotted by hamlets, there park-like and rural with forest trees, while there was no quarter that did not show the roof of a château or the tower of some rural church. There is little of magnificence in Swiss architecture, which never much surpasses, and is, perhaps, generally inferior to our own; but the beauty and quaintness of the sites, the great variety of the surfaces, the hillsides, and the purity of the atmosphere, supply charms that are peculiar to the country. Vévey lay at the water-side, many hundred feet lower, and seemingly on a narrow strand, though in truth enjoying ample space; while the houses of St. Saphorin, Corsier, Montreux, and of a dozen more villages, were clustered together, like so many of the compact habitations of wasps stuck against the mountains. But the principal charm was in the Leman. One who had never witnessed the lake in its fury, could not conceive the possibility of danger in the tranquil shining sheet that was now spread like a liquid mirror, for leagues, beneath the eye. Some six or seven barks were in view, their sails drooping in negligent forms, as if disposed expressly to become models for the artist, their yards inclining as chance had cast them, and their hulls looming large, to complete the picture. To these near objects must be added the distant view, which extended to the Jura in one direction, and which in the other was bounded by the frontiers of Italy, whose aërial limits were to be traced in that region which appears to belong neither to heaven nor to earth, the abode of eternal frosts. The Rhone was shining, in spots, among the meadows of the Valais, for the elevation of the castle admitted of its being seen, and Adelheid endeavored to trace among the mazes of the mountains the valleys which led to those sunny countries, towards which they journeyed.

The sensations of both father and daughter, when they came beneath the leafy canopy of the terrace, were those of mute delight. It was evident, by the expression of their countenances, that they were in a favorable mood to receive pleasurable impressions; for the face of each was full of that quiet happiness which succeeds sudden and lively joy. Adelheid had been weeping; but, judging from the radiance of her eyes, the healthful and brightening bloom of her cheeks, and the struggling smiles that played about her ripe lips, the tears had been sweet, rather than painful. Though still betraying enough of physical frailty to keep alive the concern of all who loved her, there was a change for the better in her appearance, which was so sensible as to strike the least observant of those who lived in daily communication with the invalid.

"If pure and mild air, a sunny sky, and ravishing scenery, be what they seek who cross the Alps, my father," said Adelheid, after they had stood a moment, gazing at the magnificent panorama, "why should the Swiss quit his native land? Is there in Italy aught more soft, more winning or more healthful, than this?"

"This spot has often been called the Italy of our mountains. The fig ripens near yonder village of Montreux, and, open to the morning sun while it is sheltered by the precipices above, the whole of that shore well deserves its happy reputation. Still they whose spirits require diversion, and whose constitutions need support, generally prefer to go into countries where the mind has more occupation, and where a greater variety of employments help the climate and nature to complete the cure."

"But thou forgettest, father, it is agreed between us that I am now to become strong, and active, and laughing, as we used to be at Willading, when I first grew into womanhood."

"If I could but see those days again, darling, my own closing hours would be calm as those of a saint--though Heaven knows I have little pretension to that blessed character in any other particular."

"Dost thou not count a quiet conscience and a sure hope as something, father?"

"Have it as thou wilt, girl. Make a saint of me, or a bishop, or a hermit, if thou wilt; the only reward I ask is, to see thee smiling and happy, as thou never failedst to be during the first eighteen years of thy life. Had I foreseen that thou wert to return from my good sister so little like thyself, I would have forbidden the visit, much as I love her, and all that are her's. But the wisest of us are helpless mortals, and scarce know our own wants from hour to hour. Thou saidst, I think, that this brave Sigismund honestly declared his belief that my consent could never be given to one who had so little to boast of, in the way of birth and fortune? There was, at least, good sense, and modesty, and right feeling, in the doubt, but he should have thought better of my heart."

"He said this;" returned Adelheid, in a timid and slightly trembling voice, though it was quite apparent by the confiding expression of her eye, that she had no longer any secret from her parent. "He had too much honor to wish to win the daughter of a noble without the knowledge and approbation of her friends."

"That the boy should love thee, Adelheid, is natural; it is an additional proof of his own merit--but that he should distrust my affection and justice is an offence that I can scarce forgive. What are ancestry and wealth to thy happiness?"

"Thou forget'st, dear sir, he is yet to learn that my happiness, in any measure, depends on his."

Adelheid spoke quickly and with warmth.

"He knew I was a father and that thou art an only child; one of his good sense and right way of thinking should have better understood the feelings of a man in my situation, than to doubt his natural affection."

"As he has never been the parent of an only daughter, father," answered the smiling Adelheid, for, in her present mood, smiles came easily, "he may not have felt or anticipated all that thou imagin'st. He knew the prejudices of the world on the subject of noble blood, and they are few indeed, that, having much, are disposed to part with it to him who hath little."

"The lad reasoned more like an old miser than a young soldier, and I have a great mind to let him feel my displeasure for thinking so meanly of me. Have we not Willading, with all its fair lands, besides our rights in the city, that we need go begging money of others, like needy mendicants! Thou hast been in the conspiracy against my character, girl, or such a fear could not have either uneasiness for a moment."

"I never thought, father, that thou would'st reject him on account of poverty, for I knew our own means sufficient for all our own wants; but I did believe that he who could not boast the privileges of nobility might fail to gain thy favor."

"Are we not a republic?--is not the right of the bürgerschaft the one essential right in Berne--why should I raise obstacles about that on which the laws are silent?"

Adelheid listened, as a female of her years would be apt to listen to words so grateful, with a charmed ear; and yet she shook her head, in a way to express an incredulity that was not altogether free from apprehension.

"For thy generous forgetfulness of old opinions in behalf of my happiness, dearest father," she resumed, the tears starting unbidden to her thoughtful blue eye, "I thank thee fervently. It is true that we are inhabitants of a republic, but we are not the less noble."

"Dost thou turn against thyself, and hunt up reasons why I should not do that which thou hast just acknowledged to be so necessary to prevent thee from following thy brothers and sisters to their early graves?"

The blood rushed in a torrent to the face of Adelheid, for though, weeping and in the moment of tender confidence which succeeded her thanksgivings for the baron's safety, she had thrown herself on his bosom, and confessed that the hopelessness of the sentiments with which she met the declared love of Sigismund was the true cause of the apparent malady that had so much alarmed her friends, the words which had flowed spontaneously from her heart, in so tender a scene, had never appeared to her to convey a meaning so strong, or one so wounding to virgin-pride, as that which her father, in the strength of his masculine habits, had now given them.

"In God's mercy, father, I shall live, whether united to Sigismund or not, to smooth thine own decline, and to bless thy old age. A pious daughter will never be torn so cruelly from one to whom she is the last and only stay. I may mourn this disappointment, and foolishly wish, perhaps, it might have been otherwise; but ours is not a house of which the maidens die for their inclinations in favor of any youths, however deserving!"

"Noble or simple," added the baron, laughing, for he saw that his daughter spoke in sudden pique, rather than from her excellent heart. Adelheid, whose good sense, and quick recollections, instantly showed her the weakness of this little display of female feeling, laughed faintly in her turn, though she repeated his words as if to give still more emphasis to her own.

"This will not do, my daughter. They who profess the republican doctrine, should not be too rigid in their constructions of privileges. If Sigismund be not noble, it will not be difficult to obtain for him that honorable distinction, and, in failure of male line, he may bear the name and sustain the honors of our family. In any case he will become of the bürgerschaft, and that of itself will be all that is required in Berne."

"In Berne, father," returned Adelheid, who had so far forgotten the recent movement of pride as to smile on her fond and indulgent parent, though, yielding to the waywardness of the happy, she continued to trifle with her own feelings--"it is true. The bürgerschaft will be sufficient for all the purposes of office and political privileges, but will it suffice for the opinions of our equals, for the prejudices of society, or for your own perfect contentment, when the freshness of gratitude shall have passed?"

"Thou puttest these questions, girl, as if employed to defeat thine own cause--Dost not truly love the boy, after all?"

"On this subject, I have spoken sincerely and as became thy child," frankly returned Adelheid. "He saved my life from imminent peril, as he has now saved thine, and although my aunt, fearful of thy displeasure, would not that thou should'st hear the tale, her prohibition could not prevent gratitude from having its way. I have told thee that Sigismund has declared his feelings, although he nobly abstained from even asking a return, and I should not have been my mother's child, could I have remained entirely indifferent to so much worth united to a service so great What I have said of our prejudices is, then, rather for your reflection, dearest sir, than for myself. I have thought much of all this, and am ready to make any sacrifice to pride, and to bear all the remarks of the world, in order to discharge a debt to one to whom I owe so much. But, while it is natural, perhaps unavoidable, that I should feel thus, thou art not necessarily to forget the other claims upon thee. It is true that, in one sense, we are all to each other, but there is a tyrant that will scarce let any escape from his reign; I mean opinion. Let us then not deceive ourselves--though we of Berne affect the republic, and speak much of liberty, it is a small state, and the influence of those that are larger and more powerful among our neighbors rules in every thing that touches opinion. A noble is as much a noble in Berne, in all but what the law bestows, as he is in the Empire--and thou knowest we come of the German root, which has struck deep into these prejudices."

The Baron de Willading had been much accustomed to defer to the superior mind and more cultivated understanding of his daughter, who, in the retirement of her father's castle, had read and reflected far more than her years would have probably permitted in the busier scenes of the world. He felt the justice of her remark, and they had walked the entire length of the terrace in profound silence, before he could summon the ideas necessary to make a suitable answer.

"The truth of what thou sayest, is not to be denied," he at length said, "but it may be palliated. I have many friends in the German courts, and favors may be had; letters of nobility will give the youth the station he wants, after which he can claim thy hand without offence to any opinions, whether of Berne or elsewhere."

"I doubt if Sigismund will willingly become a party to this expedient. Our own nobility is of ancient origin; it dates from a period anterior to the existence of Berne as a city, and is much older than our institutions. I remember to have heard him say, that when a people refuse to bestow these distinctions themselves, their citizens can never receive them from others without a loss of dignity and character, and one of his moral firmness might hesitate to do what he thinks wrong for a boon so worthless as that we offer."

"By the soul of William Tell! should the unknown peasant dare--But he is a brave boy, and twice has he done the last service to my race! I love him, Adelheid, little less than thyself; and we will win him ever to our purpose gently, and by degrees. A maiden of thy beauty and years to say nothing of thy other qualities, thy name the lands of Willading, and the rights of Berne are matters, after all, not to me lightly refused by a nameless soldier who hath naught--"

"But his courage, his virtues, his modesty, and his excellent sense, father!"

"Thou wilt not let me have the naked satisfaction of vaunting my own wares! I see Gaetano Grimaldi making signs at his window, as if he were about to come forth: go thou to thy chamber, that I may discourse of this troublesome matter with that excellent friend; in good season thou shalt know the result."

Adelheid kissed the hand that she held in her own, and left him with a thoughtful air. As she descended from the terrace, it was not with the same elastic step as she had come up half an hour before.

Early deprived of her mother, this strong-minded but delicate girl had long been accustomed to make her father a confidant of all her hopes, thoughts, and pictures of the future. Owing to her peculiar circumstances, she would have had less hesitation than is usual to her sex in avowing to her parent any of her attachments; but a dread that the declaration might conduce to his unhappiness, without in any manner favoring her own cause, had hitherto kept her silent. Her acquaintance with Sigismund had been long and intimate. Rooted esteem and deep respect lay at the bottom of her sentiments, which were, however, so lively as to have chased the rose from her cheek in the endeavor to forget them, and to have led her sensitive father to apprehend that she was suffering under that premature decay which had already robbed him of his other children. There was in truth no serious ground for this apprehension, so natural to one in the place of the Baron de Willading; for, until thought, and reflection paled her cheek, a more blooming maiden than Adelheid, or one that united more perfect health with feminine delicacy, did not dwell among her native mountains. She had quietly consented to the Italian journey, in the expectation that it might serve to divert her mind from brooding over what she had long considered hopeless, and with the natural desire to see lands so celebrated, but not under any mistaken opinions of her own situation. The presence of Sigismund, so far as she was concerned, was purely accidental, although she could not prevent the pleasing idea from obtruding--an idea so grateful to her womanly affections and maiden pride--that the young soldier, who was in the service of Austria, and who had become known to her in one of his frequent visits to his native land, had gladly seized this favorable occasion to return to his colors. Circumstances, which it is not necessary to recount, had enabled Adelheid to make the youth acquainted with her father, though the interdictions of her aunt, whose imprudence had led to the accident which nearly proved so fatal, and from whose consequences she had been saved by Sigismund, prevented her from explaining all the causes she had for showing him respect and esteem. Perhaps the manner in which this young and imaginative though sensible girl was compelled to smother a portion of her feelings gave them intensity, and hastened that transition of sentiment from gratitude to affection, which, in another case, might have only been produced by a more open and prolonged association. As it was, she scarcely knew herself how irretrievably her happiness was bound up in that of Sigismund, though she had so long cherished his image in most of her day-dreams, and had unconsciously admitted his influence over her mind and hopes, until she learned that they were reciprocated.

The Signor Grimaldi appeared on one end of the terrace, as Adelheid de Willading descended at the other. The old nobles had separated late on the previous night, after a private and confidential communication that had shaken the soul of the Italian, and drawn strong and sincere manifestations of sympathy from his friend. Though so prone to sudden shades of melancholy, there was a strong touch of the humorous in the native character of the Genoese, which came so quick upon his more painful recollection, as greatly to relieve their weight, and to render him, in appearance at least, a happy, while the truth would have shown that he was a sorrowing man. He had been making his orisons with a grateful heart, and he now came forth into the genial mountain air, like one who had relieved his conscience of a heavy debt. Like most laymen of the Catholic persuasion, he thought himself no longer bound to maintain a grave and mortified exterior, when worship and penitence were duly observed, and he joined his friend with a cheerfulness of air and voice that an ascetic, or a puritan, might have attributed to levity, after the scenes through which he had so lately passed.

"The Virgin and San Francesco keep thee in mind, old friend!" said the Signor Grimaldi, cordially kissing the two cheeks of the Baron de Willading. "We both have reason to remember their care, though; heretic as thou art, I doubt not thou hast already found some other mediators to thank, that we now stand on this solid terrace of the Signor de Blonay, instead of being worthless clay at the bottom of yonder treacherous lake."

"I thank God for this, as for all his mercies--for thy life, Gaetano, as well as for mine own."

"Thou art right, thou art right, good Melchior: 'twas no affair for any but Him who holds the universe in the hollow of his hand, in good faith, for a minute later would have gathered both with our lathers. Still thou wilt permit me, Catholic as I am, to remember the intercessors on whom I called in the moment of extremity."

"This is a subject on which we have never agreed, and on which we probably never shall," answered the Bernese, with somewhat of the reserve of one conscious of a stronger dissidence than he wished to express, as they turned and commenced their walk up and down the terrace, "though I believe it is the only matter of difference that ever existed between us."

"Is it not extraordinary," returned the Genoese, "that men should consort together in good and evil, bleed for each other, love each other, do all acts of kindness to each other, as thou and I have done, Melchior, nay, be in the last extremity, and feel more agony for the friend than for one's self, and yet entertain such opinions of their respective creeds, as to fancy the unbeliever in the devil's claws all this time, and to entertain a latent distrust that the very soul which, in all other matters, is deemed so noble and excellent, is to be everlastingly damned for the want of certain opinions and formalities that we ourselves have been taught to think essential?"

"To tell thee the truth," returned the Swiss, rubbing his forehead like a man who wished to brighten up his ideas, as one would brighten old silver, by friction; "this subject, as thou well knowest, is not my strong side. Luther and Calvin, with other sages, discovered that it was weakness to submit to dogmas, without close examination, merely because they were venerable, and they winnowed the wheat from the chaff. This we call a reform. It is enough for me that men so wise were satisfied with their researches and changes, and I feel little inclination to disturb a decision that has now received the sanction of nearly two centuries of practice. To be plain with thee, I hold it discreet to reverence the opinions of my fathers."

"Though it would seem not of thy grandfathers," said the Italian, drily, but in perfect good humor. "By San Francesco! thou wouldst have made a worthy cardinal, had chance brought thee into the world fifty leagues farther south, or west, or east. But this is the way with the world, whether it be your Turk, your Hindoo, or your Lutheran, and I fear it is much the same with the children of St. Peter too. Each has his arguments for faith, or politics, or any interest that may be named, which he uses like a hammer to knock down the bricks of his opponent's reasons, and when he finds himself in the other's intrenchments, why he gathers together the scattered materials in order to build a wall for his own protection. Then what was oppression yesterday is justifiable defence to-day; fanaticism becomes logic; and credulity and pliant submission get, in two centuries, to be deference to the venerable opinion of our fathers! But let it go--thou wert speaking of thanking God, and in that; Roman though I am, I fervently and devoutly join with or without saints' intercession."

The honest baron did not like his friend's allusions, though they were much too subtle for his ready comprehension, for the intellect of the Swiss was a little frosted by constant residence among snows and in full view of glaciers, and it wanted the volatile play of the Genoese's fancy, which was apt to expand like air rarefied by the warmth of the sun. This difference of temperament, however, so far from lessening their mutual kindness, was, most probably, the real cause of its existence, since it is well known that friendship, like love, is more apt to be generated by qualities that vary a little from our own than by a perfect homogeneity of character and disposition which is more liable to give birth to rivalry and contention, than when each party has some distinct capital of his own on which to adventure, and with which to keep alive the interest of him who, in that particular feature, may be but indifferently provided. All that is required for a perfect community of feeling is a mutual recognition of, and a common respect for, certain great moral rules, without which there can exist no esteem between the upright. The alliance of knaves depends on motives so hackneyed and obvious, that we abstain from any illustration of its principle as a work of supererogation. The Signor Grimaldi and Melchior de Willading were both very upright and justly-minded men, as men go, in intention at least, and their opposite peculiarities and opinions had served, during hot youth, to keep alive the interest of their communications, and were not likely, now that time had mellowed their feelings and brought so many recollections to strengthen the tie, to overturn what they had been originally the principal instruments in creating.

"Of thy readiness to thank God, I have never doubted," answered the baron, when his friend had ended the remark just recorded, "but we know that his favors are commonly shown to us here below by means of human instruments. Ought we not, therefore, to manifest another sort of gratitude in favor of the individual who was so serviceable in last night's gust?"

"Thou meanest my untractable countryman? I have bethought me much since we separated of his singular refusal, and hope still to find the means of conquering his obstinacy."

"I hope thou may'st succeed, and thou well know'st that I am always to be counted on as an auxiliary. But he was not in my thoughts at the instant; there is still another who nobly risked more than the mariner in our behalf, since he risked life."

"This is beyond question, and I have already reflected much on the means of doing him good. He is a soldier of fortune, I learn, and if he will take service in Genoa, I will charge myself with the care of his preferment. Trouble not thyself, therefore, concerning the fortunes of young Sigismund; thou knowest my means, and canst not doubt my will."

The baron cleared his throat, for he had a secret reluctance to reveal his own favorable intentions towards the young man, the last lingering feeling of worldly pride, and the consequence of prejudices which were then universal, and which are even now far from being extinct. A vivid picture of the horrors of the past night luckily flashed across his mind, and the good genius of his young preserver triumphed.

"Thou knowest the youth is a Swiss," he said, "and, in virtue of the tie of country, I claim at least an equal right to do him good."

"We will not quarrel for precedence in this matter, but thou wilt do well to remember that I possess especial means to push his interests;--means that thou canst not by possibility use."

"That is not proved;" interrupted the Baron de Willading. "I have not thy particular station, it is true, Signor Gaetano, nor thy political power, nor thy princely fortune; but, poor as I am in these, there is a boon in my keeping that is worth them all, and which will be more acceptable to the boy, or I much mistake his mettle, than any favors that thou hast named or canst name."

The Signor Grimaldi had pursued his walk, with eyes thoughtfully fastened on the ground; but he now raised them, in surprise, to the countenance of his friend, as if to ask an explanation. The baron was not only committed by what had escaped him, but he was warming with opposition, for the best may frequently do very excellent things under the influence of motives of but a very indifferent aspect.

"Thou knowest I have a daughter," resumed the Swiss firmly, determined to break the ice at once, and expose a decision which he feared his friend might deem a weakness.

"Thou hast; and a fairer, or a modester, or a tenderer, and yet, unless my judgment err, a firmer at need, is not to be found among all the excellent of her excellent sex. But thou wouldst scarce think of bestowing Adelheid in reward for such a service on one so little known, or without her wishes being consulted?"

"Girls of Adelheid's birth and breeding are ever ready to do what is meet to maintain the honor of their families. I deem gratitude to be a debt that must not stand long uncancelled against the name of Willading."

The Genoese looked grave, and it was evident he listened to his friend with something like displeasure.

"We who have so nearly passed through life, good Melchior," he said, "should know its difficulties and its hazards. The way is weary, and it has need of all the solace that affection and a community of feeling can yield to lighten its cares. I have never liked this heartless manner of trafficking in the tenderest ties, to uphold a failing line or a failing fortune; and better it were that Adelheid should pass her days unwooed in thy ancient castle, than give her hand, under any sudden impulse of sentiment, not less than under a cold calculation of interest. Such a girl, my friend, is not to be bestowed without much care and reflection."

"By the mass! to use one of thine own favorite oaths, I wonder to hear thee talk thus!--thou, whom I knew a hot-blooded Italian, jealous as a Turk, and maintaining at thy rapier's point that women were like the steel of thy sword, so easily tarnished by rust, or evil breath, or neglect, that no father or brother could be easy on the score of honor, until the last of his name was well wedded, and that, too, to such as the wisdom of her advisers should choose! I remember thee once saying thou couldst not sleep soundly till thy sister was a wife or a nun."

"This was the language of boyhood and thoughtless youth, and bitterly rebuked have I been for having used it. I wived a beauteous and noble virgin, de Willading; but I much fear that, while my fair conduct in her behalf won her respect and esteem, I was too late to win her love. It is a fearful thing to enter on the solemn and grave ties of married life, without enlisting in the cause of happiness the support of the judgment, the fancy, the tastes, with the feelings that are dependent on them, and, more than all, those wayward inclinations, whose workings too often baffle human foresight. If the hopes of the ardent and generous themselves are deceived in the uncertain lottery of wedlock, the victim will struggle hard to maintain the delusion; but when the calculations of others are parent to the evil, a natural inducement, that comes of the devil I fear, prompts us to aggravate, instead of striving to lessen, the evil."

"Thou dost not speak of wedlock as one who found the condition happy, poor Gaetano?"

"I have told thee what I fear was but too true," returned the Genoese, with a heavy sigh. "My birth, vast means, and I trust a fair name, induced the kinsmen of my wife to urge her to a union, that I have since had reason to fear her feelings not lead her to form. I had a terrible ally too in the acknowledged unworthiness of him who had captivated her young fancy, and whom, as age brought reflection, her reason condemned. I was accepted, therefore, as a cure to a bleeding heart and broken peace, and my office, at the best, was not such as a good man could desire, or a proud man tolerate. The unhappy Angiolina died in giving birth to her first child, the unhappy son of whom I have told thee so much. She found peace at last in the grave!"

"Thou hadst not time to give thy manly tenderness and noble qualities an opportunity; else, my life on it, she would have come to love thee, Gaetano, as all love thee who know thee!" returned the baron, warmly.

"Thanks, my kind friend; but beware of making marriage a mere convenience. There may be folly in calling each truant inclination that deep sentiment and secret sympathy which firmly knits heart to heart, and doubtless a common fortune may bind the worldly-minded together; but this is not the holy union which keeps noble qualities in a family, and which fortifies against the seductions of a world that is already too strong for honesty. I remember to have heard from one that understood his fellow-creatures well, that marriages of mere propriety tend to rob woman of her greatest charm, that of superiority to the vulgar feeling of worldly calculations, and that all communities in which they prevail become, of necessity, selfish beyond the natural limits, and eventually corrupt"

"This may be true;--but Adelheid loves the youth."

"Ha! This changes the complexion of the affair. How dost thou know this?"

"From her own lips. The secret escaped her, under the warmth and sincerity of feeling that the late events so naturally excited."

"And Sigismund!--he has thy approbation?--for I will not suppose that one like thy daughter yielded her affections unsolicited."

"He has--that is--he has. There is what the world will be apt to call an obstacle, but it shall count for nothing with me. The youth is not noble."

"The objection is serious, my honest friend. It is not wise to tax human infirmity too much, where there is sufficient to endure from causes that cannot be removed. Wedlock is a precarious experiment, and all unusual motives for disgust should be cautiously avoided.--I would he were noble."

"The difficulty shall be removed by the Emperor's favor. Thou hast princes in Italy, too, that might be prevailed on to do us this grace, at need?"

"What is the youth's origin and history, and by what means has a daughter of thine been placed in a situation to love one that is simply born?"

"Sigismund is a Swiss, and of a family of Bernese burghers, I should think, though, to confess the truth, I know little more than that he has passed several years in foreign service, and that he saved my daughter's life from one of our mountain accidents, some two years since, as he has now saved thine and mine. My sister, near whose castle the acquaintance commenced, permitted the intercourse, which it would now be too late to think of prohibiting. And, to speak honestly, I begin to rejoice the boy is what he is, in order that our readiness to receive him to our arms may be the more apparent. If the young fellow were the equal of Adelheid in other things, as he is in person and character, he would have too much in his favor.--No, by the faith of Calvin!--him whom thou stylest a heretic--I think I rejoice that the boy is not noble!"

"Have it as thou wilt," returned the Genoese whose countenance continued to express distrust and thought, for his own experience had made him wary on the subject of doubtful or ill-assorted alliances; "let his origin be what it may, he shall not need gold. I charge myself with seeing that the lands of Willading shall be fairly balanced: and here comes our hospitable host to be witness of the pledge."

Roger de Blonay advanced upon the terrace to greet his guests, as the Signor Grimaldi concluded. The three old men continued their walk for an hour longer, discussing the fortunes of the young pair, for Melchior de Willading was as little disposed to make a secret of his intentions with one of his friends as with the other.

Chapter X

--But I have not the time to pause
Upon these gewgaws of the heart.

Werner.

Though the word castle is of common use in Europe, as applied to ancient baronial edifices, the thing itself is very different in style, extent, and cost, in different countries. Security, united to dignity and the means of accommodating a train of followers suited to the means of the noble, being the common object, the position and defences of the place necessarily varied according to the general aspect of the region in which it stood. Thus ditches and other broad expanses of water were much depended on in all low countries, as in Flanders, Holland, parts of Germany, and much of France; while hills, spurs of mountains, and more especially the summits of conical rocks, were sought in Switzerland, Italy, and wherever else these natural means of protection could readily found. Other circumstances, such as climate wealth, the habits of a people, and the nature of the feudal rights, also served greatly to modify the appearance and extent of the building. The ancient hold in Switzerland was originally little more than a square solid tower, perched upon a rock, with turrets at its angles. Proof against fire from without, it had ladders to mount from floor to floor and often contained its beds in the deep recesses of the windows, or in alcoves wrought in the massive wall. As greater security or greater means enabled, offices and constructions of more importance arcse around its base, inclosing a court. These necessarily followed the formation of the rock, until, in time, the confused and inartificial piles, which are now seen mouldering on so many of the minor spurs of the Alps, were created.

As is usual in all ancient holds, the Rittersaal--the Salle des Chevaliers-- or the knights' hall, of Blonay, as it is differently called in different languages, was both the largest and the most laboriously decorated apartment of the edifice. It was no longer in the rude gaol-like keep that grew, as it were, from the living rock, on which it had been reared with so much skill as to render it difficult to ascertain where nature ceased and art commenced; but it had been transferred, a century before the occurrences; related in our tale, to a more modern portion of the buildings that formed the south-eastern angle of the whole construction. The room was spacious, square, simple, for such is the fashion of the country, and lighted by windows that looked on one side towards Valais, and on the other over the whole of the irregular, but lovely declivity, to the margin of the Leman, and along that beautiful sheet, embracing hamlet, village, city, castle, and purple mountain, until the view was limited by the hazy Jura. The window on the latter side of the knights' hall, had an iron balcony at a giddy height from the ground, and in this airy look-out Adelheid had taken her seat, when, after quitting her father, she mounted to the apartment common to all the guests of the castle.

We have already alluded generally to the personal appearance and to the moral qualities of the Baron de Willading's daughter, but we now conceive it necessary to make the reader more intimately acquainted with one who is destined to act no mean part in the incidents of our tale. It has been said that she was pleasing to the eye, but her beauty was of a kind that depended more on expression, on a union of character with feminine grace, than on the vulgar lines of regularity and symmetry. While she had no feature that was defective, she had none that was absolutely faultless, though all were combined with so much harmony and the soft expression of the mild blue eye accorded so well with the gentle play of a sweet mouth, that the soul of their owner seemed ready at all times to appear through these ingenuous tell-tales of her thoughts. Still, maidenly reserve sate in constant watch over all, and it was when the spectator thought himself most in communion with her spirit, that he most felt its pure and correcting influence. Perhaps a cast of high intelligence, of a natural power to discriminate, which much surpassed the limited means accorded to females of that age, contributed their share to hold those near her in respect, and served in some degree as a mild and wise repellant, to counteract the attractions of her gentleness and candor. In short, one cast unexpectedly in her society would not have been slow to infer, and he would have decided correctly, that Adelheid de Willading was a girl of warm and tender affections, of a playful but regulated fancy, of a firm and lofty sense of all her duties, whether natural or merely the result of social obligations, of melting pity, and yet of a habit and quality to think and act for herself, in all those cases in which it was fitting for a maiden of her condition and years to assume such self-control.

It was now more than a year since Adelheid had become fully sensible of the force of her attachment for Sigismund Steinbach, and during all that time she had struggled hard to overcome a feeling which she believed could lead to no happy result. The declaration of the young man himself, a declaration that was extorted involuntarily and in a moment of powerful passion, was accompanied by an admission of its uselessness and folly, and it first opened her eyes to the state of her own feelings. Though she had listened, as all of her sex will listen, even when the passion is hopeless, to such words coming from lips they love, it was with a self-command that enabled her to retain her own secret, and with a settled and pious resolution to do that which she believed to be her duty to herself, to her father, and to Sigismund. From that hour she ceased to see him, unless under circumstances when it would have drawn suspicion on her motives to refuse, and while she never appeared to forget her heavy obligations to the youth, she firmly denied herself the pleasure of even mentioning his name when it could be avoided. But of all ungrateful and reluctant tasks, that of striving to forget is the least likely to succeed. Adelheid was sustained only by her sense of duty and the desire not to disappoint her father's wishes, to which habit and custom had given nearly the force of law with maidens of her condition, though her reason and judgment no less than her affections were both strongly enlisted on the other side. Indeed, with the single exception of the general unfitness of a union between two of unequal stations, there was nothing to discredit her choice, if that may be termed choice which, after all, was more the result of spontaneous feeling and secret sympathy than of any other cause, unless it were a certain equivocal reserve, and a manifest uneasiness, whenever allusion was made to the early history and to the family of the soldier. This sensitiveness on the part of Sigismund had been observed and commented on by others as well as by herself, and it had been openly ascribed to the mortification of one who had been thrown, by chance, into an intimate association that was much superior to what he was entitled to maintain by birth; a weakness but too common, and which few have strength of mind to resist or sufficient pride to overcome. The intuitive watchfulness of affection, however, led Adelheid to a different conclusion; she saw that he never affected to conceal, while with equal good taste he abstained from obtrusive allusions to the humble nature of his origin, but she also perceived that there were points of his previous history on which he was acutely sensitive, and which at first she feared must be attributed to the consciousness of acts that his clear perception of moral truth condemned, and which he could wish forgotten. For some time Adelheid clung to this discovery as to a healthful and proper antidote to her own truant inclinations, but native rectitude banished a suspicion which had no sufficient ground, as equally unworthy of them both. The effects of a ceaseless mental struggle, and of the fruitlessness of her efforts to overcome her tenderness in behalf of Sigismund, have been described in the fading of her bloom, in the painful solicitude of a countenance naturally so sweet, and in the settled melancholy of her playful and mellow eye. These were the real causes of the journey undertaken by her father, and, in truth, of most of the other events which we are about to describe.

The prospect of the future had undergone a sudden change. The color, though more the effect of excitement than of returning health--for he tide of life, when rudely checked, does not resume its currents at the first breath of happiness--again brightened her cheek and imparted brilliancy to her looks, and smiles stole easily to those lips which had long been growing pallid with anxiety. She leaned forward from the balcony, and never before had the air of her native mountains seemed so balmy and healing. At that moment the subject of her thoughts appeared on the verdant declivity, among the luxuriant nut-trees that shade the natural lawn of Blonay. He saluted her respectfully, and pointed to the glorious panorama of the Leman. The heart of Adelheid beat violently; she struggled for an instant with her fears and her pride, and then, for the first time in her life, she made a signal that she wished him to join her.

Notwithstanding the important service that the young soldier had rendered to the daughter of the Baron de Willading, and the long intimacy which had been its fruit, so great had been the reserve she had hitherto maintained, by placing a constant restraint on her inclinations, though the simple usages of Switzerland permitted greater familiarity of intercourse than was elsewhere accorded to maidens of rank, that Sigismund at first stood rooted to the ground, for he could not imagine the waving of the hand was meant for him. Adelheid saw his embarrassment, and the signal was repeated. The young man sprang up the acclivity with the rapidity of the wind, and disappeared behind the walls of the castle.

The barrier of reserve, so long and so successfully observed by Adelheid, was now passed, and she felt as if a few short minutes must decide her fate. The necessity of making a wide circuit in order to enter the court still afforded a little time for reflection, however, and this she endeavored to improve by collecting her thoughts and recovering her self-possession.

When Sigismund entered the knights' hall, he found the maiden still seated near the open window of the balcony, pale and serious, but perfectly calm, and with such an expression of radiant happiness in her countenance as he had not seen reigning in those sweet lineaments for many painful, months. The first feeling was that of pleasure at perceiving how well she bore the alarms and dangers of the past night. This pleasure he expressed, with the frankness admitted, by the habits of the Germans.

"Thou wilt not suffer, Adelheid, by the exposure on the lake!" he said, studying her face until the tell-tale blood stole to her very temples.

"Agitation of the mind is a good antidote to the consequences of bodily exposure. So far from suffering by what has passed, I feel stronger to-day and better able to endure fatigue, than at any time since we came through the gates of Willading. This balmy air, to me, seems Italy, and I see no necessity to journey farther in search of what they said was necessary to my health, agreeable objects and a generous sun."

"You will not cross the St. Bernard!" he exclaimed in a tone of disappointment.

Adelheid smiled, and he felt encouraged, though the smile was ambiguous. Notwithstanding the really noble sincerity of the maiden's disposition, and her earnest desire to set his heart at ease, nature, or habit, or education, for we scarcely know to which the weakness ought to be ascribed, tempted her to avoid a direct explanation.

"Why need one desire aught that is more lovely than this?" she answered, evasively. "Here is a warm air, such a scene as Italy can scarcely surpass, and a friendly roof. The experience of the last twenty-four hours gives little encouragement for attempting the St. Bernard, notwithstanding the fair promises of hospitality and welcome that have been so liberally held out by the good canon."

"Thy eye contradicts thy tongue, Adelheid; thou art happy and well enough to use pleasantry to-day. For heaven's sake, do not neglect to profit by this advantage, however, under a mistaken opinion that Blonay is the well-sheltered Pisa. When the winter shall arrive, thou wilt see that these mountains are still the icy Alps, and the winds will whistle through this crazy castle, as they are wont to sing in the naked corridors of Willading."

"We have time before us, and can think of this. Thou wilt proceed to Milan, no doubt, as soon as the revels of Vévey are ended."

"The soldier has little choice but duty. My long and frequent leaves of absence of late,--leaves that have been liberally granted to me on account of important family-concerns,--impose an additional obligation to be punctual, that I may not seem forgetful of favors already enjoyed. Although we all owe a heavy debt to nature, our voluntary engagements have ever seemed to me the most serious."

Adelheid listened with breathless attention. Never before had he uttered the word family, in reference to himself, in her presence. The allusion appeared to have created unpleasant recollections in the mind of the young man himself, for when he ceased to speak his countenance fell, and he even appeared to be fast forgetting the presence of his fair companion. The latter turned sensitively from a subject which she saw gave him pain, and endeavored to call his thoughts to other things. By an unforeseen fatality, the very expedient adopted hastened the explanation she would now have given so much to postpone.

"My father has often extolled the site of the Baron de Blonay's castle," said Adelheid, gazing from the window, though all the fair objects of the view floated unheeded before her eyes: "but, until now, I have always suspected that friendly feeling had a great influence on his descriptions."

"You did him injustice then," answered Sigismund, advancing to the opening: "of all the ancient holds of Switzerland, Blonay is perhaps entitled to the palm, for possessing the fairest site. Regard yon treacherous lake, Adelheid! Can we fancy that sleeping mirror the same boiling cauldron on which we were so lately tossed, helpless and nearly hopeless?"

"Hopeless, Sigismund, but for thee!"

"Thou forgett'st the daring Italian, without whose coolness and skill we must indeed have irredeemably perished."

"And what would it be to me if the worthless bark were saved, while my father and his friend were abandoned to the frightful fate that befell the patron and that unhappy peasant of Berne!"

The pulses of the young man beat high, for there was a tenderness in the tones of Adelheid to which he was unaccustomed, and which, indeed, he had never before discovered in her voice.

"I will go seek this brave mariner," he said, trembling lest his self-command should be again lost by the seductions of such a communion:--"it is time he had more substantial proofs of our gratitude."

"No, Sigismund," returned the maiden; firmly, and in a way to chain him to the spot, "thou must not quit me yet--I have much to say--much that touches my future happiness, and, I am perhaps weak enough to believe, thine."

Sigismund was bewildered, for the manner of his companion, though the color went and came in sudden and bright flashes across her pure brows, was miraculously calm and full of dignity. He took the seat to which she silently pointed, and sat motionless as if carved in stone, his faculties absorbed in the single sense of hearing. Adelheid saw that the crisis was arrived, and that retreat, without an appearance of levity that her character and pride equally forbade, was impossible. The inbred and perhaps the inherent feelings of her sex would now have caused her again to avoid the explanation, at least as coming from herself, but that she was sustained by a high and holy motive.

"Thou must find great delight, Sigismund, in reflecting on thine own good acts to others. But for thee Melchior de Willading would have long since been childless; and but for thee his daughter would now be an orphan. The knowledge that thou hast had the power and the will to succor thy friends must be worth all other knowledge!"

"As connected with thee, Adelheid, it is," he answered in a low voice: "I would not exchange the secret happiness of having been of this use to thee, and to those thou lovest, for the throne of the powerful prince I serve. I have had my secret wrested from me already, and it is vain attempting to deny it, if I would. Thou knowest I love thee; and, in spite of myself, my heart cherishes the weakness. I rather rejoice, than dread, to say that it will cherish it until it cease to feel. This is more than I ever intended to repeat to thy modest ears, which ought not to be wounded by idle declarations like these, but--thou smilest--Adelheid!--can thy gentle spirit mock at a hopeless passion!"

"Why should my smile mean mockery?"

"Adelheid!--nay--this never can be. One of my birth--my ignoble, nameless origin, cannot even intimate his wishes, with honor, to a lady of thy name and expectations!"

"Sigismund, it *can* be. Thou hast not well calculated either the heart of Adelheid de Willading, or the gratitude of her father."

The young man gazed earnestly at the face of the maiden, which, now that she had disburdened her soul of its most secret thought, reddened to the temples, more however with excitement than with shame, for she met his ardent look with the mild confidence of innocence and affection. She believed, and she had every reason so to believe, that her words would give pleasure, and, with the jealous watchfulness of true love, she would not willingly let a single expression of happiness escape her. But, instead of the brightening eye, and the sudden expression of joy that she expected, the young man appeared overwhelmed with feelings of a very opposite, and indeed of the most painful, character. His breathing was difficult, his look wandered, and his lips were convulsed. He passed his hand across his brow, like a man in intense agony, and a cold perspiration broke out, as by a dreadful inward working of the spirit, upon his forehead and temples, in large visible drops.

"Adelheid--dearest Adelheid--thou knowest not what thou sayest!--One like me can never become thy husband."

"Sigismund!--why this distress? Speak to me--ease thy mind by words. I swear to thee that the consent of my father is accompanied on my part by a willing heart. I love thee, Sigismund--wouldst thou have me--can I say more?"

The young man gazed at her incredulously, and then, as thought became more clear, as one regards a much-prized object that is hopelessly lost. He shook his head mournfully, and buried his face in his hands.

"Say no more, Adelheid--for my sake--for thine own sake, say no more--in mercy, be silent! Thou never canst be mine--No, no--honor forbids it; in thee it would be madness, in me dishonor--we can never be united. What fatal weakness has kept me near thee--I have long dreaded this--"

"Dreaded!"

"Nay, do not repeat my words,--for I scarce know what I say. Thou and thy father have yielded, in a moment of vivid gratitude, to a generous, a noble impulse--but it is not for me to profit by the accident that has enabled me to gain this advantage. What would all of thy blood, all of the republic say, Adelheid, were the noblest born, the best endowed, the fairest, gentlest, best maiden of the canton, to wed a nameless, houseless, soldier of fortune, who has but his sword and some gifts of nature to recommend him? Thy excellent father will surely think better of this, and we will speak of it no more!"

"Were I to listen to the common feelings of my sex, Sigismund, this reluctance to accept what both my father and myself offer might cause me to feign displeasure. But, between thee and me, there shall be naught but holy truth. My father has well weighed all these objections, and he has generously decided to forget them. As for me, placed in the scale against thy merits, they have never weighed at all. If thou canst not become noble in order that we may be equals, I shall find more happiness in descending to thy level, than by living in heartless misery at the vain height where I have been placed by accident."

"Blessed, ingenuous girl!--But what does it all avail? Our marriage is impossible."

"If thou knowest of any obstacle that would render it improper for a weak, but virtuous girl--"

"Hold, Adelheid!--do not finish the sentence. I am sufficiently humbled--sufficiently debased--without this cruel suspicion."

"Then why is our union impossible--when my father not only consents, but wishes it may take place?"

"Give me time for thought--thou shalt know all, Adelheid, sooner or later. Yes, this is, at the least, due to thy noble frankness, Thou shouldst in justice have known it long before."

Adelheid regarded him in speechless apprehension, for the evident and violent physical struggles of the young man too fearfully announced the mental agony he endured. The color had fled from her own face, in which the beauty of expression now reigned undisputed distress; but it was the expression of the mingled sentiments of wonder, dread, tenderness, and alarm. He saw that his own sufferings were fast communicating themselves to his companion, and, by a powerful effort, he so far mastered his emotions as to regain a portion of his self-command.

"This explanation has been too heedlessly delayed," he continued: "cost what it may, it shall be no longer postponed. Thou wilt not accuse me of cruelty, or of dishonest silence, but remember the failing of human nature, and pity rather than blame a weakness which may be the cause of as much future sorrow to thyself, beloved Adelheid, as it is now of bitter regret to me. I have never concealed from thee that my birth is derived from that class which throughout Europe, is believed to be of inferior rights to thine own; on this head, I am proud rather than humble, for the invidious distinctions of usage have too often provoked comparisons, and I have been in situations to know that the mere accidents of descent bestow neither personal excellence, superior courage, nor higher intellect. Though human inventions may serve to depress the less fortunate, God has given fixed limits to the means of men. He that would be greater than his kind, and illustrious by unnatural expedients, must debase others to attain his end. By different means than these there is no nobility, and he who is unwilling to admit an inferiority which exists only in idea can never be humbled by an artifice so shallow. On the subject of mere birth, as it is ordinarily estimated, whether it come from pride, or philosophy, or the habit of commanding as a soldier those who might be deemed my superiors as men, I have never been very sensitive. Perhaps the heavier disgrace which crushes me may have caused this want to appear lighter than it otherwise might."

"Disgrace!" repeated Adelheid, in a voice that was nearly choked. "The word is fearful, coming from one of thy regulated mind, and as applied to himself."

"I cannot choose another. Disgrace it is by the common consent of men--by long and enduing opinion--it would almost seem by the just judgment of God. Dost thou not believe, Adelheid, that there are certain races which are deemed accursed, to answer some great and unseen end--races on whom the holy blessings of Heaven never descend, as they visit the meek and well-deserving that come of other lines!"

"How can I believe this gross injustice, on the part of a Power that is wise without bounds, and forgiving to parental love?"

"Thy answer would be well, were this earth the universe, or this state of being the last. But he whose sight extends beyond the grave, who fashions justice, and mercy, and goodness, on a scale commensurate with his own attributes, and not according to our limited means, is not to be estimated by the narrow rules that we apply to men. No, we must not measure the ordinances of God by laws that are plausible in our own eyes. Justice is a relative and not an abstract quality; and, until we understand the relations of the Deity to ourselves as well as we understand our own relations to the Deity, we reason in the dark."

"I do not like to hear thee speak thus, Sigismund, and, least of all, with a brow so clouded, and in a voice so hollow!"

"I will tell my tale more cheerfully, dearest. I have no right to make thee the partner of my misery; and yet this is the manner I have reasoned, and thought, and pondered--ay, until my brain has grown heated, and the power to reason itself has nearly tottered. Ever since that accursed hour, in which the truth became known to me, and I was made the master of the fatal secret, have I endeavored to feel and reason thus."

"What truth?--what secret?--If thou lovest me, Sigismund, speak calmly and without reserve."

The young man gazed at her anxious face in a way to show how deeply he felt the weight of the blow he was about to give. Then, after a pause he continued.

"We have lately passed through a terrible scene together, dearest Adelheid. It was one that may well lessen the distances set between us by human laws and the tyranny of opinions. Had it been the will of God that the bark should perish, what a confused crowd of ill-assorted spirits would have passed together into eternity! We had them, there, of all degrees of vice, as of nearly all degrees of cultivation, from the subtle iniquity of the wily Neapolitan juggler to thine own pure soul. There would have died in the Winkelried the noble of high degree, the reverend priest, the soldier in the pride of his strength, and the mendicant! Death is an uncompromising leveller, and the depths of the lake, at least, might have washed out all our infamy, whether it came of real demerits or merely from received usage; even the luckless Balthazar, the persecuted and hated headsman, might have found those who would have mourned his loss."

"If any could have died unwept in meeting such a fate, it must have been one that, in common, awakes so little of human sympathy; and one too, who, by dealing himself in the woes of others, has less claim to the compassion that we yield to most of our species."

"Spare me--in mercy, Adelheid, spare me--thou speakest of my father!"

Chapter XI

> Fortune had smil'd upon Guelberto's birth.
> The heir of Valdespesa's rich domain;
> An only child, he grew in years and worth,
> And well repaid a father's anxious pain.
>
> Southey.

As Sigismund uttered this communication, so terrible to the ear of his listener, he arose and fled from the room. The possession of a kingdom would not have tempted him to remain and note troubled air and rapid strides as he passed them, but, too simple to suspect more than the ordinary impetuosity of youth, he succeeded in getting through the inferior gate of the castle and into the fields, without attracting any embarrassing attention to his movements. Here he began to breathe more freely, and the load which had nearly choked his respiration became lightened. For half an hour the young man paced the greensward scarcely conscious whither he went, until he found that his steps had again led him beneath the window of the knights' hall. Glancing an eye upward, he saw Adelheid still seated at the balcony, and apparently yet alone. He thought she had been weeping, and he cursed the weakness which had kept him from effecting the often-renewed resolution to remove himself, and his cruel fortunes, for ever from before her mind. A second look, however, showed him that he was again beckoned to ascend! The revolutions in the purposes of lovers are sudden and easily effected; and Sigismund, through whose mind a dozen ill-digested plans of placing the sea between himself and her he loved had just been floating, was now hurriedly retracing his steps to her presence.

Adelheid had necessarily been educated under the influence of the prejudices of the age and of the country in which she lived. The existence of the office of headsman in Berne, and the nature of its hereditary duties, were well known to her: and, though superior to the inimical feeling which had so lately been exhibited against the luckless Balthazar, she had certainly never anticipated a shock so cruel as was now produced, by abruptly learning that this despised and persecuted being was the father of the youth to whom she had yielded her virgin affections. When the words which proclaimed the connexion had escaped the lips of Sigismund, she listened like one who fancied that her ears deceived her. She had prepared herself to learn that he derived his being from some peasant or ignoble artisan, and, once or twice, as he drew nearer to the fatal declaration, awkward glimmerings of a suspicion that some repulsive moral unworthiness was connected with his origin troubled her imagination; but her apprehensions could not, by possibility, once turn in the direction of the revolting truth. It was some time before she was able to collect her thoughts, or to reflect on the course it most became her to pursue. But, as has been seen, it was long before she could summon the self-command to request what she now saw was doubly necessary, another meeting with her lover. As both had thought of nothing but his last words during the short separation, there appeared no abruptness in the manner in which he resumed the discourse, on seating himself at her side, exactly as if they had not parted at all.

"The secret has been torn from me, Adelheid. The headsman of the canton is my father; were the fact publicly known, the heartless and obdurate laws would compel me to be his successor. He has no other child, except a gentle girl--one innocent and kind as thou."

Adelheid covered her face with both her hands, as if to shut out a view of the horrible truth. Perhaps an instinctive reluctance to permit her companion to discover how great a blow had been given by this avowal of his birth, had also its influence in producing the movement. They who have passed the period of youth, and who can recall those days of inexperience and hope, when the affections are fresh and the heart is untainted with too much communion with the world,--and, especially, they who know of what a delicate compound of the imaginative and the real the master-passion is formed, how sensitively it regards all that can reflect credit on the beloved object, and with what ingenuity it endeavors to find plausible excuses for every blot that may happen, either by accident or demerit, to tarnish the lustre of a picture that fancy has so largely aided in drawing, will understand the rude nature of the shock that she had received. But Adelheid de Willading, though a woman in the liveliness and fervor of her imagination, as well as in the proneness to conceive her own ingenuous conceptions to be more founded in reality than a sterner view of things might possibly have warranted, was a woman also in the more generous qualities of the heart, and in those enduring principles, which seem to have predisposed the better part of the sex to make the heaviest sacrifices rather than be false to their affections. While her frame shuddered, therefore, with the violence and abruptness of the emotions she had endured, dawnings of the right gleamed upon her pure mind, and it was not long before she was able to contemplate the truth with the steadiness of principle, though it might, at the same time, have been with much of the lingering weakness of humanity. When she lowered her hands, she looked towards the mute and watchful Sigismund, with a smile that caused the deadly paleness of her features to resemble a gleam of the sun lighting upon a spotless peak of her native mountains.

"It would be vain to endeavor to conceal from thee, Sigismund," she said, "that I could wish this were not so. I will confess even more--that when the truth first broke upon me, thy repeated services, and, what is even less pardonable, thy tried worth, were for an instant forgotten in the reluctance I felt to admit that my fate could ever be united with one so unhappily situated. There are moments when prejudices and habits are stronger than reason; but their triumph is short in well-intentioned minds. The terrible injustice of our laws have never struck me with such force before, though last night, while those wretched travellers were so eager for the blood of-- of--?"

"My father, Adelheid."

"Of the author of thy being, Sigismund," she continued, with a solemnity that proved to the young man how deeply she reverenced the tie, "I was compelled to see that society might be cruelly unjust; but now I find its laws and prohibitions visiting one like thee, so far from joining in its oppression, my soul revolts against the wrong."

"Thanks--thanks--a thousand thanks!" returned the young man, fervently. "I did not expect less than this from thee, Mademoiselle de Willading."

"If thou didst not expect more--far more, Sigismund," resumed the maiden, her ashen hue brightened to crimson, "thou hast scarcely been less unjust than the world; and I will add, thou hast never understood that Adelheid de Willading, whose name is uttered with so cold a form. We all have moments of weakness; moments when the seductions of life, the worthless ties which bind together the thoughtless and selfish in what are called the interests of the world, appear of more value than aught else. I am no visionary, to fancy imaginary and factitious obligations superior to those which nature and wisdom have created--for if there be much unjustifiable cruelty in the practices, there is also much that is wise in the ordinances, of society--or to think that a wayward fairy is to be indulged at any and every expense to the feelings and opinions of others. On the contrary; I well know that so long as men exist in the condition in which they are, it is little more than common prudence to respect their habits; and that ill-assorted unions, in general, contain in themselves a dangerous enemy to happiness. Had I always known thy history, dread of the consequences, or those cold forms which protect the fortunate would probably have interposed to prevent either from learning much of the other's character.--I say not this, Sigismund, as by thy eye I see thou wouldst think, in reproach for any deception, for I well know the accidental nature of our acquaintance, and that the intimacy was forced upon thee by our own importunate gratitude, but simply, and in explanation of my own feelings. As it is, we are not to judge of our situation by ordinary rules, and I am not now to decide on your pretensions to my hand merely as the daughter of the Baron de Willading receiving a proposal from one whose birth is not noble, but as Adelheid should weigh the claims of Sigismund, subject to some diminution of advantages, if thou wilt, that is perhaps greater than she had at first anticipated."

"Dost thou consider the acceptance of my hand possible, after what thou knowest!" exclaimed the young man, in open wonder.

"So far from regarding the question in that manner, I ask myself if it will be right--if it be possible, to reject the preserver of my own life, the preserver of my father's life, Sigismund Steinbach, because he is the son of one that men persecute?"

"Adelheid!"

"Do not anticipate my words," said the maiden calmly, but in a way to check his impatience by the quiet dignity of her manner, "This is an important, I might say a solemn decision, and it has been presented to me suddenly and without preparation. Thou wilt not think the worse of me, for asking time to reflect before I give the pledge-that in my eyes, will be for ever sacred. My father, believing thee to be of obscure origin, and thoroughly conscious of thy worth, dear Sigismund, authorized me to speak as I did in the beginning of our interview; but my father may possibly think the conditions of his consent altered by this unhappy exposure of the truth. It is meet that I tell him all, for thou knowest I must abide by his decision. This thine own sense and filial piety will approve."

In spite of the strong objectionable facts that he had just revealed, hope had begun to steal upon the wishes of the young man, as he listened to the consoling words of the single-minded and affectionate Adelheid. It would scarcely have been possible for a youth so endowed by nature, and one so inevitably conscious of his own value, though so modest in its exhibition, not to feel encouraged by her ingenuous and frank admission, as she betrayed his influence over her happiness in the undisguised and simple manner related. But the intention to appeal to her father caused him to view the subject more dispassionately, for his strong sense was not slow in pointing out the difference between the two judges, in a case like his.

"Trouble him not, Adelheid; the consciousness that his prudence denies what a generous feeling might prompt him to bestow, may render him unhappy. It is impossible that Melchior de Willading should consent to give an only child to a son of the headsman of his canton. At some other time, when the recollections of the late storm shall be less vivid, thine own reason will approve of his decision."

His companion, who was thoughtfully leaning her spotless brow on her hand, did not appeal to hear his words. She had recovered from the shock given by the sudden announcement of his origin, and was now musing intently, and with cooler discrimination, on the commencement of their acquaintance, its progress and all its little incidents, down to the two grave events which had so gradually and firmly cemented the sentiments of esteem and admiration in the stronger and indelible tie of affection.

"If thou art the son of him thou namest, why art thou known by the name of Steinbach, when Balthazar bears another?" demanded Adelheid anxious to seize even the faintest hold of hope.

"It was my intention to conceal nothing, but to lay before thee the history of my life, with all the reasons that may have influenced my conduct," returned Sigismund: "at some other time, when both are in a calmer state of mind, I shall dare to entreat a hearing--"

"Delay is unnecessary--it might even be improper. It is my duty to explain every thing to my father, and he may wish to know why thou hast not always appeared what thou art. Do not fancy, Sigismund, that I distrust thy motive, but the wariness of the old and the confidence of the young have so little in common!--I would rather that thou told me now."

He yielded to the mild earnestness of her manner, and to the sweet, but sad, smile with which she seconded the appeal.

"If thou wilt hear the melancholy history, Adelheid," he said, "there is no sufficient reason why I should wish to postpone the little it will be necessary to say. You are probably familiar with the laws of the canton, I mean those cruel ordinances by which a particular family is condemned, for a better word can scarcely be found, to discharge the duties of this revolting office. This duty may have been a privilege in the dark ages but it is now become a tax that none, who have been educated with better hopes, can endure to pay. My father, trained from infancy to expect the employment, and accustomed to its discharge in contemplation, succeeded to his parent while yet young; and, though formed by nature a meek and even a compassionate man, he has never shrunk from his bloody tasks, whenever required to fulfil them by the command of his superiors. But, touched by a sentiment of humanity, it was his wish to avert from me what his better reason led him to think the calamity of our race. I am the eldest born, and, strictly, I was the child most liable to be called to assume the office, but, as I have heard, the tender love of my mother induced her to suggest a plan by which I, at least, might be rescued from the odium that had so long been attached to our name. I was secretly conveyed from the house while yet an infant; a feigned death concealed the pious fraud, and thus far, Heaven be praised! the authorities are ignorant of my birth!"

"And thy mother, Sigismund; I have great respect for that noble mother, who, doubtless, is endowed with more than her sex's firmness and constancy, since she must have sworn faith and love to thy father, knowing his duties and the hopelessness of their being evaded? I feel a reverence for a woman so superior to the weaknesses, and yet so true to the real and best affections, of her sex!"

The young man smiled so painfully as to cause his enthusiastic companion to regret that she had put the question.

"My mother is certainly a woman not only to be loved, but in many particulars deeply to be revered. My poor and noble mother has a thousand excellencies, being a most tender parent, with a heart so kind that it would grieve her to see injury done even to the meanest living thing. She was not a woman, surely, intended by God to be the mother of a line of executioners!"

"Thou seest, Sigismund," said Adelheid, nearly breathless in the desire to seek an excuse for her own predilections, and to lessen the mental agony he endured--"thou seest that one gentle and excellent woman, at least, could trust her happiness to thy family. No doubt she was the daughter of some worthy and just-viewing burgher of the canton, that had educated his child to distinguish between misfortune and crime?"

"She was an only child and an heiress, like thy self, Adelheid;" he answered, looking about him as if he sought some object on which he might cast part of the bitterness that loaded his heart. "Thou art not less the Beloved and cherished of thine own parent than was my excellent mother of her's!"

"Sigismund, thy manner is startling!--What wouldst thou say?"

"Neufchâtel, and other countries besides Berne, have their privileged! My mother was the only child of the headsman of the first. Thus thou seest, Adelheid, that I boast my quarterings as well as another. God be praised! we are not legally compelled, however, to butcher the condemned of any country but our own!"

The wild bitterness with which this was uttered, and the energy of his language, struck thrilling chords on every nerve of his listener.

"So many honors should not be unsupported;" he resumed. "We are rich, for people of humble wishes, and have ample means of living without the revenues of our charge--I love to put forth our long-acquired honors! The means of a respectable livelihood are far from being wanted. I have told you of the kind intentions of my mother to redeem one of her children, at least, from stigma which weighed upon us all, and the birth of a second son enabled her to effect this charitable purpose, without attracting attention. I was nursed and educated apart, for many years, in ignorance of my birth. At a suitable age, notwithstanding the early death of my brother, I was sent to seek advancement in the service of the house of Austria, under the feigned name I bear. I will not tell thee the anguish I felt, Adelheid, when the truth was at length revealed! Of all the cruelties inflicted by society, there is none so unrighteous in its nature as the stigma it entails in the succession of crime or misfortune: of all its favors, none can find so little justification, in right and reason, as the privileges accorded to the accident of descent." "And yet we are much accustomed to honor those that come of an ancient line, and to see some part of the glory of the ancestor even in the most remote descendant."

"The more remote, the greater is the world's deference. What better proof can we have of the world's weakness? Thus the immediate child of the hero, he whose blood is certain, who bears the image of the father in his face, who has listened to his counsels, and may be supposed to have derived, at least, some portion of his greatness from the nearness of his origin, is less a prince than he who has imbibed the current through a hundred vulgar streams, and, were truth but known, may have no natural claim at all upon the much-prized blood! This comes of artfully leading the mind to prejudices, and of a vicious longing in man to forget his origin and destiny, by wishing to be more than nature ever intended he should become."

"Surely, Sigismund, there is something justifiable in the sentiment of desiring to belong to the good and noble!"

"If good and noble were the same. Thou hast well designated the feeling; so long as it is truly a sentiment, it is not only excusable but wise; for who would not wish to come of the brave, and honest, and learned, or by what other greatness they may be known?--it is wise, since the legacy of his virtues is perhaps the dearest incentive that a good man has for struggling against the currents of baser interest; but what hope is left to one like me, who finds himself so placed that he can neither inherit nor transmit aught but disgrace! I do not affect to despise the advantages of birth, simply because I do not possess them; I only complain that artful combinations have perverted what should be sentiment and taste, into a narrow and vulgar prejudice, by which the really ignoble enjoy privileges greater than those perhaps who are worthy of the highest honors man can bestow."

Adelheid had encouraged the digression which, with one less gifted with strong good sense than Sigismund, might have only served to wound his pride, but she perceived that he eased his mind by thus drawing on his reason, and by setting up that which should be in opposition to that which was.

"Thou knowest," she answered, "that neither my father nor I am disposed to lay much stress on the opinions of the world, as it concerns thee."

"That is, neither will insist on nobility; but will either consent to share the obloquy of a union with an hereditary executioner?"

"Thou hast not yet related all it may be necessary to know that we may decide."

"There is left little to explain. The expedient of my kind parents has thus far succeeded. Their two surviving children, my sister and myself, were snatched, for a time at least, from their accursed fortune, while my poor brother, who promised little, was left, by a partiality I will not stop to examine, to pass as the inheritor of our infernal privileges-- Nay, pardon, dearest Adelheid, I will be more cool; but death has saved the youth from the execrable duties, and I am now the only male child of Balthazar--yes," he added, laughing frightfully, "I, too have now a narrow monopoly of all the honors of our house!"

"Thou--thou, Sigismund--with thy habits, thy education, thy feelings, thou surely canst not be required to discharge the duties of this horrible office!"

"It is easy to see that my high privileges do not charm you, Mademoiselle de Willading; nor can I wonder at the taste. My chief surprise should be, that you so long tolerate an executioner in your presence."

"Did I not know and understand the bitterness of feeling natural to one so placed, this language would cruelly hurt me, Sigismund; but thou canst not truly mean there is a real danger of thy ever being called to execute this duty? Should there be the chance of such a calamity, may not the influence of my father avert it? He is not without weight in the councils of the canton."

"At present his friendship need not be taxed, for none but my parents, my sister, and thou, Adelheid, are acquainted with the facts I have just related. My poor sister is an artless, but an unhappy girl, for the well-intentioned design of our mother has greatly disqualified her from bearing the truth, as she might have done, had it been kept constantly before her eyes. To the world, a young kinsman of my father appears destined to succeed him, and there the matter must stand until fortune shall decide differently. As respects my poor sister, there is some little hope that the evil may be altogether averted. She is on the point of a marriage here at Vévey, that may be the means of concealing her origin in new ties. As for me, time must decide my fate."

"Why should the truth be ever known!" exclaimed Adelheid, nearly gasping for breath, in her eagerness to propose some expedient that should rescue Sigismund for ever from so odious an office.

"Thou sayest that there are ample means in thy family--relinquish all to this youth, on condition that he assume thy place!"

"I would gladly beggar myself to be quit of it--"

"Nay, thou wilt not be a beggar while there is wealth among the de Willadings. Let the final decision, in respect to other things, be what it may, this can we at least promise!"

"My sword will prevent me from being under the necessity of accepting the boon thou wouldst offer. With this good sword I can always command an honorable existence, should Providence save me from the disgrace of exchanging it for that of the executioner. But there exists an obstacle of which thou hast not yet heard. My sister, who has certainly no admiration for the honors that have humiliated our race for so many generations--I might say ages--have we not ancient honors, Adelheid, as well as thou?--my sister is contracted to one who bargains for eternal secrecy on this point, as the condition of his accepting the hand and ample dowry of one of the gentlest of human beings! Thou seest that others are not as generous as thyself, Adelheid! My father, anxious to dispose of his child, has consented to the terms and as the youth who is next in succession to the family-honors is little disposed to accept them, and has already some suspicion of the deception as respects her, I may be compelled to appear in order to protect the offspring of my unoffending sister from the curse."

This was assailing Adelheid in a point where she was the weakest. One of her generous temperament and self-denying habits could scarce entertain the wish of exacting that from another which she was not willing to undergo herself, and the hope that had just been reviving in her heart was nearly extinguished by the discovery. Still she was so much in the habit of feeling under the guidance of her excellent sense, and it was so natural to cling to her just wishes, while there was a reasonable chance of their being accomplished, that she did not despair.

"Thy sister and her future husband know her birth, and understand the chances they run."

"She knows all this, and such is her generosity, that she is not disposed to betray me in order to serve herself. But this self-denial forms an additional obligation on my part to declare myself the wretch I am. I cannot say that my sister is accustomed to regard our long-endured fortunes with all the horror I feel, for she has been longer acquainted with the facts, and the domestic habits of her sex have left her less exposed to the encounter of the world's hatred, and perhaps she is partly ignorant of all the odium we sustain. My long absences in foreign services delayed the confidence as respects myself, while the yearnings of a mother towards an only daughter caused her to be received into the family, though still in secret, several years before I was told the truth. She is also much my junior; and all these causes, with some difference in our education, have less disposed her to misery than I am; for while my father, with a cruel kindness, had me well and even liberally instructed, Christine was taught as better became the hopes and origin of both. Now tell me, Adelheid, that thou hatest me for my parentage, and despisest me for having so long dared to intrude on thy company, with the full consciousness of what I am for ever present to my thoughts!"

"I like not to hear thee make these bitter allusions to an accident of this nature, Sigismund. Were I to tell thee that I do not feel this circumstance with nearly, if not quite, as much poignancy as thyself," added the ingenuous girl, with a noble frankness, "I should do injustice to my gratitude and to my esteem for thy character. But there is more elasticity in the heart of woman than in that of thy imperious and proud sex. So far from thinking of thee as thou wouldst fain believe, I see naught but what is natural and justifiable in thy reserve. Remember, thou hast not tempted my ears by professions and prayers, as women are commonly entreated, but that the interest I feel in thee has been modestly and fairly won. I can neither say nor hear more at present for this unexpected announcement has in some degree unsettled my mind. Leave me to reflect on what I ought to do, and rest assured that thou canst not have a kinder or more partial advocate of what truly belongs to thy honor and happiness than my own heart."

As the daughter of Melchior de Willading concluded, she extended her hand with affection to the young man, who pressed it against his breast with manly tenderness, when he slowly and reluctantly withdrew.

Chapter XII

To know no more
Is woman's happiest knowledge, and her praise.

Milton.

Our heroine was a woman in the best meaning of that endearing, and, we might add, comprehensive word. Sensitive, reserved, and at times even timid, on points that did not call for the exercise of higher qualities, she was firm in her principles, constant as she was fond in her affections, and self-devoted when duty and inclination united to induce the concession, to a degree that placed the idea of sacrifice out of the question. On the other hand, the liability to receive lively impressions, a distinctive feature of her sex, and the aptitude to attach importance to the usages by which she was surrounded, and which is necessarily greatest in those who lead secluded and inactive lives, rendered it additionally difficult for her mind to escape from the trammels of opinion, and to think with indifference of circumstances which all near her treated with high respect, or to which they attached a stigma allied to disgust. Had the case been reversed, had Sigismund been noble, and Adelheid a headsman's child, it is probable the young man might have found the means to indulge his passion without making too great a sacrifice of his pride. By transporting his wife to his castle, conferring his own established name, separating her from all that was unpleasant and degrading in the connexion, and finding occupation for his own mind in the multiplied and engrossing employments of his station, he would have diminished motives for contemplating, and consequently for lamenting, the objectionable features of the alliance he had made. These are the advantages which nature and the laws of society give to man over the weaker but the truer sex: and yet how few would have had sufficient generosity to make even the sacrifice of feeling which such a course required! On the other hand, Adelheid would be compelled to part with the ancient and distinguished appellation of her family, to adopt one which was deemed infamous in the canton, or, if some politic expedient were found to avert this first disgrace, it would unavoidably be of a nature to attract, rather than to avert, the attention of all who knew the facts, from the humiliating character of his origin. She had no habitual relief against the constant action of her thoughts, for the sphere of woman narrows the affections in such a way as to render them most dependent on the little accidents of domestic life; she could not close her doors against communication with the kinsmen of her husband, should it be his pleasure to command or his feeling to desire it; and it would become obligatory on her to listen to the still but never-ceasing voice of duty, and to forget, at his request, that she had ever been more fortunate, or that she was born for better hopes.

We do not say that all these calculations crossed the mind of the musing maiden, though she certainly had a general and vague view of the consequences that were likely to be drawn upon herself by a connexion with Sigismund. She sat motionless, buried in deep thought, long after his disappearance. The young man had passed by the postern around the base of the castle, and was descending the mountain-side, across the sloping meadows, with rapid steps, and probably for the first time since their acquaintance her eye followed his manly figure vacantly and with indifference.

Her mind was too intently occupied for the usual observation of the senses. The whole of that grand and lovely landscape was spread before her without conveying impressions, as we gaze into the void of the firmament with our looks on vacuum. Sigismund had disappeared among the walls of the vineyards, when she arose, and drew such a sigh as is apt to escape us after long and painful meditation. But the eyes of the high-minded girl were bright and her cheek flushed, while the whole of her features wore an expression of loftier beauty than ordinarily distinguished even her loveliness. Her own resolution was formed. She had decided with the rare and generous self-devotion of a female heart that loves, and which can love in its freshness and purity but once. At that instant footsteps were heard in the corridor, and the three old nobles whom we so lately left on the castle-terrace, appeared together in the knights' hall.

Melchior de Willading approached his daughter with a joyous face, for he too had lately gained what he conceived to be a glorious conquest over his prejudices, and the victory put him in excellent humor with himself.

"The question is for ever decided," he said, kissing the burning forehead of Adelheid with affection, and rubbing his hands, in the manner of one who was glad to be free from a perplexing doubt "These good friends agree with me, that, in a case like this, it becomes even our birth to forget the origin of the youth. He who has saved the lives of the two last of the Willadings at least deserves to have some share in what is left of them. Here is my good Grimaldi, too, ready to beard me if I will not consent to let him enrich the brave fellow--as if we were beggars, and had not the means of supporting our kinsman in credit at borne. But we will not be indebted even to so tried a friend for a tittle of our happiness. The work shall be all our own, even to the letters of nobility, which I shall command at an early day from Vienna; for it would be cruel to let the noble fellow want so simple an advantage, which will at once raise him to our own level, and make him as good--ay, by the beard of Luther! better than the best man in Berne."

"I have never known thee niggardly before, though I have known thee often well intrenched behind Swiss frugality;" said the Signor Grimaldi, laughing. "Thy life, my dear Melchior, may have excellent value in thine own eyes, but I am little disposed to set so mean a price on my own, as thou appearest to think it should command. Thou hast decided well, I will say nobly, in the best meaning of the word, in consenting to receive this brave Sigismund as a son; but thou art not to think, young lady, because this body of mine is getting the worse for use, that I hold it altogether worthless, and that it is to be dragged from yonder lake like so much foul linen, and no questions are to be asked touching the manner in which the service has been done. I claim to portion thy husband, that he may at least make an appearance that becomes the son-in-law of Melchior de Willading. Am I of no value, that ye treat me so unceremoniously as to say I shall not pay for my own preservation?

"Have it thine own way, good Gaetano--have it as thou wilt, so thou dost but leave us the youth--"

"Father--"

"I will have no maidenly affectation, Adelheid I expect thee to receive the husband we offer with as good a grace as if he wore a crown. It has been agreed upon between us that Sigismund Steinbach is to be my son; and from time immemorial, the daughters of our house have submitted, in these affairs, to what has been advised by the wisdom of their seniors, as became their sex and inexperience."

The three old men had entered the hall full of good-humor, and it would have been sufficiently apparent, by the manner of the Baron de Willading, that he trifled with Adelheid, had it not been well known to the others that her feelings were chiefly consulted in the choice that had just been made.

But, notwithstanding the high glee in which the father spoke, the pleasure and buoyancy of his manner did not communicate itself to the child as quickly as he could wish. There was far more than virgin embarrassment in the mien of Adelheid. Her color went and came, and her look turned from one to the other painfully, while she struggled to speak. The Signor Grimaldi whispered to his companions, and Roger de Blonay discreetly withdrew, under the pretence that his services were needed at Vévey, where active preparations were making for the Abbaye des Vignerons. The Genoese would then have followed his example, but the baron held his arm, while he turned an inquiring eye towards his daughter, as if commanding her to deal more frankly with him.

"Father," said Adelheid, in a voice that shook in spite of the effort to control her feelings, "I have something important to communicate, before this acceptance of Herr Steinbach is a matter irrevocably determined."

"Speak freely, my child; this is a tried friend, and one entitled to know all that concerns us, especially in this affair. Throwing aside all pleasantry, I trust, Adelheid, that we are to have no girlish trifling with a youth like Sigismund; to whom we owe so much, even to our lives, and in whose behalf we should be ready to sacrifice every feeling of prejudice, or habit-- all that we possess, ay, even to our pride."

"All, father?"

"I have said all. I will not take back a letter of the word, though it should rob me of Willading, my rank in the canton, and an ancient name to boot. Am I not right, Gaetano? I place the happiness of the boy above all other considerations, that of Adelheid being understood to be so intimately blended with his. I repeat it, therefore, all."

"It would be well to hear what the young lady has to say, before we urge this affair any farther;" said the Signor Grimaldi, who, having achieved no conquest over himself, was not quite so exuberant in his exultation as his friend; observing more calmly, and noting what he saw with the clearness of a cooler-headed and more sagacious man. "I am much in error, or thy daughter has that which is serious, to communicate."

The paternal affection of Melchior now took the alarm, and he gave an eager attention to his child. Adelheid returned his evident solicitude by a smile of love, but its painful expression was so unequivocal as to heighten the baron's fears.

"Art not well, love? It cannot be that we have been deceived--that some peasant's daughter is thought worthy to supplant thee? Ha!--Signor Grimaldi, this matter begins, in sooth, to seem offensive;--but, old as I am-- Well, we shall never know the truth, unless thou speakest frankly--this is a rare business, after all, Gaetano--that a daughter of mine should be repulsed by a hind!"

Adelheid made an imploring gesture for her father to forbear, while she resumed her seat from farther inability to stand. The two anxious old men followed her example, in wondering silence.

"Thou dost both the honor and modesty of Sigismund great injustice, father;" resumed the maiden, after a pause, and speaking with a calmness of manner that surprised even herself. "If thou and this excellent and tried friend will give me your attention for a few minutes, nothing shall be concealed."

Her companions listened in wonder, for they plainly saw that the matter was more grave than either had at first imagined. Adelheid paused again, to summon force for the ungrateful duty, and then she succinctly, but clearly, related the substance of Sigismund's communication. Both the listeners eagerly caught each syllable that fell from the quivering lips of the maiden, for she trembled, notwithstanding a struggle to be calm that was almost superhuman, and when her voice ceased they gazed at each other like men suddenly astounded by some dire and totally unexpected calamity. The baron, in truth, could scarcely believe that he had not been deceived by a defective hearing, for age had begun a little to impair that useful faculty, while his friend admitted the words as one receives impressions of the most revolting and disheartening nature.

"This is a damnable and fearful fact!" muttered the latter, when Adelheid had altogether ceased to speak.

"Did she say that Sigismund is the son of Balthazar, the public headsman of the canton!" asked the father of his friend, in the way that one reluctantly assures himself of some half-comprehended and unwelcome truth,--"of Balthazar--of that family accursed!"

"Such is the parentage it hath been the will of God to bestow on the preserver of our lives," meekly answered Adelheid.

"Hath the villain dared to steal into my family-circle, concealing this disgusting and disgraceful fact!--Hath he endeavored to engraft the impurity of his source on the untarnished stock of a noble and ancient family! There is something exceeding mere duplicity in this, Signor Grimaldi. There is a dark and meaning crime."

"There is that which much exceeds our means of remedying, good Melchior. But let us not rashly blame the boy, whose birth is rather to be imputed to him as a misfortune than as a crime. If he were a thousand Balthazars, he has saved all our lives!"

"Thou sayest true--thou sayest no more than the truth. Thou wert always of a more reasonable brain than I, though thy more southern origin would seem to contradict it. Here, then, are all our fine fancies and liberal schemes of generosity blown to the winds!"

"That is not so evident," returned the Genoese, who had not failed the while to study the countenance of Adelheid, as if he would fully ascertain her secret wishes. "There has been much discourse, fair Adelheid, between thee and the youth on this matter?"

"Signore, there has. I was about to communicate the intentions of my father; for the circumstances in which we were placed, the weight of our many obligations, the usual distance which rank interposes between the noble and the simply born, perhaps justified this boldness in a maiden," she added, though the tell-tale blood revealed her shame. "I was making Sigismund acquainted with my father's wishes, when he met my confidence by the avowal which I have just related."

"He deems his birth--?"

"An insuperable barrier to the connexion. Sigismund Steinbach, though so little favored in the accident of his origin, is not a beggar to sue for that which his own generous feelings would condemn."

"And thou?"

Adelheid lowered her eyes, and seemed to reflect on the nature of her answer.

"Thou wilt pardon this curiosity, which may wear too much the aspect of unwarrantable meddling, but my age and ancient friendship, the recent occurrences, and a growing love for all that concerns thee, must plead my excuses. Unless we know thy wishes, daughter, neither Melchior nor I can act as we might wish?"

Adelheid was long and thoughtfully silent. Though every sentiment of her heart, and all that inclination which is the offspring of the warm and poetical illusions of love, tempted her to declare a readiness to sacrifice every other consideration to the engrossing and pure affections of woman, opinion with its iron gripe still held her in suspense on the propriety of braving the prejudices of the world. The timidity of that sex which, however ready to make an offering of its most cherished privileges on the shrine of connubial tenderness, shrinks with a keen sensitiveness from the appearance of a forward devotion to the other, had its weight also, nor could a child so pious altogether forget the effect her decision might have on the future happiness of her sole surviving parent.

The Genoese understood the struggle, though he foresaw its termination, and he resumed the discourse himself, partly with the kind wish to give the maiden time to reflect maturely before she answered, and partly following a very natural train of his own thoughts.

"There is naught sure in this fickle state of being;" he continued. "Neither the throne, nor riches, nor health, nor even the sacred affections are secure against change. Well may we pause then and weigh every chance of happiness, ere we take the last and final step in any great or novel measure. Thou knowest the hopes with which I entered life, Melchior, and the chilling disappointments with which my career is likely to close. No youth was born to fairer hopes, nor did Italy know one more joyous than myself, the morning I received the hand of Angiolina; and yet two short years saw all those hopes withered, this joyousness gone, and a cloud thrown across my prospects which has never disappeared. A widowed husband, a childless father, may not prove a bad counsellor, my friend, in a moment when there is so much doubt besetting thee and thine."

"Thy mind naturally returns to thine own unhappy child, poor Gaetano, when there is so much question of the fortunes of mine."

The Signor Grimaldi turned his look on his friend, but the gleam of anguish, which was wont to pass athwart his countenance when his mind was drawn powerfully towards that painful subject, betrayed that he was not just then able to reply.

"We see in all these events," continued the Genoese, as if too full of his subject to restrain his words, "the unsearchable designs of Providence. Here is a youth who is all that a father could desire; worthy in every sense to be the depository of a beloved and only daughter's weal; manly, brave, virtuous, and noble in all but the chances of blood, and yet so accursed by the world's opinion that we might scarce venture to name him as the associate of an idle hour, were the fact known that he is the man he has declared himself to be!"

"You put the matter in strong language Signor Grimaldi;" said Adelheid, starting.

"A youth of a form so commanding that a king might exult at the prospect of his crown descending on such a head; of a perfection of strength and masculine excellence that will almost justify the dangerous exultation of health and vigor; of a reason that is riper than his years; of a virtue of proof; of all qualities that we respect, and which come of study and not of accident, and yet a youth condemned of men to live under the reproach of their hatred and contempt, or to conceal for ever the name of the mother that bore him! Compare this Sigismund with others that may be named; with the high-born and pampered heir of some illustrious house, who riots in men's respect while he shocks men's morals; who presumes on privilege to trifle with the sacred and the just; who lives for self, and that in base enjoyments; who is fitter to be the lunatic's companion than any other's, though destined to rule in the council; who is the type of the wicked, though called to preside over the virtuous; who cannot be esteemed, though entitled to be honored; and let us ask why this is so, what is the wisdom which hath drawn differences so arbitrary, and which, while proclaiming the necessity of justice, so openly, so wantonly, and so ingeniously sets its plainest dictates at defiance?"

"Signore, it should not be thus--God never intended it should be so!"

"While every principle would seem to say that each must stand or fall by his own good or evil deeds, that men are to be honored as they merit, every device of human institutions is exerted to achieve the opposite. This is exalted, because his ancestry is noble; that condemned for no better reason than that he is born vile. Melchior! Melchior! our reason is unhinged by subtleties, and our boasted philosophy and right are no more than unblushing mockeries, at which the very devils laugh!"

"And yet the commandments of God tell us, Gaetano, that the sins of the father shall be visited on the descendants from generation to generation. You of Rome pay not this close attention, perhaps, to sacred writ, but I have heard it said that we have not in Berne a law for which good warranty cannot be found in the holy volume itself."

"Ay, there are sophists to prove all that they wish. The crimes and follies of the ancestor leave their physical, or even their moral taint, on the child, beyond a question, good Melchior;--but is not this sufficient? Are we blasphemously, even impiously, to pretend that God has not sufficiently provided for the punishment of the breaches of his wise ordinances, that we must come forward to second them by arbitrary and heartless rules of our own? What crime is imputable to the family of this youth beyond that of poverty, which probably drove the first of his race to the execution of their revolting office. There is little in the mien or morals of Sigismund to denote the visitations of Heaven's wise decrees, but there is everything in his present situation to proclaim the injustice of man."

"And dost thou, Gaetano Grimaldi, the ally of so many ancient and illustrious houses--thou, Gaetano Grimaldi, the honored of Genoa--dost thou counsel me to give my only child, the heiress of my lands and name, to the son of the public executioner, nay, to the very heritor of his disgusting duties!"

"There thou hast me on the hip, Melchior; the question is put strongly, and needs reflection for an answer. Oh! why is this Balthazar so rich in offspring, and I so poor? But we will not press the matter; it is an affair of many sides, and should be judged by us as men, as well as nobles. Daughter, thou hast just learned, by the words of thy father, that I am against thee, by position and heritage, for, while I condemn the principle of this wrong, I cannot overlook its effects, and never before did a case of as tangled difficulty, one in which right was so palpably opposed by opinion, present itself for my judgment. Leave us, that we may command ourselves; the required decision exacts much care, and greater mastery of ourselves than I can exercise, with that sweet pale face of thine appealing so eloquently to my heart in behalf of the noble boy."

Adelheid arose, and first offering her marble-like brow to the salutations of both her parents, for the ancient friendship and strong sympathies of the Genoese, gave him a claim to this appellation in her affections at least, she silently withdrew.

As to the conversation which ensued between the old nobles, we momentarily drop the curtain, to proceed to other incidents of our narrative. It may, however, be generally observed that the day passed quietly away, without the occurrence of any event which it is necessary to relate, all in the château, with the exception of the travellers, being principally occupied by the approaching festivities. The Signor Grimaldi sought an occasion to have a long and confidential communication with Sigismund, who, on his part, carefully avoided being seen again by her who had so great an influence on his feelings, until both had time to recover their self-command.

Chapter XIII

Hold, hurt him not, for God's sake;--he is mad.
Comedy of Errors.

The festivals of Bacchus are supposed to have been the models of those long-continued festivities, which are still known in Switzerland by the name of the Abbaye des Vignerons.

This fête was originally of a simple and rustic character, being far from possessing the labored ceremonies and classical allegories of a later day, the severity of monkish discipline most probably prohibiting the introduction of allusions to the Heathen mythology, as was afterwards practised; for certain religious communities that were the proprietors of large vineyards in that vicinity appear to have been the first known patrons of the custom. So long as a severe simplicity reigned in the festivities, they were annually observed; but, when heavier expenses and greater preparations became necessary, longer intervals succeeded; the Abbaye, at first, causing its festival to become triennial, and subsequently extending the period of vacation to six years. As greater time was obtained for the collection of means and inclination, the festival gained in *éclat*, until it came at length to be a species of jubilee, to which the idle, the curious, and the observant of all the adjacent territories were accustomed to resort in crowds. The town of Vévey profited by the circumstance, the usual motive of interest being enlisted in behalf of the usage, and, down to the epoch of the great European revolution, there would seem to have been an unbroken succession of the fêtes. The occasion to which there has so often been allusion, was one of the regular and long-expected festivals; and, as report had spoken largely of the preparations, the attendance was even more numerous than usual.

Early on the morning of the second day after the arrival of our travellers at the neighboring castle of Blonay, a body of men, dressed in the guise of halberdiers, a species of troops then known in most of the courts of Europe, marched into the great square of Vévey, taking possession of all its centre, and posting its sentries in such a manner as to interdict the usual passages of the place. This was the preliminary step in the coming festivities; for this was the spot chosen for the scene of most of the ceremonies of the day.

The curious were not long behind the guards, and by the time the sun had fairly arisen above the hills of Fribourg, some thousands of spectators were pressing in and about the avenues of the square, and boats from the opposite shores of Savoy were arriving at each instant, crowded to the water's edge with peasants and their families.

Near the upper end of the square, capacious scaffoldings had been erected to contain those who were privileged by rank, or those who were able to buy honors with the vulgar medium; while humbler preparations for the less fortunate completed the three sides of a space that was in the form of a parallelogram, and which was intended to receive the actors in the coming scene. The side next the water was unoccupied, though a forest of latine spars, and a platform of decks, more than supplied the deficiency of scaffolding and room. Music was heard, from time to time, intermingled or relieved by those wild Alpine cries which characterize the songs of the mountaineers. The authorities of the town were early afoot, and, as is customary with the important agents of small concerns, they were exercising their municipal function with a bustle, which of itself contained reasonable evidence that they were of no great moment, and a gravity of mien with which the chiefs of a state might have believed it possible to dispense.

The estrade, or stage, erected for the superior class of spectators was decorated with flags, and a portion near its centre had a fair display of tapestry and silken hangings. The chateau-looking edifice near the bottom of the square, and whose windows, according to a common Swiss and German usage, showed the intermingled stripes that denoted it to be public property, were also gay in colors, for the ensign of the Republic floated over its pointed roofs, and rich silks waved against the walls. This was the official residence of Peter Hofmeister, the functionary whom we have already introduced to the reader.

An hour later, a shot gave the signal for the various *troupes* to appear, and soon after, parties of the different actors arrived in the square. As the little processions approached to the sound of the trumpet or horn, curiosity became more active and the populace was permitted to circulate in those portions of the square that were not immediately required for other purposes. About this time, a solitary individual appeared on the stage. He seemed to enjoy peculiar privileges, not only from his situation, but by the loud salutations and noisy welcomes with which he was greeted from the crowd below. It was the good monk of St. Bernard, who, with a bare head and a joyous contented face, answered to the several calls of the peasants, most of whom had either bestowed hospitality on the worthy Augustine, in his many journeyings among the charitable of the lower world, or had received it at his hands in their frequent passages of the mountain. These recognitions and greetings spoke well for humanity; for in every instance they wore the air of cordial good-will, and a readiness to do honor to the benevolent character of the religious community that was represented in the person of its clavier or steward.

"Good luck to thee, Father Xavier, and a rich *quête*" cried a burly peasant; "thou hast of late unkindly forgotten Benoit Emery and his. When did a clavier of St. Bernard ever knock at my door, and go away with an empty hand? We look for thee, reverend monk, with thy vessel, to-morrow; for the summer has been hot, the grapes are rich, and the wine is beginning to run freely in our tubs. Thou shalt dip without any to look at thee, and, take it of which color thou wilt, thou shalt take it with a welcome."

"Thanks, thanks, generous Benoit; St. Augustine will remember the favor, and thy fruitful vines will be none the poorer for thy generosity. We ask only that we may give, and on none do we bestow more willingly than on the honest Vaudois whom may the saints keep in mind for their kindness and good-will!"

"Nay, I will have none of thy saints; thou knowest we are St. Calvin's men in Vaud, if there must be any canonized. But what is it to us that thou hearest mass, while we love the simple worship! Are we not equally men? Does not the frost nip the members of Catholic and Protestant the same? or does the avalanche respect one more than the other? I never knew thee, or any of thy convent, question the frozen traveller of his faith, but all are fed, and warmed, and, at need, administered to from the pharmacy, with brotherly care, and as Christians merit. Whatever thou mayest think of the state of our souls, thou on thy mountain there, no one will deny thy tender services to our bodies. Say I well, neighbors, or is this only the foolish gossip of old Benoit, who has crossed the Col so often, that he has forgotten that out churches have quarrelled, and that the learned will have us go to heaven by different roads?"

A general movement among the people, and a tossing of hands, appeared in support of the truth and popularity of the honest peasant's sentiments, for in that age the hospice of St. Bernard, more exclusively a refuge for the real and poor traveller than at present, enjoyed a merited reputation in all the country round.

"Thou shalt always be welcome on the pass, thou and thy friends, and all others in the shape of men, without other interference in thy opinions than secret prayers;" returned the good-humored and happy-looking clavier, whose round contented face shone partly in habitual joy, partly in gratification at this public testimonial in favor of the brotherhood, and a little in satisfaction perhaps at the promise of an ample addition to the convent's stores; for the community of St. Bernard, while so much was going out, had a natural and justifiable desire to see some return for its incessant and unwearied liberality. "Thou wilt not deny us the happiness of praying for those we love, though it happen to be in a manner different from that in which they ask blessings for themselves."

"Have it thine own way, good canon; I am none of those who are ready to refuse a favor because it savors of Rome. But what has become of our friend Uberto? He rarely comes into the valleys, that we are not anxious to see his glossy coat."

The Augustine gave the customary call, and the mastiff mounted the stage with a grave deliberate step, as if conscious of the dignity and usefulness of the life he led, and like a dog accustomed to the friendly notice of man. The appearance of this well-known and celebrated brute caused another stir in the throng, many pressing upon the guards to get a nearer view, and a few casting fragments of food from their wallets, as tokens of gratitude and regard. In the midst of this little by-play of good feeling, a dark shaggy animal leaped upon the scaffolding, and very coolly commenced, with an activity that denoted the influence of the keen mountain air on his appetite, picking up the different particles of meat that had, as yet, escaped the eye of Uberto. The intruder was received much in the manner that an unpopular or an offending actor is made to undergo the hostilities of pit and galleries, to revenge some slight or neglect for which he has forgotten or refused to atone. In other words, he was incontinently and mercilessly pelted with such missiles as first presented themselves. The unknown animal, which the reader, however, will not be slow in recognizing to be the water-dog of Il Maledetto, received these unusual visitations with some surprise, and rather awkwardly; for, in his proper sphere, Nettuno had been quite as much accustomed to meet with demonstrations of friendship from the race he so faithfully served, as any of the far-famed and petted mastiffs of the convent. After dodging sundry stones and clubs, as well as a pretty close attention to the principal matter in hand would allow, and with a dexterity that did equal credit to his coolness and muscle, a missile of formidable weight took the unfortunate follower of Maso in the side, and sent him howling from the stage. At the next instant, his master was at the throat of the offender, throttling him till he was black in the face.

The unlucky stone had come from Conrad. Forgetful of his assumed character, he had joined in the hue and cry against a dog whose character and service should have been sufficiently known to him, at least, to prove his protection, and had given; the crudest blow of all. It has been already seen that there was little friendship between Maso and the pilgrim, for the former appeared to have an instinctive dislike of the latter's calling, and this little occurrence was not of a character likely to restore the peace between them.

"Thou, too!" cried the Italian, whose blood had mounted at the first attack on his faithful follower, and which fairly boiled when he witnessed the cowardly and wanton conduct of this new assailant--"art not satisfied with feigning prayers and godliness with the credulous, but thou must even feign enmity to my dog, because it is the fashion to praise the cur of St. Bernard at the expense of all other brutes! Reptile!--dost not dread the arm of an honest man, when raised against thee in just anger?"

"Friends--Vévaisans--honorable citizens!" gasped the pilgrim, as the gripe of Maso permitted breath. "I am Conrad, a poor, miserable, repentant pilgrim--Will ye see me murdered for a brute?"

Such a contest could not continue long in such a place. At first the pressure of the curious, and the great density of the crowd, rather favored the attack of the mariner; but in the end they proved his enemies by preventing the possibility of escaping from those who were especially charged with the care of the public peace. Luckily for Conrad, for passion had fairly blinded Maso to the consequences of his fury, the halberdiers soon forced their way into the centre of the living mass, and they succeeded in seasonably rescuing him from the deadly gripe of his assailant. Il Maledetto trembled with the reaction of this hot sally, the moment his gripe was forcibly released, and he would have disappeared as soon as possible, had it been the pleasure of those into whose hands he had fallen to permit so politic a step. But now commenced the war of words, and the clamor of voices, which usually succeed, as well as precede, all contests of a popular nature. The officer in charge of this portion of the square questioned; twenty answered in a breath, not only drowning each other's voices, but effectually contradicting all that was said in the way of explanation. One maintained that Conrad had not been content with attacking Maso's dog, but that he had followed up the blow by offering a personal indignity to the master himself; this was the publican in whose house the mariner had taken up his abode, and in which he had been sufficiently liberal in his expenditure fairly to entitle him to the hospitable support of its landlord. Another professed his readiness to swear that the dog was the property of the pilgrim, being accustomed to carry his wallet, and that Maso, owing to an ancient grudge against both master and beast, had hurled the stone which sent the animal away howling, and had resented a mild remonstrance of its owner in the extraordinary manner that all had seen. This witness was the Neapolitan juggler, Pippo, who had much attached himself to the person of Conrad since the adventure of the bark, and who was both ready and willing to affirm anything in behalf of a friend who had so evident need of his testimony, if it were only on the score of boon-companionship. A third declared that the dog belonged truly to the Italian, that the stone had been really hurled by one who stood near the pilgrim, who had been wrongfully accused of the offence by Maso; that the latter had made his attack under a false impression, and richly merited punishment for the unceremonious manner in which he had stopped Conrad's breath. This witness was perfectly honest, but of a vulgar and credulous mind. He attributed the original offence to one near that happened to have a bad name, and who was very liable to father every sin that, by possibility, could be laid at his door, as well as some that could not. On the other hand, he had also been duped that morning by the pilgrim's superabundant professions of religious zeal a circumstance that of itself would have prevented him from detecting Conrad's arm in the air as it cast the stone, and which served greatly to increase his certainty that the first offence came from the luckless wight just alluded to; since they who discriminate under general convictions and popular prejudices, usually heap all the odium they pertinaciously withhold from the lucky and the favored, on those who seem fated by general consent to be the common target of the world's darts.

The officer, by the time he had deliberately heard the three principal witnesses, together with the confounding explanations of those who professed to be only half-informed in the matter, was utterly at a loss to decide which had been right and which wrong. He came, therefore, to the safe conclusion to send all the parties to the guard-house, including the witnesses, being quite sure that he had hit on an effectual method of visiting the true criminal with punishment, and of admonishing all those who gave evidence in future to have a care of the manner in which they contradicted each other. Just as this equitable decision was pronounced, the sound of a trumpet proclaimed the approach of a division of the principal mummers, if so irreverent a term can be applied to men engaged in a festival as justly renowned as that of the vine-dressers. This announcement greatly quickened the steps of Justice, for they who were charged with the execution of her decrees felt the necessity of being prompt, under the penalty of losing an interesting portion of the spectacle. Actuated by this new impulse, which, if riot as respectable, was quite as strong, as the desire to do right, the disturbers of the peace, even to those who had shown a quarrelsome temper by telling stories that gave each other the lie, were hurried away in a body, and the public was left in the enjoyment of that tranquillity which, in these perilous times of revolution and changes, is thought to to be so necessary to its dignity, so especially favorable to commerce, and so grateful to those whose duty it is to preserve the public peace with as little inconvenience to themselves as possible.

A blast of the trumpet was the signal for a more general movement, for it announced the commencement of the ceremonies. As it will be presently necessary to speak of the different personages who were represented on this joyous occasion, we shall only say here, that group after group of the actors came into the square, each party marching to the sound of music from its particular point of rendezvous to the common centre. The stage now began to fill with the privileged, among whom were many of the high aristocracy of the ruling canton, most of its officials, who were too dignified to be more than complacent spectators of revels like these, many nobles of mark from Prance and Italy, a few travellers from England, for in that age England was deemed a distant country and sent forth but a few of her *élite* to represent her on such occasions, most of those from the adjoining territories who could afford the time and cost, and who by rank or character were entitled to the distinction, and the wives and families of the local officers who happened to be engaged as actors in the representation. By the time the different parts of the principal procession were assembled in the square, all the seats of the estrade were crowded, with the exception of those reserved for the bailiff and his immediate friends.

Chapter XIV

> So once were ranged the sons of ancient Rome,
> A noble show! While Roscius trod the stage.
>
> Cowper.

The day was not yet far advanced, when all the component parts of the grand procession had arrived in the square. Shortly after, a flourish of clarions gave notice of the approach of the authorities. First came the bailiff, filled with the dignity of station, and watching, with a vigilant but covert eye, every indication of feeling that might prove of interest to his employers, even while he most affected sympathy with the occasion and self-abandonment to the follies of the hour; for Peter Hofmeister owed his long-established favor with the bürgerschaft more to a never-slumbering regard to its exclusive interests and its undivided supremacy, than to any particular skill in the art of rendering men comfortable and happy. Next to the worthy bailiff, for apart from an indomitable resolution to maintain the authority of his masters, for good or for evil, the Herr Hofmeister merited the appellation of a worthy man, came Roger de Blonay and his guest the Baron de Willading, marching, *pari passu*, at the side of the representative of Berne himself. There might have been some question how far the bailiff was satisfied with this arrangement of the difficult point of etiquette, for he issued from his own gate with a sort of side-long movement that kept him nearly confronted to the Signor Grimaldi, though it left him the means of choosing his path and of observing the aspect of things in the crowd. At any rate, the Genoese, though apparently occupying a secondary station, had no grounds to complain of indifference to his presence. Most of the observances and not a few of the sallies of honest Peter, who had some local reputation as a joker and a *bel esprit*, as is apt to be the case with your municipal magistrate, more especially when he holds his authority independently of the community with whom he associates, and perhaps as little likely to be the fact when he depends on popular favor for his rank, were addressed to the Signor Grimaldi. Most of these good things were returned in kind, the Genoese meeting the courtesies like a man accustomed to be the object of peculiar attentions, and possibly like one who rather rioted in the impunity from ceremonies and public observation, that he now happened to enjoy. Adelheid, with a maiden of the house of Blonay, closed the little train.

As all commendable diligence was used by the officers of the peace to make way for the bailiff, Herr Hofmeister and his companions were soon in their allotted stations, which, it is scarcely necessary to repeat, were the upper places on the estrade. Peter had seated himself, after returning numerous salutations, for none in a situation to catch his eye neglected so fair an opportunity to show their intimacy with the bailiff, when his wandering glance fell upon the happy visage of Father Xavier. Rising hastily, the bailiff went through a multitude of the formal ceremonies that distinguished the courtesy of the place and period, such as frequent wavings and liftings of the beaver, profound reverences, smiles that seemed to flow from the heart, and a variety of other tokens of extraordinary love and respect. When all were ended, he resumed his place by the side of Melchior de Willading, with whom he commenced a confidential dialogue.

"We know not, noble Freiherr," (he spoke in the vernacular of their common canton,) "whether we have most reason to esteem or to disrelish these Augustines. While they do so many Christian acts to the travellers on their mountain yonder, they are devils incarnate in the way of upholding popery and its abominations among the people. Look you, the commonalty--God bless them as they deserve!--have no great skill at doctrinal discussions, and are much disposed to be led away by appearances. Numberless are the miserable dolts who fancy the godliness which is content to pass its time on the top of a frozen hill, doing good, feeding the hungry, dressing the wounds of the fallen, and--but thou knowest the manner in which these sayings run--the ignorant, as I was about to add, are but too ready to believe that the religion which leads men to do this, must have some savor of Heaven in it, after all!"

"Are they so very wrong, friend Peter, that we were wise to disturb the monks in the enjoyment of a favor that is so fairly earned?"

The bailiff looked askance at his brother burgher, for such was the humble appellation that aristocracy assumed in Berne, appearing desirous to probe the depth of the other's political morals before he spoke more freely.

"Though of a house so honored and trusted, I believe thou art not much accustomed of late to mingle with the council?" he evasively observed.

"Since this heavy losses in my family, of which thou may'st have heard, the care of this sole surviving child has been my principal solace and occupation, I know not whether the frequent and near sight of death among those so tenderly loved may have softened my heart towards the Augustines, but to me theirs seems a self-denying and a right worthy life."

"'Tis doubtless as you say, noble Melchior, and we shall do well to let our love for the holy canons be seen. Ho! Mr. Officer--do us the favor to request the reverend monk of St. Bernard to draw nearer, that the people may learn the esteem in which their patient charities and never-wearying benevolence are held by the lookers-on. As you will have occasion to pass a night beneath the convent's roof, Herr von Willading, in your journey to Italy, a little honor shown to the honest and pains-taking clavier will not be lost on the brotherhood, if these churchmen have even a decent respect for the usages of their fellow-creatures."

Father Xavier took the proffered place, which was nearer to the person of the bailiff than the one he had just quitted, and insomuch the more honorable, with the usual thanks, but with a simplicity which proved that he understood the compliment to be due to the fraternity of which he was a member, and not to himself. This little disposition made, as well as all other preliminary matters properly observed, the bailiff seemed satisfied with himself and his arrangements, for the moment.

The reader must imagine the stir in the throng the importance of the minor agents appointed to marshal the procession, and the mixture of weariness and curiosity that possessed the spectators, while the several parts of so complicated and numerous a train were getting arranged, each in its prescribed order and station. But, as the ceremonies which followed were of a peculiar character, and have an intimate connexion with the events of the tale, we shall describe them with a little detail, although the task we have allotted to ourselves is less that of sketching pictures of local usages, and of setting before the reader's imagination scenes of real or fancied antiquarian accuracy, than the exposition of a principle, and the wholesome moral which we have always flattered ourselves might, in a greater or less degree, follow from our labors.

A short time previously to the commencement of the ceremonies, a guard of honor, composed of shepherds, gardeners, mowers, reapers, vine-dressers, escorted by halberdiers and headed by music, had left the square in quest of the abbé, as the regular and permanent presiding officer of the abbaye, or company, is termed. This escort, all the individuals of which were dressed in character, was not long in making its appearance with the officer in question, a warm, substantial citizen and proprietor of the place, who, otherwise attired in the ordinary costume of his class in that age, had decorated his beaver with a waving plume, and, in addition to a staff or baton, wore a flowing scarf pendent from his shoulder. This personage, on whom certain judicial functions had devolved, took a convenient position in the front of the stage, and soon made a sign for the officials to proceed with their duties.

Twelve vine-dressers led by a chief, each having his person more or less ornamented with garlands of vine-leaves, and bearing other emblems of his calling, marched in a body, chanting a song of the fields. They escorted two of their number who had been pronounced the most skilful and successful in cultivating the vineyards of the adjacent côtes. When they reached the front of the estrade, the abbé pronounced a short discourse in honor of the cultivators of the earth in general, after which he digressed into especial eulogiums on the successful candidates, two pleased, abashed, and unpractised peasants, who received the simple prizes with throbbing hearts. This little ceremony observed, amid the eager and delightful gaze of friends, and the oblique and discontented regards of the few whose feelings were too contracted to open to the joys of others, even on this simple and grateful festival, the trumpets sounded again, and the cry was raised to make room.

A large group advanced from among the body of the actors to an open space, of sufficient size and elevation, immediately in front of the stage. When in full view of the multitude, those who composed it arranged themselves in a prescribed and seemly order. They were the officials of Bacchus. The high-priest, robed in a sacrificial dress, with flowing beard, and head crowned with the vine, stood foremost, chanting in honor of the craft, of the vine-dresser. His song also contained a few apposite allusions to the smiling blushing candidates. The whole joined in the chorus, though the leader of the band scarce needed the support of any other lungs than those with which he had been very amply furnished by nature.

The hymn ended, a general burst of instrumental music succeeded; and, the followers of Bacchus regaining their allotted station, the general procession began to move, sweeping around the whole area of the square in a manner to pass in order before the bailiff.

The first body in the march was composed of the council of the abbaye, attended by the shepherds and gardeners. One in an antique costume, and bearing a halberd, acted as marshal. He was succeeded by the two crowned vine-dressers, after whom came the abbé with his counsellors, and large groups of shepherds and shepherdesses, as well as a number of both sexes who toiled in gardens, all attired in costumes suited to the traditions of their respective pursuits. The marshal and the officers of the abbaye moved slowly past, with the gravity and decorum that became their stations, occasionally halting to give time for the evolutions of those who followed; but the other actors now began in earnest to play their several parts. A group of young shepherdesses, clad in closely fitting vests of sky-blue with skirts of white, each holding her crook, came forward dancing, and singing songs that imitated the bleatings of their flocks and all the other sounds familiar to the elevated pasturages of that region. These were soon joined by an equal number of young shepherds also singing their pastorals, the whole exhibiting an active and merry group of dancers, accustomed to exercise their art on the sward of the Alps; for, in this festival, although we have spoken of the performers as actors, it is not in the literal meaning of the term, since, with few exceptions none appeared to represent any other calling than that which, in truth, formed his or her daily occupation. We shall not detain the narrative to say more of this party, than that they formed a less striking exception to the conventional picture of the appearance of those engaged in tending flocks, than the truth ordinarily betrays; and that their buoyant gaiety, blooming faces, and unweaned action, formed a good introductory preparation for the saltation that was to follow.

The male gardeners appeared in their aprons, carrying spades, rakes, and the other implements of their trade; the female supporting baskets on their heads filled with rich flowers, vegetables, and fruits. When in front of the bailiff, the young men formed a sort of fasces of their several implements, with a readiness that denoted much study while the girls arranged their baskets in a circle at its foot. Then, joining hands, the whole whirled around, filling the air with a song peculiar to their pursuits.

During the whole of the preparations of the morning, Adelheid had looked on with a vacant eye, as if her feelings had little connexion with that which was passing before her face. It is scarcely necessary to say, that her mind, in spite of herself, wandered to other scenes, and that her truant thoughts were busy with interests very different from those which were here presented to the senses. But, by the time the group of gardeners had passed dancing away, her feelings began to enlist with those who were so evidently pleased with themselves and all around them, and her father, for the first time that morning, was rewarded for the deep attention with which he watched the play of her features, by an affectionate and natural smile.

"This goes off right merrily, Herr Bailiff;" exclaimed the baron, animated by that encouraging smile, as the blood is quickened by a genial ray of the sun's heat when it has been long chilled and deadened by cold.--"This goes off with a joyful will, and is likely to end with credit to thy town! I only wonder that you have not more of this, and monthly. When joy can be had so cheap, it is churlish to deny it to a people."

"We complain not of the levities, noble Freiherr, for your light thinker makes a sober and dutiful subject; but we shall have more of this, and of a far better quality, or our time is wasted.--What is thought at Berne, noble Melchior, of the prospects of the Emperor's obtaining a new concession for the levy of troops in our cantons!"

"I cry thy mercy, good Peterchen, but by thy leave, we will touch on these matters more at our leisure. Boyish though it seem to thy eyes, so long accustomed to look at matters of state, I do confess that these follies begin to have their entertainment and may well claim an hour of idleness from him that has nothing better in hand."

Peter Hofmeister ejaculated a little expressively. He then examined the countenance of the Signor Grimaldi, who had given himself to the merriment with the perfect good-will and self-abandonment of a man of strong intellect, and who felt his powers too sensibly to be jealous of appearances. Shrugging his shoulders, like one that was disappointed, the pragmatical bailiff turned his look towards the revellers, in order to detect, if possible, some breach of the usages of the country, that might require official reproof; for Peter was of that class of governors who have an itching to see their fingers stirring even the air that is breathed by the people, lest they should get it of a quality or in a quantity that might prove dangerous to a monopoly which it is now the fashion to call the conservative principle. In the mean time the revels proceeded.

No sooner had the gardeners quitted the arena, than a solemn and imposing train appeared to occupy the sward. Four females marched to the front, bearing an antique altar that was decorated with suitable devices. They were clad in emblematical dresses, and wore garlands of flowers on their heads. Boys carrying censers preceded an altar that was dedicated to Flora, and her ministering official came after it, mitred and carrying flowers. Like all the priestesses that followed, she was laboriously attired in the robes that denoted her sacred duty. The goddess herself was borne by four females on a throne canopied by flowers, and from whose several parts sweeping festoons of every hue and die descended to the earth. Haymakers of both sexes, gay and pastoral in their air and attire, succeeded, and a car groaning with the sweet-scented grass of the Alps, accompanied by females bearing rakes, brought up the rear.

The altar and the throne being deposited on the sward, the priestess offered sacrifice, hymning the praise of the goddess with mountain lungs. Then followed the dance of the haymakers, as in the preceding exhibition, and the train went off as before.

"Excellent well, and truer than it could be done by your real pagan!" cried the bailiff, who, in spite of his official longings, began to watch the mummery with a pleased eye. "This beateth greatly our youthful follies in the Genoese and Lombard carnivals, in which, to say truth, there are sometimes seen rare niceties in the way of representing the old deities."

"Is it the usage, friend Hofmeister," demanded the baron, "to enjoy these admirable pleasantries often here in Vaud?"

"We partake of them, from time to time, as the abbaye desires, and much as thou seest. The honorable Signor Grimaldi--who will pardon me that he gets no better treatment than he receives, and who will not fail to ascribe what, to all who know him, might otherwise pass for inexcusable neglect, to his own desire for privacy--he will tell us, should he be pleased to honor us with his real opinion, that the subject is none the worse for occasions to laugh and be gay. Now, there is Geneva, a town given to subtleties as ingenious and complicated as the machinery of their own watches; it can never have a merry-making without a leaven of disputation and reason, two as damnable ingredients in the public humor as schism in religion, or two minds in a *ménage*. There is not a knave in the city who does not fancy himself a better man than Calvin, and some there are who believe if they are not cardinals, it is merely because the reformed church does not relish legs cased in red stockings. By the word of a bailiff! I would not be the ruler, look ye, of such a community, for the hope of becoming Avoyer of Berne itself. Here it is different. We play our antics in the shape of gods and goddesses like sober people, and, when all is over, we go train our vines, or count our herds, like faithful subjects of the great canton. Do I state the matter fairly to our friends, Baron de Blonay?"

Roger de Blonay bit his lip, for he and his had been of Vaud a thousand years, and he little relished the allusion to the quiet manner in which his countrymen submitted to a compelled and foreign dictation. He bowed a cold acquiescence to the bailiff's statement, however, as if no farther answer were needed.

"We have other ceremonies that invite our attention," said Melchior de Willading, who had sufficient acquaintance with his friend's opinions to understand his silence.

The next group that approached was composed of those who lived by the products of the dairy. Two cowherds led their beasts, the monotonous tones of whose heavy bells formed a deep and rural accompaniment to the music that regularly preceded each party, while a train of dairy-girls, and of young mountaineers of the class that tend the herds in the summer pasturages, succeeded, a car loaded with the implements of their calling bringing up the rear. In this little procession, no detail of equipment was wanting. The milking-stool was strapped to the body of the dairyman; one had the peculiarly constructed pail in his hand, while another bore at his back the deep wooden vessel in which milk is carried up and down the precipices to the chalet. When they reached the sodded arena, the men commenced milking the cows, the girls set in motion the different processes of the dairy, and the whole united in singing the Ranz des Vaches of the district. It is generally and erroneously believed that there is a particular air which is known throughout Switzerland by this name, whereas in truth nearly every canton has its own song of the mountains, each varying from the others in the notes, as well as in the words, and we might almost add in the language. The Ranz des Vaches of Vaud is in the patois of the country, a dialect that is composed of words of Greek and Latin origin, mingled on a foundation of Celtic. Like our own familiar tune, which was first bestowed in derision, and which a glorious history has enabled us to continue in pride, the words are far too numerous to be repeated. We shall, however, give the reader a single verse of a song which Swiss feeling has rendered so celebrated, and which is said often to induce the mountaineer in foreign service to desert the mercenary standard and the tame scenes of towns; to return to the magnificent nature that haunts his waking imagination and embellishes his dreams. It will at once be perceived that the power of this song is chiefly to be found in the recollections to which it gives birth, by recalling the simple charms of rural life, and by reviving the indelible impressions that are made by nature wherever she has laid her hand on the face of the earth with the same majesty as in Switzerland.

> [The cowherds of the Alps
> Arise at an early hour.
>
> Chorus.
> Ha, ah! ha, ah!
> Liauba! Liauba! in order to milk.
> Come all of you,
> Black and white,
> Red and mottled,
> Young and old;
> Beneath this oak
> I am about to milk you.
> Beneath this poplar,
> I am about to press,
> Liauba! Liauba! in order to milk.]

Lé zermailli dei Colombietté
Dé bon matin, sé san léha.--

Refrain.
Ha, ah! ha, ah!
Liauba! Liauba! por aria.
  Venidé toté,
  Bllantz' et naire,
  Rodz et motaile,
  Dzjouvan' et etro
  Dezó ou tzehano,
  Io vo z' ario
  Dezo ou triembllo,
  Io ië triudzo,
  Liauba! Liauba! por aris.

The music of the mountains is peculiar and wild, having most probably received its inspiration from the grandeur of the natural objects. Most of the sounds partake of the character of echoes, being high-keyed but false notes; such as the rocks send back to the valleys, when the voice is raised above its natural key in order to reach the caverns and savage recesses of inaccessible precipices. Strains like these readily recall the glens and the magnificence amid which they were first heard, and hence, by an irresistible impulse, the mind is led to indulge in the strongest of all its sympathies, those which are mixed with the unalloyed and unsophisticated delights of buoyant childhood.

The herdsmen and dairymaids no sooner uttered the first notes of this magic song, than a deep and breathing stillness pervaded the crowd. As the peculiar strains of the chorus rose on the ear, murmuring echoes issued from among the spectators, and ere the wild intonations could be repeated which accompanied the words "Liauba! Liauba!" a thousand voices were lifted simultaneously, as it were, to greet the surrounding mountains with the salutations of their children. From that moment the remainder of the Ranz des Vaches was a common burst of enthusiasm, the offspring of that national fervor, which forms so strong a link in the social chain, and which is capable of recalling to the bosom that, in other respects, has been hardened by vice and crime, a feeling of some of the purest sentiments of our nature.

The last strain died amid this general exhibition of healthful feeling. The cowherds and the dairy-girls collected their different implements, and resumed their march to the melancholy music of the bells, which formed a deep contrast to the wild notes that had just filled the square.

To these succeeded the followers of Ceres, with the altar, the priestess, and the enthroned goddess, as has been already described in the approach of Flora. Cornucopiæ ornamented the chair of the deity, and the canopy was adorned with the gifts of autumn. The whole was surmounted by a sheaf of wheat. She held the sickle as her sceptre, and a tiara composed of the bearded grain covered her brow. Reapers followed, bearing emblems of the season of abundance, and gleaners closed the train. There was the halt, the chant, the chorus, and the song in praise of the beneficent goddess of autumn, as had been done by the votaries of the deity of flowers. A dance of the reapers and gleaners followed, the threshers flourished their flails, an the whole went their way.

After these came the grand standard of the abbaye and the vine-dresse the real objects of the festival, succeeded. The laborers of the spring led t advance, the men carrying their picks and spades, and the women vessels contain the cuttings of the vines. Then came a train bearing baskets load with the fruit, in its different degrees of perfection and of every shade color. Youths holding staves topped with miniature representations of th various utensils known in the culture of the grape, such as the laborer with the tub on his back, the butt, and the vessel that first receives the flowing juice, followed. A great number of men, who brought forward the forge that is used to prepare the tools, closed this part of the exhibition. The song and the dance again succeeded, when the whole disappeared at a signal given by the approaching music of Bacchus. As we now touch upon the most elaborate part of the representation, we seize the interval that is necessary to bring it forward, in order to take breath ourselves.

Chapter XV

And thou, O wall, O sweet, O lovely wall,
That stand'st between her father's ground and mine
Thou wall, O wall, O sweet and lovely wall,
Show me thy chink, to blink through with mine eyne.

Midsummer Night's Dream.

"'Odds my life, but this goes off with a grace, brother Peter!" exclaimed the Baron de Willading, as he followed the vine-dressers in their retreat, with an amused eye--"If we have much more like it, I shall forget the dignity of the bürgerschaft, and turn mummer with the rest, though my good for wisdom were the forfeit of the folly."

"That is better said between ourselves than performed before the vulgar eye, honorable Melchior It would sound ill, of a truth, were these Vaudois to boast that a noble of thy estimation in Berne were thus to forget himself!"

"None of this!--are we not here to be merry and to laugh, and to be pleased with any folly that offers? A truce, then, to thy official distrusts and superabundant dignity, honest Peterchen," for such was the good-natured name by which the worthy bailiff was most commonly addressed by his friend; "let the tongue freely answer to the heart, as if we were boys rioting together, as was once the case, long ere thou wert thought of for this office, or I knew a sorrowful hour."

"The Signor Grimaldi shall judge between us: I maintain that restraint is necessary to those in high trusts."

"I will decide when the actors have all played their parts," returned the Genoese, smiling; "at present, here cometh one to whom all old soldiers pay homage. We will not fail of respect in so great a presence, on account of a little difference in taste."

Peter Hofmeister was not a small drinker, and as the approach of the god of the cup was announced by a flourish from some twenty instruments made to speak on a key suited to the vault of heaven, he was obliged to reserve his opinions for another time. After the passage of the musicians, and a train of the abbaye's servants, for especial honors were paid to the ruby deity, there came three officials of the sacrifice, one leading a goat with gilded horns, while the two others bore the knife and the hatchet. To these succeeded the altar adorned with vines, the incense-bearers, and the high-priest of Bacchus, who led the way for the appearance of the youthful god himself. The deity was seated astride on a cask, his head encircled with a garland of generous grapes, bearing a cup in one hand, and a vine entwined and fruit-crowned sceptre in the other. Four Nubians carried him on their shoulders, while others shaded his form with an appropriate canopy; fauns wearing tiger-skins, and playing their characteristic antics, danced in his train, while twenty laughing and light-footed Bacchantes flourished their instruments, moving in measure in the rear.

A general shout in the multitude preceded the appearance of Silenus, who was sustained in his place on an ass by two blackamoors. The half-empty skin at his side, the vacant laugh, the foolish eye, the lolling tongue, the bloated lip, and the idiotic countenance, gave reason to suspect that there was a better motive for their support than any which belonged to the truth of the representation. Two youths then advanced, bearing on a pole a cluster of grapes that nearly descended to the ground, and which was intended to represent the fruit brought from Canaan by the messengers of Joshua--a symbol much affected by the artists and mummers of the other hemisphere, on occasions suited to its display. A huge vehicle, ycleped the ark of Noah, closed the procession. It held a wine-press, having its workmen embowered among the vines, and it contained the family of the second father of the human race. As it rolled past, traces of the rich liquor were left in the tracks of its wheels.

Then came the sacrifice, the chant, and the dance, as in most of the preceding exhibitions, each of which, like this of Bacchus, had contained allusions to the peculiar habits and attributes of the different deities. The bacchanal that closed the scene was performed in character; the trumpets flourished, and the procession departed in the order in which it had arrived.

Peter relented a little from his usual political reserve, as he witnessed these games in honor of a deity to whom he so habitually did practical homage, for it was seldom that this elaborate functionary, who might be termed quite a doctrinaire in his way, composed his senses in sleep, without having pretty effectually steeped them in the liquor of the neighboring hills; a habit that was of far more general use among men of his class in that age than in this of ours, which seems so eminently to be the season of sobriety.

"This is not amiss, of a verity;" observed the contented bailiff, as the Fauns and Bacchantes moved off the sward, capering and cutting their classical antics with far more agility and zeal than grace. "This looks like the inspiration of good wine, Signior Genoese, and were the truth known, it would be found that the rogue who plays the part of the fat person on the ass--how dost call the knave, noble Melchior?"

"Body o' me! if I am wiser than thyself, worthy bailiff; it is clearly a rogue who can never have done his mummery so expertly, without some aid from the flask."

"Twill be well to know the fellow's character, for there may be the occasion to commend him to the gentlemen of the abbaye, when all is over. Your skilful ruler has two great instruments that he need use with discretion, Baron de Willading, and these are, fear and flattery; and Berne hath no servant more ready to apply both, or either, as there may be necessity, than one of her poor bailiffs that hath not received all his dues from the general opinion, if truth were spoken. But it is well to be prepared to speak these good people of the abbaye fairly, touching their exploits. Harkee master halberdier; thou art of Vévey, I think, and a warm citizen in thy every-day character, or my eyes do us both injustice."

"I am, as you have said, Monsieur le Bailli, a Vévaisan, and one that is well known among our artisans."

"True, that was visible, spite of thy halberd. Thou art, no doubt, rarely gifted, and taught to the letter in these games. Wilt name the character that has just ridden past on the ass--he that hath so well enacted the drunkard, I mean? His name hath gone out of our minds for the moment, though his acting never can, for a better performance of one overcome by liquor is seldom seen."

"Lord keep you! worshipful bailiff, that is Antoine Giraud, the fat butcher of La Tour de Peil, and a better at the cup there is not in all the country of Vaud! No wonder that he hath done his part so readily; for, while the others have been reading in books, or drilling like so many awkward recruits under the school-master, Antoine hath had little more to perform than to dip into the skin at his elbow. When the officers of the abbaye complain, lest he should disturb the ceremonies, he bids them not to make fools of themselves, for every swallow he gives is just so much done in honor of the representation; and he swears, by the creed of Calvin! that there shall be more truth in his acting than in that of any other of the whole party."

"'Odds my life! the fellow hath humor as well as good acting in him--this Antoine Giraud! Will you look into the written order they have given as, fair Adelheid, that we may make sure this artisan-halberdier hath not deceived us? We in authority must not trust a Vévaisan too lightly."

"It will be vain, I fear, Herr Bailiff, since the characters, and not the names of the actors, appear in the lists. The man in question represents Silenus I should think, judging from his appearance and all the other circumstances."

"Well, let it be as thou wilt. Silenus himself could not play his own part better than it hath been done by this Antoine Giraud. The fellow would gain gold like water at the court of the emperor as a mime, were he only advised to resort thither. I warrant you, now, he would do Pluto or Minerva, or any other god, just as well as he hath done this rogue Silenus!"

The honest admiration of Peter, who, sooth to say, had not much of the learning of the age, as the phrase is, raised a smile on the lip of the beauteous daughter of the baron, and she glanced a look to catch the eye of Sigismund, towards whom all her secret sympathies, whether of sorrow or of joy, so naturally and so strongly tended. But the averted head, the fixed attention, and the nearly immovable and statue-like attitude in which he stood, showed that a more powerful interest drew his gaze to the next group. Though ignorant of the cause of his intense regard, Adelheid instantly forgot the bailiff, his dogmatism, and his want of erudition, in the wish to examine those who approached.

The more classical portion of the ceremonies was now duly observed. The council of the abbaye intended to close with an exhibition that was more intelligible to the mass of the spectators than anything which had preceded it, since it was addressed to the sympathies and habits of every people, and in all conditions of society. This was the spectacle that so engrossingly attracted the attention of Sigismund. It was termed the procession of the nuptials, and it was now slowly advancing to occupy the space left vacant by the retreat of Antoine Giraud and his companions.

There came in front the customary band, playing a lively air which use has long appropriated to the festivities of Hymen. The lord of the manor, or, as he was termed, the baron, and his lady-partner led the train, both apparelled in the rich and quaint attire of the period. Six ancient couples, the representatives of happy married lives, followed by a long succession of offspring of every age, including equally the infant at the breast and the husband and wife in the flower of their days, walked next to the noble pair. Then appeared the section of a dwelling, which was made to portray the interior of domestic economy, having its kitchen, its utensils, and most of the useful and necessary objects that may be said to compose the material elements of an humble *ménage*. Within this moiety of a house, one female plied the wheel, and another was occupied in baking. The notary, bearing the register beneath an arm, with hat in hand, and dressed in an exaggerated costume of his profession, strutted in the rear of the two industrious housemaids. His appearance was greeted with a general laugh, for the spectators relished the humor of the caricature with infinite goût. But this sudden and general burst of merriment was as quickly forgotten in the desire to behold the bride and bridegroom, whose station was next to that of the officer of the law. It was understood that these parties were not actors, but that the abbaye had sought out a couple, of corresponding rank and means, who had consented to join their fortunes in reality on the occasion of this great jubilee, thereby lending to it a greater appearance of that genuine joy and festivity which it was the desire of the heads of the association to represent. Such a search had not been made without exciting deep interest in the simple communities which surrounded Vévey. Many requisites had been proclaimed to be necessary in the candidates--such as beauty, modesty, merit, and the submission of her sex, in the bride; and in her partner those qualities which might fairly entitle him to be the repository of the happiness of a maiden so endowed.

Many had been the speculations of the Vévaisans touching the individuals who had been selected to perform these grave and important characters which, for fidelity of representation, were to outdo that of Silenus himself; but so much care had been taken by the agents of the abbaye to conceal the names of those they had selected, that, until this moment, when disguise was no longer possible, the public was completely in the dark on the interesting point. It was so usual to make matches of this kind on occasions of public rejoicing, and marriages of convenience, as they are not unaptly termed, enter so completely into the habits of all European communities-- perhaps we might say of all old communities--that common opinion would not have been violently outraged had it been known that the chosen pair saw each other for the second or third time in the procession, and that they had now presented themselves to take the nuptial vow, as it were, at the sound of the trumpet or the beat of drum. Still, it was more usual to consult the inclinations of the parties, since it gave greater zest to the ceremony, and these selections of couples on public occasions were generally supposed to have more than the common interest of marriages, since they were believed to be the means of uniting, through the agency of the rich and powerful, those whom poverty or other adverse circumstances had hitherto kept asunder. Rumor spoke of many an inexorable father who had listened to reason from the mouths of the great, rather than balk the public humor; and thousands of pining hearts, among the obscure and simple, are even now gladdened at the approach of some joyous ceremony, which is expected to throw open the gates of the prison to the debtor and the criminal, or that of Hymen to those who are richer in constancy and affection than in any other stores.

A general murmur and a common movement betrayed the lively interest of the spectators, as the principal and real actors in this portion of the ceremonies drew near. Adelheid felt a warm glow on her cheek, and a gentler flow of kindness at her heart, when her eye first caught a view of the bride and bridegroom, whom she was fain to believe a faithful pair that a cruel fortune had hitherto kept separate, and who were now willing to brave such strictures as all must encounter who court public attention, in order to receive the reward of their enduring love and self-denial. This sympathy, which was at first rather of an abstract and vague nature, finding its support chiefly in her own peculiar situation and the qualities of her gentle nature, became intensely heightened, however, when she got a better view of the bride. The modest mien, abashed eye, and difficult breathing of the girl, whose personal charms were of an order much superior to those which usually distinguish rustic beauty in those countries in which females are not exempted from the labors of the field, were so natural and winning as to awaken all her interest; and, with instinctive quickness, the lady of Willading bent her look on the bridegroom, in order to see if one whose appearance was so eloquent in her favor was likely to be happy in her choice. In age, personal appearance, and apparently in condition of life, there was no very evident unfitness, though Adelheid fancied that the mien of the maiden announced a better breeding than that of her companion--a difference which she was willing to ascribe, however, to a greater aptitude in her own sex to receive the first impress of the moral seal, than that which belongs to man.

"She is fair," whispered Adelheid, slightly bending her head towards Sigismund, who stood at her side, "and must deserve her happiness."

"She is good, and merits a better fate!" muttered the youth, breathing so hard as to render his respiration audible.

The startled Adelheid raised her eyes, and strong but suppressed agitation was quivering in every lineament of her companion's countenance. The attention of those near was so closely drawn towards the procession, as to allow an instant of unobserved communication.

"Sigismund, this is thy sister!"

"God so cursed her."

"Why has an occasion, public as this, been chosen to wed a maiden of her modesty and manner?"

"Can the daughter of Balthazar be squeamish? Gold, the interest of the abbaye, and the foolish *éclat* of this silly scene, have enabled my father to dispose of his child to yonder mercenary, who has bargained like a Jew in the affair, and who, among other conditions, has required that the true name of his bride shall never be revealed. Are we not honored by a connexion which repudiates us even before it is formed!"

The hollow stifled laugh of the young man thrilled on the nerves of his listener, and she ceased the stolen dialogue to return to the subject at a more favorable moment. In the mean time the procession had reached the station in front of the stage, where the mummers had already commenced their rites.

A dozen groomsmen and as many female attendants accompanied the pair who were about to take the nuptial vow. Behind these came the *trousseau* and the *corbeille*; the first being that portion of the dowry of the bride which applies to her personal wants, and the last is an offering of the husband, and is figuratively supposed to be a pledge of the strength of his passion. In the present instance the trousseau was so ample, and betokened so much liberality, as well as means, on the part of the friends of a maiden who would consent to become a wife in a ceremony so public, as to create general surprise; while, on the other hand, a solitary chain of gold, of rustic fashion, and far more in consonance with the occasion, was the sole tribute of the swain. This difference between the liberality of the friends of the bride, and that of the individual, who, judging from appearances, had much the most reason to show his satisfaction, did not fail to give rise to many comments. They ended as most comments do, by deductions drawn against the weaker and least defended of the parties. The general conclusion was so uncharitable as to infer that a girl thus bestowed must be under peculiar disadvantages, else would there have been a greater equality between the gifts; an inference that was sufficiently true, though cruelly unjust to its modest but unconscious subject.

While speculations of this nature were rife among the spectators, the actors in the ceremony began their dances, which were distinguished by the quaint formality that belonged to the politeness of the age The songs that succeeded were in honor of Hymen and his votaries, and a few couplets that extolled the virtues and beauty of the bride were chanted in chorus. A sweep appeared at the chimney-top, raising his cry, in allusion to the business of the ménage, and then all moved away, as had been done by those who had preceded them. A guard of halberdiers closed the procession.

That part of the mummeries which was to be enacted in front of the estrade was now ended for the moment, and the different groups proceeded to various other stations in the town, where the ceremonies were to be repeated for the benefit of those who, by reason of the throng, had not been able to get a near view of what had passed in the square. Most of the privileged profited by the pause to leave their seats, and to seek such relaxation as the confinement rendered agreeable. Among those who entirely quitted the square were the bailiff and his friends, who strolled towards the promenade on the lake-shore, holding discourse, in which there was blended much facetious merriment concerning what they had just seen.

The bailiff soon drew his companions around him, in a deep discussion of the nature of the games, during which the Signor Grimaldi betrayed a malicious pleasure in leading on the dogmatic Peter to expose the confusion that existed in his head touching the characters of sacred and profane history. Even Adelheid was compelled to laugh at the commencement of this ludicrous exhibition, but her thoughts were not long in recurring to a subject in which she felt a nearer and a more tender interest. Sigismund walked thoughtfully at her side, and she profited by the attention of all around them being drawn to the laughable dialogue just mentioned, to renew the subject that had been so lightly touched on before.

"I hope thy fair and modest sister will never have reason to repent her choice," she said, lessening her speed, in a manner to widen the distance between herself and those she did not wish to overhear the words, while it brought her nearer to Sigismund; "It is a frightful violence to all maiden feeling to be thus dragged before the eyes of the curious and vulgar, in a scene; trying and solemn as that in which she plights her marriage vows!"

"Poor Christine! her fate from infancy has been pitiable. A purer or milder spirit than hers, one that more sensitively shrinks from rude collision, does not exist, and yet, on whichever side she turns her eyes, she meets with appalling prejudices or opinions to drive a gentle nature like hers to madness It may be a misfortune, Adelheid, to want instruction, and to be fated to pass a life in the depths of ignorance, and in the indulgence of brutal passions, but it is scarcely a blessing to have the mind elevated above the tasks which a cruel and selfish world so frequently imposes."

"Thou wast speaking of thy mild and excellent sister?--"

"Well hast thou described her! Christine is mild, and more than modest--she is meek. But what can meekness itself do to palliate such a calamity? Desirous of averting the stigma of his family from all he could with prudence, my father caused my sister, like myself, to be early taken from the parental home. She was given in charge to strangers, under such circumstances of secrecy, as left her long, perhaps too long, in ignorance of the stock from which she sprang. When maternal pride led my mother to seek her daughter's society, the mind of Christine was in some measure formed, and she had to endure the humiliation of learning that she was one of a family proscribed. Her gentle spirit, however, soon became reconciled to the truth, at least so far as human observation could penetrate, and, from the moment of the first terrible agony, no one has heard her murmur at the stern decree of Providence. The resignation of that mild girl has ever been a reproach to my own rebellious temper, for, Adelheid, I cannot conceal the truth from thee--I have cursed all that I dared include in my wicked imprecations, in very madness at this blight on my hopes! Nay, I have even accused my father of injustice, that he did not train me at the side of the block, that I might take a savage pride in that which is now the bane of my existence. Not so with Christine; she has always warmly returned the affection of our parents, as a daughter should love the authors of her being, while I fear I have been repining when I should have loved. Our origin is a curse entailed by the ruthless laws of the land, and it is not to be attributed to any, at least to none of these later days, as a fault; and such has ever been the language of my poor sister when she has seen a merit in their wishes to benefit us at the expense of their own natural affection. I would I could imitate her reason and resignation!"

"The view taken by thy sister is that of a female, Sigismund, whose heart is stronger than her pride; and, what is more, it is just."

"I deny it not; 'tis just. But the ill-judged mercy has for ever disqualified me to sympathize as I could wish with those to whom I belong. 'Tis an error to draw these broad distinctions between our habits and our affections. Creatures stern as soldiers cannot bend their fancies like pliant twigs, or with the facility of female--"

"Duty," said Adelheid gravely, observing that he hesitated.

"If thou wilt, duty. The word has great weight with thy sex, and I do not question that it should have with mine."

"Thou canst not be wanting in affection for thy father, Sigismund. The manner in which thou interposedst to save his life, when we were in that fearful jeopardy of the tempest, disproves thy words."

"Heaven forbid that I should be wanting in natural feeling of this sort, and yet, Adelheid, it is horrible not to be able to respect, to love profoundly, those to whom we owe our existence! Christine in this is far happier than I, an advantage that I doubt not she owes to her simple life, and to the closer intimacies which unite females. I am the son of a headsman; that bitter fact is never absent from my thoughts when they turn to home and those scenes in which I could so gladly take pleasure. Balthazar may have meant a kindness when he caused me to be trained in habits so different from his own, but, to complete the good work, the veil should never have been removed."

Adelheid was silent. Though she understood the feelings which controlled one educated so very differently from those to whom he owed his birth, her habits of thought were opposed to the indulgence of any reflections that could unsettle the reverence of the child for its parent.

"One of a heart like thine, Sigismund, cannot hate his mother!" she said, after a pause.

"In this thou dost me no more than justice; my words have ill represented my thoughts, if they have left such an impression. In cooler moments, I have never considered my birth as more than a misfortune, and my education I deem a reason for additional respect and gratitude to my parents, though it may have disqualified me in some measure to enter deeply into their feelings. Christine herself is not more true, nor of more devoted love, than my poor mother. It is necessary, Adelheid, to see and know that excellent woman in order to understand all the wrongs that the world inflicts by its ruthless usages."

"We will now speak only of thy sister. Has she been here bestowed without regard to her own wishes, Sigismund?"

"I hope not. Christine is meek;, but, while neither word nor look betrays the weakness, still she feels the load that crushes us both. She has long accustomed herself to look at all her own merits through the medium of this debasement, and has set too low a value on her own excellent qualities. Much, very much depends, in this life, on our own habits of self-estimation, Adelheid; for he who is prepared to admit unworthiness--I speak not of demerit towards God but towards men--will soon become accustomed to familiarity with a standard below his just pretensions, and will end perhaps in being the thing he dreaded. Such has been the consequence of Christine's knowledge of her birth, for, to her meek spirit, there is an appearance of generosity in overlooking this grand defect, and it has too well prepared her mind to endow the youth with a hundred more of the qualities that are absolutely necessary to her esteem, but which I fear exist only in her own warm fancy."

"This is touching on the most difficult branch of human knowledge," returned Adelheid, smiling sweetly on the agitated brother; "a just appreciation of ourselves. If there is danger of setting too low a value on our merits, there is also some danger of setting too high; though I perfectly comprehend the difference you would make between vulgar vanity, and that self-respect which is certainly in some degree necessary to success. But one, like her thou hast described, would scarce yield her affections without good reason to think them well bestowed."

"Adelheid, thou, who hast never felt the world's contempt, cannot understand how winning respect and esteem can be made to those who pine beneath its weight! My sister hath so long accustomed herself to think meanly of her hopes, that the appearance of liberality and justice in this youth would have been sufficient of itself to soften her feelings in his favor. I cannot say I think--for Christine will soon be his wife--but I will say, I fear that the simple fact of his choosing one that the world persecutes has given him a value in her eyes he might not otherwise have possessed."

"Thou dost not appear to approve of thy sister's choice?"

"I know the details of the disgusting bargain better than poor Christine," answered the young man, speaking between his teeth, like one who repressed bitter emotion. "I was privy to the greedy exactions on the one side, and to the humiliating concessions on the other. Even money could not buy this boon for Balthazar's child, without a condition that the ineffaceable stigma of her birth should be for ever concealed."

Adelheid saw, by the cold perspiration that stood on the brow of Sigismund, how intensely he suffered, and she sought an immediate occasion to lead his thoughts to a less disturbing subject. With the readiness of her sex, and with the sensitiveness and delicacy of a woman that sincerely loved, she found means to effect the charitable purpose, without again alarming his pride. She succeeded so far in calming his feelings, that, when they rejoined their companions, the manner of the young man had entirely regained the quiet and proud composure in which he appeared to take refuge against the consciousness of the blot that darkened his hopes, frequently rendering life itself a burthen nearly too heavy to be borne.

Chapter XVI

--Come apace, good Audrey, I will fetch
Up your goats, Audrey: and how, Audrey? am
I the man yet? Doth my simple features content
You.

As You Like It.

While the mummeries related were exhibiting in the great square, Maso, Pippo, Conrad, and the others concerned in the little disturbance connected with the affair of the dog, were eating their discontent within the walls of the guard-house. Vévey has several squares, and the various ceremonies of the gods and demigods were now to be repeated in the smaller areas. On one of the latter stands the town-house and prison. The offenders in question had been summarily transferred to the gaol, in obedience to the command of the officer charged with preserving the peace. By an act of grace, however, that properly belonged to the day, as well as to the character of the offence, the prisoners were permitted to occupy a part of the edifice that commanded a view of the square, and consequently were not precluded from all participation in the joyousness of the festivities. This indulgence had been accorded on the condition that the parties should cease their wrangling, and otherwise conduct themselves in a way not to bring scandal on the exhibition in which the pride of every Vévaisan was so deeply enlisted. All the captives, the innocent as well as the guilty, gladly subscribed to the terms; for they found themselves in a temporary duresse which did not admit of any fair argument of the merits of the case, and there is no leveller so effectual as a common misfortune.

The anger of Maso, though sudden and violent, the effect of a hot temperament, had quickly subsided in a calm which more probably belonged to his education and opinions, in all of which he was much superior to his profligate antagonist. Contempt, therefore, soon took the place of resentment; and though too much accustomed to rude contact with men of the pilgrim's class to be ashamed of what had occurred, the manner strove to forget the occurrence. It was one of those moral disturbances to which he was scarcely less used than he was accustomed to encounter physical contests of the elements like that in which he had lately rendered so essential service on the Leman.

"Give me thy hand, Conrad;" he said, with the frank forgiveness which is apt to distinguish the reconciliation of men who pass their lives amid the violent, but sometimes ennobling, scenes of adventure and lawlessness. "Thou hast thy humors and habits, and I have mine. If thou findest this traffic in penances and prayers to thy fancy, follow the trade, of Heaven's sake, and leave me and my dog to live by other means!"

"Thou ought'st to have bethought thee how much reason we pilgrims have to prize the mastiffs of the mountain," answered Conrad, "and how likely it was to stir my blood to see another cur devouring that which was intended for old Uberto. Thou hast never toiled up the sides of St. Bernard, friend Maso, loaded with the sins of a whole parish, to say nothing of thine own, and therefore canst not know the value of these brutes, who so often stand between us pilgrims and a grave of snow."

Il Maledetto smiled grimly, and muttered a sentence between his teeth; for, in perfect consonance with the frank lawlessness of his own life, there was a reckless honesty in his nature, which caused him to despise hypocrisy as unworthy of the bold attributes of manhood.

"Have it as thou wilt, pious Conrad," he said sneeringly, "so there be peace between us. I am, as thou knowest, an Italian, and though we of the south seek revenge occasionally of those who wrong us, it is not often that we do violence after giving a willing palm--I trust ye of Germany are no less honest?"

"May the Virgin be deaf to every ave I have sworn to repeat, and the good fathers of Loretto refuse absolution, if I think more of it! 'Twas but the gripe of a throat, and I am not so tender in that part of the body as to fear it is to be the forerunner of a closer squeeze. Didst ever hear of a churchman that suffered in this way?"

"Men often escape with less than their deserts;" Maso drily answered. "Well, fortune, or the saints, or Calvin, or whatever power most suits your tastes, good friends, has at length put a roof over our heads,--an honor that rarely arrives to most of us, if I may judge by appearances and some little knowledge of the different trades we follow. Thou wilt have a fair occasion to suffer Policinello to rest from his uneasy antics, Pippo, while his master breathes the air through a window for the first time in many a day, as I will answer."

The Neapolitan had no difficulty in laughing at this sally; for his was a nature that took all things pleasantly, though it took nothing under the corrective of principle or a respect for the rights of others.

"Were this Napoli, with her gentle sky and hot volcano," he said, smiling at the allusion, "no one would have less relish for a roof than myself."

"Thou wast born beneath the arch of some Duca's gateway," returned Maso, with a sort of reckless sarcasm, that as often cut his friends as his enemies; "thou wilt probably die in the hospital of the poor, and wilt surely be shot from the death-cart into one of the daily holes of thy Campo Santo, among a goodly company of Christians, in which legs and arms will be thrown at random like jack-straws, and in which the wisest among ye all will be puzzled to tell his own limbs from those of his neighbors, at the sound of the last trumpet."

"Am I a dog, to meet this end!" demanded Pippo, fiercely--"or that I should not know my own bones from those of some infidel rascal, who may happen to be my neighbor!"

"We have had one disturbance about brutes, let us not have another;" sarcastically rejoined Il Maledetto. "Princes and nobles," he added, with affected gravity, "we are here bound by the heels, during the good pleasure of those who rule in Vévey; the wisest course will be to pass the time in good-humor with each other, and as pleasantly as our condition will allow. The reverend Conrad shall have all the honors of a cardinal, Pippo shall have the led horse at his funeral, and, as for these worthy Vaudois, who, no doubt, are men of substance in their way, they shall be bailiffs sent by Berne to rule between the four walls of our palace! Life is but a graver sort of mummery, gentlemen, and the second of its barest secrets is to make others fancy us what we wish to appear--the first being, without question, the faculty of deceiving ourselves. Now each one has only to imagine that he is the high personage I have just named, and the most difficult part of the work is achieved to his hands."

"Thou hast forgotten to name thine own quality," cried Pippo, who was too much used to buffoonery not to relish the whim of Maso, and who, with Neapolitan fickleness, forgot his anger the instant he had given it vent.

"I will represent the sapient public, and, being well disposed to be duped, the whole job is complete. Practise away, worthies, and ye shall see with what open eyes and wide gullet I am ready to admire and swallow all your philosophy."

This sally produced a hearty laugh, which rarely fails to establish momentary good fellowship. The Vaudois, who had the thirsty propensities of mountaineers, ordered wine, and, as their guardians looked upon their confinement more as a measure of temporary policy than of serious moment, the command was obeyed. In a short time, this little group of worldlings were making the best of circumstances, by calling in the aid of physical stimulants to cheer their solitude. As they washed their throats with the liquor, which was both good and cheap and by consequence doubly agreeable, the true characters of the different individuals began to show themselves in stronger colors.

The peasants of Vaud, of whom there were three and all of the lowest class, became confused and dull in their faculties though louder and more vehement in speech, each man appearing to balance the increasing infirmities of his reason by stronger physical demonstrations of folly.

Conrad, the pilgrim, threw aside the mask entirely, if, indeed, so thin a veil as that he ordinarily wore when not in the presence of his employers deserved such a name, and appeared the miscreant he truly was,--a strange admixture of cowardly superstition, (for few meddle with superstition without getting more or less entangled in its meshes,) of low cunning, and of the most abject and gross sensuality and vice. The invention and wit of Pippo, at all times ready and ingenious, gained increased powers, but the torrent of animal spirits that were let loose by his potations swept before it all reserve, and he scarce opened his mouth but to betray the thoughts of a man long practised in frauds and all other evil designs on the rights of his fellow-creatures. On Maso the wine produced an effect that might almost be termed characteristic, and which it is in some sort germane to the moral of the tale to describe.

Il Maledetto had indulged freely and with apparent recklessness in the frequent draughts. He was long familiarized to the habits of this wild and uncouth fellowship, and a singular sentiment, that men of his class choose to call honor, and which perhaps deserves the name as much as half of the principles that are described by the same appellation, prevented him from refusing to incur an equal risk in the common assault on their faculties, inducing him to swallow his full share of the intoxicating fluid as the cup passed from one reeking mouth to another. He liked the wine, too, and tasted its perfume, and cherished its glowing influence, with the perfect good-will of a man who knew how to profit by the accident which placed such generous liquor at his command. He had also his designs in wishing to unmask his companions, and he thought the moment favorable to such an intention. In addition to these motives, Maso had his especial reasons for being uneasy at finding himself in the hands of the authorities, and he was not sorry to bring about a state of things that might lead to his being confounded with the others in a group of vulgar devotees of Bacchus.

But Maso yielded to the common disposition in a manner peculiar to himself. His eyes became even more lustrous than usual, his face reddened, and his voice even grew thick, while his senses retained their powers. His reason, instead of giving way, like those of the men around him, rather brightened under the excitement, as if it foresaw the danger it incurred, and the greater necessity there existed for vigilance. Though born in a southern clime, he was saturnine and cold when unexcited, and such temperaments rather gain their tone than lose their powers by stimulants under which men of feebler organizations sink. He had passed his life amid wild adventure and in scenes of peril which suited such a disposition, and it most probably required either some strong motive of danger, like that of the tempest on the Leman, or a stimulant of another quality, to draw out the latent properties of his mind, which so well fitted him to lead when others were the most disposed to follow. He was, therefore, without fear for himself while he aroused his companions; and he was free of his purse, which did not, however, appear to be sufficiently stored to answer very heavy demands, by ordering cup after cup to supply the place of those which were so quickly drained to the dregs. In this manner an hour or two passed swiftly, they who were charged with the care of the jolly party in the town-house being much more occupied in noting the festivities without, than those within, the prison.

"Thou hast a merry life of it, honest Pippo," cried Conrad with swimming eyes, answering a remark of the buffoon. "Thou art but a laugh at the best, and wilt go through the world grinning and making others grin. Thy Policinello is a rare fellow, and I never meet one of thy set that weary legs and sore feet are not forgotten in his fooleries!"

"Corpo di Bacco!--I wish this were so; but thou hast much the best of the matter, even in the way of amusement, reverend pilgrim, though to the looker-on it would seem otherwise. The difference between us, pious Conrad, is just this--that thou laughest in thy sleeve without seeming to be merry, whereas I yawn ready to split my jaws while I seem to be dying with fun. Your often-told joke is a bad companion, and gets at last to be as gloomy as a dirge. Wine can be swallowed but once, and laughter will not come for ever for the same folly. Cospetto! I would give the earnings of a year for a set of new jokes, such as might come fresh from the wit of one who never saw a mountebank, and are not worn threadbare with being rubbed against the brains of all the jokers in Europe."

"There was a wise man of old, of whom it is not probable that any of you have ever heard," observed Maso, "who has said there was nothing new under the sun."

"He who said that never tasted of this liquor, which is as raw as if it were still running from the press," rejoined the pilgrim. "Knave, dost think that we are unknowing in these matters, that thou darest bring a pot of such lees to men of our quality? Go to, and see that thou doest us better justice in the next!"

"The wine is the same as that which first pleased you, but it is the nature of drunkenness to change the palate; and therein Solomon was right as in all other points," coolly remarked Il Maledetto. "Nay, friend, thou wilt scarce bring thy liquors again to those who do not know how to do them proper honor."

Maso thrust the lad who served them from the room, and he slipped a small coin in his hand, ordering him not to return. Inebriety had made sufficient ravages for his ends, and he was now desirous of stopping farther excesses.

"Here come the mummers--gods and goddesses, shepherds and their lasses and all the other pleasantries, to keep us in humor! To do these Vévaisans justice, they treat us rarely; for ye see they send their players to amuse our retirement!"

"Wine! liquor! raw or ripe, bring us liquor!" roared Conrad, Pippo, and their pot-companions, who were much too drunk to detect the agency of Maso in defeating their wishes, though they were just drunk enough to fancy that what he said of the attention of the authorities was not only true but merited.

"How now, Pippo! art ashamed to be outdone in thine own craft, that thou bellowest for wine at the moment when the actors have come into the square to exhibit their skill?" cried the mariner. "Truly, we shall have a mean opinion of thy merit, if thou art afraid to meet a few Vaudois peasants in thy trade,--and thou a buffoon of Napoli!"

Pippo swore with pot-oaths that he defied the cleverest of Switzerland; for that he had not only acted on every mall and mole of Italy, but that he had exhibited in private before princes and cardinals, and that he had no superior on either side of the Alps. Maso profited by his advantage, and, by applying fresh goads to his vanity, soon succeeded in causing him to forget the wine, and in drawing him, with all the others, to the windows.

The processions, in making the circuit of the city, had now reached the square of the town-house, where the acting and exhibition were repeated, as has been already related in general terms to the reader. There were the officers of the abbaye, the vine-dressers, the shepherds and the shepherdesses, Flora, Ceres, Pales, and Bacchus, with all the others, attended by their several trains and borne in state as became their high attributes. Silenus rolled from his ass, to the great joy of a thousand shouting blackguards, and to the infinite scandal of the prisoners at the windows, the latter affirming to a man that there was no acting in the case, but that the demigod was shamefully under the influence of too many potations that had been swallowed in his own honor.

We shall not go over the details of these scenes, which all who have ever witnessed a public celebration will readily imagine, nor is it necessary to record the different sallies of wit that, under the inspiration of the warm wines of Vévey and the excitement of the revels, issued from the group that clustered around the windows of the prison. All who have ever listened to low humor, that is rather deadened than quickened by liquor, will understand their character, and they who have not will scarcely be losers by the omission.

At length the different allegories drawn from the heathen mythology ended, and the procession of the nuptials came into the square. The meek and gentle Christine had appeared nowhere that day without awakening strong sympathy in her youth, beauty, and apparent innocence. Murmurs of approbation accompanied her steps, and the maiden, more accustomed to her situation, began to feel, probably for the first time since she had known the secret of her origin, something like that security which is an indispensable accompaniment of happiness. Long used to think of herself as one proscribed of opinion, and educated in the retirement suited to the views of her parents, the praises that reached her ear could not but be grateful, and they went warm and cheeringly to her heart, in spite of the sense of apprehension and uneasiness that had so long harbored there. Throughout the whole of the day, until now, she had scarce dared to turn her eyes to her future husband,--him who, in her simple and single-minded judgment, had braved prejudice to do justice to her worth; but, as the applause, which had been hitherto suppressed, broke out in loud acclamations in the square of the town-house, the color mantled brightly on her cheek, and she looked with modest pride at her companion, as if she would say in the silent appeal, that his generous choice would not go entirely without its reward. The crowd responded to the sentiment, and never did votaries of Hymen approach the altar seemingly under happier auspices.

The influence of innocence and beauty is universal. Even the unprincipled and half-intoxicated prisoners were loud in praise of the gentle Christine. One praised her modesty, another extolled her personal appearance, and all united with the multitude in shouting to her honor. The blood of the bridegroom began to quicken, and, by the time the train had halted in the open space near the building, immediately beneath the windows occupied by Maso and his fellows, he was looking about him in the exultation of a vulgar mind, which finds its delight in, as it is apt to form its judgments from, the suffrages of others.

"Here is a grand and beautiful festa!" said the hiccoughing Pippo, "and a most willing bride San Gennaro bless thee, bella sposina, and the worthy man who is the stem of so fair a rose! Send us wine, generous groom and happy bride, that we may drink to the health of thee and thine!"

Christine changed color, and looked furtively around, for they who lie under the weight of the world's displeasure, though innocent, are sensitively jealous of allusions to the sore points in their histories. The feeling communicated itself to her companion, who threw distrustful glances at the crowd, in order to ascertain if the secret of his bride's birth were not discovered.

"A braver festa never honored an Italian corso," continued the Neapolitan, whose head was running on his own fancies, without troubling itself about the apprehensions and wishes of others. "A gallant array and a fair bride! Send us wine, felicissimi sposi, that we may drink to your eternal fame and happiness! Happy the father that calls thee daughter, bella sposa, and most honored the mother that bare so excellent a child! Scellerati, ye of the crowd, why do ye not bear the worthy parents in your arms, that all may see and do homage to the honorable roots of so rich a branch! Send us wine, buona gente, send us cups of merry wine!"

The cries and figurative language of Pippo attracted the attention of the multitude, who were additionally amused by the mixture of dialects in which he uttered his appeals. The least important trifles, by giving a new direction to popular sympathies, frequently become the parents of grave events. The crowd, which followed the train of Hymen, had begun to weary with the repetition of the same ceremonies, and it now gladly lent itself to the episode of the felicitations and entreaties of the half-intoxicated Neapolitan.

"Come forth, and act the father of the happy bride, thyself, reverend and grave stranger;" cried one in derision, from the throng. "So excellent an example will descend to thy children's children, in blessings on thy line!"

A shout of laughter rewarded this retort. It put the quick-witted Neapolitan on his mettle, to produce a prompt and suitable reply.

"My blessing on the blushing rose!" he answered in an instant. "There are worse parents than Pippo, for he who lives by making others laugh deserves well of men, whereas there is your medico, who eats the bread of colics, and rheumatisms, and other foul diseases, of which he pretends to be the enemy, though, San Gennaro to aid!--who is there so silly, as not to see that the knavish doctor and the knavish distemper play into each others hands, as readily as Policinello and the monkey."

"Hast thou another worse than thyself that can be named," cried he of the crowd.

"A score, and thou shalt be of the number. My blessing on the fair bride! thrice happy is she that hath a right to receive the benediction from one of so honest life as the merry Pippo. Speak not I the truth, figligiola?"

Christine perceived that the hand of her companion was coldly releasing her own, and she felt the creeping sensation of the blood which is the common attendant of extreme and humiliating shame. Still she bore up against the weakness, with that deep reliance on the justice of others which is usually the most strongly seated in those who are the most innocent; and she followed the procession, in its circuit, with a step whose trembling was mistaken for no more than the embarrassment natural to her situation.

At this moment, as the mummers were wheeling past the town-house, and the air was filled with music, while a general movement stirred the multitude, a cry of alarm arose in the building. It was immediately succeeded by such a rush of bodies towards the spot, as indicates, in a throng, a sudden and general interest in some new and extraordinary event.

The crowd was beaten back and dispersed, the procession had disappeared, and there was an unusual appearance of activity and mystery among the officials of the place, before the cause of this disturbance began to be whispered among the few who remained in the square. The rumor ran that one of the prisoners, an athletic Italian mariner had profited by the attention of all the other guardians of the place being occupied by the ceremonies, to knock down the solitary sentinel, and to effect his escape, followed by all the drunkards who were able to run.

The evasion of a few lawless blackguards from their prison was not an event likely long to divert the attention of the curious from the amusements of the day, especially as it was understood that their confinement would have terminated of itself with the setting sun. But when the fact was communicated to Peter Hofmeister, the sturdy bailiff swore fifty harsh oaths at the impudence of the knaves, at the carelessness of their keepers, and in honor of the good cause of justice in general. After which he incontinently commanded that the runaways should be apprehended. This material part of the process achieved, he moreover, ordered that they should be brought forthwith into his presence, even should he be engaged in the most serious of the ceremonies of the day. The voice of Peter speaking in anger was not likely to be unheard, and the stern mandate had scarcely issued from his lips, when a dozen of the common thief-takers of Vaud set about the affair in good earnest, and with the best possible intentions to effect their object. In the mean time the sports continued, and, as the day drew on, and the hour for the banquet approached, the good people began to collect once more in the great square to witness the closing scenes, and to be present at the nuptial benediction, which was to be pronounced over Jacques Colis and Christine by a real servitor of the altar, as the last and most important of the ceremonies of that eventful day.

Chapter XVII

Ay, marry; now unmuzzle your wisdom.

Rosalind.

The hour of noon was past, when the stage was a second time filled with the privileged. The multitude was again disposed around the area of the square, and the bailiff and his friends once more occupied the seats of honor in the centre of the long estrade. Procession after procession now began to reappear, for all had made the circuit of the city, and each had repeated its mummeries so often that the actors grew weary of their sports. Still, as the several groups came again into the high presence of the bailiff and the élite not only of their own country but of so many others, pride overcame fatigue, and the songs and dances were renewed with the necessary appearance of good will and zeal. Peter Hofmeister and divers others of the magnates of the canton, were particularly loud in their plaudits on this repetition of the games, for, by a process that will be easily understood, they, who had been revelling and taking their potations in the marquees and booths while the mummers were absent, were more than qualified to supply the deficiencies of the actors by the warmth and exuberance of their own warmed imaginations. The bailiff, in particular, as became, his high office and determined character, was unusually talkative and decided, both as respects the criticisms and encomiums he uttered on the various performances, making as light of his own peculiar qualifications to deal with the subject, as if he were a common hack-reviewer of our own times, who is known to keep in view the quantity rather than the quality of his remarks, and the stipulated price he is to receive per line. Indeed the parallel would hold good in more respects than that of knowledge, for his language was unusually captious and supercilious, his tone authoritative, and his motive the desire to exhibit his own endowments, rather than the wish he affected to manifest of setting forth the excellences of others. His speeches were more frequently than ever directed to the Signor Grimaldi, for whom there had suddenly arisen in his mind a still stronger gusto than that he had so liberally manifested, and which had already drawn so much attention to the deportment of this pleasing but modest stranger. Still he never failed to compel all, within reach of a reasonable exercise of his voice, to listen to his oracles.

"Those that have passed, brother Melchior," said the bailiff, addressing the Baron de Willading in the fraternal style of the bürgerschaft, while his eye was directed to the Genoese, in whom in reality he wished to excite admiration for his readiness in Heathen lore, "are no more than shepherds and shepherdesses of our mountains, and none of your gods and demigods, the former of which are to be known in this ceremony from all others by the fact that they are carried on men's shoulders, and the latter that they ride on asses, or have other conveniences natural to their wants. Ah! here we have the higher orders of the mummers in person --this comely creature is, in reality, Mariette Marron of this country, as strapping a wench as there is in Vaud, and as impudent--but no matter! She is now the Priestess of Flora, and I'll warrant you there is not a horn in all our valleys that will bring a louder echo out of the rocks than this very priestess will raise with her single throat! That yonder on the throne is Flora herself, represented by a comely young woman, the daughter of a warm citizen here in Vévey, and one able to give her all the equipments she bears, without taxing the abbaye a doit. I warrant you that every flower about her was culled from their own garden!"

"Thou treatest the poetry of the ceremonies with so little respect, good Peterchen, that the goddess and her train dwindle into little more than vine-dressers and milk-maids beneath thy tongue."

"Of Heaven's sake, friend Melchior," interrupted the amused Genoese, "do not rob us of the advantage of the worthy bailiff's graphic remarks. Your Heathen may be well enough in his way, but surely he is none the worse for a few notes and illustrations, that would do credit to a Doctor of Padova. I entreat you to continue, learned Peter, that we strangers may lose none of the niceties of the exhibition."

"Thou seest, baron," returned the well-warmed bailiff, with a look of triumph, "a little explanation can never injure a good thing, though it were even the law itself. Ah! yon is Ceres and her company, and a goodly train they appear! These are the harvest-men and harvest-women, who represent the abundance of our country of Vaud, Signor Grimaldi, which, truth to say, is a fat land, and worthy of the allegory. These knaves, with the stools strapped to their nether parts, and carrying tubs, are cowherds, and all the others are more or less concerned with the dairy. Ceres was a personage of importance among the ancients, beyond dispute, as may be seen by the manner in which, she is backed by the landed interest. There is no solid respectability, Herr von Willading, that is not fairly bottomed on broad lands. Ye perceive that the goddess sits on a throne whose ornaments are all taken from the earth; a sheaf of wheat tops the canopy; rich ears of generous grain are her jewels, and her sceptre is the sickle. These are but allegories, Signor Grimaldi, but they are allusions that give birth to wholesome thoughts in the prudent. There is no science that may not catch a hint from our games; politics, religion, or law--'tis all the same for the well-disposed and cunning."

"An ingenious scholar might even find an argument for the bürgerschaft in an allegory that is less clear;" returned the amused Genoese. "But you have overlooked, Signor Bailiff, the instrument that Ceres carries in the other hand, and which is full to overflowing with the fruits of the earth;--that which so much resembles a bullock's horn, I mean."

"That is, out of question, some of the utensils of the ancients; perhaps a milking vessel in use among the gods and goddesses, for your deities of old were no bad housewives, and made a merit of their economy; and Ceres here, as is seen, is not ashamed of a useful occupation. By my faith, but this affair has been gotten up with a very creditable attention to the moral! But our dairy-people are about to give us some of their airs."

Peterchen now put a stop to his classic lore, while the followers of Ceres arranged themselves in order, and began to sing. The contagious and wild melody of the Ranz des Vaches rose in the square, and soon drew the absorbed and delighted attention of all within hearing which, to say the truth, was little less than all who were within the limits of the town, for, the crowd chiming in with the more regular artists, a, sort of musical enthusiasm seized upon all present who came of Vaud and her valleys. The dogmatical, but well-meaning bailiff; though usually jealous of his Bernese origin, and alive on system to the necessity of preserving the superiority of the great canton by all the common observances of dignity and reserve, yielded to the general movement, and shouted with the rest, under favor of a pair of lungs that nature had admirably fitted to sustain the chorus of a mountain song. This condescension in the deputy of Berne was often spoken of afterwards with admiration, the simple-minded and credulous ascribing the exaltation of Peterchen to a generous warmth in their happiness and interests, while the more wary and observant were apt to impute the musical excess to a previous excess of another character, in which the wines of the neighboring côtes were fairly entitled to come in for a full share of the merit. Those who were, nearest the bailiff were secretly much diverted-with his awkward attempts at graciousness, which one fair and witty Vaudoise likened to the antics of one of the celebrated animals that are still fostered in the city which ruled so much of Switzerland, and from whom, indeed, the town and canton are both vulgarly supposed to have derived their common name; for, while the authority of Berne weighed so imperiously and heavily on its subsidiary countries, as is usual in such cases, the people of the latter were much addicted to taking an impotent revenge, by whispering the pleasantest sarcasms they could invent against their masters. Notwithstanding this and many more criticisms on his performance, the bailiff enacted his part in the representation to his own entire satisfaction; and he resumed his seat with a consciousness of having at least merited the applause of the people, for having entered with so much spirit into their games, and with the hope that this act of grace might be the means of causing them to forget some fifty, or a hundred, of his other acts, which certainly had not possessed the same melodious and companionable features.

After this achievement the bailiff was reasonably quiet, until Bacchus and his train again entered the square. At the appearance of the laughing urchin who bestrode the cask, he resumed his dissertations with a confidence that all are apt to feel who are about to treat on a subject with which they have had occasion to be familiar.

"This is the god of good liquor," said Peterchen, always speaking to any who would listen although, by an instinct of respect, he chiefly preferred favoring the Signor Grimaldi with his remarks, "as may plainly be seen by his seat; and these are dancing attendants to show that wine gladdens the heart;--yonder is the press at work, extracting the juices, and that huge cluster is to represent the grapes which the messengers of Joshua brought back from Canaan when sent to spy out the land, a history which I make no doubt you Signore, in Italy, have at your fingers' ends."

Gaetano Grimaldi looked embarrassed, for, although well skilled in the lore of the heathen mythology, his learning as a male papist and a laic was not particularly rich in the story of the Christian faith. At first he supposed that the bailiff had merely blundered in his account of the mythology, but, by taxing his memory a little, he recovered some faint glimpses of the truth, a redemption of his character as a book-man for which he was materially indebted to having seen some celebrated pictures on this very subject, a species of instruction in holy writ that is sufficiently common those who inhabit the Catholic countries of the other hemisphere.

"Thou surely hast not overlooked the history of the gigantic cluster of grapes, Signore" exclaimed Peterchen, astonished at the apparent hesitation of the Italian. "'Tis the most beautiful of all the legends of the holy book. Ha! as I live, there is the ass without his rider;--what has become of the blackguard Antoine Giraud? The rogue has alighted to swallow a fresh draught from some booth, after draining his own skin to the bottom. This comes of neglect; a sober man, or at least one of a harder head, should have been put to the part;--for, look you,'tis a character that need stand at least a gallon, since the rehearsals alone are enough to take a common drinker off his centre."

The tongue of the bailiff ran on in accompaniment, during the time that the followers of Bacchus were going through with their songs and pageants, and when they disappeared, it gained a louder key, like the "rolling river that murmuring flows and flows for ever," rising again on the ear, after the din of any adventitious noise has ceased.

"Now we may expect the pretty bride and her maids," continued Peterchen, winking at his companions, as the ancient gallant is wont to make a parade of his admiration of the fair; "the solemn ceremony is to be pronounced here, before the authorities, as a suitable termination to this happy day. Ah! my good old friend Melchior, neither of us is the man he was, or these skipping hoydens would not go through their pirouettes without some aid from our arms! Now, dispose of yourselves, friends; for this is to be no acting, but a downright marriage, and it is meet that we keep a graver air. How! what means the movement among the officers?"

Peterchen had interrupted himself, for just at that moment the thief-takers entered the square in a body, inclosing in their centre a group, who had the mien of captives too evidently to be mistaken for honest men. The bailiff was peculiarly an executive officer; one of that class who believe that the enactment of a law is a point of far less interest than its due fulfilment. Indeed, so far did he push his favorite principle, that he did not hesitate sometimes to suppose shades of meaning in the different ordinances of the great council that existed only in his own brain, but which were, to do him justice, sufficiently convenient to himself in carrying out the constructions which he saw fit to put on his own duties. The appearance of an affair of justice was unfortunate for the progress of the ceremonies, Peterchen having some such relish for the punishment of rogues, and more especially for such as seemed to be an eternal reproach to the action of the Bernese system by their incorrigible misery and poverty, as an old coachman is proverbially said to retain for the crack of the whip. All his judicial sympathies were not fully awakened, on the present occasion, however: the criminals, though far from belonging to the more lucky of their fellow-creatures, not being quite miserable enough in appearance to awaken all those powers of magisterial reproach and severity that lay dormant in the bailiff's moral temperament, ready, at any time, to vindicate the right of the strong against the innovations of the feeble and unhappy. The reader will at once have anticipated that the prisoners were Maso and his companions, who had been more successful in escaping from their keepers, than fortunate in evading the attempts to secure their persons a second time.

"Who are these that dare affront the ruling powers on this day of general good-will and rejoicing?" sternly demanded the bailiff, when the minions of the law and their captives stood fairly before him. "Do ye not know, knaves, that this is a solemn, almost a religious ceremony at Vévey--for so it would be considered by the ancients at least--and that a crime is doubly a crime when committed either in an honorable presence, on a solemn and dignified occasion, like this, or against the authorities;--this last being always the gravest and greatest of all?"

"We are but indifferent scholars, worshipful bailiff, as you may easily perceive by our outward appearance, and are to be judged leniently," answered Maso. "Our whole offence was a hot but short quarrel touching a dog, in which hands were made to play the part of reason, and which would have done little harm to any but ourselves, had it been the pleasure of the town authorities to have left us to decide the dispute in our own way. As you well say, this is a joyous occasion, and we esteem it hard that we of all Vévey should be shut up on account of so light an affair, and cut off from the merriment of the rest."

"There is reason in this fellow, after all," said Peterchen, in a low voice. "What is a dog more or less to Berne, and a public rejoicing to produce its end should go deep into the community. Let the men go, of God's name! and look to it, that all the dogs be beaten out of the square, that we have no more folly."

"Please you, these are the men that have escaped from the authorities, after knocking down their keeper;" the officer humbly observed.

"How is this! Didst thou not say, fellow, that it was all about a dog?"

"I spoke of the reason of our being shut up. It is true that, wearied with breathing pent air, and a little heated with wine, we left the prison without permission; but we hope this little sally of spirit will be overlooked on account of the extraordinary occasion."

"Rogue, thy plea augments the offence. A crime committed on an extraordinary occasion becomes an extraordinary crime, and requires an extraordinary punishment, which I intend to see inflicted, forthwith. You have insulted the authorities, and that is the unpardonable sin in all communities. Draw nearer, friends, for I love to let my reasons be felt and understood by those who are to be affected by my decisions, and this is a happy moment, to give a short lesson to the Vévaisans--let the bride and bridegroom wait--draw nearer all, that ye may better hear what I have to say."

The crowd pressed more closely around the foot of the stage, and Peterchen, assuming a didactic air, resumed his discourse.

"The object of all authority is to find the means of its own support," continued the bailiff; "for unless it can exist, it must fall to the ground; and you all are sufficiently schooled to know that when a thing becomes of indifferent value, it loses most of its consideration. Thus government is established in order that it may protect itself; since without this power it could not remain a government, and there is not a man existing who is not ready to admit that even a bad government is better than none. But ours is particularly a good government, its greatest care on all occasions being to make itself respected, and he who respects himself is certain to have esteem in the eyes of others. Without this security we should become like the unbridled steed, or the victims of anarchy and confusion, ay, and damnable heresies in religion. Thus you see my friends, your choice lies between the government of Berne, or no government at all; for when only two things exist, by taking one away the number is reduced half, and as the great canton will keep its own share of the institutions, by taking half away, Vaud is left as naked as my hand. Ask yourselves if you have any government but this? You know you have not. Were you quit of Berne, therefore, you clearly would have none at all. Officer, you have a sword at your side, which is a good type of our authority; draw it and hold it up, that all may see it. You perceive, my friends, that the officer hath a sword; but that he hath only one sword. Lay it at thy feet, officer. You perceive, friends, that having but one sword, and laying that sword aside, he no longer hath a sword at all! That weapon represents our authority, which laid aside becomes no authority, leaving us with an unarmed hand."

This happy comparison drew a murmur of applause; the proposition of Peterchen having most of the properties of a popular theory, being deficient in neither a bold assertion, a brief exposition, nor a practical illustration. The latter in particular was long afterwards spoken of in Vaud, as an exposition little short of the well-known judgment of Solomon, who had resorted to the same keen-edged weapon in order to solve a point almost as knotty as this settled by the bailiff. When the approbation had a little subsided, the warmed Peterchen continued his discourse, which possessed the random and generalized logic of most of the dissertations that are uttered in the interests of things as they are, without paying any particular deference to things as they should be.

"What is the use of teaching the multitude to read and write?" he asked. "Had not Franz Kauffman known how to write, could he have imitated his master's hand, and would he have lost his head for mistaking another man's name for his own? a little reflection shows us he would not. Now, as for the other art, could the people read bad books had they never learned the alphabet? If there is a man present who can say to the contrary, I absolve him from his respect, and invite him to speak boldly, for there is no Inquisition in Vaud, but we invite argument. This is a free government, and a fatherly government, and a mild government, as ye all know; but it is not a government that likes reading and writing; reading that leads to the perusal of bad books, and writing that causes false signatures. Fellow-citizens, for we are all equal, with the exception of certain differences that need not now be named, it is a government for your good, and therefore it is a government that likes itself, and whose first duty it is to protect itself and its officers at all hazards, even though it might by accident commit some seeming injustice. Fellow, canst thou read?"

"Indifferently, worshipful bailiff," returned Maso. "There are those who get through a book with less trouble than myself."

"I warrant you, now, he means a good book but, as for a bad one, I'll engage the varlet goes through it like a wild boar! This comes of education among the ignorant! There is no more certain method to corrupt a community, and to rivet it in beastly practices, than to educate the ignorant. The enlightened can bear knowledge, for rich food does not harm the stomach that is used to it, but it is hellebore to the ill-fed. Education is an arm, for knowledge is power, and the ignorant man is but an infant, and to give him knowledge is like putting a loaded blunderbuss into the hands of a child. What can an ignorant man do with knowledge? He is as likely to use it wrong end uppermost as in any other manner. Learning is a ticklish thing; it was said by Festus to have maddened even the wise and experienced Paul and what may we not expect it to do with your downright ignoramus? What is thy name prisoner?"

"Tommaso Santi; sometimes known among my friends as San Tommaso; called by my enemies, Il Maledetto, and by my familiars, Maso."

"Thou hast a formidable number of aliases, the certain sign of a rogue. Thou hast confessed that thou canst read----"

"Nay, Signor Bailiff, I would not be taken to have said----"

"By the faith of Calvin, thou didst confess it, before all this goodly company! Wilt thou deny thine own words, knave, in the very face of justice? Thou canst read--thou hast it in thy countenance, and I would go nigh to swear, too, that thou hast some inkling of the quill, were the truth honestly said. Signor Grimaldi, I know not how you find this affair on the other side of the Alps, but with us, our greatest troubles come from these well-taught knaves, who, picking up knowledge fraudulently, use it with felonious intent, without thought of the wants and rights of the public."

"We have our difficulties, as is the fact wherever man is found with his selfishness and passions Signor Bailiff; but are we not doing an ungallant act towards yonder fair bride, by giving the precedency to men of this cast? Would it not be better to dismiss the modest Christine, happy in Hymen's chains, before we enter more deeply into the question of the manacles of these prisoners?"

To the amazement of all who knew the bailiff's natural obstinacy, which was wont to increase instead of becoming more manageable in his cups, Peterchen assented to this proposition with a complaisance and apparent good-will, that he rarely manifested towards any opinion of which he did not think himself legitimately the father; though, like many others who bear that honorable title, he was sometimes made to yield the privileges of paternity to other men's children. He had shown an unusual deference to the Italian, however, throughout the whole of their short intercourse, and on no occasion was it less equivocal, than in the promptness with which he received the present hint. The prisoners and officers were commanded to stand aside, but so near as to remain beneath his eye, while some of the officials of the abbaye were ordered to give notice to the train, which awaited these arrangements in silent wonder, that it might now approach.

Chapter XVIII

> Go, wiser thou! and in thy scale of sense
> Weigh thy opinion against Providence;
> Call imperfection what thou fanciest such;
> Say, here he gives too little, there too much;
> Destroy all creatures for thy sport or gust,
> And say, if man's unhappy, God's unjust.
>
> Pope.

It is unnecessary to repeat the list of characters that acted the different parts in the train of the village nuptials. All were there at the close of the ceremonies, as they had appeared earlier in the day, and as the last of the legal forms of the marriage was actually to take place in presence of the bailiff, preparatory to the more solemn rites of the church, the throng yielded to its curiosity, breaking through the line of those who were stationed to restrain its inroads, and pressing about the foot of the estrade in the stronger interest which reality is known to possess over fiction. During the day, a thousand new inquiries had been made concerning the bride, whose beauty and mien were altogether so superior to what might have been expected in one who could consent to act the part she did on so public an occasion, and whose modest bearing was in such singular contradiction to her present situation. None knew, however, or, if it were known, no one chose to reveal, her history; and, as curiosity had been so keenly whetted by mystery, the rush of the multitude was merely a proof of the power which expectation, aided by the thousand surmises of rumor, can gain over the minds of the idle.

Whatever might have been the character of the conjectures made at the expense of poor Christine--and they were wanting in neither variety nor malice--most were compelled to agree in commending the diffidence of her air, and the gentle sweetness of her mild and peculiar beauty. Some, indeed, affected to see artifice in the former, which was pronounced to be far too excellent, or too much overdone, for nature. The usual amount of common-place remarks were made, too, on the lucky diversity that was to be found in tastes, and on the happy necessity there existed of all being able to find the means to please themselves. But these were no more than the moral blotches that usually disfigure human commendation. The sentiment and the sympathies of the mass were powerfully and irresistibly enlisted in favor of the unknown maiden--feelings that were very unequivocally manifested as she drew nearer the estrade, walking timidly through a dense lane of bodies, all of which were pressing eagerly forward to get a better view of her person.

The bailiff, under ordinary circumstances, would have taken in dudgeon this violation of the rules prescribed for the government of the multitude; for he was perfectly sincere in his opinions, absurd as so many of them were, and, like many other honest men who defeat the effects they would produce by forced constructions of their principles, he was a little apt to run into excesses of discipline. But in the present instance, he was rather pleased than otherwise to see the throng within the reach of his voice. The occasion was, at best, but semi-official, and he was so far under the influence of the warm liquors of the côtes as to burn with the desire of putting forth still more liberally his flowers of eloquence and his stores of wisdom. He received the inroad, therefore, with an air of perfect good-humor, a manifestation of assent that encouraged still greater innovations on the limits until the space occupied by the principal actors in this closing scene was reduced to the smallest possible size that was at all compatible with their movements and comforts. In this situation of things the ceremonies proceeded.

The gentle flow of hope and happiness which was slowly increasing in the mild bosom of the bride, from the first moment of her appearance in this unusual scene to that in which it was checked by the cries of Pippo, had been gradually lessening under a sense of distrust, and she now entered the square with a secret and mysterious dread at the heart, which her inexperience and great ignorance of life served fearfully to increase. Her imagination magnified the causes of alarm into some prepared and designed insult. Christine, fully aware of the obloquy that pressed upon her race, had only consented to adopt this unusual mode of changing her condition, under a sensitive, apprehension that any other would have necessarily led to the exposure of her origin. This fear, though exaggerated, and indeed causeless, was the result of too much brooding of late over her own situation, and of that morbid sensibility in which the most pure and innocent are, unhappily, the most likely to indulge. The concealment, as has already been explained, was that of her intended husband, who, with the subterfuge of an interested spirit, had hoped to mislead the little circle of his own acquaintances and gratify his cupidity at the cheapest possible rate to himself. But there is a point of self-abasement beyond which the perfect consciousness of right rarely permits even the most timid to proceed. As the bride moved up the lane of human bodies, her eye grew less disturbed and her step firmer,--for the pride of rectitude overcame the ordinary girlish sensibilities of her sex, and made her the steadiest at the very instant that the greater portion of females would have been the most likely to betray their weakness. She had just attained this forced but respectable tranquillity, as the bailiff, signing to the crowd to hush its murmurs and to remain motionless, arose, with a manner that he intended to be dignified, and which passed with the multitude for a very successful experiment in its way, to open the business in hand by a short address. The reader is not to be surprised at the volubility of honest Peterchen, for it was getting to be late in the day, and his frequent libations throughout the ceremonies would have wrought him up to even a much higher flight of eloquence, had the occasion and the company at all suited such a display of his powers.

"We have had a joyous day, my friends" he said; "one whose excellent ceremonies ought to recall to every one of us our dependence on Providence, our frail and sinful dispositions, and particularly our duties to the councils. By the types of plenty and abundance, we see the bounty of nature, which is a gift from Heaven; by the different little failures that have been, perhaps, unavoidably made in some of the nicer parts of the exhibition--and I would here particularly mention the besotted drunkenness of Antoine Giraud, the man who has impudently undertaken to play the part of Silenus, as a fit subject of your attention, for it is full of profit to all hard-drinking knaves-- we may see our own awful imperfections; while, in the order of the whole, and the perfect obedience of the subordinates, do we find a parallel to the beauty of a vigilant and exact police and a well-regulated community. Thus you see, that though the ceremony hath a Heathen exterior, it hath a Christian moral; God grant that we all forget the former, and remember the latter, as best becomes our several characters and our common country. And now, having done with the divinities and their legends--with the exception of that varlet Silenus, whose misconduct, I promise you, is not to be so easily overlooked--we will give some attention to mortal affairs. Marriage is honorable before God and man, and although I have never had leisure to enter into this holy state myself, owing to a variety of reasons, but chiefly from my being wedded, as it were, to the State, to which we all owe quite as much, or even greater duty, than the most faithful wife owes to her husband, I would not have you suppose that I have not a high veneration for matrimony. So far from this, I have looked on no part of this day's ceremonies with more satisfaction than these of the nuptials, which we are now called upon to complete in a manner suitable to the importance of the occasion. Let the bridegroom and the bride stand forth, that all may the better see the happy pair."

At the bidding of the bailiff, Jacques Colis led Christine upon the little stage prepared for their reception, where both were more completely in view of the spectators than they had yet been. The movement, and the agitation consequent on so public an exposure, deepened the bloom on the soft cheeks of the bride, and another and a still less equivocal murmur of applause arose in the multitude. The spectacle of youth, innocence, and feminine loveliness, strongly stirred the sympathies of even the most churlish and rude; and most present began to feel for her fears, and to participate in her hopes.

"This is excellent!" continued the well-pleased Peterchen, who was never half so happy as when he was officially providing for the happiness of others; "it promises a happy *ménage*. A loyal, frugal, industrious, and active groom, with a fair and willing bride, can drive discontent up any man's chimney. That which is to be done next, being legal and binding, must be done with proper gravity and respect. Let the notary advance-- not him who hath so aptly played this character, but the commendable and upright officer who is rightly charged with these respectable functions--and we will listen to the contract. I recommend a decent silence, my friends, for the true laws and real matrimony are at the bottom--a grave affair at the best, and one never to be treated with levity; since a few words pronounced now in haste may be repented of for a whole life hereafter."

Every thing was conducted according to the wishes of the bailiff, and with great decency of form. A true and authorized notary read aloud the marriage-contract, the instrument which contained the civic relations and rights of the parties, and which only waited for the signatures to be complete. This document required, of course, that the real names of the contracting parties, their ages, births, parentage, and all those facts which are necessary to establish their identity, and to secure the rights of succession, should be clearly set forth in a way to render the instrument valid at the most remote period, should there ever arrive a necessity to recur to it in the way of testimony. The most eager attention pervaded the crowd as they listened to these little particulars, and Adelheid trembled in this delicate part of the proceedings, as the suppressed but still audible breathing of Sigismund reached her ear, lest something might occur to give a rude shock to his feelings. But it would seem the notary had his cue. The details touching Christine were so artfully arranged, that while they were perfectly binding in law, they were so dexterously concealed from the observation of the unsuspecting, that no attention was drawn to the point most apprehended by their exposure. Sigismund breathed freer when the notary drew near the end of his task, and Adelheid heard the heavy breath he drew at the close, with the joy one feels at the certainty of having passed an imminent danger.

Christine herself seemed relieved, though hor inexperience in a great degree prevented her from foreseeing all that the greater practice of Sigismund had led him to anticipate.

"This is quite in rule, and naught now remains but to receive the signatures of the respective parties and their friends," resumed the bailiff. "A happy ménage is like a well-ordered state, a foretaste of the joys and peace of Heaven; while a discontented household and a turbulent community may be likened at once to the penalties and the pains of hell! Let the friends of the parties step forth, in readiness to sign when the principals themselves shall have discharged this duty."

A few of the relatives and associates of Jacques Colis moved out of the crowd and placed themselves at the side of the bridegroom, who immediately wrote his own name, like a man impatient to be happy. A pause succeeded, for all were curious to see who claimed affinity to the trembling girl on this the most solemn and important event of her life. An interval of several minutes elapsed, and no one appeared. The respiration of Sigismund became more difficult; he seemed about to choke, and then yielding to a generous impulse, he arose.

"For the love of God!--for thine own sake!--for mine! be not too hasty!" whispered the terrified Adelheid; for she saw the hot glow that almost blazed on his brow.

"I cannot desert poor Christine to the scorn of the world, in a moment like this! If I die of shame, I must go forward and own myself."

The hand of Mademoiselle de Willading was laid upon his arm, and he yielded to this silent but impressive entreaty, for just then he saw that his sister was about to be relieved from her distressing solitude. The throng yielded, and a decent pair, attired in the guise of small but comfortable proprietors, moved doubtingly towards the bride. The eyes of Christine filled with tears, for terror and the apprehension of disgrace yielded suddenly to joy. Those who advanced to support her in that moment of intense trial were her father and mother. The respectable-looking pair moved slowly to the side of their daughter, and, having placed themselves one on each side of her, they first ventured to cast furtive and subdued glances at the multitude.

"It is doubtless painful to the parents to part with so fair and so dutiful a child," resumed the obtuse Peterchen, who rarely saw in any emotion more than its most common-place and vulgar character; "Nature pulls them one way, while the terms of the contract and the progress of our ceremonies pull another. I have often weaknesses of this sort myself, the most sensitive hearts being the most liable to these attacks. But my children are the public, and do riot admit of too much of what I may call the detail of sentiment, else, by the soul of Calvin! were I but an indifferent bailiff for Berne!--Thou art the father of this fair and blushing maiden, and thou her mother?"

"We are these," returned Balthazar mildly.

"Thou art not of Vévey, or its neighborhood, by thy speech?"

"Of the great canton, mein Herr;" for the answer was in German, these contracted districts possessing nearly as many dialects as there are territorial divisions. "We are strangers in Vaud."

"Thou hast not done the worse for marrying thy daughter with a Vévaisan, and, more especially, under the favor of our renowned and liberal Abbaye. I warrant me thy child will be none the poorer for this compliance with the wishes of those who lead our ceremonies!"

"She will not go portionless to the house of her husband," returned the father, coloring with secret pride; for to one to whom the chances of life left so few sources of satisfaction, those that were possessed became doubly dear.

"This is well! A right worthy couple! And I doubt not, a meet companion will your offspring prove. Monsieur le Notaire, call off the names of those good people aloud, that they may sign, at least, with a decent parade."

"It is settled otherwise." hastily answered the functionary of the quill, who was necessarily in the secret of Christine's origin, and who had been well bribed to observe discretion. "It would altogether derange the order and regularity of the proceedings."

"As thou wilt; for I would have nothing illegal, and least of all, nothing disorderly. But o' Heaven's sake! let us get through with our penmanship, for I hear there are symptoms that the meats are likely to be overbaked. Canst thou write, good man?"

"Indifferently, mein Herr: but in a way to make what I will binding before the law."

"Give the quill to the bride, Mr. Notary, and let us protract the happy event no longer."

The bailiff here bent his head aside and whispered to an attendant to hurry towards the kitchens and to look to the affairs of the banquet. Christine took the pen with a trembling hand and pallid cheek, and was about to apply it to the paper, when a sudden cry from the throng diverted the attention of all present to a new matter of interest.

"Who dares thus indecently interrupt this grave scene, and that, too, in so great a presence?" sternly demanded the bailiff.

Pippo, who with the other prisoners had unavoidably been inclosed in the space near the estrade by the pressure of the multitude, staggered more into view, and removing his cap with a well-managed respect, presented himself humbly to the sight of Peterchen.

"It is I, illustrious and excellent governor," returned the wily Neapolitan, who retained just enough of the liquor he had swallowed to render him audacious, without weakening his means of observation. "It is I, Pippo; an artist of humble pretensions, but, I hope, a very honest man and, as I know, a great reverencer of the laws and a true friend to order."

"Let the good man speak up boldly. A man of these principles has a right to be heard. We live in a time of damnable innovations, and of most atrocious attempts to overturn the altar, the state, and the public trusts, and the sentiments of such a man are like dew to the parched grass."

The reader is not to imagine, from the language of the bailiff, that Vaud stood on the eve of any great political commotion, but, as the Government was in itself an usurpation, and founded on the false principle of exclusion, it was quite as usual then, as now, to cry out against the moral throes of violated right, since the same eagerness to possess, the same selfishness in grasping, however unjustly obtained, and the same audacity of assertion with a view to mystify, pervaded the Christian world a century since as exist to-day. The cunning Pippo saw that the bait had taken, and, assuming a still more respectful and loyal mien, he continued:--

"Although a stranger, illustrious governor, I have had great delight in these joyous and excellent ceremonies. Their fame will be spread far and near, and men will talk of little less for the coming year but of Vévey and its festival. But a great scandal hangs over your honorable heads which it is in my power to turn aside, and San Gennaro forbid! that I, a stranger, that hath been well entertained in your town, should hesitate about raising his voice on account of any scruples of modesty. No doubt, great governor, your eccellenza believes that this worthy Vévaisan is about to wive a creditable maiden, whose name could be honorably mentioned with those of the ceremonies and your town, before the proudest company in Europe?"

"What of this, fellow? the girl is fair, and modest enough, at least to the eye, and if thou knowest aught else, whisper thy secret to her husband or her friends, but do not come in this rude manner to disturb our harmony with thy raven throat, just as we are ready to sing an epithalamium in honor of the happy pair. Your excessive particularity is the curse of wedlock, my friends, and I have a great mind to send this knave, in spite of all this profession of order, which is like enough to produce disorder, for a month or two into our Vévey dungeon for his pains."

Pippo was staggered, for, just drunk enough to be audacious, he had not all his faculties at his perfect command, and his usual acumen was a little at fault. Still, accustomed to brave public opinion, and to carry himself through the failures of his exhibitions by heavier drafts on the patience and credulity of his audience, he determined to persevere as the most likely way of extricating himself from the menaced consequences of his indiscretion.

"A thousand pardons, great bailiff;" he answered. "Naught, but a burning desire to do justice to your high honor, and to the reputation of the abbaye's festival, could have led me so far, but--"

"Speak thy mind at once, rogue, and have done with circumlocution."

"I have little to say, Signore, except that the father of this illustrious bride, who is about to honor Vévey by making her nuptials an occasion for all in the city to witness and to favor, is the common headsman of Berne--a wretch who lately came near to prove the destruction of more Christians than the law has condemned, and who is sufficiently out of favor with Heaven to bring the fate of Gomorrah upon your town!"

Pippo tottered to his station among the prisoners with the manner of one who had delivered himself of an important trust, and was instantly lost to view. So rapid and unlooked for had been the interruption, and so vehement the utterance of the Italian while delivering his facts, that, though several present saw their tendency when it was too late, none had sufficient presence of mind to prevent the exposure. A murmur arose in the crowd, which stirred like a vast sheet of fluid on which a passing gust had alighted, and then became fixed and calm. Of all present, the bailiff manifested the least surprise or concern, for to him the last minister of the law was an object, if not precisely of respect, of politic good-will rather than of dishonor.

"What of this!" he answered, in the way of one who had expected a far more important revelation. "What of this, should it be true! Harkee, friend,--art thou, in sooth, the noted Balthazar, he to whose family the canton is indebted for so much fair justice?"

Balthazar saw that his secret was betrayed, and that it were wiser simply to admit the facts, than to have recourse to subterfuge or denial. Nature, moreover, had made him a man with strong and pure propensities for the truth, and he was never without the innate consciousness of the injustice of which he had been made the victim by the unfeeling ordinance of society. Raising his head, he looked around him with firmness, for he too, unhappily, had been accustomed to act in the face of multitudes, and he answered the question of the bailiff, in his usual mild tone of voice, but with composure.

"Herr Bailiff, I am by inheritance the last avenger of the law."

"By my office! I like the title; it is a good one! The last avenger of the law! If rogues will offend, or dissatisfied spirits plot, there must be a hand to put the finishing blow to their evil works, and why not thou as well as another! Harkee, officers, shut me up yonder Italian knave for a week on bread and water, for daring to trifle with the time and good-nature of the public in this impudent manner. And this worthy dame is thy wife, honest Balthazar; and that fair maiden thy child--Hast thou more of so goodly a race?"

"God has blessed me in my offspring, mein Herr."

"Ay; God hath blessed thee!--and a great blessing it should be, as I know by bitter experience--that is, being a bachelor, I understand the misery of being childless--I would say no more. Sign the contract, honest Balthazar, with thy wife and daughter, that we may have an end of this."

The family of the proscribed were about to obey this mandate, when Jacques Colis abruptly threw down the emblems of a bridegroom, tore the contract in fragments, and publicly announced that he had changed his intention, and that he would not wive a headsman's child. The public mind is usually caught by any loud declaration in favor of the ruling prejudice, and, after the first brief pause of surprise was past, the determination of the groom was received with a shout of applause that was immediately followed by general, coarse, and deriding laughter. The throng pressed upon the keepers of the limits in a still denser mass, opposing an impenetrable wall of human bodies to the passage of any in either direction, and a dead stillness succeeded, as if all present breathlessly awaited the result of the singular scene.

So unexpected and sudden was the purpose of the groom, that they who were most affected by it, did not, at first, fully comprehend the extent of the disgrace that was so publicly heaped upon them The innocent and unpractised Christine stood resembling the cold statue of a vestal, with the pen raised ready to affix her as yet untarnished name to the contract, in an attitude of suspense, while her wondering look followed the agitation of the multitude, as the startled bird, before it takes wing, regards a movement among the leaves of the bush. But there was no escape from the truth. Conviction of its humiliating nature came too soon, and, by the time the calm of intense curiosity had succeeded to the momentary excitement of the spectators, she was standing an exquisite but painful picture of wounded feminine feeling and of maiden shame. Her parents, too, were stupified by the suddenness of the unexpected shock, and it was longer before their faculties recovered the tone proper to meet an insult so unprovoked and gross.

"This is unusual;" drily remarked the bailiff, who was the first to break the long and painful silence.

"It is brutal!" warmly interposed the Signor Grimaldi. "Unless there has been deception practised on the bridegroom, it is utterly without excuse."

"Your experience, Signore, has readily suggested the true points in a very knotty case, and I shall proceed without delay to look into its merits."

Sigismund resumed his seat, his hand releasing the sword-hilt that it had spontaneously grasped when he heard this declaration of the bailiff's intentions.

"For the sake of thy poor sister, forbear!" whispered the terrified Adelheid. "All will ye be well--all must be well--it is impossible that one so sweet and innocent should long remain with her honor unavenged!"

The young man smiled frightfully, at least so it seemed to his companion: but he maintained the appearance of composure. In the mean time Peterchen, having secretly dispatched another messenger to the cooks, turned his serious attention to the difficulty that had just arisen.

"I have long been intrusted by the council with honorable duties," he said, "but never, before to-day, have I been required to decide upon a domestic misunderstanding, before the parties were actually wedded. This is a grave interruption of the ceremonies of the abbaye, as well as a slight upon the notary and the spectators, and needs be well looked to. Dost thou really persist in putting this unusual termination to a marriage-ceremony, Herr Bridegroom?"

Jacques Colis had lost a little of the violent impulse which led him to the precipitate and inconsiderate act of destroying an instrument he had legally executed; but his outbreaking of feeling was followed by a sullen and fixed resolution to persevere in the refusal at every hazard to himself.

"I will not wive the daughter of a man hunted of society, and avoided by all;" he doggedly answered.

"No doubt the respectability of the parent is the next thing to a good dowry, in the choice of a wife," returned the bailiff, "but one of thy years has not come hither, without having first inquired into the parentage of her thou wert about to wed?"

"It was sworn to me that the secret should be kept. The girl is well endowed, and a promise was solemnly made that her parentage should never be known. The family of Colis is esteemed in Vaud, and I would not have it said that the blood of the headsman of the canton hath mixed in a stream as fair as ours."

"And yet thou wert not unwilling, so long as the circumstance was unknown? Thy objection is less to the fact, than to its public exposure."

"Without the aid of parchments and tongues, Monsieur le Bailli, we should all be equal in birth. Ask the noble Baron de Willading, who is seated there at your side, why he is better than another. He will tell you that he is come of an ancient and honorable line; but had he been taken from his castle in infancy, and concealed under a feigned name, and kept from men's knowledge as being that he is, who would think of him for the deeds of his ancestors? As the Sire de Willading would, in such a case, have lost in the world's esteem, so did Christine gain; but as opinion would return to the baron, when the truth should be published, so does it desert Balthazar's daughter, when she is known to be a headsman's child. I would have married the maiden as she was, but, your pardon, Monsieur le Bailli, if I say, I will not wive her as she is."

A murmur of approbation followed this plausible and ready apology, for, when antipathies are active and bitter, men are easily satisfied with a doubtful morality and a weak argument.

"This honest youth hath some reason in him," observed the puzzled bailiff, shaking his head. "I would he had been less expert in disputation, or that the secret had been better kept! It is apparent as the sun in the heavens, friend Melchior, that hadst thou not been known as thy father's child, thou wouldst not have succeeded to thy castle and lands--nay, by St Luke! not even to the rights of the bürgerschaft."

"In Genoa we are used to hear both parties," gravely rejoined the Signor Grimaldi, "that we may first make sure that we touch the true merits of the case. Were another to claim the Signor de Willading's honors and name, thou wouldst scarce grant his suit, without questioning our friend here, touching his own rights to the same."

"Better and better! This is justice, while that which fell from the bridegroom was only argument. Harkee, Balthazar, and thou good woman, his wife--and thou too, pretty Christine--what have ye all to answer to the reasonable plea of Jacques Colis?"

Balthazar, who, by the nature of his office, and by his general masculine duties, had been so much accustomed to meet with harsh instances of the public hatred, soon recovered his usual calm exterior, even though he felt a father's pang and a father's just resentment at witnessing this open injury to one so gentle and deserving as his child. But the blow had been far heavier on Marguerite, the faithful and long-continued sharer of his fortunes. The wife of Balthazar was past the prime of her days, but she still retained the presence, and some of the personal beauty, which had rendered her, in youth, a woman of extraordinary mien and carriage. When the words which announced the slight to her daughter first fell on her ears, she paled to the hue of the dead. For several minutes she stood looking more like one that had taken a final departure from the interests and emotions of life, than one that, in truth, was a prey to one of the strongest passions the human breast can ever entertain, that of wounded maternal affection. Then the blood stole slowly to her temples, and, by the time the bailiff put his question, her entire face was glowing under a tumult of feeling that threatened to defeat its own wishes, by depriving her of the power of speech.

"Thou canst answer him, Balthazar," she said huskily, motioning for her husband to arouse his faculties; "thou art used to these multitudes and to their scorn. Thou art a man, and canst do us justice."

"Herr Bailiff," said the headsman, who seldom lost the mild deportment that characterized his manner, "there is much truth in what Jacques hath urged, but all present may have seen that the fault did not come of us, but of yonder heartless vagabond. The wretch sought my life on the lake, in our late unfortunate passage hither; and, not content with wishing to rob my children of their father, he comes now to injure me still more cruelly. I was born to the office I hold, as you well know, Herr Hofmeister, or it would never have been sought by me; but what the law wills, men insist upon as right. This girl can never be called upon to strike a head from its shoulders, and, knowing from childhood up the scorn that awaits all who come of my race, I sought the means of releasing her, at least, from some part of the curse that hath descended on us."

"I know not if this were legal!" interrupted the bailiff, quickly. "What is your opinion, Her von Willading? Can any in Berne escape their heritable duties, any more than hereditary privileges can be assumed? This is a grave question; innovation leads to innovation, and our venerable laws and our sacred usages must be preserved, if we would avert the curse of change!"

"Balthazar hath well observed that a female cannot exercise the executioner's office."

"True, but a female may bring forth them that can. This is a cunning question for the doctors-in-law, and it must be examined; of all damnable offences, Heaven keep me from that of a wish for change. If change is ever to follow, why establish? Change is the unpardonable sin in politics, Signor Grimaldi; since that which is often changed becomes valueless in time, even if it be coin.

"The mother hath something she would utter, said the Genoese, whose quick but observant eye had been watching the workings of the countenances of the repudiated family, while the bailiff was digressing in his usual prolix manner on things in general, and who detected the throes of feeling which heaved the bosom of the respectable Marguerite, in a way to announce a speedy birth to her thoughts.

"Hast thou aught to urge, good woman?" demanded Peterchen, who was well enough disposed to hear both sides in all cases of controversy, unless they happened to touch the supremacy of the great canton. "To speak the truth, the reasons of Jacques Colis are plausible and witty, and are likely to weigh heavy against thee."

The color slowly disappeared from the brow of the mother, and she turned such a look of fondness and protection on her child, as spoke a complete condensation of all her feelings in the engrossing, sentiment of a mother's love.

"Have I aught to urge!" slowly repeated Marguerite, looking steadily about her at the curious and unfeeling crowd which, bent on the indulgence of its appetite for novelty, and excited by its prejudices, still pressed upon the halberds of the officers--"Has a mother aught to say in defence of her injured and insulted child! Why hast thou not also asked, Herr Hofmeister, if I am human? We come of proscribed races, I know, Balthazar and I, but like thee, proud bailiff, and the privileged at thy side, we come too of God! The judgment and power of men have crushed us from the beginning, and we are used to the world's scorn and to the world's injustice!"

"Say not so, good woman, for no more is required than the law sanctions. Thou art now talking against thine own interests, and I interrupt thee in pure mercy. 'Twould be scandalous in me to sit here and listen to one that hath bespattered the law with an evil tongue."

"I know naught of the subtleties of thy laws, but well do I know their cruelty and wrongs, as respects me and mine! All others come into the world with hope, but we have been crushed from the beginning. That surely cannot be just which destroys hope. Even the sinner need not despair, through the mercy of the Son of God! but we, that have come into the world under thy laws, have little before us in life but shame and the scorn of men!"

"Nay, thou quite mistakest the matter, dame; these privileges were first bestowed on thy families in reward for good services, I make no doubt, and it was long accounted profitable to be of this office."

"I do not say that in a darker age, when oppression stalked over the land, and the best were barbarous as the worst to-day, some of those of whom we are born may not have been fierce and cruel enough to take upon themselves this office with good will; but I deny that any short of Him who holds the universe in his hand, and who controls an endless future to compensate for the evils of the present time, has the power to say to the son, that he shall be the heritor of the father's wrongs!"

"How! dost question the doctrine of descents? We shall next hear thee dispute the rights of the bürgerschaft!"

"I know nothing, Herr Bailiff, of the nice distinctions of your rights in the city, and wish to utter naught for or against. But an entire life of contumely and bitterness is apt to become a life of thoughtfulness and care; and I see sufficient difference between the preservation of privileges fairly earned, though even these may and do bring with them abuses hard to be borne, and the unmerited oppression of the offspring for the ancestors' faults. There is little of that justice which savors of Heaven in this, and the time will come when a fearful return will be made for wrongs so sore!"

"Concern for thy pretty daughter, good Marguerite, causes thee to speak strongly."

"Is not the daughter of a headsman and a headsman's wife their offspring, as much as the fair maiden who sits near thee is the child of the noble at her side? Am I to love her less, that she is despised by a cruel world? Had I not the same suffering at the birth, the same joy in the infant smile, the same hope in the childish promise, and the same trembling for her fate when I consented to trust her happiness to another, as she that bore that more fortunate but not fairer maiden hath had in her? Hath God created two natures--two yearnings for the mother--two longings for our children's weal--those of the rich and honored, and those of the crushed and despised?"

"Go to, good Marguerite; thou puttest the matter altogether in a manner that is unusual. Are our reverenced usages nothing--our solemn edicts --our city's rule--and our resolution to govern and that fairly and with effect?"

"I fear that these are stronger than the right, and likely to endure when the tears of the oppressed are exhausted, when they and their fates shall be forgotten!"

"Thy child is fair and modest," observed the Signor Grimaldi, "and will yet find a youth who will more than atone for this injury. He that has rejected her was not worthy of her faith."

Marguerite turned her look, which had been glowing with awakened feeling, on her pale and still motionless daughter. The expression of her softened, and she folded her child to her bosom, as the dove shelters its young. All her aroused feelings appeared to dissolve in the sentiment of love.

"My child is fair, Herr Peter;" she continued, without adverting to the interruption; "but better than fair, she is good! Christine is gentle and dutiful, and not for a world would she bruise the spirit of another as hers has been this day bruised. Humbled as we are, and despised of men, bailiff, we have our thoughts, and our wishes, and our hopes, and memory, and all the other feelings of those that are more fortunate; and when I have racked my brain to reason on the justice of a fate which has condemned all of my race to have little other communion with their kind but that of blood, and when bitterness has swollen at my heart, ay, near to bursting, and I have been ready to curse Providence and die, this mild, affectionate girl hath been near to quench the fire that consumed me, and to tighten the cords of life, until her love and innocence have left me willing to live even under a heavier load than this I bear. Thou art of an honored race, bailiff, and canst little understand most of our suffering; but thou art a man, and shouldst know what it is to be wounded through another, and that one who is dearer to thee than thine own flesh."

"Thy words are strong, good Marguerite," again interrupted the bailiff, who felt an uneasiness, of which he would very gladly be rid. "Himmel! Who can like any thing better than his own flesh? Besides, thou shouldst remember that I am a bachelor, and bachelors are apt, naturally, to feel more for their own flesh than for that of others. Stand aside, and let the procession pass, that we may go to the banquet, which waits. If Jacques Colis will none of thy girl, I hove not the power to make him. Double the dowry, good woman, and thou shalt have a choice of husbands, in spite of the axe and the sword that are in thy escutcheon. Let the halberdiers make way for those honest people there who, at least, are functionaries of the law, and are to be protected as well as ourselves."

The crowd obeyed, yielding readily to the advance of the officers, and, in a few minutes, the useless attendants of the village nuptials, and the train of Hymen, slunk away, sensible of the ridicule that, in a double degree, attaches itself to folly when it fails of effecting even its own absurdities.

Chapter XIX

>The weeping blood in woman's breast
>Was never known to thee;
>Nor the balm that drops on wounds of woe
>From woman's pitying e'e.
>
>Burns.

A large portion of the curious followed the disconcerted mummers from the square, while others hastened to break their fasts at the several places selected for this important feature in the business of the day. Most of those who had been on the estrade now left it, and, in a few minutes, the living carpet of heads around the little area in front of the bailiff was reduced to a few hundreds of those whose better feelings were stronger than their self indulgence. Perhaps this distribution of the multitude is about in the proportion that is usually found in those cases in which selfishness draws in one direction, while feeling or sympathy with the wronged pulls in another, among all masses of human beings that are congregated as spectators of some general and indifferent exhibition of interests in which they have no near personal concern.

The bailiff and his immediate friends, the prisoners, and the family of the headsman, with a sufficient number of the guards, were among those who remained. The bustling Peterchen had lost some of his desire to take his place at the banquet, in the difficulties of the question which had arisen, and in the certainty that nothing material, in the way of gastronomy, would be attempted until he appeared. We should do injustice to his heart, did we not add, also, that he had troublesome qualms of conscience, which intuitively admonished him that the world had dealt hardly with the family of Balthazar. There remained the party of Maso, too, to dispose of, and his character of an upright as well as of a firm magistrate to maintain. As the crowd diminished, however, he and those near him descended from their high places, and mixed with the few who occupied the still guarded area in front of the stage.

Balthazar had not stirred from his riveted posture near the table of the notary, for he shrunk from encountering, in the company of his wife and daughter, the insults to which he should be exposed now his character was known, by mingling with the crowd, and he waited for a favorable moment to withdraw unseen. Marguerite still stood folding Christine to her bosom, as if jealous of farther injury to her beloved. The recreant bridegroom had taken the earliest opportunity to disappear, and was seen no more in Vevey during the remainder of the revels.

Peterchen cast a hurried glance at this group, as his foot reached the ground, and then turning towards the thief-takers he made a sign for them to advance with their prisoners.

"Thy evil tongue has balked one of the most engaging rites of this day's festival, knave;" observed the bailiff, addressing Pippo with a certain magisterial reproof in his voice. "I should do well to send thee to Berne, to serve a month among those who sweep the city streets, as a punishment for thy raven throat. What, in the name of all thy Roman saints and idols, hadst thou against the happiness of these honest people, that thou must come, in this unseemly manner, to destroy it?"

"Naught but the love of truth, eccellenza, and a just horror of the man of blood."

"That thou and all like thee should have a horror of the ministers of the law, I can understand; and it is more than probable that thy dislike will extend to me, for I am about to pronounce a just judgment on thee and thy fellows for disturbing the harmony of the day, and especially for having been guilty of the enormous crime of an outrage on our agents."

"Couldst thou grant me a moment's leave?" asked the Genoese in his ear.

"An hour, noble Gaetano, if thou wilt."

The two then conversed apart, for a minute or more. During the brief dialogue, the Signor Grimaldi occasionally looked at the quiet and apparently contrite Maso, and stretched his arm towards the Leman, in a way to give the observers an inkling of his subject. The countenance of the Herr Hofmeister changed from official sternness to an expression of decent concern as he listened, and ere long it took a decidedly forgiving laxity of muscle. When the other had done speaking, he bowed a ready assent to what he had just heard, and returned to the prisoners.

"As I have just observed," he resumed, "it is my duty now to pronounce finally on these men and their conduct. Firstly they are strangers, and as such are not only ignorant of our laws, but entitled to our hospitality; next, they have been punished sufficiently for the original offence, by being abridged of the day's sports; and as to the crime committed against ourselves, in the person of our agents, it is freely forgiven, for forgiveness is a generous quality, and becomes a paternal form of rule. Depart therefore, of God's name! all of ye to a man, and remember henceforth to be discreet. Signore, and you, Herr Baron, shall we to the banquet?"

The two old friends had already moved onward, in close and earnest discourse, and the bailiff was obliged to seek out another companion. None offered, at the moment, but Sigismund, who had stood, since quitting the stage, in an attitude of complete indecision and helplessness, notwithstanding his great physical energy and his usual moral readiness to act. Taking the arm of the young soldier, with the disregard of ceremony that denotes a sense of condescension, the bailiff drew him away from the spot, heedless himself of the other's reluctance, and without observing that, in consequence of the general desertion, for few were disposed to indulge their compassion unless it were in company with the honored and noble, Adelheid was left absolutely alone with the family of Balthazar.

"This office of a headsman, Herr Sigismund," commenced the unobservant Peterchen, too full of his own opinions, and much too sensible of his right to be delivered of them in the presence of his junior and inferior, to note the youth's trouble, "is at the best but a disgusting affair; though we, of station and authority, are obliged prudently to appear to deem it otherwise before the people, in our own interest. Thou hast had occasion to remark often, in the discipline of thy military followers, that a false coloring must be put upon things, lest they who are very necessary to the state should not think the state quite so necessary to them. What is thy opinion, Captain Sigismund, as a man who has yet his hopes and his views on the softer sex, of this act of Jacques Colis?--Is it conduct to be approved of, or to be condemned?"

"I deem him a heartless, mercenary, miscreant!"

The suppressed energy with which these unexpected words were uttered caused the bailiff to stop and to look up in his companion's face, as if to ask its reason. But there all was already calm, for the young man had too long been accustomed to drill its expression, when the sensitive sore of his origin was probed, as so frequently happened, to permit the momentary weakness long to maintain its ascendency.

"Ay, this is the opinion of thy years;" resumed Peterchen. "Thou art at a time of life when we esteem a pretty face and a mellow eye of more account even than gold. But we put on our interested spectacles after thirty, and seldom see any thing very admirable, that is not at the same time very lucrative. Here is Melchior de Willading's daughter, now, a woman to set a city in a blaze, for she hath wit, and lands, and beauty, besides good blood;--what, for instance, is thy opinion of her merit?"

"That she is deserving of all the happiness that every human excellence ought to confer!"

"Hum--thou art nearer to thirty than I had thought thee, Herr Sigismund! But touching this Balthazar, thou art not to believe, on account of the few words of grace which fell from me, that my aversion for the wretch is less than thine, or than that of any other honest man; but it would be unseemly and unwise in a bailiff to desert the last minister of the law's decrees in the face of the public. There are feelings and sentiments that are natural to us all, and among them are to be classed respect and honor for the well and nobly born," (the discourse was in German,) "and hatred and contempt for those who are condemned of men. These are feelings which belong to human nature itself, and God forbid that I, a man already past the age of romance, should really entertain any sentiments that are not strictly human."

"Do they not rather belong to abuses--to our prejudices?"

"The difference is not material, in a practical view, young man. That which is fairly bred into the mind, by discipline and habit, gets to be stronger than instinct, or even than one of the senses. Let there be an unseemly sight, or a foul smell near thee, and thou hast only to turn thy eyes, or hold thy nose, to be rid of it; but I could never find the means to lessen a prejudice that was once fairly seated in the mind. Thou mayest look whither thou wilt, and shut out the unsavory odors of the imagination by all the means thou canst invent, but if a man is, in truth, condemned of opinion, he might as well make his appeal to God at once for justice, as to any mercy he is likely to receive from men. This much have I learned in my experience as a public functionary."

"I should hope that these are not the legal dogmas of our ancient canton," returned the youth, conquering his feelings, though it cost him a severe effort.

"As far from it as Basle is from Coire. We hold no such discreditable doctrines. I challenge the world to show a state that possesses a fairer set of maxims than ourselves, and we even endeavor to make our practice chime in with our opinions, whenever it can be done in safety. No in these particulars, Berne is a paragon of a community, and as rarely says one thing and does another, as any government you shall see. What I now tell thee, young man, is said to thee in the familiarity of a fête, as thou know'st, in which there have been some fooleries, to open confidence and to loosen the tongue. We openly and loudly profess great truth and equality before the law saving the city's rights, and take holy, heavenly, upright justice for our guide in all matters of theory. Himmel! If thou would'st have thy affair decided on principle, go before the councils, or the magistracy of the canton, and thou shalt hear such wisdom, and witness such keen-sightedness into chicanery, as would have honored Solomon himself!"

"And notwithstanding this, prejudice is a general master."

"How canst thou have it otherwise? Is not a man a man? Will he not lean as he has been weighed upon?--does not the tree grow in the way the twig is bent? No, while I adore justice, Herr Sigismund, as becomes a bailiff, I confess to both prejudice and partiality, mentally considered. Now, yonder maiden, the pretty Christine, lost some of her grace in my eyes, as no doubt she did in thine, when the truth came to be known that she was Balthazar's child. The girl is fair and modest and winning in her way; but there is something--I cannot tell thee what--but a certain damnable something--a taint--a color--a hue--a--a--that showed her origin the instant I heard who was her parent--was it not so with thee?"

"When her origin was proved, but not previously."

"Ay, of a certainty; I mean not otherwise. But a thing is not seen any the worse because it is seen thoroughly, although it may be seen falsely when there are false covers to conceal its ugliness. Particularity is necessary to philosophy. Ignorance is a mask to conceal the little details that are necessary to knowledge. Your Moor might pass for a Christian in a mask, but strip him of his covering and the true shade of the skin is seen. Didst thou not observe, for instance, in all that touches feminine grace and perfection, the manifest difference between the daughter of Melchior de Willading and the daughter of this Balthazar?"

"There was the difference between a maiden of most honored and happy extraction and a maiden most miserably condemned!"

"Nay, the Demoiselle de Willading is the fairer."

"Nature has certainly been most bountiful to the heiress of Willading, Herr Bailiff, who is scarcely less attractive for her female grace and goodness, than she is fortunate in the accidents of birth and condition."

"I knew thou couldst not, in secret, be of a different mind from the rest of men!" exclaimed Peterchen in triumph, for he, took the warmth of his companion's manner to be a reluctant and half-concealed assent to his own proposition. Here the discourse ended: for, the earnest conference between Melchior and the Signor Grimaldi having terminated, the bailiff hastened to join his more important guests, and Sigismund was released from an examination that had harrowed every feeling of his soul, while he even despised the besotted loquacity of the man who had been the instrument of his torture.

The separation of Adelheid from her father was anticipated and previously provided for; since the men were expected to resort to the banquet at this hour. She had continued near Christine and her mother, therefore, without attracting any unusual attention to her movements, even in those who were the objects of her sympathy, a feeling that was so natural in one of her years and sex. A male attendant, in the livery of her father's house remained near her person, a protector who certain to insure not only her safety in the thronged streets of the town, but to exact from those whose faculties were beginning to yield to the excesses of the occasion the testimonials of respect that were due to her station. It was under these circumstances, then, that the more honored, and, to the eyes of the uninstructed, the happier of these maidens, approached the other, when curiosity was so far appeased as to have left the family of Balthazar nearly alone in the centre of the square.

"Is there no friendly roof near, to which thou canst withdraw?" asked the heiress of Willading of the mother of the pallid and scarcely conscious Christine; "thou wouldst do better to seek some shelter and privacy for thy unoffending and much injured child. If any that belong to me can be of service, I pray that thou wilt command as freely as if they were followers of thine own."

Marguerite had never before spoken with a female of a rank superior to the ordinary classes. The ample means of both her father's and her husband's family had furnished all that was necessary to the improvement of the mind of one in her station, and perhaps she had been the gainer, in mere deportment, by having been greatly excluded, by their prejudices, from association with females of her own condition. As is often seen among those who have the thoughts without the conventional usages of a better caste in life, she was slightly tinctured with an exhibition of what might be termed an exaggerated manner, while at the same time it was perfectly free from vulgarity or coarseness. The gentle accents of Adelheid fell on her ear soothingly, and she gazed long and earnestly at the beautiful speaker without a reply.

"Who and what art thou that canst think a headman's child may receive an insult that is unmerited, and who offerest the service of thy menials, as if the very vassal would not refuse his master's bidding in our behalf!"

"I am Adelheid de Willading, the daughter of the baron of that name, and one much disposed to temper this cruel blow to the feelings of poor Christine. Suffer that my people seek the means to convey thy child to some other place!"

Marguerite folded her daughter still closer to her bosom, passing a hand across her brow, as if to recall some half-obscured idea.

"I have heard of thee, lady.--'Tis said that thou art kind to the wronged, and of excellent dispositions towards the unhappy--that thy father's castle is an honored and hospitable abode, which those who enter rarely love to quit. But hast thou well weighed the consequences of this liberality towards a race, that is and has been proscribed of men, from generation to generation--from him who first lent himself to his bloody office, with a cruel heart and a greedy desire for gold, to him whose courage is scarcely equal to the disgusting duty? Hast thou bethought thee of this, or hast thou yielded, heedlessly, to a sudden and youthful impulse?"

"Of all this have I thought," said Adelheid, eagerly; "whatever may be the injustice of others, thou hast none to fear from me."

Marguerite yielded the form of her child to the support of her father's arm, and drew nearer, with a gaze of earnest and pleased interest, to the blushing but still composed Adelheid. She took the hand of the latter, and, with a look of recognition and intelligence, said slowly, as if communing with herself, rather than speaking to another----

"This is getting to be intelligible!" she murmured; "there is still gratitude and creditable feeling in the world. I can understand why we are not revolting to this fair being: she has a sense of justice that is stronger than her prejudices. We have done her service, and she is not ashamed of the source whence it has come!"

The heart of Adelheid throbbed quick and violently; and, for a moment, she doubted her ability to command her feelings. But the pleasing conviction that Sigismund had been honorable and delicate, even in his most sacred and confidential communications with his own mother, came to relieve her, and to make her momentarily happy; since nothing is so painful to the pure mind, as to think those they love have acted unworthily; or nothing so grateful, as the assurance that they merit the esteem we have been induced liberally and confidingly to bestow.

"You do me no more than justice," returned the pleased listener of this flattering and seemingly involuntary opinion--"we are indeed--indeed we are truly grateful; but had we not reason for the sacred obligations of gratitude, I think we could still be just. Will you not now consent that my people should aid you?"

"This is not necessary, lady. Send away thy followers, for their presence will draw unpleasant observations on our movements. The town is now occupied with feasts, and, as we have not blindly overlooked the necessity of a retreat for the hunted and persecuted, we will take the opportunity to withdraw unseen. As for thyself--"

"I would be near this innocent at a moment so trying,"--added Adelheid earnestly, and with that visible sympathy which rarely fails to meet an echo.

"Heaven bless thee! Heaven bless thee, sweet girl! And Heaven will bless thee, for few wrongs go unrequited in this life, and little good without its reward. Send thy followers away, or if thy habits require their watchfulness, let them be near unseen, whilst thou wateriest our movements; and when the eyes of all are turned on their own pleasures, thou canst follow. Heaven bless thee--ay, and Heaven will!"

Marguerite then led her daughter towards one of the least frequented streets. She was accompanied by the silent Balthazar, and closely watched by one of the menials of Adelheid. When fairly housed, the domestic returned to show the spot to his mistress, who had appeared to occupy herself with the hundred silly devices that were invented to amuse the multitude. Dismissing her attendants, with an order to remain at hand, however, the heiress of Willading soon found means to enter the humble abode in which the proscribed family had taken refuge, and, as she was expected, she was soon introduced into the chamber where Christine and her mother had taken refuge.

The sympathy of the young and tender Adelheid was precious to one of the character of Christine. They wept together, for the weakness of her sex prevailed over the pride of the former, when she found herself unrestrained by the observation of the world, and she gave way to the torrent of feeling that broke through its bounds, in spite of her endeavors to control it. Marguerite was the only spectator of this silent but intelligible communion between these two young and pure spirits, and her soul was shaken by the unlooked-for commiseration of one so honored, and who was usually esteemed so happy.

"Thou hast the consciousness of our wrongs," she said, when the first burst of emotion had a little subsided. "Thou canst then believe that a headsman's child is like the offspring of another and is not to be hunted of men like the young of a wolf."

"Mother, this is the Baron de Willading's heiress," said Christine: "would she come here, did she not pity us?"

"Yes, she can pity us--and yet I find it hard even to be pitied! Sigismund has told us of her goodness, and she may, in truth, feel for the wretched!"

The allusion to her son caused the temples of Adelheid to burn like fire, while there was a chill, resembling that of death, at her heart. The first arose from the quick and uncontrollable alarm of female sensitiveness; the last was owing to the shock inseparable from being presented with this vivid, palpable picture of Sigismund's close affinity with the family of an executioner. She could have better borne it, had Marguerite spoken of her son less familiarly, or with more of that feigned ignorance of each other, which, without stopping to scan its fitness, she had been led to think existed between the young man and his family.

"Mother!" exclaimed Christine reproachfully, and in surprise, as if a great indiscretion had been thoughtlessly committed.

"It matters not, child; it matters not. I saw by the kindling eye of Sigismund to-day, that our secret will not much longer be kept. The noble boy must show more energy than those who have gone before him; he must quit for ever a country in which he was condemned, even before he was born."

"I shall not deny that your connexion with Monsieur Sigismund is known to me," said Adelheid, summoning all her resolution to make an avowal which put her at once into the confidence of Balthazar's family. "You are acquainted with the heavy debt of gratitude we owe your son, and it will explain the nature of the interest I now feel in your wrongs."

The keen eye of Marguerite studied the crimsoned features of Adelheid till forgetfulness got the better of discretion. The search was anxious, rather than triumphant, the feeling most dreaded by its subject; and, when her eyes were withdrawn, the mother of the youth became thoughtful and pensive. This expressive communion produced a deep and embarrassing silence, which each would gladly have broken, had they not both been irresistibly tongue-tied by the rapidity and intensity of their thoughts.

"We know that Sigismund hath been of service to thee," observed Marguerite, who always addressed her gay companion with the familiarity that belonged to her greater age, rather than with the respect which Adelheid had been accustomed to receive from those who were of a rank inferior to her own. "The brave boy hath spoken of it, though he hath spoken of it modestly."

"He had every right to do himself justice in his communications with those of his own family. Without his aid, my father would have been childless; and without his brave support, the child fatherless. Twice has he stood between us and death."

"I have heard of this," returned Marguerite, again fastening her penetrating eye on the tell-tale features of Adelheid, which never failed to brighten and glow, whenever there was allusion to the courage and self-devotion of him she secretly loved, "As to what thou say'st of the intimacy of our poor boy with those of his blood, cruel circumstances stand between us and our wishes. If Sigismund has told thee of whom he comes he has also most probably told thee of the manner in which he passes, in the world, for that which he is not."

"I believe he has not withheld any thing that he knew, and which it was proper to communicate to me;" answered Adelheid, dropping her eyes before the attentive, expectant look of Marguerite. "He has spoken freely, and--"

"Thou wouldst have said--"

"Honorably, and as became a soldier;" continued Adelheid, firmly.

"He has done well! This lightens my heart of one burthen at least. No; God has destined us to this fate, and it would have grieved me that a son of mine should have failed of principle in an affair, of all others, in which it is most wanted. You look amazed, lady!"

"These sentiments, in one so situated, surprise as much as they delight me! If any thing could excuse some looseness in the manner of regarding the usual ties of life, it would surely be to find oneself so placed, by no misconduct of our own, as to be a but to the world's dislike and injustice; and yet here, where there was reason to expect some resentment against fortune, I meet with sentiments that would honor a throne!"

"Thou thinkest as one more accustomed to consider thy fellow-creatures through the means of what men fancy, than through things as they are. This is the picture of youth, and inexperience, and innocence; but it is not the picture of life. 'Tis misfortune, and not prosperity that chasteneth, by proving our insufficiency for true happiness, and by leading the soul to depend on a power greater than any that is to be found on earth. We fall before the temptation of happiness, when we rise in adversity. If thou thinkest, innocent one, that noble and just sentiments belong to the fortunate, thou trustest to a false guide. There are evils which flesh cannot endure, it is true; but, removed from these overwhelming wants, we are strongest in the right, when least tempted by vanity and ambition. More starving beggars abstain from stealing the crust they crave, than pampered gluttons deny themselves the luxury that kills them. They that live under the rod, see and dread the hand that holds it; they who riot in earth's glories, come at last to think they deserve the short-lived distinctions they enjoy. When thou goest down into the depths of misery, thou hast naught to fear except the anger of God! It is when raised above others, that thou shouldst tremble most for thine own safety."

"This is not the manner in which the world is used to reason."

"Because the world is governed by those whose interest it is to pervert truth to their own objects, and not by those whose duties run hand-in-hand with the right. But we will say no more of this, lady; here is one that feels too acutely just now to admit truth to be too freely spoken."

"Dost, feel thyself better, and more able to listen to thy friends, dear Christine?" asked Adelheid, taking the hand of the repudiated and deserted girl with the tenderness of an affectionate sister.

Until now the sufferer had only spoken the few words related, in mild reproof of her mother's indiscretion. That little had been uttered with parched lips and a choked voice, while the hue of her features was deadly pale, and her whole countenance betrayed intense mental anguish. But this display of interest in one of her own years and sex, of whose excellencies she had been accustomed to hear such fervid descriptions from the warm-hearted Sigismund, and of whose sincerity she was assured by the subtle and quick instinct that unites the innocent and young, caused a quick and extreme change in her sensibilities. The grief which had been struggling and condensed, now flowed more freely from her eyes, and she threw herself, sobbing and weeping, in a paroxysm of gentle, but overwhelming, feeling, on the bosom of this new found friend. The experienced Marguerite smiled at this manifestation of kindness on the part of Adelheid, though even this expression of satisfaction was austere and regulated in one who had so long stood at bay with the world. And, after a short pause, she left the room, under the belief that such a communion with a spirit, pure and inexperienced as her own, a communion so unusual to her daughter, would be more likely to produce a happy effect, if left to themselves, than when restrained by her presence.

The two girls wept in common, for a long time after Marguerite had disappeared. This intercourse, chastened as it was by sorrow, and rendered endearing on the one side by a confiding ingenuousness, and on the other by generous pity, caused both to live in that short period, as it were, months together in a near and dear intimacy. Confidence is not always the growth of time. There are minds that meet each other with a species of affinity that resembles the cohesive property of matter, and with a promptitude and faith that only belongs to the purer essence of which they are composed. But when this attraction of the ethereal part of the being is aided by the feelings that have been warmed by an interest so tender as that which the hearts of both the maidens felt in a common object, its power is not only stronger, but quicker, in making itself felt. So much was already known by each of the other's character, fortunes, and hopes (always with the exception of Adelheid's most sacred secret, which Sigismund cherished as a deposit by far too sacred to be shared even with his sister) that the meeting under no circumstances could have been that of strangers, and their mutual knowledge came as an assistant to break down the barriers of those forms which were so irksome to their longings for a freer interchange of feeling and thought. Adelheid possessed too much intellectual tact to have recourse to the every-day language of consolation. When she did speak, which, as became her superior rank and less embarrassed situation, she was the first to do, it in general but friendly allusions.

"Thou wilt go with us to Italy, in the morning," she said, drying her eyes; "my father quits Blonay, in company with the Signor Grimaldi, with to-morrow's sun, and thou wilt be of our company?"

"Where thou wilt--anywhere with thee--anywhere to hide my shame!"

The blood mounted to the temples of Adelheid; her air even appeared imposing to the eyes of the artless and unpractised Christine, as she answered--

"Shame is a word that applies to the mean and mercenary, to the vile and unfaithful," she said, with womanly and virtuous indignation; "but not to thee, love."

"O! do not, do not condemn him;" whispered Christine, covering her face with her hands. "He has found himself unequal to bearing the burthen of our degradation, and he should be spoken of in pity rather than with hatred."

Adelheid was silent; but she regarded the poor trembling girl, whose head now nestled in her bosom, with melancholy concern.

"Didst thou know him well?" she asked in a low tone, following rather the chain of her own thoughts, than reflecting on the nature of the question she put. "I had hoped that this refusal would bring no other pain than the unavoidable mortification which I fear belongs to the weakness of our sex and our habits."

"Thou knowest not how dear preference is to the despised!--how cherished the thought of being loved becomes to those, who, out of their own narrow limits of natural friends, have been accustomed to meet only with contempt and aversion! Thou hast always been known, and courted, and happy! Thou canst not know how dear it is to the despised to seem even to be preferred!"

"Nay, say not this, I pray thee!" answered Adelheid, hurriedly, and with a throb of anguish at her heart; "there is little in this life that speaks fairly for itself. We are not always what we seem; and if we were, and far more miserable than anything but vice can make us, there is another state of being, in which justice--pure, unalloyed justice--will be done."

"I will go with thee to Italy," answered Christine, looking calm and resolved, while a glow of holy hope bloomed on each cheek; "when all is over, we will go together to a happier world!"

Adelheid folded the stricken and sensitive plant to her bosom. Again they wept together, but it was with a milder and sweeter sorrow than before.

Chapter XX

I'll show thee the best springs; I'll pluck thee berries.

Tempest.

The day dawned clear and cloudless on the Leman, the morning that succeeded the Abbaye des Vignerons. Hundreds among the frugal and time-saving Swiss had left the town before the appearance of the light, and many strangers were crowding into the barks, as the sun came bright and cheerfully over the rounded and smiling summits of the neighboring côtes. At this early hour, all in and around the rock-seated castle of Blonay were astir, and in motion. Menials were running, with hurried air, from room to room, from court to terrace and from lawn to tower. The peasants in the adjoining fields rested on their utensils of husbandry, in gaping, admiring attention to the preparations of their superiors. For though we are not writing of a strictly feudal age, the events it is our business to record took place long before the occurrence of those great political events, which have since so materially changed the social state of Europe. Switzerland was then a sealed country to most of those who dwelt even in the adjoining nations, and the present advanced condition of roads and inns was quite unknown, not only to these mountaineers, but throughout the rest of what was then much more properly called the exclusively civilized portion of the globe, than it is to-day. Even horses were not often used in the passage of the Alps, but recourse was had to the surer-footed mule by the traveller, and, not unfrequently, by the more practised carrier and smuggler of those rude paths. Roads existed, it is true, as in other parts of Europe, in the countries of the plain, if any portion of the great undulating surface of that region deserve the name; but once within the mountains, with the exception of very inartificial wheel-tracks in the straitened and glen-like valleys, the hoof alone was to be trusted or indeed used.

The long train of travellers, then, that left the gates of Blonay just as the fog began to stir on the wide alluvial meadows of the Rhone, were all in the saddle. A courier, accompanied by a sumpter-mule, had departed overnight to prepare the way for those who were to follow, and active young mountaineers had succeeded, from time to time, charged with different orders, issued in behalf of their comforts.

As the cavalcade passed beneath the arch of the great gate, the lively, spirit-stirring horn sounded a fare well air, to which custom had attached the signification of good wishes. It took the way towards the level of the Leman by means of a winding and picturesque bridle-path that led, among alpine meadows, groves, rocks, and hamlets, fairly to the water-side. Roger de Blonay and his two principal guests rode in front, the former seated on a war-horse that he had ridden years before as a soldier, and the two latter well mounted on beasts prepared for, and accustomed to, the mountains. Adelheid and Christine came next, riding by themselves, in the modest reserve of their maiden condition. Their discourse was low, confidential, and renewed at intervals. A few menials followed, and then came Sigismund at the side of the Signor Grimald's friend, and one of the family of Blonay, the latter of whom was destined to return with the baron, after doing honor to their guests by seeing them as far as Villeneuve The rear was brought up by muleteers, domestics, and those who led the beasts that bore the baggage. All of the former who intended to cross the Alps carried the fire-arms of the period at their saddle-bows, and each had his rapier, his *couteau de chasse*, or his weapon of more military fashion, so disposed about his person as to denote it was considered an arm for whose use some occasion might possibly occur.

As the departure from Blonay was unaccompanied by any of those leave-takings which usually impress a touch of melancholy on the traveller, most of the cavalcade, as they issued into the pure and exhilarating air of the morning, were sufficiently disposed to enjoy the loveliness of the landscape, and to indulge in the cheerfulness and delight that a scene so glorious is apt to awaken, in all who are alive to the beauties of nature.

Adelheid gladly pointed out to her companion the various objects of the view, as a means of recalling the thoughts of Christine from her own particular griefs, which were heightened by regret for the loss of her mother, from whom she was now seriously separated for the first time in her life, since their communications, though secret, had been constant during the years she had dwelt under another roof. The latter gratefully lent herself to the kind intentions of her new friend, and endeavored to be pleased with all she beheld, though it was such pleasure as the sad and mourning admit with a jealous reservation of their own secret causes of woe.

"Yonder tower, towards which we advance, is Châtelard," said the heiress of Willading to the daughter of Balthazar, in the pursuit of her kind intention; "a hold, nearly as ancient and honorable as this we have just quitted, though not so constantly the dwelling of the same family; for these of Blonay have been a thousand years dwellers on the same rock, always favorably known for their faith and courage."

"Surely, if there is anything in life that can compensate for its every-day evils," observed Christine, in a manner of mild regret and perhaps with the perversity of grief, "it must be to have come from those who have always been known and honored among the great and happy! Even virtue and goodness, and great deeds, scarce give a respect like that we feel for the Sire de Blonay, whose family has been seated, as thou hast just said, a thousand years on that rock above us!"

Adelheid was mute. She appreciated the feeling which had so naturally led her companion to a reflection like this, and she felt the difficulty of applying balm to a wound as deep as that which had been inflicted on her companion.

"We are not always to suppose those the most happy that the world most honors," she at length answered; "the respect to which we are accustomed comes in time to be necessary, without being a source of pleasure; and the hazard of incurring its loss is more than equal to the satisfaction of its possession."

"Thou wilt at least admit that to be despised and shunned is a curse to which nothing can reconcile us."

"We will speak now of other things, dear. It may be long ere either of us again sees this grand display of rock and water, of brown mountain and shining glacier; we will not prove ourselves ungrateful for the happiness we have, by repining for that which is impossible."

Christine quietly yielded to the kind intention of her new friend, and they rode on in silence, picking their way along the winding path, until the whole party, after a long but pleasant descent, reached the road, which is nearly washed by the waters of the lake. There has already been allusion, in the earlier pages of our work, to the extraordinary beauties of the route near this extremity of the Leman. After climbing to the heigh of the mild and healthful Montreux, the cavalcade again descended, under a canopy of nut-trees, to the gate of Chillon, and, sweeping around the margin of the sheet, it reached Villeneuve by the hour that had been named for an early morning repast. Here all dismounted, and refreshed themselves awhile, when Roger de Blonay and his attendants, after many exchanges of warm and sincere good wishes, took their final leave.

The sun was scarcely yet visible in the deep glens, when those who were destined for St. Bernard were again in the saddle. The road now necessarily left the lake, traversing those broad alluvial bottoms which have been deposited during thirty centuries by the washings of the Rhone, aided, if faith is to be given to geological symptoms and to ancient traditions, by certain violent convulsions of nature. For several hours our travellers rode amid such a deep fertility, and such a luxuriance of vegetation, that their path bore more analogy to an excursion on the wide plains of Lombardy, than to one amid the usual Swiss scenery; although, unlike the boundless expanse of the Italian garden, the view was limited on each side by perpendicular barriers of rock, that were piled for thousands of feet into the heavens, and which were merely separated from each other by a league or two, a distance that dwindled to miles in its effect on the eye, a consequence of the grandeur of the scale on which nature has reared these vast piles.

It was high-noon when Melchior de Willading and his venerable friend led the way across the foaming Rhone, at the celebrated bridge of St Maurice. Here the country of the Valais, then like Geneva, an ally, and not a confederate of the Swiss cantons, was entered, and all objects, both animate and inanimate, began to assume that mixture of the grand, the sterile, the luxuriant, and the revolting, for which this region is so generally known. Adelheid gave an involuntary shudder, her imagination having been prepared by rumor for even more than the truth would have given reason to expect, when the gate of St. Maurice swung back upon its hinges, literally inclosing the party in this wild, desolate, and yet romantic region. As they proceeded along the Rhone, however, she and those of her companions to whom the scene was new, were constantly wondering at some unlooked-for discrepancy, that drove them from admiration to disgust--from the exclamations of delight to the chill of disappointment. The mountains on every side were dreary, and without the rich relief of the pastured eminences, but most of the valley was rich and generous. In one spot a sac d'eau, one of those reservoirs of water which form among the glaciers on the summits of the rocks, had broken, and, descending like a water-spout, it had swept before it every vestige of cultivation, covering wide breadths of the meadows with a débris that resembled chaos. A frightful barrenness, and the most smiling fertility, were in absolute contact: patches of green, that had been accidentally favored by some lucky formation of the ground, sometimes appearing like oases of the desert, in the very centre of a sterility that would put the labor and the art of man at defiance for a century. In the midst of this terrific picture of want sat a crétin, with his semi-human attributes, the lolling tongue, the blunted faculties, and the degraded appetites, to complete the desolation. Issuing from this belt of annihilated vegetation, the scene became again as pleasant as the fancy could desire, or the eye crave. Fountains leaped from rock to rock in the sun's rays; the valley was green and gentle; the mountains began to show varied and pleasing forms; and happy smiling faces appeared, whose freshness and regularity were perhaps of a cast superior to that of most of the Swiss. In short, the Valais was then; as now, a country of opposite extremes, but in which, perhaps, there is a predominance of the repulsive and inhospitable.

It was fairly nightfall, notwithstanding the trifling distance they had journeyed, when the travellers reached Martigny, where dispositions had previously been made for their reception during the hours of sleep. Here preparations were made to seek their rest at an early hour, in order to be in readiness for the fatiguing toil of the following day.

Martigny is situated at the point where the great valley of the Rhone changes its direction from a north and south to an east and west course, and it is the spot whence three of the celebrated mountain paths diverge, to make as many passages of the upper Alps. Here are the two routes of the great and little St. Bernard, both of which lead into Italy, and that of the Col-de-Balme, which crosses a spur of the Alps into Savoy toward the celebrated valley of Chamouni. It was the intention of the Baron de Willading and his friend to journey by the former of these roads, as has so often been mentioned in these pages, their destination being the capital of Piedmont. The passage of the great St. Bernard, though so long known by its ancient and hospitable convent, the most elevated habitation in Europe, and in these later times so famous for the passage of a conquering army is but a secondary alpine pass, considered in reference to the grandeur of its scenery. The ascent, so inartificial even to this hour, is loner and comparatively without danger, and in general it is sufficiently direct, there being no very precipitous rise like those of the Gemmi, the Grimsel, and various other passes in Switzerland and Italy, except at the very neck, or col, of the mountain, where the rock is to be literally climbed on the rude and broad steps that so frequently occur among the paths of the Alps and the Apennines. The fatigue of this passage comes, therefore, rather from its length, and the necessity of unremitted diligence, than from any excessive labor demanded by the ascent; and the reputation acquired by the great captain of our age, in leading an army across its summit, has been obtained more by the military combinations of which it formed the principal feature, the boldness of the conception, and the secrecy and promptitude with which so extensive an operation was effected, than by the physical difficulties that were overcome. In the latter particular, the passage of St. Bernard, as this celebrated coup-de-main is usually called, has frequently been outdone in our own wilds; for armies have often traversed regions of broad streams, broken mountains, and uninterrupted forests, for weeks at a time, in which the mere bodily labor of any given number of days would be found to be greater than that endured on this occasion by the followers of Napoleon. The estimate we attach to every exploit is so dependent on the magnitude of its results, that men rarely come to a perfectly impartial judgment on its merits; the victory or defeat, however simple or bloodless, that shall shake or assure the interests of civilized society, being always esteemed by the world an event of greater importance, than the happiest combinations of thought and valor that affect only the welfare of some remote and unknown people. By the just consideration of this truth, we come to understand the value of a nation's possessing confidence in itself, extensive power, and a unity commensurate to its means; since small and divided states waste their strength in acts too insignificant for general interest, frittering away their mental riches, no less than their treasure and blood, in supporting interests that fail to enlist the sympathies of any beyond the pale of their own borders. The nation which, by the adverse circumstances of numerical inferiority, poverty of means, failure of enterprise, or want of opinion, cannot sustain its own citizens in the acquisition of a just renown, is deficient in one of the first and most indispensable elements of greatness; glory, like riches, feeding itself, and being most apt to be found where its fruits have already accumulated. We see, in this fact, among other conclusions, the importance of an acquisition of such habits of manliness of thought, as will enable us to decide on the merits and demerits of what is done among ourselves, and of shaking off that dependence on others which it is too much the custom of some among us to dignify with the pretending title of deference to knowledge and taste, but which, in truth, possesses some such share of true modesty and diffidence, as the footman is apt to exhibit when exulting in the renown of his master.

This little digression has induced us momentarily to overlook the incidents of the tale. Few who possess the means, venture into the stormy regions of the upper Alps, at the late season in which the present party reached the hamlet of Martigny, without seeking the care of one or more suitable guides. The services of these men are useful in a variety of ways, but in none more than in offering the advice which long familiarity with the signs of the heavens, the temperature of the air, and the direction of the winds, enables them to give. The Baron de Willading, and his friend, immediately dispatched a messenger for a mountaineer, of the name of Pierre Dumont, who enjoyed a fair name for fidelity, and who was believed to be better acquainted with all the difficulties of the ascent and descent, than any other who journeyed among the glens of that part of the Alps. At the present day, when hundreds ascend to the convent from curiosity alone, every peasant of sufficient strength and intelligence becomes a guide, and the little community of the lower Valais finds the transit of the idle and rich such a fruitful source of revenue, that it has been induced to regulate the whole by very useful and just ordinances; but at the period of the tale, this Pierre was the only individual, who, by fortunate concurrences, had obtained a name among affluent foreigners, and who was at all in demand with that class of travellers. He was not long in presenting himself in the public room of the inn--a hale, florid, muscular man of sixty, with every appearance of permanent health and vigor, but with a slight and nearly imperceptible difficulty of breathing.

"Thou art Pierre Dumont?" observed the baron, studying the open physiognomy and well-set frame of the Valaisan, with satisfaction. "Thou hast been mentioned by more than one traveller in his book."

The stout mountaineer raised himself in pride, and endeavored to acknowledge the compliment in the manner of his well-meant but rude courtesy; for refinement did not then extend its finesse and its deceit among the glens of Switzerland.

"They have done me honor, Monsieur," he said: "it has been my good fortune to cross the Col with many brave gentlemen and fair ladies--and in two instances with princes." (Though a sturdy republican, Pierre was not insensible to worldly rank.) "The pious monks know me well; and they who enter the convent are not the worse received for being my companions. I shall be glad to lead so fair a party from our cold valley into the sunny glens of Italy, for, if the truth must be spoken, nature has placed us on the wrong side of the mountain for our comfort, though we have our advantage over those who live even in Turin and Milan, in matters of greater importance."

"What can be the superiority of a Valaisan over the Lombard, or the Piedmontese?" demanded the Signor Grimaldi quickly, like a man who was curious to hear the reply. "A traveller should seek all kind of knowledge, and I take this to be a newly-discovered fact."

"Liberty, Signore! We are our own masters; we have been so since the day when our fathers sacked the castles of the barons, and compelled their tyrants to become their equals. I think of this each time I reach the warm plains of Italy, and return to my cottage a more contented man, for the reflection."

"Spoken like a Swiss, though it is uttered by an ally of the cantons!" cried Melchior de Willading, heartily. "This is the spirit, Gaetano, which sustains our mountaineers, and renders them more happy amid their frosts and rocks, than thy Genoese on his warm and glowing bay."

"The word liberty, Melchior, is more used than understood, and as much abused as used;" returned the Signor Grimaldi gravely. "A country on which God hath laid his finger in displeasure as on this, needs have some such consolation as the phantom with which the honest Pierre appears to be so well satisfied.--But, Signor guide, have many travellers tried the passage of late, and what dost thou think of our prospects in making the attempt? We hear gloomy tales, sometimes, of thy alpine paths in that Italy thou hold'st so cheap."

"Your pardon, noble Signore, if the frankness of a mountaineer has carried me too far. I do not undervalue your Piedmont, because I love our Valais more. A country may be excellent, even though another should be better. As for the travellers, none of note have gone up the Col of late, though there have been the usual number of vagabonds and adventurers. The savor of the convent kitchen will reach the noses of these knaves here in the valley, though we have a long twelve leagues to journey in getting from one to the other."

The Signor Grimaldi waited until Adelheid and Christine, who were preparing to retire for the night, were out of hearing, and he resumed his questions.

"Thou hast not spoken of the weather?"

"We are in one of the most uncertain and treacherous months of the good season, Messieurs. The winter is gathering among the upper Alps, and in a month in which the frosts are flying about like uneasy birds that do not know where to alight, one can hardly say whether he hath need of his cloak or not."

"San Francesco! Dost think I am dallying with thee, friend, about a thickness more or less of cloth! I am hinting at avalanches and falling rocks--at whirlwinds and tempests?"

Pierre laughed and shook his head, though he answered vaguely as became his business.

"These are Italian opinions of our hills, Signore," he said; "they savor of the imagination. Our pass is not as often troubled with the avalanche as some that are known, even in the melting snows. Had you looked at the peaks from the lake, you would have seen that, the hoary glaciers excepted, they are still all brown and naked. The snow must fall from the heavens before it can fall in the avalanche, and we are yet, I think, a few days from the true winter."

"Thy calculations are made with nicety, friend," returned the Genoese, not sorry, however, to hear the guide speak with so much apparent confidence of the weather, "and we are obliged to thee in proportion. What of the travellers thou hast named? Are there brigands on our path?"

"Such rogues have been known to infest the place, but, in general, there is too little to be gained for the risk. Your rich traveller is not an every-day sight among our rocks; and you well know Signore, that there may be too few, as well as too many, on a path, for your freebooter."

The Italian was distrustful by habit on all such subjects, and he threw a quick suspicious glance at the guide. But the frank open countenance of Pierre removed all doubt of his honesty, to say nothing of the effect of a well-established reputation.

"But thou hast spoken of certain vagabonds who have preceded us?"

"In that particular, matters might be better;" answered the plain-minded mountaineer, dropping his head in an attitude of meditation so naturally expressed as to give additional weight to his words. "Many of bad appearance have certainly gone up to-day; such as a Neapolitan named Pippo, who is anything but a saint--a certain pilgrim, who will be nearer heaven at the convent than he will be at the death--St. Pierre pray for me if I do the man injustice!--and one or two more of the same brood. There is another that hath gone up also, post haste, and with good reason as they say, for he hath made himself the but of all the jokers in Vévey on account of some foolery in the games of the Abbaye--a certain Jacques Colis."

The name was repeated by several near the speaker.

"The same, Messieurs. It would seem that the Sieur Colis would fain take a maiden to wife in the public sports, and, when her birth came to be be known, that his bride was no other than the child of Balthazar, the common headsman of Berne!"

A general silence betrayed the embarrassment of most of the listeners.

"And that tale hath already reached this glen," said Sigismund, in a tone so deep and firm as to cause Pierre to start, while the two old nobles looked in another direction, feigning not to observe what was passing.

"Rumor hath a nimbler foot than a mule, young officer;" answered the honest guide. "The tale, as you call it, will have travelled across the mountains sooner than they who bore it--though I never knew how such a miracle could pass--but so it is; report goes faster than the tongue that spreads it, and if there be a little untruth to help it along, the wind itself is scarcely swifter. Honest Jacques Colis has bethought him to get the start of his story, but, my life on it, though he is active enough in getting away from his mockers, that he finds it, with all the additions, safely housed at the inn at Turin when he reaches that city himself."

"These, then, are all?" interrupted the Signor Grimaldi, who saw, by the heaving bosom of Sigismund, that it was time in mercy to interpose.

"Not so, Signore--there is still another and one I like less than any. A countryman of your own, who, impudently enough, calls himself Il Maledetto."

"Maso!"

"The very same."

"Honest, courageous Maso, and his noble dog!"

"Signore, you describe the man so well in some things, that I wonder you know so little of him in others. Maso hath not his equal on the road for activity and courage, and the beast is second only to our mastiffs of the convent for the same qualities; but when you speak of the master's honesty, you speak of that for which the world gives him little credit, and do great disparagement to the brute, which is much the best of the two, in this respect."

"This may be true enough," rejoined the Signore Grimaldi, turning anxiously towards his companions:--"man is a strange compound of good and evil; his acts when left to natural impulses are so different from what they become on calculation that one can scarcely answer for a man of Maso's temperament. We know him to be a most efficient friend, and such a man would be apt to make a very dangerous enemy! His qualities were not given to him by halves. And yet we have a strong circumstance in our favor; for he who hath once done the least service to a fellow-creature feels a sort of paternity in him he hath saved, and would be little likely to rob himself of the pleasure of knowing, that there are some of his kind who owe him a grateful recollection."

This remark was answered by Melchior de Willading in the same spirit, and the guide, perceiving he was no longer wanted, withdrew.

Soon after, the travellers retired to rest.

Chapter XXI

As yet the trembling year is unconfirmed,
And winter oft, at eve, resumes the breeze,
Chills the pale morn, and bids his driving sleets
Deform the day delightful:----

Thomson.

The horn of Pierre Dumont was blowing beneath the windows of the inn of Martigny, with the peep of dawn. Then followed the appearance of drowsy domestics, the saddling of unwilling mules, and the loading of baggage. A few minutes later the little caravan was assembled, for the cavalcade almost deserved this name, and the whole were in motion for the summits of the Alps.

The travellers now left the valley of the Rhone to bury themselves amid those piles of misty and confused mountains, which formed the background of the picture they had studied from the castle of Blonay and the sheet of the Leman. They soon plunged into a glen, and, following the windings of a brawling torrent, were led gradually, and by many turnings, into a country of bleak upland pasturage, where the inhabitants gained a scanty livelihood, principally by means of their dairies.

A few leagues above Martigny, the paths again separated, one inclining to the left towards the elevated valley that has since become so celebrated in the legends of this wild region, by the formation of a little lake in its glacier, which, becoming too heavy for its foundation, broke through its barrier of ice, and descended in a mountain of water to the Rhone, a distance of many leagues, sweeping before it every vestige of civilization that crossed its course, and even changing, in many places, the face of nature itself. Here the glittering peak of Vélan became visible, and, though so much nearer to the eye than when viewed from Vévey, it was still a distant shining pile, grand in its solitude and mystery, on which the sight loved to dwell, as it studies the pure and spotless edges of some sleepy cloud.

It has already been said, that the ascent of the great St. Bernard, with the exception of occasional hills and hollows, is nowhere very precipitous but at the point at which the last rampart of rock is to be overcome. On the contrary, the path, for leagues at a time, passes along tolerably even valleys, though of necessity the general direction is upward, and for most of the distance through a country that admits of cultivation, though the meagreness of the soil, and the shortness of the seasons, render but an indifferent return to the toil of the husbandman. In this respect it differs from most of the other Alpine passes; but if it wants the variety, wildness, and sublimity of the Splugen. the St. Gothard, the Gemmi, and the Simplon, it is still an ascent on a magnificent scale, and he who journeys on its path is raised, as it were, by insensible degrees, to an elevation that gradually changes all his customary associations with the things of the lower world.

From the moment of quitting the inn to that of the first halt, Melchior de Willading and the Signor Grimaldi rode in company, as on the previous day. These old friends had much to communicate in confidential discourse which the presence of Roger de Blonay, and the importunities of the bailiff, had hitherto prevented them from freely saying. Both had thought maturely, too, on the situation of Adelheid, of her hopes, and of her future fortunes, and both had reasoned much as two old nobles of that day, who were not without strong sympathies for their kind, while they were too practised to overlook the world and its ties, would be likely to reason on an affair of this delicate nature.

"There came a feeling of regret, perhaps I might fairly call it by its proper name, of envy," observed the Genoese, in the pursuance of the subject which engrossed most of their time and thoughts, as they rode slowly along, the bridles dangling from the necks of their mules,--"there came a feeling of regret, when I first saw the fair creature that calls thee father, Melchior. God has dealt mercifully by me, in respect to many things that make men happy; but he rendered my marriage accursed, not only in its bud, but in its fruit. Thy child is dutiful and loving, all that a father can wish; and yet here is this unusual attachment come to embarrass, if not to defeat, thy fair and just hopes for her welfare! This is no common affair, that a few threats of bolts and a change of scene will cure, but a rooted affection that is but too firmly based on esteem.--By San Francesco, but I think, at times, thou wouldst do well to permit the ceremony!"

"Should it be our fortune to meet with the absconding Jacques Colis at Turin, he might give us different counsel," answered the old baron drily.

"That is a dreadful barrier to our wishes! Were the boy anything but a headsman's child! I do not think thou couldst object, Melchior, had he merely come of a hind, or of some common follower of thy family?"

"It were far better that he should have come of one like ourselves, Gaetano. I reason but little on the dogmas of this or that sect in politics; but

I feel and think, in this affair, as the parent of an only child. All those usages and opinions in which we are trained, my friend, are so many ingredients in our happiness, let them be silly or wise, just or oppressive; and though I would fain do that which is right to the rest of mankind, I could wish to begin to practise innovation with any other than my own daughter. Let them who like philosophy and justice, and natural rights, so well, commence by setting us the example."

"Thou hast hit the stumbling-block that causes a thousand well-digested plans for the improvement of the world to fail, honest Melchior. Could we toil with others' limbs, sacrifice with others' groans, and pay with others' means, there would be no end to our industry, our disinterestedness, or our liberality--and yet it were a thousand pities that so sweet a girl and so noble a youth should not yoke!"

"'Twould be a yoke indeed, for a daughter of the house of Willading;" returned the graver father, with emphasis. "I have looked at this matter in every face that becomes me, Gaetano, and though I would not rudely repulse one that hath saved my life, by driving him from my company, at a moment when even strangers consort for mutual aid and protection, at Turin we must part for ever!"

"I know not how to approve, nor yet how to blame thee, poor Melchior! 'Twas a sad scene, that of the refusal to wed Balthazar's daughter, in the presence of so many thousands!"

"I take it as a happy and kind warning of the precipice to which a foolish tenderness was leading us both, my friend."

"Thou may'st have reason; and yet I wish thou wert more in error than ever Christian was! These are rugged mountains, Melchior, and, fairly passed, it might be so arranged that the boy should forget Switzerland for ever. He might become a Genoese, in which event, dost thou not see the means of overcoming some of the present difficulty?"

"Is the heiress of my house a vagrant, Signor Grimaldi, to forget her country and birth?"

"I am childless, in effect, if not in fact; and where there are the will and the means, the end should not be wanting. We will speak of this under the warmer sun of Italy, which they say is apt to render hearts tender."

"The hearts of the young and amorous, good Gaetano, but, unless much changed of late, it is as apt to harden those of the old, as any sun I know of;" returned the baron, shaking his head, though it much exceeded his power to smile at his own pleasantry when speaking on this painful subject. "Thou knowest that in this matter I act only for the welfare of Adelheid, without thought of myself; and it would little comport with the honor of a baron of an ancient house, to be the grandfather of children who come of a race of executioners."

The Signor Grimaldi succeeded better than his friend in raising a smile, for, more accustomed to dive into the depths of human feeling, he was not slow in detecting the mixture of motives that were silently exercising their long-established influence over the heart of his really well-intentioned companion.

"So long as thou speakest of the wisdom of respecting men's opinions, and the danger of wrecking thy daughter's happiness by running counter to their current, I agree with thee to the letter; but, to me, it seems possible so to place the affair, that the world shall imagine all is in rule, and, by consequence, all proper. If we can overcome ourselves, Melchior, I apprehend no great difficulty in blinding others." The head of the Bernois dropped upon his breast, and he rode a long distance in that attitude, reflecting on the course it most became him to pursue, and struggling with the conflicting sentiments which troubled his upright but prejudiced mind. As his friend understood the nature of this inward strife, he ceased to speak, and a long silence succeeded the discourse.

It was different with those who followed. Though long accustomed to gaze at their native mountains from a distance, this was the first occasion on which Adelheid and her companion had ever actually penetrated into their glens, or journeyed on their broken and changing faces. The path of St. Bernard, therefore, had all the charm of novelty, and their youthful and ardent minds were soon won from meditating on their own causes of unhappiness, to admiration of the sublime works of nature. The cultivated taste of Adelheid, in particular, was quick in detecting those beauties of a more subtle kind which the less instructed are apt to overlook, and she found additional pleasure in pointing them out to the ingenuous and wondering Christine, who received these, her first, lessons in that grand communion with nature which is pregnant with so much unalloyed delight, with gratitude and a readiness of comprehension, that amply repaid her instructress. Sigismund was an attentive and pleased listener to what was passing, though one who had so often passed the mountains, and who had seen them familiarly on their warmer and more sunny side, had little to learn, himself, even from so skilful and alluring a teacher.

As they ascended, the air became purer and less impregnated with the humidity of its lower currents; changing, by a process as fine as that wrought by a chemical application, the hues and aspect of every object in the view. A vast hill-side lay basking in the sun, which illuminated on its rounded swells a hundred long stripes of grain in every stage of verdure, resembling so much delicate velvet that was thrown in a variety of accidental faces to the light, while the shadows ran away, to speak technically, from this *foyer de lumière* of the picture, in gradations of dusky russet and brown, until the *colonne de vigueur* was obtained in the deep black cast from the overhanging branches of a wood of larch in the depths of some ravine, into which the sight with difficulty penetrated. These were the beauties on which Adelheid most loved to dwell, for they are always the charms that soonest strike the true admirer of nature, when he finds himself raised above the lower and less purified strata of the atmosphere, into the regions of more radiant light and brightness. It is thus that the physical, no less than the moral, vision becomes elevated above the impurities that cling to this nether world, attaining a portion of that spotless and sublime perception as we ascend, by which we are nearly assimilated to the truths of creation; a poetical type of the greater and purer enjoyment we feel, as morally receding from earth we draw nearer to heaven.

The party rested for several hours, as usual, at the little mountain hamlet of Liddes. At the present time, it is not uncommon for the traveller, favored by a wheel-track along this portion of the route, to ascend the mountain and to return to Martigny in the same day. The descent in particular, after reaching the village just named, is soon made; but at the period of our tale, such an exploit, if ever made, was of very rare occurrence. The fatigue of being in the saddle so many hours compelled our party to remain at the inn much longer than is now practised, and their utmost hope was to be able to reach the convent before the last rays of the sun had ceased to light the glittering peak of Vélan.

There occurred here, too, some unexpected detention on the part of Christine, who had retired with Sigismund soon after reaching the inn, and who did not rejoin the party until the impatience of the guide had more than once manifested itself in such complaints as one in his situation is apt to hazard. Adelheid saw with pain, when her friend did at length rejoin them, that she had been weeping bitterly; but, too delicate to press her for an explanation on a subject in which it was evident the brother and sister did not desire to bestow their confidence, she communicated her readiness to depart to the domestics, without the slightest allusion to the change in Christine's appearance, or to the unexpected delay of which she had been the cause.

Pierre muttered an ave in thankfulness that the long halt was ended. He then crossed himself with one hand, while with the other he flourished his whip, among a crowd of gaping urchins and slavering crétins, to clear the way for those he guided. His followers were, in the main of a different mood. If the traveller too often reaches the inn hungry and disposed to find fault, he usually quits it good-humored and happy. The restoration, as it is well called in France, effected by means of the larder and the resting of wearied limbs, is usually communicated to the spirits; and it must be a crusty humor indeed, or singularly bad fare, that prevents a return to a placid state of mind. The party, under the direction of Pierre, formed no exception to the general rule. The two old nobles had so far forgotten the subject of their morning dialogue, as to be facetious; and, ere long, even their gentle companions were disposed to laugh at some of their sallies, in spite of the load of care that weighed so constantly and so heavily on both. In short, such is the waywardness of our feelings, and so difficult is it to be always sorrowful as well as always happy, that the well-satisfied landlady, who had, in truth, received the full value of a very indifferent fare, was ready to affirm, as she curtsied her thanks on the dirty threshold, that a merrier party had never left her door.

"We shall take our revenge out of the casks of the good Augustines to-night for the sour liquor of this inn; is it not so, honest Pierre?" demanded the Signor Grimaldi, adjusting himself in the saddle, as they got clear of the stones, sinuosities, projecting roofs, and filth of the village, into the more agreeable windings of the ordinary path, again. "Our friend, the clavier, is apprized of the visit, and as we have already gone through fair and foul in company, I look to his fellowship for some compensation for the frugal meal of which we have just partaken."

"Father Xavier is a hospitable and a happy-minded priest, Signore; and that the saints will long leave him keeper of the convent-keys, is the prayer of every muleteer, guide, or pilgrim, who crosses the col. I wish we were going up the rough steps, by which we are to climb the last rock of the mountain, at this very moment, Messieurs, and that all the rest of the way were as fairly done as this we have so happily passed."

"Dost thou anticipate difficulty, friend?" demanded the Italian, leaning forward on his saddle-bow, for his quick observation had caught the examining glance that the guide threw around at the heavens.

"Difficulty is a meaning not easily admitted by a mountaineer, Signore; and I am one of the last to think of it, or to feel its dread. Still, we are near the end of the season, and these hills are high and bleak, and those that follow are delicate flowers for a stormy heath. Toil is always sweeter in the remembrance than in the expectation.--I mean no more, if I mean that."

Pierre stopped his march as he ceased speaking. He stood on a little eminence of the path, whence, by looking back, he commanded a view of the opening among the mountains which indicates the site of the valley of the Rhone. The look was long and understanding; but, when it was ended, he turned and resumed his march with the business-like air of one more disposed to act than to speculate on the future. But for the few words which had just escaped him, this natural movement would have attracted no attention; and, as it was, it was observed by none but the Signor Grimaldi, who would himself have attached little importance to the whole, had the guide maintained Ins usual pace.

As is common in the Alps, the conductor of the travellers went on foot, leading the whole party at such a gait as he thought most expedient for man and beast. Hitherto, Pierre had proceeded with sufficient leisure, rendering it necessary for those who followed to observe the same moderation; but he now walked sensibly faster, and frequently so fast as to make it necessary for the mules to break into easy trots, in order to maintain their proper stations. All this, however, was ascribed by most of the party to the formation of the ground, for, after leaving Liddes, there is a long reach of what, among the upper valleys of the Alps, may by comparison be called a level road. This industry, too, was thought to be doubly necessary, in order to repair the time lost at the inn, for the sun was already dipping towards the western boundary of their narrow view of the heavens, and the temperature announced, if not a sudden change in the weather, at least the near approach of the periodical turn of the day.

"We travel by a very ancient path;" observed the Signore Grimaldi, when his thoughts had reverted from their reflections on the movements of the guide to the circumstance of their present situation. "A very reverend path, it might be termed in compliment to the worthy monks who do so much to lessen its dangers, and to its great antiquity. History speaks often of its use by different leaders of armies, for it has long been a thoroughfare for those who journey between the north and the south, whether it be in strife, or in amity. In the time of Augustus it was the route commonly used by the Roman legions in their passages to and from Helvetia and Gaul; the followers of Cæcinna went by these gorges to their attack upon Otho; and the Lombards made the same use of it, five hundred years later. It was often trod by armed bands, in the wars of Charles of Burgundy, those of Milan, and in the conquests of Charlemagne. I remember a tale, in which it is said that a horde of infidel Corsairs from the Mediterranean penetrated by this road, and seized upon the bridge of St. Maurice with a view to plunder. As we are not the first so it is probable that we are not to be the last, who have trusted themselves in these regions of the upper air, bent on our objects, whether of love or of strife."

"Signore," observed Pierre respectfully, when the Genoese ceased speaking, "if your eccellenza would make your discourse less learned, and more in those familiar words which can be said under a brisk movement, it might better suit the time and the great necessity there is to be diligent."

"Dost thou apprehend danger? Are we behind our time?--Speak; for I dislike concealment."

"Danger has a strong meaning in the mouth of a mountaineer, Signore; for what is security on this path, might be thought alarming lower down in the valleys; I say it not. But the sun is touching the rocks, as you see, and we are drawing near to places where a miss-step of a mule in the dark might cost us dear. I would that all diligently improve the daylight, while they can."

The Genoese did not answer, but he urged his mule again to a gait that was more in accordance with the wishes of Pierre. The movement was followed, as a matter of course, by the rest; and the whole party was once more in a gentle trot, which was scarcely sufficient, however, to keep even pace with the long, impatient, and rapid strides of Pierre, who, notwithstanding his years, appeared to get over the ground with a facility that cost him no effort. Hitherto, the heat had not been small, and, in that pure atmosphere, all its powers were felt during the time the sun's rays fell into the valley; but, the instant they were intercepted by a brown and envious peak of the mountains, their genial influence was succeeded by a chill that sufficiently proved how necessary was the presence of the luminary to the comfort of those who dwelt at that great elevation. The females sought their mantles the moment the bright light was followed by the usual shadow; nor was it long before even the more aged of the gentlemen were seen unstrapping their cloaks, and taking the customary precautions against the effects of the evening air.

The reader is not to suppose, however, that all these little incidents of the way occurred in a time as brief as that which has been consumed in the narration. A long line of path was travelled over before the Signor Grimaldi and his friend were cloaked, and divers hamlets and cabins were successively passed. The alteration from the warmth of day to the chill of evening also was accompanied by a corresponding change in the appearance of the objects they passed. St. Pierre, a cluster of stone-roofed cottages, which bore all the characteristics of the inhospitable region for which they had been constructed, was the last village; though there was a hamlet, at the bridge of Hudri, composed of a few dreary abodes, which, by their aspect, seemed the connecting link between the dwellings of man and the caverns of beasts. Vegetation had long been growing more and more meagre, and it was now fast melting away into still deeper and irretrievable traces of sterility, like the shadows of a picture passing through their several transitions of color to the depth of the back-ground. The larches and cedars diminished gradually in size and numbers, until the straggling and stinted tree became a bush, and the latter finally disappeared in the shape of a tuft of pale green, that adhered to some crevice in the rocks like so much moss. Even the mountain grasses, for which Switzerland is so justly celebrated, grew thin and wiry; and by the time the travellers reached the circular basin at the foot of the peak of Vélan, which is called La Plaine de Prou, there only remained, in the most genial season of the year, and that in isolated spots between the rocks, a sufficiency of nourishment for the support of a small flock of adventurous, nibbling, and hungry goats.

The basin just alluded to is an opening among high pinnacles, and is nearly surrounded by naked and ragged rocks. The path led through its centre, always ascending on an inclined plane, and disappeared through a narrow gorge around the brow of a beetling cliff. Pierre pointed out the latter as the pass by far the most dangerous on this side the Col, in the season of the melting snows, avalanches frequently rolling from its crags. There was no cause for apprehending this well-known Alpine danger, however, in the present moment; for, with the exception of Mont-Vélan, all above and around them lay in the same dreary dress of sterility. Indeed, it would not be easy for the imagination to conceive a more eloquent picture of desolation than that which met the eyes of the travellers, as, following the course of the run of water that trickled through the middle of the inhospitable valley, the certain indication of the general direction of their course, they reached its centre.

The time was getting to be that of early twilight, but the sombre color of the rocks, streaked and venerable by the ferruginous hue with which time had coated their sides, and the depth of the basin, gave to their situation a melancholy gloom passing the duskiness of the hour. On the other hand, the light rested bright and gloriously on the snowy peak of Vélan, still many thousand feet above them, though in plain, and apparently, in near view; while rich touches of the setting sun were gleaming on several of the brown, natural battlements of the Alps, which, worn with eternal exposure to the storms, still lay in sublime confusion at a most painful elevation in their front. The azure vault that canopied all, had that look of distant glory and of grand repose, which so often meets the eye, and so forcibly strikes the mind, of him who travels in the deep valleys and embedded lakes of Switzerland. The glacier of Valsorey descended from the upper region nearly to the edge of the valley, bright and shining, its lower margin streaked and dirty with the *débris* of the overhanging rocks, as if doomed to the fate of all that came upon the earth, that of sharing its impurities.

There no longer existed any human habitation between the point which the travellers had now attained and the convent, though more modern speculation, in this age of curiosity and restlessness, has been induced to rear a substitute for an inn in the spot just described, with the hope of gleaning a scanty tribute from those who fail of arriving in season to share the hospitality of the monks. The chilliness of the air increased faster even than the natural change of the hour would seem to justify, and there were moments when the dull sound of the wind descended to their ears, though not a breath was stirring a withered and nearly solitary blade of grass at their feet. Once or twice, large black clouds drove across the opening above them, resembling heavy-winged vultures sailing in the void, preparatory to a swoop upon their prey.

Chapter XXII

Through this gap
On and say nothing, lest a word, a breath,
Bring down a winter's snow, enough to whelm
The armed files that, night and day, were seen
Winding from cliff to cliff in loose array,
To conquer at Marengo.

Italy.

Pierre Dumont halted in the middle of the sterile little plain, while he signed for those he conducted to continue their ascent. As each mule passed, it received a blow or a kick from the impatient guide, who did not seem to think it necessary to be very ceremonious with the poor beasts, and had taken this simple method to give a general and a brisker impulsion to the party. The expedient was so natural, and so much in accordance with the practice of the muleteers and others of their class, that it excited no suspicion in most of the travellers, who pursued their way, either meditating on and enjoying the novel and profound emotions that their present situation so naturally awakened, or discoursing lightly, in the manner of the thoughtless and unconcerned. The Signor Grimaldi alone, whose watchfulness had already been quickened by previous distrust, took heed of the movement. When all had passed, the Genoese turned in his saddle, and cast an apparently careless look behind. But the glance in truth was anxious and keen. Pierre stood looking steadily at the heavens, one hand holding his hat, and the other extended with an open palm. A glittering particle descended to the latter, when the guide instantly resumed his place in advance. As he passed the Italian, however, meeting an inquiring look, he permitted the other to see a snow-drop so thoroughly congealed, as to have not yet melted with the natural heat of his skin. The eye of Pierre appeared to impose discretion on his confidant, and the silent communion escaped the observation of the rest of the travellers. Just at this moment, too, the attention of the others was luckily called to a different object, by a cry from one of the muleteers, of whom there were three as assistants to the guide. He pointed out a party which, like themselves, was holding the direction of the Col. There was a solitary individual mounted on a mule, and a single pedestrian, without any guide, or other traveller, in their company. Their movements were swift, and they had not been more than a minute in view, before they disappeared behind an angle of the crags which nearly closed the valley on the side of the convent, and which was the precise spot already mentioned as being so dangerous in the season of the melting snows.

"Dost thou know the quality and object of the travellers before us?" demanded the Baron de Willading of Pierre.

The latter mused. It was evident he did not expect to meet with strangers in that particular part of the passage.

"We can know little of those who come from the convent, though few would be apt to leave so safe a roof at this late hour," he answered; "but, until I saw yonder travellers with my own eyes, I could have sworn there were none on this side of the Col going the same way as ourselves? It is time that all the others were already arrived."

"They are villagers of St. Pierre, going up with supplies;" observed one of the muleteers. "None bound to Italy have passed Liddes since the party of Pippo, and they by this tine should be well housed at the hospice. Didst not see a dog among them?--'twas one of the Augustines' mastiffs."

"'Twas the dog I noted, and it was on account of his appearance that I spoke;" returned the baron. "The animal had the air of an old acquaintance, Gaetano, for to me it seemed to resemble our tried friend Nettuno; and he at whose heels it kept so close wore much the air of our acquaintance of the Leman, the bold and ready Maso."

"Who has gone unrequited for his eminent services!" answered the Genoese, thoughtfully "The extraordinary refusal of that man to receive our money is quite as wonderful as any other part of his unusual and inexplicable conduct. I would he had been less obstinate or less proud, for the unrequited obligation rests like a load upon my spirits."

"Thou art wrong. I employed our young friend Sigismund secretly on this duty, while we were receiving the greetings of Roger de Blonay and the good bailiff, but thy countryman treated the escape lightly, as the mariner is apt to consider past danger, and he would listen to no offer of protection or gold. I was, therefore more displeased than surprised by what thou hast well enough termed obstinacy."

"Tell your employers, he said," added Sigismund, "that they may thank the saints, Our Lady, or brother Luther, as best suits their habits, but that they had better forget that such a man as Maso lives. His acquaintance can bring them neither honor nor advantage. Tell this especially to the Signor Grimaldi, when you are on your journey to Italy, and we have parted for ever, as on my suggestion. This was said to me, in the interview I held with the I rave fellow after his liberation from prison."

"The answer was remarkable for a man of his condition, and the especial message to myself of singular exception. I observed that his eye was often on me, with peculiar meaning, during the passage of the lake, and to this hour I have not been able to explain the motive!"

"Is the Signore of Genoa?"--asked the guide: "or is he, by chance, in any way connected with her authorities?"

"Of that republic and city, and certainly of some little interest with the authorities;" answered the Italian, a slight smile curling his lip, as he glanced a look at his friend.

"It is not necessary to look farther for Maso's acquaintance with your features," returned Pierre, laughing; "for of all who live in Italy, there is not a man who has more frequent occasions to know the authorities; but we linger, in this gossip. Urge the beasts upwards, Etienne--presto!--presto!"

The muleteers answered this appeal by one of their long cries, which has a resemblance to the rattling that is the well-known signal of the venomous serpent of this country when he would admonish the traveller to move quickly, and which certainly produces the same startling effect on the nerves of the mule as the signal of the snake is very apt to excite in man. This interruption caused the dialogue to be dropped, all riding onward, musing in their several fashions on what had just passed. In a few minutes the party turned the crag in question, and, quitting the valley, or sterile basin, in which they had been journeying for the last half hour, they entered by a narrow gorge into a scene that resembled a crude collection of the materials of which the foundations of the world had been originally formed. There was no longer any vegetation at all, or, if here and there a blade of grass had put forth under the shelter of some stone, it was so meagre, and of so rare occurrence, as to be unnoticed in that sublime scene of chaotic confusion. Ferruginous, streaked, naked, and cheerless rocks arose around them, and even that snowy beacon, the glowing summit of Vélan, which had so long lain bright and cheering on their path, was now hid entirely from view. Pierre Dumont soon after pointed out a place on the visible summit of the mountain, where a gorge between the neigh boring peaks admitted a view of the heavens beyond. This he informed those he guided was the Col, through whose opening the pile of the Alps was to be finally surmounted. The light that still tranquilly reigned in this part of the heavens was in sublime contrast to the gathering gloom of the passes below, and all hailed this first glimpse of the end of their day's toil as a harbinger of rest, and we might add of security; for, although none but the Signor Grimaldi had detected the secret uneasiness of Pierre, it was not possible to be, at that late hour, amid so wild and dreary a display of desolation, and, as it were, cut off from communion with their kind, without experiencing an humbling sense of the dependence of man upon the grand and ceaseless Providence of God.

The mules were again urged to increase their pace, and images of the refreshment and repose that were expected from the convent's hospitality, became general and grateful among the travellers. The day was fast disappearing from the glens and ravines through which they rode, and all discourse ceased in the desire to get on. The exceeding purity of the atmosphere, which, at that great elevation, resembled a medium of thought rather than of matter, rendered objects defined, just, and near; and none but the mountaineers and Sigismund, who were used to the deception, (for in effect truth obtains this character with those who have been accustomed to the false) and who understood the grandeur of the scale on which nature has displayed her power among the Alps, knew how to calculate the distance which still separated them from their goal. More than a league of painful and stony ascent was to be surmounted, and yet Adelheid and Christine had both permitted slight exclamations of pleasure to escape them, when Pierre pointed to the speck of blue sky between the hoary pinnacles above, and first gave them to understand that it denoted the position of the convent. Here and there, too, small patches of the last year's snow were discovered, lying under the shadows of overhanging rocks, and which were likely to resist the powers of the sun till winter came again; another certain sign that they had reached a height greatly exceeding that of the usual habitations of men. The keenness of the air was another proof of their situation, for all the travellers had heard that the Augustines dwelt among eternal frosts, a report which is nearly literally true.

At no time during the day had the industry of the party been as great as it now became. In this respect, the ordinary traveller is apt to resemble him who journeys on the great highway of life, and who finds himself obliged, by a tardy and ill-requited diligence in age, to repair those omissions and negligences of youth which would have rendered the end of his toil easy and profitable. Improved as their speed had become, it continued to increase rather than to diminish, for Pierre Dumont kept his eye riveted on the heavens, and each moment of time seemed to bring new incentives to exertion. The wearied beasts manifested less zeal than the guide, and they who rode them were beginning to murmur at the unreasonableness of the rate at which they were compelled to proceed on the narrow, uneven, stony path, where footing for the animals was not always obtained with the necessary quickness, when a gloom deeper that cast by the shadows of the rocks fell upon their track, and the air filled with snow, as suddenly as if all its particles had been formed and condensed by the application of some prompt chemical process.

The change was so unexpected, and yet so complete, that the whole party checked their mules, and sat looking up at the millions of flakes that were descending on their heads, with more wonder and admiration than fear. A shout from Pierre first aroused them from this trance, and recalled them to a sense of the real state of things. He was standing on a knoll, already separated from the party by some fifty yards, white with snow, and gesticulating violently for the travellers to come on.

"For the sake of the Blessed Maria! quicken the beasts," he cried; for Pierre, like most who dwell in Valais, was a Catholic, and one accustomed to bethink him most of his heavenly mediator when most oppressed with present dangers; "quicken their speed, if ye value your lives! This is no moment to gaze at the mountains, which are well enough in their way, and no doubt both the finest and largest known," (no Swiss ever seriously vituperates or loses his profound veneration for his beloved nature,) "but which had better be the humblest plain on earth for our occasions than what they truly are. Quicken the mules then, for the love of the Blessed Virgin!"

"Thou betrayest unnecessary, and, for one that had needs be cool, indiscreet alarm, at the appearance of a little snow, friend Pierre," observed the Signer Grimaldi, as the mules drew near the guide, and speaking with a little of the irony of a soldier who had steeled his nerves by familiarity with danger. "Even we Italians, though less used to the frosts than you of the mountains, are not so much disturbed by the change, as thou, a trained guide of St. Bernard!"

"Reproach me as you will, Signore," said Pierre turning and pursuing his way with increased diligence, though he did not entirely succeed in concealing his resentment at an accusation which he knew to be unmerited, "but quicken your pace; until you are better acquainted with the country in which you journey, your words pass for empty breath in my ears. This is no trifle of a cloak doubled about the person, or of balls rolled into piles by the sport of children; but an affair of life or death. You are a half league in the air, Signor Genoese, in the region of storms, where the winds work their will, at times, as if infernal devils wore rioting to cool themselves, and where the stoutest limbs and the firmest hearts are brought but too often to see and confess their feebleness!"

The old man had uncovered his blanched locks in respect to the Italian, as he uttered this energetic remonstrance, and when he ended, he walked on with professional pride, as if disdaining to protect a brow that had already weathered so many tempests among the mountains.

"Cover thyself, good Pierre, I pray thee:" urged the Genoese in a tone of repentance. "I have shown the intemperance of a boy, and intemperance of a quality that little becomes my years. Thou art the best judge of the circumstances in which we are placed, and thou alone shalt lead us."

Pierre accepted the apology with a manly but respectful reverence, continuing always to ascend with unremitted industry.

Ten gloomy and anxious minutes succeeded. During this time, the falling snows came faster and in finer flakes, while, occasionally, there were fearful intimations that the winds were about to rise. At the elevation in which the travellers now found themselves, phenomena, that would ordinarily be of little account, become the arbiters of fate. The escape of the caloric from the human system, at the height of six or seven thousand feet above the sea, and in the latitude of forty-six, is, under the most favorable circumstances, frequently of itself the source of inconvenience; but here were grave additional reasons to heighten the danger. The absence of the sun's rays alone left a sense of chilling cold, and a few hours of night were certain to bring frost, even at midsummer. Thus it is that storms of trifling import in themselves gain power over the human frame, by its reduced means of resistance, and when to this fact is added the knowledge that the elements are far fiercer in their workings in the upper than in the nether regions of the earth, the motives of Pierre's concern will be better understood by the reader than they probably wese by himself, though the honest guide had a long and severe experience to supply the place of theory.

Men are rarely loquacious in danger. The timid recoil into themselves, yielding most of their faculties to a tormenting imagination, that augments the causes of alarm and diminishes the means of security, while the firm of mind rally and condense their powers to the point necessary to exertion. Such were the effects in the present instance, on those who followed Pierre. A general and deep silence pervaded the party, each one seeing their situation in the colors most suited to his particular habits and character. The men, without an exception, were grave and earnest in their efforts to force the mules forward; Adelheid became pale, but she preserved her calmness by the sheer force of character; Christine was trembling and dependent, though cheered by the presence of, and her confidence in, Sigismund; while the attendants of the heiress of Willading covered their heads, and followed their mistress with the blind faith in their superiors that is apt to sustain people of their class in serious emergencies.

Ten minutes sufficed entirely to change the aspect of the view. The frozen element could not adhere to the iron-like and perpendicular faces of the mountains, but the glens, and ravines, and valleys became as white as the peak of Vélan. Still Pierre continued his silent and upward march, in a way to keep alive a species of trembling hope among those who depended so helplessly upon his intelligence and faith. They wished to believe that the snow was merely one of those common occurrences that were to be expected on the summits of the Alps at this late season of the year, and which were no more than so many symptoms of the known rigor of the approaching winter. The guide himself was evidently disposed to lose no time in explanation, and as the secret excitement stole over all his followers, he no longer had cause to complain of the tardiness of their movements. Sigismund kept near his sister and Adelheid, having a care that their mules did not lag; while the other males performed the same necessary office for the beasts ridden by the female domestics. In this manner passed the few sombre minutes which immediately preceded the disappearance of day. The heavens were no longer visible. In that direction the eye saw only an endless succession of falling flakes, and it was getting to be difficult to distinguish even the ramparts of rock that bounded the irregular ravine in which they rode. They were known to be, however, at no great distance from the path, which indeed occasionally brushed their sides. At other moments they crossed rude, stony, mountain heaths, if such a word can be applied to spots without the symbol or hope of vegetation. The traces of the beasts that had preceded them, became less and less apparent, though the trickling stream that came down from the glaciers, and along which they had now journeyed-for hours, was occasionally seen, as it was crossed in pursuing their winding way. Pierre, though still confident that he held the true direction, alone knew that this guide was not longer to be relied on; for, as they drew nearer to the top of the mountains, the torrent gradually lessened both in its force and in the volume of its water, separating into twenty small rills, which came rippling from the vast bodies of snow that lay among the different peaks above.

As yet, there had been no wind. The guide, as minute after minute passed without bringing any change in this respect, ventured at last to advert to the fact, cheering his companions by giving them reasons to hope that they should yet reach the convent without any serious calamity. As if in mockery of this opinion, the flakes of snow began to whirl in the air, while the words were on his lips, and a blast came through the ravine, that set the protection of cloaks and mantles at defiance. Notwithstanding his resolution and experience, the stout-hearted Pierre suffered an exclamation of despair to escape him, and he instantly stopped, in the manner of a man who could no longer conceal the dread that had been collecting in his bosom for the last interminable and weary hour. Sigismund, as well as most of the men of the party, had dismounted a little previously, with a view to excite warmth by exercise. The youth had often traversed the mountains, and the cry no sooner reached his ear, than he was at the side of him who uttered it.

"At what distance, are we still from the convent?" he demanded eagerly.

"There is more than a league of steep and stone path to mount, Monsieur le Capitaine;" returned the disconsolate Pierre, in a tone that perhaps said more than his words.

"This is not a moment for indecision. Remember that thou art not the leader of a party of carriers with their beasts of burthen, but that there are those with us, who are unused to exposure, and are feeble of body. What is the distance from the last hamlet we passed?"

"Double that to the convent!"

Sigismund turned, and with the eye he made a silent appeal to the two old nobles, as if to ask for advice or orders.

"It might indeed be better to return," observed the Signore Grimaldi, in the way one utters a half-formed resolution. "This wind is getting to be piercingly cutting, and the night is hard upon us. What thinkest thou, Melchior; for, with Monsieur Sigismund, I am of opinion that there is little time to lose."

"Signore, your pardon," hastily interrupted the guide. "I would not undertake to cross the plain of the Vélan an hour later, for all the treasures of Einsideln and Loretto! The wind will have an infernal sweep in that basin, which will soon be boiling like a pot, while here we shall get, from time to time, the shelter of the rocks. The slightest mishap on the open ground might lead us astray a league or more, and it would need an hour to regain the course. The beasts too mount faster than they descend, and with far more surety in the dark; and even when at the village there is nothing fit for nobles, while the brave monks have all that a king can need."

"Those who escape from these wild rocks need not be critical about their fare, honest Pierre, when fairly housed. Wilt thou answer for our arrival at the convent unharmed, and in reasonable time?"

"Signore, we are in the hands of God. The pious Augustines, I make no doubt, are praying for all who are on the mountain at this moment; but there is not a minute to lose. I ask no more than that none lose sight of their companions, and that each exert his force to the utmost. We are not far from the House of Refuge, and should the storm increase to a tempest, as, to conceal the danger no longer, well may happen in this late month, we will seek its shelter for a few hours."

This intelligence was happily communicated, for the certainty that there was a place of safety within an attainable distance, had some such cheering effect on the travellers as is produced on the mariner who finds that the hazards of the gale are lessened by the accidental position of a secure harbor under his lee. Repeating his admonitions for the party to keep as close together as possible, and advising all who felt the sinister effects of the cold on their limbs to dismount, and to endeavor to restore the circulation by exercise, Pierre resumed his route.

But even the time consumed in this short conference had sensibly altered the condition of things for the worse. The wind, which had no fixed direction, being a furious current of the upper air diverted from its true course by encountering the ragged peaks and ravines of the Alps, was now whirling around them in eddies, now aiding their ascent by seeming to push against their backs, and then returning in their faces with a violence that actually rendered advance impossible. The temperature fell rapidly several degrees, and the most vigorous of the party began to perceive the benumbing influence of the chilling currents, at their lower extremities especially, in a manner to excite serious alarm. Every precaution was used to protect the females that tenderness could suggest; but though Adelheid, who alone retained sufficient self-command to give an account of her feelings, diminished the danger of their situation with the wish not to alarm their companions uselessly, she could not conceal from herself the horrible truth that the vital heat was escaping from her own body, with a rapidity that rendered it impossible for her much longer to retain the use of her faculties. Conscious of her own mental superiority over that of all her female companions, a superiority which in such moments is even of more account than bodily force, after a few minutes of silent endurance, she checked her mule, and called upon Sigismund to examine the condition of his sister and her maids, neither of whom had now spoken for some time.

This startling request was made at a moment when the storm appeared to gather new force, and when it had become absolutely impossible to distinguish even the whitened earth at twenty paces from the spot where the party stood collected in a shivering group. The young soldier threw open the cloaks and mantles in which Christine was enveloped, and the half-unconscious girl sank on his shoulder, like a drowsy infant that was willing to seek its slumbers in the arms of one it loved.

"Christine!--my sister!--my poor, my much-abused, angelic sister!" murmured Sigismund, happily for his secret in a voice that only reached the ears of Adelheid. "Awake! Christine; for the love of our excellent and affectionate mother, exert thyself. Awake! Christine, in the name of God, awake!"

"Awake, dearest Christine!" exclaimed Adelheid, throwing herself from the saddle, and folding the smiling but benumbed girl to her bosom. "God protect me from the pang of feeling that thy loss should be owing to my wish to lead thee amid these cruel and inhospitable rocks! Christine, if thou hast love or pity for me, awake!"

"Look to the maids!" hurriedly said Pierre, who found that he was fast touching on one of those mountain catastrophes, of which, in the course of his life, he had been the witness of a few of fearful consequences. "Look to all the females, for he who now sleeps, dies!"

The muleteers soon stripped the two domestics of their outer coverings, and it was immediately proclaimed that both were in imminent danger, one having already lost all consciousness. A timely application of the flask of Pierre, and the efforts of the muleteers, succeeded so far in restoring life as to remove the grounds of immediate apprehension; though it was apparent to the least instructed of them all, that half an hour more of exposure would probably complete the fatal work that had so actively and vigorously commenced. To add to the horror of this conviction, each member of the party, not excepting the muleteers, was painfully conscious of the escape of that vital warmth whose total flight was death.

In this strait all dismounted. They felt that the occasion was one of extreme jeopardy, that nothing could save them but resolution, and that every minute of time was getting to be of the last importance. Each female, Adelheid included, was placed between two of the other sex, and, supported in this manner, Pierre called loudly and in a manful voice for the whole to proceed. The beasts were driven after them by one of the muleteers.

The progress of travellers, feeble as Adelheid and her companions, on a stony path of very uneven surface, and of a steep ascent, the snow covering the feet, and the tempest cutting their faces, was necessarily slow, and to the last degree toilsome. Still, the exertion increased the quickness of the blood, and, for a short time, there was an appearance of recalling those who most suffered to life. Pierre, who still kept his post with the hardihood of a mountaineer, and the fidelity of a Swiss, cheered them on with his voice, continuing to raise the hope that the place of refuge was at hand.

At this instant, when exertion was most needed, and when, apparently, all were sensible of its importance and most disposed to make it, the muleteer charged with the duty of urging on the line of beasts deserted his trust, preferring to take his chance of regaining the village by descending the mountain, to struggle uselessly, and at a pace so slow, to reach the convent. The man was a stranger in the country, who had been adventitiously employed for this expedition, and was unconnected with Pierre by any of those ties which are the best pledges of unconquerable faith, when the interests of self press hard upon our weaknesses. The wearied beasts, no longer driven, and indisposed to toil, first stopped, then turned aside to avoid the cutting air and the ascent, and were soon wandering from the path it was so vitally necessary to keep.

As soon as Pierre was informed of the circumstance, he eagerly issued an order to collect the stragglers without delay, and at every hazard. Benumbed, bewildered, and unable to see beyond a few yards, this embarrassing duty was not easily performed. One after another of the party joined in the pursuit, for all the effects of the travellers were on the beasts; and after some ten minutes of delay, blended with an excitement which helped to quicken the blood and to awaken the faculties of even the females, the mules were all happily regained. They were secured to each other head and tail, in the manner so usual in the droves of these animals, and Pierre turned to resume the order of the march. But on seeking the path, it was not to be found! Search was made on every side, and yet none could meet with the smallest of its traces. Broken, rough fragments of rock, were all that rewarded the most anxious investigation; and after a few precious minutes uselessly wasted, they all assembled around the guide, as if by common consent, to seek his counsel. The truth was no longer to be concealed--the party was lost!

Chapter XXIII

Let no presuming railer tax
Creative wisdom, as if aught was form'd
In vain, or not for admirable ends.

Thomson.

So long as we possess the power to struggle, hope is the last feeling to desert the human mind. Men are endowed with every gradation of courage, from the calm energy of reflection, which is rendered still more effective by physical firmness, to the headlong precipitation of reckless spirit: from the resolution that grows more imposing and more respectable as there is greater occasion for its exercise, to the fearful and ill-directed energies of despair. But no description with the pen can give the reader a just idea of the chill that comes over the heart when accidental causes rob us, suddenly and without notice, of those resources on which we have been habitually accustomed to rely. The mariner without his course or compass loses his audacity and coolness, though the momentary danger be the same; the soldier will fly, if you deprive him of his arms; and the hunter of our own forests who has lost his landmarks, is transformed from the bold and determined foe of its tenants, into an anxious and dependent fugitive, timidly seeking the means of retreat. In short, the customary associations of the mind being rudely and suddenly destroyed, we are made to feel that reason, while it elevates us so far above the brutes as to make man their lord and governor, becomes a quality less valuable than instinct, when the connecting link in its train of causes and effects is severed.

It was no more than a natural consequence of his greater experience, that Pierre Dumont understood the horrors of their present situation far better than any with him. It is true, there yet remained enough light to enable him to pick his way over the rocks and stones, but he had sufficient experience to understand that there was less risk in remaining stationary than in moving; for, while there was only one direction that led towards the Refuge, all the rest would conduct them to a greater distance from the shelter, which was now the only hope. On the other hand, a very few minutes of the intense cold, and of the searching wind to which they were exposed, would most probably freeze the currents of life in the feebler of those intrusted to his care.

"Hast thou aught to advise?" asked Melchior de Willading, folding Adelheid to his bosom, beneath his ample cloak, and communicating, with a father's love, a small portion of the meagre warmth that still remained in his own aged frame to that of his drooping daughter--"canst thou bethink thee of nothing, that may be done, in this awful strait?"

"If the good monks have been active--" returned the wavering Pierre. "I fear me that the dogs have not yet been exercised, on the paths, this season!"

"Has it then come to this! Are our lives indeed dependent on the uncertain sagacity of brutes!"

"Mein Herr, I would bless the Virgin, and her holy Son, if it were so! But I fear this storm has been so sudden and unexpected, that we may not even hope for their succor."

Melchior groaned. He folded his child still nearer to his heart, while the athletic Sigismund shielded his drooping sister, as the fowl shelters its young beneath the wing.

"Delay is death," rejoined the Signor Grimaldi. "I have heard of muleteers that have been driven to kill their beasts, that shelter and warmth might be found in their entrails."

"The alternative is horrible!" interrupted Sigismund. "Is return impossible? By always descending, we must, in time reach the village below."

"That time would be fatal," answered Pierre. "I know of only one resource that remains. If the party will keep together, and answer my shouts I will make another effort to find the path."

This proposal was gladly accepted, for energy and hope go hand-in-hand, and the guide was about to quit the group, when he felt the strong grasp of Sigismund on his arm.

"I will be thy companion," said the soldier firmly.

"Thou hast not done me justice, young man," answered Pierre, with severe reproach in his manner. "Had I been base enough to desert my trust, these limbs and this strength are yet sufficient to carry me safely down the mountain; but though a guide of the Alps may freeze like another man, the last throb of his heart will be in behalf of those he serves!"

"A thousand pardons brave old man--a thousand pardons; still, will I be thy companion; the search that is conducted by two will be more likely to succeed, than that on which thou goes alone."

The offended Pierre, who liked the spirit of the youth as much as he disliked his previous suspicions, met the apology frankly. He extended his hand and forgot the feelings, that, even amid the tempests of those wild mountains, were excited by a distrust of his honesty. After this short concession to the ever-burning, though smothered volcano, of human passion, they left the group together, in order to make a last search for their course.

The snow by this time was many inches deep, and as the road was at best but a faint bridle-path that could scarcely be distinguished by day-light from the débris which strewed the ravines, the undertaking would have been utterly hopeless, had not Pierre known that there was the chance of still meeting with some signs of the many mules that daily went up and down the mountain. The guide called to the muleteers, who answered his cries every minute, for so long as they kept within the sound of each other's voices, there was no danger of their becoming entirely separated. But, amid the hollow roaring of the wind, and the incessant pelting of the storm, it was neither safe nor practicable to venture far asunder. Several little stony knolls were ascended and descended, and a rippling rill was found, but without bringing with it any traces of the path. The heart of Pierre began to chill with the decreasing; warmth of his body, and the firm old man, overwhelmed with his responsibility while his truant thoughts would unbidden recur to those whom he had left in his cottage at the foot of the mountain, gave way at last to his emotions in a paroxysm of grief, wringing his hands, weeping and calling loudly on God for succor. This fearful evidence of their extremity worked upon the feelings of Sigismund until they were wrought up nearly to frenzy. His great physical force still sustained him, and in an access of energy that was fearfully allied to madness, he rushed forward into the vortex of snow and hail, as if determined to leave all to the Providence of God, disappearing from the eyes of his companion. This incident recalled the guide to his senses. He called earnestly on the thoughtless youth to return. No answer was given, and Pierre hastened back to the motionless and shivering party, in order to unite all their voices in a last effort to be heard. Cry upon cry was raised, but each shout was answered merely by the hoarse rushing of the winds.

"Sigismund! Sigismund!" called one after another, in hurried and alarmed succession.

"The noble boy will be irretrievably lost!" exclaimed the Signor Grimaldi, in despair, the services already rendered by the youth, together with his manly qualities, having insensibly and closely wound themselves around his heart. "He will die a miserable death, and without the consolation of meeting his fate in communion with his fellow-sufferers!"

A shout from Sigismund came whirling past, as if the sound were embodied in the gale.

"Blessed ruler of the earth, this is alone the mercy!" exclaimed Melchior de Willading,--"he has found the path!"

"And honor to thee, Maria--thou mother of God!" murmured the Italian.

At that moment, a dog came leaping and barking through the snow. It immediately was scenting and whining among the frozen travellers. The exclamations of joy and surprise were scarcely uttered before Sigismund, accompanied by another, joined the party.

"Honor and thanks to the good Augustines!" cried the delighted guide; "this is the third good office of the kind, for which I am their debtor!"

"I would it were true, honest Pierre," answered the stranger. "But Maso and Nettuno are poor substitutes, in a tempest like this, for the servants and beasts of St. Bernard. I am a wanderer, and lost like yourselves, and my presence brings little other relief than that which is known to be the fruit of companionship in misery. The saints have brought me a second time into your company when matters were hanging between life and death!"

Maso made this last remark when, by drawing nearer the group, he had been able to ascertain, by the remains of the light, of whom the party was composed.

"If it is to be as useful now as thou hast already been," answered the Genoese, "it will be happier for us all, thyself included: bethink thee quickly of thy expedients, and I will make thee an equal sharer of all that a generous Providence hath bestowed."

Il Maledetto rarely listened to the voice of the Signor Grimaldi, without a manner of interest and curiosity which, as already mentioned, had more than once struck the latter himself, but which he quite naturally attributed to the circumstance of his person being known to one who had declared himself to be a native of Genoa. Even at this terrible moment, the same manner was evident and the noble, thinking it a favorable symptom, renewed the already neglected offer of fortune, with a view to quicken a zeal which he reasonably enough supposed would be most likely to be awakened by the hopes of a substantial reward.

"Were there question here, illustrious Signore," answered Maso, "of steering a barge, of shortenning sail, or of handling a craft of any rig or construction, in gale, squall, hurricane, or a calm among breakers, my skill and experience might be turned to good account; but setting aside the difference in our strength and hardihood, even that lily which is in so much danger of being nipped by the frosts, is not more helpless than I am myself at this moment. I am no better than yourselves, Signori, and, though a better mountaineer perhaps, I rely on the favor of the saints to be succored, or my time must finish among the snows instead of in the surf of a sea-shore, as, until now, I had always believed would be my fate."

"But the dog--thy admirable dog!"

"Ah, eccellenza, Nettuno is but a useless beast, here! God has given him a thicker mantle, and a warmer dress than to us Christians, but even this advantage will soon prove a curse to my poor friend. The long hair he carries will quickly be covered with icicles, and, as the snow deepens, it will retard his movements. The dogs of St. Bernard are smoother, have longer limbs, a truer scent and possess the advantage of being trained to the paths."

A tremendous shout of Sigismund's interrupted Maso,--the youth, on finding that the accidental meeting with the mariner was not likely to lead to any immediate advantages, having instantly, accompanied by Pierre and one of his assistants, renewed the search. The cry was echoed from the guide and the muleteer, and then all three were seen flying through the snow, preceded by a powerful mastiff. Nettuno, who had been crouching with his bushy tail between his legs, barked, seemed to arouse with renewed courage, and then leaped with evident joy and good-will upon the back of his old antagonist Uberto.

The dog of St. Bernard was alone. But his air and all his actions were those of an animal whose consciousness was wrought up to the highest pitch permitted by the limits nature had set to the intelligence of a brute. He ran from one to another, rubbed his glossy and solid side against the limbs of all, wagged his tail, and betrayed the usual signs that creatures of his species manifest, when their instinct is most alive. Luckily he had a good interpreter of his meaning in the guide, who, knowing the habits, and, if it may be so expressed, the intentions of the mastiff, feeling there was not a moment to lose if they would still preserve the feebler members of their party, begged the others to hasten the necessary dispositions to profit by this happy meeting. The females were supported as before, the mules fastened together, and Pierre, placing himself in front, called cheerfully to the dog, encouraging him to lead the way.

"Is it quite prudent to confide so implicitly to the guidance of this brute?" asked the Signor Grimaldi a little doubtingly, when he saw the arrangement on which, by the increasing gloom and the growing intensity of the cold, it was but too apparent, even to one as little accustomed to the mountains as himself, that the lives of the whole party depended.

"Fear not to trust to old Uberto, Signore," answered Pierre, moving onward as he spoke, for to think of further delay was out of the question; "fear nothing for the faith or the knowledge of the dog. These animals are trained by the servants of the convent to know and keep the paths, even when the snows lie on them fathoms deep. God has given them stout hearts, long limbs, and short hair expressly, as it has often seemed to me, for this end; and nobly do they use the gifts! I am acquainted with all their ways, for we guides commonly learn the ravines of St. Bernard by first serving the claviers of the convent, and many a day have I gone up and down these rocks with a couple of these animals in training for this very purpose. The father and mother of Uberto were my favorite companions, and their son will hardly play an old friend of the family false."

The travellers followed their leader with more confidence, though blindly. Uberto appeared to perform his duty with the sobriety and steadiness that became his years, and which, indeed, were very necessary for the circumstances in which they were placed. Instead of bounding ahead and becoming lost to view, as most probably would have happened with a younger animal, the noble and half-reasoning brute maintained a pace that was suited to the slow march of those who supported the females, occasionally stopping to look back, as if to make sure that none were left.

The dogs of St. Bernard are, or it might perhaps be better to say were,--for it is affirmed that the ancient race is lost,--chosen for their size, their limbs, and the shortness of their coats, as has just been stated by Pierre; the former being necessary to convey the succor with which they were often charged, as well as to overcome the difficulties of the mountains, and the two latter that they might the better wade through, and resist the influence of, the snows. Their training consisted in rendering them familiar with, and attached to, the human race; in teaching them to know and to keep the paths on all occasions, except such as called for a higher exercise of their instinct, and to discover the position of those who had been overwhelmed by the avalanches; and; to assist in disinterring their bodies. In all these duties Uberto had been so long exercised, that he was universally know to be the most sagacious and the most trusty animal on the mountain. Pierre followed his steps with so much greater-reliance on his intelligence, from being perfectly acquainted with the character of the dog. When, therefore, he saw the mastiff turn at right angles to the course he had just been taking, the guide, on reaching the spot, imitated his example, and, first removing the snow to make sure of the fact, he joyfully proclaimed to those who came after him that the lost path was found. This intelligence sounded like a reprieve from death, though the mountaineers well knew that more than an hour of painful and increasing toil was still necessary to reach the hospice. The chilled blood of the tender beings who were fast dropping into the terrible sleep which is the forerunner of death, was quickened in their veins, however, when they heard the shout of delight that spontaneously broke from all their male companions, on learning the glad tidings.

The movement was now faster, though embarrassed and difficult on account of the incessant pelting of the storm and the influence of the biting cold, which were difficult to be withstood by even the strongest of the party. Sigismund groaned inwardly, as he thought of Adelheid and his sister's being exposed to a tempest which shook the stoutest frame and the most manly heart among them. He encircled the latter with an arm, rather carrying than leading her along, for the young soldier had sufficient knowledge of the localities of the mountain to understand that they were still at a fearful distance from the Col, and that the strength of Christine was absolutely unequal to the task of reaching it unsupported.

Occasionally Pierre spoke to the dogs, Nettuno keeping close to the side of Uberto in order to prevent separation, since the path was no longer discernible without constant examination, the darkness having so far increased as to reduce the sight to very narrow limits. Each time the name of the latter was pronounced, the animal would stop, wag his tail, or give some other sign of recognition, as if to reassure his followers of his intelligence and fidelity. After one of these short halts, old Uberto and his companion unexpectedly refused to proceed. The guide, the two old nobles, and at length the whole party, were around them, and no cry or encouragement of the mountaineers could induce the dogs to quit their tracks.

"Are we again lost?" asked the Baron de Willading, pressing Adelheid closer to his beating heart, nearly ready to submit to their common fate in despair. "Has God at length forsaken us?--my daughter--my beloved child!"

This touching appeal was answered by a howl from Uberto, who leaped madly away and disappeared. Nettuno followed, barking wildly and with a deep throat. Pierre did not hesitate about following, and Sigismund, believing that the movement of the guide was to arrest the flight of the dogs, was quickly on his heels. Maso moved with greater deliberation.

"Nettuno is not apt to raise that bark with nothing but hail, and snow, and wind in his nostrils," said the calculating Italian. "We are either near another party of travellers, for such are on the mountains as I know"

"God forbid! Art sure of this?" demanded the Signor Grimaldi, observing that the other had suddenly checked himself.

"Sure that others *were*, Signore," returned the mariner deliberately, as if he measured well the meaning of each word. "Ah, here comes the trusty beast, and Pierre, and the Captain, with their tidings, be they good or be they evil."

The two just named rejoined their friends a Maso ceased speaking. They hurriedly informed the shivering travellers that the much desired Refuge was near, and that nothing but the darkness and the driving snow prevented it from being seen.

"It was a blessed thought, and one that came from St. Augustine himself, which led the holy monks to raise this shelter!" exclaimed the delighted Pierre, no longer considering it necessary to conceal the extent of the danger they had run. "I would not answer even for my own power to reach the hospice in a time like this. You are of mother church, Signore, being of Italy?"

"I am one of her unworthy children," returned the Genoese.

"This unmerited favor must have come from the prayers of St. Augustine, and a vow I made to send a fair offering to our Lady of Einsiedeln; for never before have I known a dog of St. Bernard lead the traveller to the Refuge! Their business is to find the frozen, and to guide the traveller along the paths to the hospice. Even Uberto had his doubts, as you saw, but the vow prevailed; or, I know not--it might, indeed, have been the prayer."

The Signor Grimaldi was too eager to get Adelheid under cover, and, in good sooth, to be there himself, to waste the time in discussing the knotty point of which of two means that were equally orthodox, had been the most efficacious in bringing about their rescue. In common with the others, he followed the pious and confiding Pierre in silence, making the best of his way after the credit lous guide. The latter had not yet seen the Refuge himself, for so these places are well termed on the Alpine passes, but the information of the ground had satisfied him of its proximity. Once reassured as to his precise position, all the surrounding localities presented themselves to his mind with the familiarity the seaman manifests with every cord in the intricate maze of his rigging, in the darkest night, or, to produce a parallel of more common use, with the readiness which all manifest in the intricacies of their own habitations. The broken chain of association being repaired and joined, every thing became clear, again to his apprehension, and, in diverging from the path on this occasion, the old man held his way as directly toward the spot he sought, as if he were journeying under a bright sun. There was a rough but short descent, a similar rise, and the long-desired goal was reached.

We shall not stop to dwell upon the emotions with which the travellers first touched this place of comparative security. Humility, and dependence on the providence of God, were the pre-dominant sensations even with the rude muleteers, while the pearly exhausted females were just able to express in murmurs their fervent gratitude to the omnipotent power that had permitted its agents so unexpectedly to interpose between them and death. The Refuge was not seen until Pierre laid his hand on the roof, now white with snow, and proclaimed its character with a loud, warm, and devout thanksgiving.

"Enter and thank God!" he said. "Another hopeless half-hour would have brought down from his pride the stoutest among us--enter, and thank God!"

As is the fact with all the edifices of that region the building was entirely of stone, even to the roof having the form of those vaulted cellars which in this country are use for the preservation of vegetables. It was quite free from humidity, however, the clearness of the atmosphere and the entire absence of soil preventing the accumulation of moisture, and it offered no more than the naked protection of its walls to those who sought its cover. But shelter on such a night was everything, and this it effectually afforded. The place had only one outlet, being simply formed of four walls and the roof; but it was sufficiently large to shelter a party twice as numerous as that which had now reached it.

The transition from the biting cold and piercing winds of the mountain to the shelter of this inartificial building, was so great as to produce something like a general sensation of warmth. The advantage gained in this change of feeling was judiciously improved by the application of friction and of restoratives under the direction of Pierre. Uberto carried a small supply of the latter attached to his collar, and before half an hour had passed Adelheid and Christine were sleeping sweetly, side by side, muffled in plenty of the spare garments, and pillowed on the saddles and housings of the mules. The brutes were brought within the Refuge and as no party mounted the St Bernard without carrying the provender necessary for its beasts of burthen, that sterile region affording none of its own, the very fuel being transported leagues on the backs of mules, the patient and hardy animals, too, found their solace, after the fatigues and exposure of the day. The presence of so many living bodies in lodgings so confined aided in producing warmth, and, after all had eaten of the scanty fare furnished by the foresight of the guide, drowsiness came over the whole party.

Chapter XXIV

> Side by side,
> Within they lie, a mournful company.
>
> Rogers.

The sleep of the weary is sweet. In after-life, Adelheid, when dwelling in a palace, reposing on down, and canopied by the rich stuffs of a more generous climate, was often heard to say that she had never taken rest grateful as that she found in the Refuge of St. Bernard. So easy, natural, and refreshing, had been her slumbers, unalloyed even by those dreams of precipices and avalanches which, long afterwards, haunted her slumbers, that she was the first to open her eyes on the following morning, awaking like an infant that had enjoyed a quiet and healthful repose. Her movements aroused Christine. They threw aside the cloaks and coats that covered them, and sat gazing about the place in the confusion that the novelty of their situation would be likely to produce. All the rest of the travellers still slumbered; and, arising without noise, they passed the silent and insensible sleepers, the quiet mules which had stretched themselves near the entrance of the place, and quitted the hut.

Without, the scene was wintry: but, as is usual in the Alps let what may be the season, its features of grand and imposing sublimity were prominent The day was among the peaks above them, while the shades of night still lay upon the valleys, forming a landscape like that exquisite and poetical picture of the lower world, which Guido has given in the celebrated al-fresco painting of Aurora. The ravines and glens were covered with snow, but the sides of the rugged rocks were bare in their eternal hue of ferruginous brown. The little knoll on which the Refuge stood was also nearly naked, the wind having driven the light particles of the snow into the ravine of the path. The air of the morning is keen at that great height even in midsummer, and the shivering girls drew their mantles about them, though they breathed the clear, elastic, inspiring element with pleasure. The storm was entirely past, and the pure sapphire-colored sky was in lovely contrast with the shadows beneath, raising their thoughts naturally to that heaven which shone in a peace and glory so much in harmony with the ordinary images we shadow forth of the abode of the blessed. Adelheid pressed the hand of Christine, and they knelt together, bowing their heads to a rock. As fervent, pure, and sincere orisons ascended to God, from these pious and innocent spirits, as it belongs to poor mortality to offer.

This general, and in their peculiar situation especial, duty performed, the gentle girls felt more assured. Relieved of a heavy and imperative obligation, they ventured to look about them with greater confidence. Another building, similar in form and material to that in which their companions were still sleeping, stood on the same swell of rock, and their first inquiries naturally took that direction. The entrance, or outlet to this hut, was an orifice that resembled a window rather than a door. They moved cautiously to the spot, looking into the gloomy, cavern-like room, as timidly as the hare throws his regards about him before he ventures from his cover. Four human forms were reposing deep in the vault, with their backs sustained against the walls. They slept profoundly too, for the curious but startled girls gazed at them long, and retired without causing them to awake.

"We have not been alone on the mountain in this terrible night," whispered Adelheid, gently urging the trembling Christine away from the spot; "thou seest that other travellers have been taking their rest near us; most probably after perils and fatigues like our own."

Christine drew closer to the side of her more experienced friend, like the young of the dove hovering near the mother-bird when first venturing from the nest, and they returned to the refuge they had quitted, for the cold was still so intense as to render its protection grateful. At the door they were met by Pierre, the vigilant old man having awakened as soon as the light crossed his eyes.

"We are not alone here;" said Adelheid, pointing to the other stone-covered roof--"there are travellers sleeping in yonder building, too."

"Their sleep will be long, lady;" answered the guide, shaking his head solemnly. "With two of them it has already lasted a twelvemonth and the third has slept where you saw him since the fall of the avalanche in the last days of April."

Adelheid recoiled a step, for his meaning was too plain to be misunderstood. After looking at her gentle companion, she demanded if those they had seen were in truth the bodies of travellers who had perished on the mountain.

"Of no other, lady," returned Pierre, "This hut is for the living--that for the dead. So near are the two to each other, when men journey on these wild rocks in winter. I have known him who passed a short and troubled night here, begin a sleep in the other before the turn of the day that is not only deep enough, but which will last for ever. One of the three that thou hast just seen was a guide like myself: he was buried in the falling snow at the spot where the path leaves the plain of Vélan below us. Another is a pilgrim that perished in as clear a night as ever shone on St. Bernard, and merely for having taking a cup too much to cheer his way. The third is a poor vine-dresser that was coming from Piedmont into our Swiss valleys to follow his calling, when death overtook him in an ill-advised slumber, in which he was so unwise as to indulge at nightfall. I found his body myself on that naked rock, the day after we had drunk together in friendship at Aoste, and with my own hands was he placed among the others."

"And such is the burial a Christian gets in this inhospitable country!"

"What would you, lady!--'tis the chance of the poor and the unknown. Those that have friends are sought and found; but those that die without leaving traces of their origin fare as you see. The spade is useless among these rocks; and then it is better that the body should remain where it may be seen and claimed, than it should be put out of sight. The good fathers, and all of note, are taken down into the valleys, where there is earth and are decently buried; while the poor and the stranger are housed in this vault, which is a better cover than many of them knew while living. Ay, there are three Christians there, who were all lately walking the earth in the flesh, gay and active as any."

"The bodies are four in number!"

Pierre looked surprised; he mused a little, and continued his employment.

"Then another has perished. The time may come when my own blood shall freeze. This is a fate the guide must ever keep in mind, for he is exposed to it at an hour and a season that he knows not!"

Adelheid pursued the subject no farther. She remembered to have heard that the pure atmosphere of the mountain prevented that offensive decay which is usually associated with the idea of death, and the usage lost some of its horror in the recollection.

In the mean time the remainder of the party awoke, and were collecting before the refuge. The mules were led forth and saddled, the baggage was loaded, and Pierre was calling upon the travellers to mount, when Uberto and Nettuno came leaping down the path in company, running side by side in excellent fellowship. The movements of the dogs were of a nature to attract the attention of Pierre and the muleteers, who predicted that they should soon see some of the servants of the hospice. The result showed the familiarity of the guide with his duty, for he had scarce ventured this opinion, when a party from the gorge on the summit of the mountain was seen wading through the snow, along the path that led towards the Refuge, with Father Xavier at its head.

The explanations were brief and natural. After conducting the travellers to the shelter, and passing most of the night in their company, at the approach of dawn Uberto had returned to the convent, always attended by his friend Nettuno. Here he communicated to the monks, by signs which they who were accustomed to the habits of the animal were not slow in interpreting, that travellers were on the mountain. The good clavier knew that the party of the Baron de Willading was about to cross the Col, for he had hurried home to be in readiness to receive them; and foreseeing the probability that they hod been overtaken by the storm of the previous night, he was foremost in joining the servants who went forth to their succor. The little flask of cordial, too, had been removed from the collar of Uberto, leaving no doubt of its contents having been used; and, as nothing was more probable than that the travellers should seek a cover, their steps were directed to wards the Refuge as a matter of course.

The worthy clavier made this explanation with eyes that glistened with moisture, occasionally interrupting himself to murmur a prayer of thanksgiving. He passed from one of the party to the other, not even neglecting the muleteers, examining their limbs, and more especially their ears, to see that they had quite escaped the influence of the frost, and was only happy when assured by his own observation that the terrible danger they had run was not likely to be attended by any injurious consequences.

"We are accustomed to see many accidents of this nature," he said, smilingly, when the examination was satisfactorily ended, "and practice has made us quick of sight in these matters. The blessed Maria be praised, and adoration to her holy Son, that you have all got through the night so well! There is a warm breakfast in readiness in the convent kitchen, and, one solemn duty performed, we will go up the rocks to enjoy it. The little building near us is the last earthly abode of those who perish on this side the mountain, and whose remains are unclaimed. None of our canons pass the spot without offering a prayer in behalf of their souls. Kneel with me, then, you that have so much reason to be grateful to God, and join in the petition."

Father Xavier knelt on the rocks, and all the Catholics of the party united with him in the prayer for the dead. The Baron de Willading, his daughter and their attendants stood uncovered the while for though their Protestant opinions rejected such a mediation as useless, they deeply felt the solemnity and holy character of the sacrifice. The clavier arose with a countenance that was beaming and bright as the morning sun which, just at that moment, appeared above the summits of the Alps, casting its genial and bland warmth on the group, the brown huts, and the mountain side.

"Thou art a heretic," he said affectionately to Adelheid, in whom he felt the interest, to which her youth and beauty, and the great danger they had so lately run in company, very naturally gave birth. "Thou art an impenitent heretic, but we will hot cast thee off; notwithstanding thy obstinacy and crimes, thou seest that the saints can interest themselves in the behalf of obstinate sinners, or thou and all with thee would have surely been lost."

This was said in a way to draw a smile from Adelheid, who received his accusations as so many friendly and playful reproaches. As a token of peace between them, she offered her hand to the monk, with a request that he would aid her in getting into the saddle.

"Dost thou remark the brutes!" said the Signor Grimaldi, pointing to the animals, who were gravely seated before the window of the bone-house, with relaxed jaws, keeping their eyes riveted on its entrance, or window. "Thy St. Bernard dogs, father, seem trained to serve a Christian in all ways, whether living or dead."

"Their quiet attitude and decent attention might indeed justify such a remark! Didst thou ever note such conduct in Uberto before?" returned the Augustine, addressing the servants of the convent, for the actions of the animals were a study and a subject of great interest to all of St. Bernard.

"They tell me that another fresh body has been put into the house, since I last came down the mountain" remarked Pierre, who was quietly disposing of a mule in a manner more favorable for Adelheid to mount: "the mastiff scents the dead. It was this that brought him to the Refuge last night, Heaven be praised for the mercy!"

This was said with the indifference that habit is apt to create, for the usage of leaving bodies uninterred had no influence on the feelings of the guide, but it did not the less strike those who had descended from the convent.

"Thou art the last that came down thyself," said one of the servants; "nor have any come up, but those who are now safe in the convent, taking their rest after last night's tempest."

"How canst utter this idle nonsense, Henri, when a fresh body is in the house! This lady counted them but now, and there are four; three was the number that I showed the Piedmontese noble whom I led from Aoste, the day thou meanest!"

"Look to this;" said the clavier, turning abruptly away from Adelheid, whom he was on the point of helping into the saddle.

The men entered the gloomy vault, whence they soon returned bearing a body, which they placed with its back against the wall of the building, in the open air. A cloak was over the head and face, as if the garment had been thus arranged to exclude the cold.

"He hath perished the past night, mistaking the bone-house for the Refuge!" exclaimed the clavier: "Maria and her Son intercede for his soul!"

"Is the unfortunate man truly dead?" asked the Genoese with more of worldly care, and with greater practice in the investigation of facts. "The frozen sleep long before the currents of life cease entirely to run."

The Augustine commanded his followers to remove the cloak, though with little hope that the suggestion of the other would prove true. When the cloth was raised, the collapsed and pallid features of one in whom life was unequivocally extinct were exposed to view. Unlike most of those that perish of cold, who usually sink into the long sleep of eternity by a gradual numbness and a slowly increasing unconsciousness, there was an expression of pain in the countenance of the stranger which seemed to announce that his parting struggles had been severe, and that he had resigned his hold of that mysterious principle which connects the soul to the body, with anguish. A shriek from Christine interrupted the awful gaze of the travellers, and drew their looks in another direction. She was clinging to the neck of Adelheid, her arms appearing to writhe with the effort to incorporate heir two bodies into one.

"It is he! It is he!" muttered the frightened and half frantic girl, burying her pale face in the bosom of her friend. "Oh! God!--it is he!"

"Of whom art thou speaking, dear?" demanded the wondering, but not the less awe-struck, Adelheid, believing that the weakened nerves of the poor girl were unstrung by the horror of the spectacle--"it is a traveller like ourselves, that has unhappily perished in the very storm from which, by the kindness of Providence, we have been permitted to escape. Thou shouldst not tremble thus; for, fearful as it is, he is in a condition to which we all must come."

"So soon! so soon! so suddenly--oh! it is he!" Adelheid, alarmed at the violence of Christine's feelings, was quite at a loss to account for them, when the relapsed grasp and the dying voice showed that her friend had fainted. Sigismund was one of the first to come to the assistance of his sister, who was soon restored to consciousness by the ordinary applications. In order to effect the cure she was borne to a rock at some little distance from the rest of the party, where none of the other sex presumed to come, with the exception of her brother. The latter staid but a moment, for a stir in the little party at the bone-house induced him to go thither. His return was slow, thoughtful, and sad.

"The feelings of our poor Christine have been unhinged, and she is too easily excited to undergo the vicissitudes of a journey" observed Adelheid, after having announced the restoration of the sufferer to her senses; "have you seen her thus before?"

"No angel could be more tranquil and happy than my cruelly treated sister was until this last disgrace;--you appear ignorant yourself of the melancholy truth?"

Adelheid looked her surprise.

"The dead man is he who was so lately intended to be the master of my sister's happiness, and the wounds on his body leave little doubt that he has been murdered."

The emotion of Christine needed no further explanation.

"Murdered!" repeated Adelheid, in a whisper.

"Of that frightful truth there can be no question. Your father and our friends are now employed in making the examinations which may hereafter be useful in discovering the authors of the deed."

"Sigismund?"

"What wouldst thou, Adelheid?"

"Thou hast felt resentment against this unfortunate man?"

"I deny it not: could a brother feel otherwise?"

"But now--now that God hath so fearfully visited him?"

"From my soul I forgive him. Had we met in Italy, whither I knew he was going--but this is foolish."

"Worse than that, Sigismund."

"From my inmost soul I pardon him. I never thought him worthy of her whose simple affection, were won by the first signs of his pretended into rest; but I could not wish him so cruel and sudden an end. May God have mercy on him, as he is pardoned by me!"

Adelheid received the silent pressure of the hand which followed with pious satisfaction. They then separated, he to join the group that was collected around the body, and she to take her station again near Christine. The former, however, was met by the Signor Grimaldi, who urged his immediate departure with the females for the convent, promising that the rest of the travellers should follow as soon as the present melancholy duty was ended. As Sigismund had no wish to be a party in what was going on, and there was reason to think his sister would be spared much pain by quitting the spot, he gladly acquiesced in the proposal. Immediate steps were taken for its accomplishment.

Christine mounted her mule, in obedience to her brother's desire, quietly, and without remonstrance; but her death-like countenance and fixed eye betrayed the violence of the shock she had received. During the whole of the ride to the convent she spoke not, and, as those around her felt for, and understood, her distress, the little cavalcade could not have been more melancholy and silent had it borne with it the body of the slain. In an hour they reached the long sought for and so anxiously desired place of rest.

While this disposition of the feebler portion of the party was making, a different scene had taken place near what have been already so well called the houses of the living and the dead. As there existed no human habitation within several leagues of the abode of the Augustines on either side of the mountain, and as the paths were much frequented in the summer, the monks exercised a species of civil jurisdiction in such cases as required a prompt exercise of justice, or a necessary respect for those forms that might be important in its ad ministration hereafter before the more regular authorities. It was no sooner known, therefore, that there was reason to suspect an act of violence had been committed, than the good clavier set seriously about taking the necessary steps to authenticate all those circumstances that could be accurately ascertained.

The identity of the body as that of Jacques Colis, a small but substantial proprietor of the country of Vaud, was quickly established. To this fact not only several of the travellers could testify, but he was also known to one of the muleteers, of whom he had engaged a beast to be left at Aoste and, it will also be remembered, he had been seen by Pierre at Martigny, while making his arrangements to puss the mountain. Of the mule there were no other traces than a few natural signs around the building, but which might equally be attributed to the beasts that still awaited the leisure of the travellers. The manner in which the unhappy man had come by his death admitted of no dispute. There were several wounds in the body, and a knife, of the sort then much used by travellers of an ordinary class, was left sticking in his back in a position to render it impossible to attribute the end of the sufferer to suicide. The clothes, too, exhibited proofs of a struggle, for they were torn and soiled, but nothing had been taken away. A little gold was found in the pockets, and though in no great plenty still enough to weaken the first impression that there had also been a robbery.

"This is wonderful!" observed the good clavier as he noted the last circumstance; "the dross which leads so many souls to damnation has been neglected while Christian blood has been shed! This seems an act of vengeance rather than of cupidity. Let us now examine if any proofs are to be found of the scene of this tragedy."

The search was unsuccessful. The whole of the surrounding region being composed of ferruginous rocks and their *débris*, it would not, indeed, have been an easy matter to trace the march of an army by their footsteps. The stain of blood, however, was nowhere discoverable, except on the spot where the body had been found. The house itself furnished no particular evidence of the bloody scene of which it had been a witness. The bones of those who had died long before were lying on the stones, it is true, broken and scattered; but, as the curious were wont to stop, and sometimes to enter among and handle these remains of mortality, there was nothing new or peculiar in their present condition.

The interior of the dead-house was obscure, and suited, in this particular at least, to its solemn office. While making the latter part of their examination, the monk and the two nobles, who began to feel a lively interest in the late event, stood before the window, gazing in at the gloomy but instructive scene. One body was so placed as to receive a few of the direct rays of the morning light, and it was consequently much more conspicuous than the rest, though even this was a dark and withered mummy that presented scarcely a vestige; of the being it had been. Like all the others whose parts still clung together, it had been placed against the wall, in the attitude of one that is seated, with the head fallen forward. The latter circumstance had brought the blackened and shrivelled face into the line of light. It had the ghastly grin of death, the features being distorted by the process of evaporation, and was altogether a revolting but salutary monitor of the common lot.

"'Tis the body of the poor vine-dresser;" remarked the monk, more accustomed to the spectacle than his companions, who had shrunk from the sight; "he unwisely slept on yonder naked rock, and it proved to him the sleep of death. There have been many masses for his soul, but what is left of his material remains still lie unclaimed. But--how is this! Pierre, thou hast lately passed this place; what was the number of the bodies, at thy last visit?"

"Three, reverend clavier; and yet the ladies spoke of four. I looked for the fourth when in the building, but there appeared none fresh, except this of poor Jacques Colis."

"Come hither, and say if there do not appear to be two in the far corner--here, where the body of thy old comrade the guide was placed, from respect for his calling; surely, there at least is a change in its position!"

Pierre approached, and taking off his cap in reverence, he leaned forward in the building, so as to exclude the external light from his eyes.

"Father!" he said, drawing back in surprise, "there is truly another; though I overlooked it when we entered the place."

"This must be examined into! The crime may be greater than we had believed!"

The servants of the convent and Pierre, whose long services rendered him a familiar of the brotherhood, now re-entered the building, while those without impatiently awaited the result. A cry from the interior prepared the latter for some fresh subject of horror, when Pierre and his companion quickly reappeared, dragging a living man into the open air. When the light permitted, those who knew him recognized the mild demeanor, the subdued look, and the uneasy, distrustful glance of Balthazar.

The first sensation of the spectators was that of open amazement; but dark suspicion followed. The baron, the two Genoese, and the monk, had all been witnesses of the scene in the great square of Vévey. The person of the headsman had become so well known to them by the passage on the lake and the event just alluded to, that there was not a moment of doubt touching his identity, and, coupled with the circumstances of that morning, there remained little more that the clue was now found to the cause of the murder.

We shall not stop to relate the particulars of the examination. It was short, reserved, and had the character of an investigation instituted more for the sake of form, than from any incertitude there could exist on the subject of the facts. When the necessary-inquiries were ended, the two nobles mounted. Father Xavier led the way, and the whole party proceeded towards the summit of the pass, leading Balthazar a prisoner, and leaving the body of Jacques Colis to its final rest, in that place where so many human forms had evaporated into air before him, unless those who had felt an interest in him in life should see fit to claim his remains.

The ascent between the Refuge and the summit of St. Bernard is much more severe than on any other part of the road. The end of the convent, overhanging the northern brow of the gorge, and looking like a mass of that ferruginous and melancholy rock which gave the whole region so wild and so unearthly an aspect, soon became visible, carved and moulded into the shape of a rude human habitation. The last pitch was so steep as to be formed into a sort of stair-way, up which the groaning mules toiled with difficulty. This labor overcome, the party stood on the highest point of the pass. Another minute brought them to the door of the convent.

Chapter XXV

 ------Hadst thou not been by,
A fellow by the hand of nature mark'd,
Noted, and sign'd to do a deed of shame,
This murder had not come into my mind.

 Shakspeare.

 The arrival of Sigismund's party at the hospice preceded that of the other travellers more than an hour. They were received with the hospitality with which all were then welcomed at this celebrated convent; the visits of the curious and the vulgar not having blunted the benevolence of the monks, who, mostly accustomed to entertain the low-born and ignorant, were always happy to relieve the monotony of their solitude by intercourse with guests of a superior class. The good clavier had prepared the way for their reception; for even on the wild ridge of St. Bernard, we do not fare the worse for carrying with us a prestige of that rank and consideration that are enjoyed in the world below. Although a mild Christian-like good-will were manifested to all, the heiress of Willading, a name that was generally known and honored between the Alps and the Jura, met with those proofs of *empressement* and deference which betray the secret thought, in despite of conventional forms and which told her, plainer than the words of welcome, that the retired Augustines were not sorry to see so fair and so noble a specimen of their species within their dreary walls.

 All this, however, was lost on Sigismund. He was too much occupied with the events of the morning to note other things; and, first committing Adelheid and his sister to the care of their women, he went into the open air in order to await the arrival of the rest.

 As it has been mentioned, the existence of the venerable convent of St. Bernard dates from a very remote period of Christianity. It stands on the very brow of the precipice which forms the last steep ascent in mounting to the Col. The building is a high, narrow, but vast, barrack-looking edifice, built of the ferruginous stone of the region, having its gable placed toward the Valais, and its front stretching in the direction of the gorge in which it stands. Immediately before its principal door, the rock rises in an ill-shapen hillock, across which runs the path to Italy. This is literally the highest point of the pass, as the building itself is the most elevated habitable abode in Europe. At this spot, the distance from rock to rock, spanning the gorge, may be a hundred yards, the wild and reddish piles rising on each side for more than a thousand feet. These are merely dwarfs, however, among their sister piles, several of which, in plain view of the convent, reach to the height of eternal snow. This point in the road attained, the path began immediately to descend, and the drippings of a snow-bank before the convent door, which had resisted the greatest heat of the past summer, ran partly into the valley of the Rhone, and partly into Piedmont; the waters, after a long and devious course through the plains of France and Italy, meeting again in the common basin of the Mediterranean. The path, on quitting the convent, runs between the base of the rocks on its right and a little limpid lake on its left, the latter occupying nearly the entire cavity of the valley of the gorge. It then disappears between natural palisades of rock, at the other extremity of the Col. This is the point where the superfluous waters of the lake find their outlet, descending swiftly, in a brawling little brook, on the sunny side of the Alps. The frontier of Italy is met on the margin of the lake, a long musket-shot from the abode of the Augustines, and near the site of a temple that the Romans had raised in honor of Jupiter, in his attribute of director of storms.

Such was the outline of the view which presented itself to Sigismund, when he left the building to while away the time that must necessarily elapse before the arrival of the rest of the party. The hour was still early, though the great altitude of the site of the convent had brought it beneath the influence of the sun's rays an hour before. He had learned from a servant of the Augustines, that a number of ordinary travellers, of whom in the fine season hundreds at a time frequently passed the night in their dormitories, were now breaking their fasts in the refectory of the peasants, and he was willing to avoid the questions that their curiosity might prompt when they came to hear what had occurred lower down on the mountain. One of the brotherhood was caressing four or five enormous mastiffs, that were leaping about and barking with deep throats in front of the convent, while old Uberto moved among them with a gravity and respect that better suited his years. Perceiving his guest, the Augustine quitted the dogs, and, lifting his eastern-looking cap, he gave him the salutation of the morning. Sigismund met the frank smile of the canon, who like himself was young with a fit return. The occasion was such as Sigismund desired, and a friendly discourse succeeded while they paced along the margin of the lake, holding the path that leads across the Col.

"You are young in your charitable office, brother," remarked the soldier, when familiarity was a little established. "This will be among the first of the winters you will have passed at your benevolent post?"

"It will make the eighth, as novice and as canon. We are early trained to this kind of life, though no practice will enable any of us to withstand the effect which the thin air and intense cold produce on the lungs many winters in succession. We go down to Martigny when there is occasion, and breathe an atmosphere better suited to man. Thou hadst an angry storm below, the past night?"

"So angry, that we thank God it is over, and that we are left to share your hospitality. Were there many on the mountain besides ourselves, or did any come up from Italy?"

"There were none but those who are now in the common refectory, and none came from Aoste. The season for the traveller is over. This is a month in which we see only those who are much pressed, and who have their reasons for trusting the weather. In the summer we sometimes lodge a thousand guests." "They whom ye receive have reason to be thankful, reverend Augustine; for, in sooth, this does not seem a region that abounds in its fruits."

Sigismund and the monk looked around at the vast piles of ragged naked rocks, and they smiled as their eyes met.

"Nature gives literally nothing," answered the Augustine: "even the fuel that warms us is transported leagues on the backs of mules, and thou wilt readily conceive that of all others this is a necessary we cannot forego. Happily, we have some of our ancient, and what were once rich, endowments; and--"

The young canon hesitated to proceed.

"You were about to say, father, that they who have the means to show gratitude are not always unmindful of the wants of those, who share the same hospitality without possessing the same ability to manifest their respect for the institution."

The Augustine bowed, and he turned the discourse by pointing out the frontiers of Italy, and the site of the ancient temple; both of which they had this time reached. An animal moved among the rocks, and attracted their attention.

"Can it be a chamois!" exclaimed Sigismund, whose blood began to quicken with a hunter's eagerness: "I would I had arms!"

"It is a dog, though not of our mountain breed! The mastiffs of the convent have failed in hospitality, and the poor beast has been driven to take refuge in this retired spot, in waiting for his master, who probably makes one of the party in the refectory. See, they come; their approaching footsteps have brought the cautious animal from his cover."

Sigismund saw, in truth, that a party of three pedestrians was quitting the convent, taking the path for Italy. A sudden and painful suspicion flashed upon his mind. The dog was Nettuno, most probably driven by the mastiffs, as the monk had suggested, to seek a shelter in this retreat; and one of those who approached, by his gait and stature was no other than his master.

"Thou knowest, father," he said, with a clammy tongue, for he was strangely agitated between reluctance to accuse Maso of such a crime, and horror at the fate of Jacques Colis, "that there has been a murder on the mountain?"

The monk quietly assented. One who lived on that road, and in that age, was not easily excited by an event of so frequent occurrence. Sigismund hastily recounted to his companion all the circumstances that were then known to himself, and related the manner in which he had first met the Italian on the lake, and his general impressions concerning his character.

"All come and go unquestioned here;" returned the Augustine, when the other had ended. "Our convent has been founded in charity, and we pray for the sinner without inquiring into the amount of his crime. Still we have authority, and it is especially our duty, to keep the road clear that our own purposes may not be defeated. I leave thee to do what thou judgest most prudent and proper in a matter so delicate."

Sigismund was silent; but as the pedestrians were drawing near, his resolution was soon and sternly formed. The obligations that he owed to Maso made him more prompt, for it excited a jealous distrust of his own powers to discharge what he conceived to be a duty. Even those late events in which his sister was so wronged had their share, too, on the decision of a mind so resolute to be upright. Placing himself in the middle of the path, he awaited the arrival of the party, while the monk stood quietly at his side. When the travellers were within speaking distance, the young man first discovered that the companions of Il Maledetto were Pippo and Conrad. Their several rencontres had made him sufficiently acquainted with the persons of the two latter, to enable him to recognize them at a glance; and Sigismund began to think the undertaking in which he had embarked more grave than he had at first imagined. Should there be a disposition to resist, he was but one against three.

"Buon giorno, Signor Capitano," cried Maso, saluting with his cap, when sufficiently near to those who occupied the path; "we meet often, and in all weathers; by day and by night; on the land and on the water; in the valley and on the mountain; in the city and on this naked rock, as Providence wills. As many chances try men's characters, we shall come to know each other in time!"

"Thou hast well observed, Maso; though I fear thou art a man oftener met than easily understood."

"Signore, I am amphibious, like Nettuno here, being part of the earth and part of the sea. As the learned say, I am not yet classed. We are repaid for an evil night by a fine day; and the descent into Italy will be pleasanter than we found the coming up. Shall I order honest Giacomo of Aoste to prepare the supper, and to air the beds for the noble company that is to follow? You will scarce do more than reach his holstery before the young and the beautiful will begin to think of their pillows."

"Maso, I had thought thee among our party, when I left the Refuge this morning?"

"By San Thomaso! Signore, but I had the same opinion touching yourself!"

"Thou wert early afoot it would seem, or thou couldst not have so much preceded me?"

"Look you, brave Signor Sigismondo, for brave I know you to be, and in the water a swimmer little less determined than gallant Nettuno there--I am a traveller, and have much need of my time which is the larger portion of my property. We sea-animals are sometimes rich and sometimes poor, as the wind happens to blow, and of late I have been driven to struggle with foul gales and troubled waves. To such a man, an hour of industry in the mornings often gives a heartier meal and sweeter rest at night. I left you all in the Refuge sleeping soundly, even to the mules,"--Maso laughed at his own fancies, as he included the brutes in the party,--"and I reached the convent just as the first touch of the sun tipped yonder white peak with its purple light."

"As thou left'st us so early, thou mayest not have heard, then, that the body of a murdered man was found in the bone-house--the building near that in which we slept--and that it is the body of one known?"

Sigismund spoke firmly and deliberately, as if he would come by degrees to his purpose, while, at the same time, he made the other sensible of his being in earnest. Maso started. He made a movement so unequivocally like one which would have manifested an intention to proceed, that the young man raised his hand to repulse him. But violence was unnecessary, for the mariner instantly became composed, and seemingly more disposed to listen.

"Where there has been a crime, Maso, there must have been a criminal!"

"The Bishop of Sion could not have made truth clearer to the sinner than yourself, Signor Sigismondo! Your manner leads me to ask what I have to do with this?"

"There has been a murder, Maso, and the murderer is sought. The dead was found near the spot where thou passed the night; I shall not conceal the unhappy suspicions that are so natural."

"Diamine! where did you pass the night yourself, brave Capitano, if I may be so bold as to question my superior? Where did the noble Baron de Willading take his rest, and his fair daughter and one nobler and more illustrious than he, and Pierre the guide, and--ay, and our friends, the mules again?"

Maso laughed recklessly once more, as he made this second allusion to the patient brutes. Sigismund disliked his levity, which he thought forced and unnatural.

"This reasoning may satisfy thee, unfortunate man, but it will not satisfy others. Thou wert alone, but we travelled in company; judging from thy exterior, thou art but little favored by fortune, Whereas we are more happy in this particular; and thou hast been, and art still, in haste to depart, while the discovery of the foul deed is owing to us alone. Thou must return to the convent, that this grave matter may, at least, be examined."

Il Maledetto seemed troubled. Once or twice he glanced his eye at the quiet athletic frame of the young man, and then turned them on the path in reflection. Although Sigismund narrowly watched the workings of his countenance, giving a little of his attention also, from time to time, to the movements of Pippo and the pilgrim, he preserved himself a perfectly calm exterior. Firm in his purpose, accustomed to make extraordinary exertions in his manly exercises, and conscious of his great physical force, he was not a man to be easily daunted. It is true that the companions of Maso conducted themselves in a way to excite no additional apprehensions on their account; for, on the announcement of the murder, they moved away from his person a little, as by a natural horror of the hand that could have done the deed. They now consulted together, and profiting by their situation behind the back of the Italian, they made signs to Sigismund of their readiness to assist should it be necessary. He received the signal writh satisfaction; for, though he knew them to be knaves, he sufficiently understood the difference between audacious crime and mere roguery to believe they might, in this instance at least, prove true.

"Thou wilt return to the convent, Maso," resumed the young soldier, who would gladly avoid a struggle with a man who had done him and those he loved so much service, though resolved to discharge what he conceived to be an imperious duty: "this pilgrim and his friend will be of our party, in order that, when we quit the mountain, all may leave it blameless and unsuspected."

"Signor Sigismondo, the proposal is fair; it has a touch of reason, I allow; but unluckily it does not suit my interests. I am engaged in a delicate mission, and too much time has been already lost by the way to waste more without good cause. I have great pity for poor Jacques Colis--"

"Ha! thou knowest the sufferer's name, then; thy unlucky tongue hath betrayed thee, Maso"

Il Maledetto was again troubled. His features betrayed it, for he frowned like a man who had committed a grave fault in a matter touching an important interest. His olive complexion changed, and his interrogator thought that his eye quailed before his own fixed look. But the emotion was transient, and shuddering, as if to shake off a weakness, his appearance became once more natural and composed.

"Thou makest no reply?"

"Signore, you have my answer; affairs press, and my visit to the convent of San Bernardo has been made. I am bound to Aoste, and should be happy to do your bidding with the worthy Giacomo. I have but a step to make to find myself in the dominions of the house of Savoy; and, with your leave, gallant Capitano, I will now take it."

Maso moved a little aside with the intention to pass Sigismund, when Pippo and Conrad threw themselves on him from behind, pinning his arms to his sides by main force. The face of the Italian grew livid, and he smiled with the contempt and hatred of an inveterately angered man. Assembling all his force, he suddenly exerted it with the energy and courage of a lion, shouting--

"Nettuno!"

The struggle was short but fierce. When it terminated, Pippo lay bleeding among the rocks with a broken head, and the pilgrim was gasping near him under the tremendous gripe of the animal. Maso himself stood firm, though pale and frowning like one who had collected all his energies, both physical and moral, to meet this emergency.

"Am I a brute, to be set upon by the scum of the earth?" he cried: "if thou wouldst aught with me, Signor Sigismondo, raise thine own arm, but strike not with the hands of these base reptiles; thou wilt find me a man, in strength and courage, at least not unworthy of thyself."

"The attack on thy person, Maso, was not made by my order, nor by my desire," returned Sigismund, reddening. "I believe myself sufficient to arrest thee; and, if not, here come assistants that thou wilt scarce deem it prudent to resist."

The Augustine had stepped on a rock the moment the struggle commenced, whence he made a signal which brought all the mastiffs from the convent. These powerful animals now arrived in a group, apprized by their instinct that strife was afoot. Nettuno immediately released the pilgrim and stood at bay; too faithful to desert his master in his need, and yet too conscious of the force opposed to him to court a contest so unequal. Luckily for the noble dog, the friendship of old Uberto proved his protection. When the younger animals saw their patriarch disposed to amity, they forbore their attack, waiting at least for another signal to be given. In the mean while, Maso had time to look about him, and to form his decision less under the influence of surprise and feeling than had been previously the case.

"Signore," he answered, "since it is your pleasure, I will return among the Augustines. But I ask, as simple justice, that, if I am to be hunted by dogs as a beast of prey, all who were in the same circumstances as myself may become subject to the same rule. This pilgrim and the Neapolitan came up the mountain yesterday, as well as myself, and I demand their arrest until they too can give an account of themselves. It will not be the first time that we have been inhabitants of the same prison."

Conrad crossed himself in submission, neither he nor Pippo raising any objection to the step. On the contrary, each frankly admitted it was no more than equitable on its face.

"We are poor travellers on whom many accidents have already alighted, and we may well be pressed to reach the end of our journey," said the pilgrim; "but, that justice may be done, we shall submit without a murmur. I am loaded with the sins of many besides my own, however, and St. Peter he knows that the last are not light. This holy canon will see that masses are said in the convent chapel in behalf of those for whom I travel; this duty done, I am an infant in your hands."

The good Augustine professed the perfect readiness of the fraternity to pray for all who were in necessity, with the single proviso that they should be Christians. With this amicable understanding then, the peace was made between them, and the parties immediately took the path that led back to the convent. On reaching the building, Maso, with the two travellers who had been found in his company, were; laced in safe keeping in one of the of the solid edifice, until the return of the clavier should enable them to vindicate their innocence.

Satisfied with himself for the part he had acted in the late affair, Sigismund strolled into the chapel, where, at that early hour, some of the brother hood were always occupied in saying masses in behalf of the souls of the living or of the dead He was here when he received a note from the Signor Grimaldi, apprizing him of the arrest of his father, and of the dark suspicions that were so naturally connected with the transaction. It is unnecessary to dwell on the nature of the shock he received from this intelligence. After a few moments of bitter anguish, he perceived the urgency of making his sister acquainted with the truth as speedily as possible. The arrival of the party from the Refuge was expected every moment, and by delay he increased the risk of Christine's hearing the appalling fact from some other quarter. He sought an audience, therefore, with Adelheid, the instant he had summoned sufficient self-command to undertake the duty.

Mademoiselle de Willading was struck with the pale brow and agitated air of the young soldier, at the first glance of her eye.

"Thou hast permitted this unexpected blow to affect thee unusually, Sigismund," she said, smiling, and offering her hand; for she felt that the circumstances were those in which cold and heartless forms should give place to feeling and sincerity. "Thy sister is tranquil, if not happy."

"She does not know the worst--she has yet to learn the most cruel part of the truth. Adelheid; they have found one concealed among the dead of the bone-house, and are now leading him here as the murderer of poor Jacques Colis!"

"Another!" said Adelheid, turning pale in alarm "we appear to be surrounded by assassins!"

"No, it cannot be true! I know my poor father's mildness of disposition too well; his habitual tenderness to all around him; his horror at the sight of blood, even for his odious task!"

"Sigismund, thy father!"

The young man groaned. Concealing his face with his hands, he sank into a seat. The fearful truth, with all its causes and consequences, began to dawn upon Adelheid. Sinking upon a chair herself, she sat long looking at the convulsed and working frame of Sigismund in silent horror. It appeared to her, that Providence, for some great but secret purpose, was disposed to visit them all with more than a double amount of its anger, and that a family which had been accursed for so many generations, was about to fill the measure of its woes. Still her own true heart did not change. On the contrary, its long-cherished and secret purpose rather grew stronger under this sudden appeal to its generous and noble properties, and never was the resolution to devote herself, her life, and all her envied hopes, to the solace of his unmerited wrongs, so strong and riveted as at that trying moment.

In a little time Sigismund regained enough self-command to be able to commence the narrative of what had passed. They then concerted together the best means to make Christine acquainted with that which it was absolutely necessary she should now know.

"Tell her the simple truth," added Sigismund, 'it cannot long be concealed, and it were better that she knew it; but tell her, also, my firm dependence on our father's innocence. God, for one of those inscrutable purposes which set human intelligence at defiance, has made him a common executioner, but the curse has not extended to his nature. Trust me, dearest Adelheid, a more gentle dove-like nature does not exist in man than that of the poor Balthazar--the despised and persecuted Balthazar. I have heard my mother dwell upon the nights of anguish and suffering that have preceded the day on which the duties of his office were to be discharged; and often have I heard that admirable woman, whose spirit is far more equal to support our unmerited fortunes, declare she has often prayed that he and all that are hers might die, so that they died innocently, rather than one of a temper so gentle and harmless should again be brought to endure the agony she had witnessed!"

"It is unhappy that he should be here at so luckless a moment! What unhappy motive can have led thy father to this spot, at a time so extra ordinary?"

"Christine will tell thee that she expected to see him at the convent. We are a race proscribed, Mademoiselle de Willading, but we are human."

"Dearest Sigismund--"

"I feel my injustice, and can only pray to be forgiven. But there are moments of feeling so intense, that I am ready to believe and treat all of my species as common enemies. Christine is an only daughter, and thou thyself, beloved Adelheid, kind, dutiful, and good as I know thee to be, art not more dear to the Baron de Willading than my poor sister is among us. Her parents have yielded her to thy generous kindness, for they believe it for her good;

but their hearts have been wrung by the separation. Thou didst not know it, but Christine took her last embrace of her mother here on the mountain, at Liddes, and it was then agreed that her father should watch her in safety over the Col, and bestow the final blessing at Aoste. Mademoiselle de Willading, you move in pride, surrounded by many protectors, who are honored in doing you service; but the abased and the hunted must indulge even their best affections stealthily, and without obtrusion! The love and tenderness of Balthazar would pass for mockery with the vulgar! Such is man in his habits and opinions, when wrong usurps the place of right."

Adelheid saw that the moment was not favorable for urging consolation and she abstained from a reply. She rejoiced, however, to hear the presence of the headsman so satisfactorily accounted for, though she could not quiet herself from an apprehension that the universal weakness of human nature, which so suddenly permits the perversion of the best of our passions to the worst, and the dreadful probability that Balthazar, suffering intensely by this compelled separation from his daughter, on accidentally encountering the man who was its cause, might have listened to some violent impulse of resentment and revenge. She saw also that Sigismund, in despite of his general confidence in the principles of his father, had fearful glimmerings of some such event, and that he fearfully anticipated the worst, even while he most professed confidence in the innocence of the accused. The interview was soon ended, and they separated; each endeavoring to invent plausible reasons for what had happened.

The arrival of the party from the refuge took place soon afterwards. It was followed by the necessary explanations, and a more detailed narrative of all that had passed. A consultation was held between the chiefs of the brotherhood and the two old nobles, and the course it was most expedient to pursue was calmly and prudently discussed.

The result was not known for some hours later. It was then generally proclaimed in the convent that a grave and legal investigation of all the facts was to take place with the least possible delay.

The Col of St. Bernard, as has been stated already, lies within the limits of the present canton but what then the allied state of the Valais. The crime had consequently been committed within the jurisdiction of that country; but as the Valais was thus leagued with Switzerland, there existed such an intimate understanding between the two, that it was rare any grave proceedings were had against a citizen of either in the dominion of the other, without paying great deference to the feelings and the rights of the country of the accused. Messengers were therefore dispatched to Vévey, to inform the authorities of that place of a transaction which involved the safety of an officer of the great canton, (for such was Balthazar,) and which had cost a citizen of Vaud his life. On the other hand, a similar communication was sent to Sion, the two places being about equidistant from the convent, with such pressing invitations to the authorities to be prompt, as were deemed necessary to bring on an immediate investigation. Melchior de Willading, in a letter to his friend the bailiff, set forth the inconvenience of his return with Adelheid at that late season, and the importance of the functionary's testimony, with such other statements as were likely to effect his wishes; while the superior of the brotherhood charged himself with making representations, with a similar intent, to the heads of his own republic. Justice in that age was not administered as frankly and openly as in this later period, its agents in the old world exercising even now a discretion that we are not accustomed to see confided to them. Her proceedings were enveloped in darkness, the blind deity being far more known in her decrees than in her principles, and mystery was then deemed an important auxiliary of power.

With this brief explanation we shall shift the time to the third day from that on which the travellers reached the convent, referring the reader to the succeeding chapter for an account of what it brought forth.

Chapter XXVI

> Anon a figure enters, quaintly neat,
> All pride and business, bustle and conceit;
> With looks unalter'd by these scenes of woe,
> With speed that, ent'ring, speaks his haste to go.
> He bids the gazing throng around him fly,
> And carries fate and physic in his eye.
>
> Crabbe.

There is another receptacle for those who die on the Great St. Bernard, hard by the convent itself. At the close of the time mentioned in the last, chapter, and near the approach of night, Sigismund was pacing the rocks on which this little chapel stands, buried in reflections to which his own history and the recent events had given birth. The snow that fell during the late storm had entirely disappeared, and the frozen element was now visible only on those airy pinnacles that form the higher peaks of the Alps. Twilight had already settled into the lower valleys, but the whole of the superior region was glowing with the fairy-like lustre of the last rays of the sun. The air was chill, for at that hour and season, whatever might be the state of the weather, the evening invariably brought with it a positive sensation of cold in the gorge of St. Bernard, where frosts prevailed at night, even in midsummer. Still the wind, though strong, was balmy and soft, blowing athwart the heated plains of Lombardy, and reaching the mountains charged with the moisture of the Adriatic and the Mediterranean. As the young man turned in his walk, and faced this breeze, it came over his spirit with a feeling of hope and home The greater part of his life had been past in the sunny country whence it blew, and there were moments when he was lulled into forgetfulness, by the grateful recollections imparted by its fragrance. But when compelled to turn northward again, and his eye fell on the misty hoary piles that distinguished his native land, rude and ragged faces of rock, frozen glaciers, and deep ravine-like valleys and glens, seemed to him to be types of his own stormy, unprofitable, and fruitless life, and to foretell a career which, though it might have touches of grandeur, was doomed to be barren of all that is genial and consolatory.

All in and about the convent was still. The mountain had an imposing air of deep solitude amid the wildest natural magnificence. Few travellers had passed since the storm, and, luckily for those who, under the peculiar circumstances in which they were placed, so much desired privacy, all of these had diligently gone their several ways. None were left, therefore, on the Col, but those who had an interest in the serious investigations which were about to take place. An officer of justice from Sion, wearing the livery of the Valais, appeared at a window, a sign that the regular authorities of the country had taken cognizance of the murder; but disappearing, the young man, to all external appearance, was left in the solitary possession of the pass. Even the dogs had been kennelled, and the pious monks were healthfully occupied in the religious offices of the vespers.

Sigismund turned his eye upward to the apartment in which Adelheid and his sister dwelt, but as the solemn moment in which so much was to be decided drew nearer, they also had withdrawn into themselves, ceasing to hold communion, even by means of the eyes, with aught that might divert their holy and pure thoughts from ceaseless and intense devotional reflections. Until now he had been occasionally favored with an answering and kind look from one or the other of these single hearted and affectionate girls, both of whom he so warmly loved, though with sentiments so different. It seemed that they too had at last left him to his isolated and hopeless existence. Sensible that this passing thought was weak and unmanly, the young man renewed his walk, and instead of turning as before, he moved slowly on, stopping only when he had reached the opening of the little chapel of the dead.

Unlike the building lower down the path, the bone-house at the convent is divided into two apartments; the exterior, and one that may be called the interior, though both are open to the weather. The former contained piles of disjointed human bones, bleached by the storms that beat in at the windows, while the latter is consecrated to the covering of those that still preserve, in their outward appearance at least, some of the more familiar traces of humanity. The first had its usual complement of dissevered and confounded fragments, in which the remains of young and old, of the two sexes, the fierce and the meek, the penitent and the sinner, lay in indiscriminate confusion--an eloquent reproach to the pride of man; while the walls of the last supported some twenty blackened and shrivelled effigies of the race, to show to what a pass of disgusting and frightful deformity the human form can be reduced, when deprived of that noble principle which likens it to its Divine Creator. On a table, in the centre of a group of black and grinning companions in misfortune, sat all that was left of Jacques Colis, who had been removed from the bone-house below to this at the convent for purposes connected with the coming investigation. The body was accidentally placed in such an attitude that the face was brought within the line of the parting light, while it had no other covering than the clothes worn by the murdered man in life. Sigismund gazed long at the pallid lineaments. They were still distorted with the agony produced by separating the soul from the body. All feeling of resentment for his sister's wrongs was lost in pity for the fate that had so suddenly overtaken one, in whom the passions, the interests, and the complicated machinery of this state of being, were so actively at work. Then came the bitter apprehension that his own father, in a moment of ungovernable anger, excited by the accumulated wrongs that bore so hard on him and his, might really have been the instrument of effecting the fearful and sudden change. Sickening with the thought, the young man turned and walked away towards the brow of the declivity. Voices, ascending to his ear, recalled him to the actual situation of things.

A train of mules were climbing the last acclivity where the path takes the broken precipitous appearance of a flight of steps. The light was still sufficient to distinguish the forms and general appearance of the travellers. Sigismund immediately recognized them to be the bailiff of Vévey and his attendants, for whose arrival the formal proceedings of the examination had alone been stayed.

"A fair evening, Herr Sigismund, and a happy meeting," cried Peterchen, so soon as his weary mule, which frequently halted under its unwieldy burthen, had brought him within hearing. "Little did I think to see thee again so quickly, and less still to lay eyes on this holy convent; for though the traveller might have returned in thy person nothing short of a miracle--" Here the bailiff winked, for he was one of those Protestants whose faith was most manifested in these side-hits at the opinions and practices of Rome,--"Nothing but a miracle, I say, and that too a miracle of some saint whose bones have been drying these ten thousand years, until every morsel of our weak flesh has fairly disappeared, could bring down old St. Bernard's abode upon the shores of the Leman. I have known many who have left Vaud to cross the Alps come back and winter in Vévey; but never did I know the stone that was placed upon another, in a workman-like manner, quits its bed without help from the hand of man. They say stones are particularly hard-hearted, and yet your saint and miracle-monger hath a way to move them!"

Peterchen chuckled at his own pleasantry, as men in authority are apt to enjoy that which comes exclusively of their own cleverness, and he winked round among his followers, as if he would invite them to bear witness to the rap he had given the Papists, even on their own exclusive ground. When the platform of the Col was attained, he checked the mule and continued his address, for want of wind had nipped his wit, as it might be, in the bud.

"A bad business this, Herr Sigismund; a thoroughly bad affair. It has drawn me far from home, at a ticklish season, and it has unexpectedly stopped the Herr von Willading (he spoke in German) in his journey over the mountains, and that, too, at a moment when all had need be diligent among the Alps. How does the keen air of the Col agree with the fair Adelheid?"

"God be thanked, Herr Bailiff, in bodily health that excellent young lady was never better."

"God be thanked, right truly! She is a tender flower, and one that might be suddenly cut off by the frosts of St Bernard. And the noble Genoese, who travels with so much modest simplicity, in a way to reprove the vain and idle--I hope he does not miss the sun among our rocks?"

"He is an Italian, and must think of us and our climate according to his habits; though in the way of health he seems at his ease."

"Well, this is consolatory! Herr Sigismund, were the truth known," rejoined Peterchen, bending as far forward on his mule as a certain protuberance of his body would permit, and then suddenly drawing himself up again in reserve--"but a state secret is a state secret, and least of all should it escape one who is truly and legitimately a child of the state. My love and friendship for Melchior von Willading are great, and of right excellent quality; but I should not have visited this pass, were it not to do honor to our guest the Genoese. I would not that the noble stranger went down from our hills with an unsavory opinion of our hospitality. Hath the honorable Châtelain from Sion reached the hill?"

"He has been among us since the turn of the day, mein Herr, and is now in conference with those you have just named, on matters connected with the object of your common visit."

"He is an honest magistrate! and like ourselves, Master Sigismund, he comes of the pure German root, which is a foundation to support merit, though it might better be said by another. Had he a comfortable ride?"

"I have heard no complaint of his ascent."

"'Tis well. When the magistrate goes forth to do justice, he hath a right to look for a fair time. All are then comfortable;--the noble Genoese, the honorable Melchior, and the worthy Châtelain.--And Jacques Colis?"

"You know his unhappy fate, Herr Bailiff," returned Sigismund briefly; for he was a little vexed with the other's phlegm in a matter that so nearly touched his own feelings.

"If I did not know it, Herr Steinbach, dost think I should now be here, instead of preparing for a warm bed near the great square of Vévey? Poor Jacques Colis! Well, he did the ceremonies of the abbaye an ill turn in refusing to buckle with the headsman's daughter, but I do not know that he at all deserved the fate with which he has met."

"God forbid that any who were hurt, and that perhaps not without reason, by his want of faith, should think his weakness merited a punishment so heavy!"

"Thou speakest like a sensible youth, a very Sensible youth--ay, and like a Christian, Herr Sigismund," answered Peterchen, "and I approve of thy words. To refuse to wive a maiden and to be murdered are very different offences, and should not be confounded. Dost think these Augustines keep kirschwasser among their stores? It is strong work to climb up to their abode, and strong toil needs strong drink. Well, should they not be so provided, we must make the best of their other liquors. Herr Sigismund, do me the favor to lend me thy arm."

The bailiff now alighted with stiffened limbs, and, taking the arm of the other, he moved slowly toward the building.

"It is damnable to bear malice, and doubly damnable to bear malice against the dead! Therefore I beg you to take notice that I have quite forgotten the recent conduct of the deceased in the matter of our public games, as it becomes an impartial and upright judge to do. Poor Jacques Colis! Ah, death is awful at any time, but it is tenfold terrible to die in this sudden manner, posthaste as it were, and that, too, on a path where we put one foot before the other with so much bodily pain. This is the ninth visit I have made the Augustines, and I cannot flatter the holy monks on the subject of their roads, much as I wish them well. Is the reverend clavier back at his post again?"

"He is, and has been active in taking the usual examinations."

"Activity is his strong property, and he needs be that, Herr Steinbach, who passeth the life of a mountaineer. The noble Genoese, and my ancient friend Melchior, and his fair daughter the beautiful Adelheid, and the equitable Châtelain, thou sayest, are all fairly reposed and comfortable?"

"Herr Bailiff, they have reason to thank God that the late storm and their mental troubles have done them no harm."

"So--I would these Augustines kept kirschwasser among their liquors!"

Peterchen entered the convent, where his presence alone was wanting to proceed to business. The mules were housed, the guides received as usual in the building, and then the preparations for the long-delayed examinations were seriously commenced.

It has already been mentioned that the fraternity of St. Bernard was of very ancient origin. It was founded in the year 962, by Bernard de Menthon, an Augustine canon of Aoste in Piedmont, for the double purposes of bodily succor and spiritual consolation. The idea of establishing a religious community in the midst of savage rocks, and at the highest point trod by the foot of a man, was worthy of Christian self-denial and a benevolent philanthropy. The experiment appears to have succeeded in a degree that is commensurate with its noble intention; for centuries have gone by, civilization has undergone a thousand changes, empires have been formed and upturned, thrones destroyed, and one-half the world has been rescued from barbarism, while this piously-founded edifice still remains in its simple and respectable usefulness where it was first erected, the refuge of the traveller and a shelter for the poor.

The convent buildings are necessarily vast, but, as all its other materials had to be transported to the place it occupies on the backs of mules, they are constructed chiefly of the ferruginous, hoary-looking stones that were quarried from the native rock. The cells of the monks, the long corridors, refectories for the different classes of travellers, and suited to the numbers of the guests, as well as those for the canons and their servants, and lodging rooms of different degrees of magnitude and convenience, with a chapel of some antiquity and of proper size, composed then, as now, the internal arrangements. There is no luxury, some comfort in behalf of those in whom indulgence has become a habit, and much of the frugal hospitality that is addressed to the personal wants and the decencies of life. Beyond this, the building, the entertainment, and the brotherhood, are marked by a severe monastic self-denial, which appears to have received a character of barren and stern simplicity from the unvarying nakedness of all that meets the eye in that region of frost and sterility.

We shall not stop to say much of the little courtesies and the ceremonious asseverations of mutual good-will and respect that passed between the Bailiff of Vévey and the Prior of St. Bernard, on the occasion of their present meeting. Peterchen was known to the brotherhood, and, though a Protestant, and one too that did not forbear to deliver his jest or his witticism against Rome and its flock at will, he was sufficiently well esteemed. In all the quêtes, or collections of the convent, the well-meaning Bernois had really shown himself a man of bowels, and one that was disposed to favor humanity, even while it helped the cause of his arch enemy, the Pope. The clavier was always well received, not only in his bailiwick but in his château, and in spite of numberless little skirmishes on doctrine and practice, they always met with a welcome and generally parted in peace. This feeling of amity and good-will extended to the superior and to all the others of the holy community, for in addition to a certain heartiness of character in the bailiff, there was mutual interest to maintain it. At the period of which we write, the vast possessions with which the monks of St. Bernard had formerly been endowed were already much reduced by sequestrations in different countries, that of Savoy in particular, and they were reduced then, as now, to seek supplies to meet the constant demands of travellers in the liberality of the well-disposed and charitable; and the liberality of Peterchen was thought to be cheaply purchased by his jokes, while, on the other hand, he had so many occasions, either in his own person or those of his friends, to visit the convent, that he always forbore to push contention to a quarrel.

"Welcome again, Herr Bailiff, and for the ninth time welcome!" continued the Prior, as he took the hand of Peterchen, leading the way to his own private parlor; "thou art always a welcome guest on the mountain, for we know that we entertain at least a friend."

"And a heretic," added Peterchen, laughing with all his might, though he uttered a joke which he now repeated for the ninth time. "We have met often, Herr Prior, and I hope we shall meet finally, after all our clambering of mountains, as well as our clambering after worldly benefits, is ended, and that where honest men come together, in spite of Pope or Luther, books, sermons, aves, or devils! This thought cheers me whenever I offer thee my hand," shaking that of the other with a hearty good-will; "for I should not like to think, Father Michael, that, when we set out on the last long journey, we are to travel for ever in different ways. Thou may'st tarry awhile, if thou seest fit, in thy purgatory, which is a lodging of thine own invention, and should therefore suit thee, but I trust to continue on, until fairly housed in heaven, miserable and unhappy sinner, that I am!"

Peterchen spoke in the confident voice of one accustomed to utter his sentiments to inferiors, who either dared not, or did not deem it wise, to dispute his oracles; and he ended with another deep-mouthed laugh, that filled the vaulted apartment of the smiling prior to the ceiling. Father Michael took all in good part, answering, as was his wont in mildness and good-tempered charity; for he was a priest of much learning, deep reflection, and rebuked opinions. The community over which he presided was so far worldly in its object as to keep the canons in constant communion with men, and he would not now have met for the first time one of those self-satisfied, authoritative, boisterous, well-meaning beings, of whose class Peterchen formed so conspicuous a member, had this been the first of the bailiff's visits to the Col. As it was, however, the Prior not only understood the species, but he well knew the individual specimen, and he was well enough disposed to humor the noisy pleasantry of his companion. Disburthened of his superfluous clothing, delivered of his introductory jokes, and having achieved his salutations to the several canons, with suitable words of recognition to the three or four novices who were usually found on the mountain, Peterchen declared his readiness to enter on the duty of what the French call restoration. This want had been foreseen, and the Prior led the way to a private refectory, where preparations had been made for a sufficient supper, the bailiff being very generally known to be a huge feeder.

"Thou wilt not fare as well as in thy warm and cheerful town of Vévey, which outdoes most of Italy in its pleasantness and fruits; but thou shalt, at least, drink of thine own warm wines," observed the superior, as they went along the corridor; "and a right goodly company awaits thee, to share hot only thy repast but thy good companionship."

"Hast ever a drop of kirschwasser, brother Michael, in thy convent?"

"We have not only that, but we have the Baron de Willading, and a noble Genoese who is in his company; they are ready to set to, the moment they can see thy face."

"A noble Genoese!"

"An Italian gentleman, of a certainty; I think they call him a Genoese."

Peterchen stopped, laid a finger on his nose, and looked mysterious; but he forbore to speak, for, by the open simple countenance of the monk, he saw that the other had no suspicion of his meaning.

"I will hazard my office of bailiff against that of thy worthy clavier, that he is just what he seemeth,--that is to say, a Genoese!"

"The risk will not be great, for so he has already announced himself. We ask no questions here and be he who or what he may, he is welcome to come, and welcome to depart, in peace."

"Ay, this is well enough for an Augustine on the top of the Alps,--he hath attendants?"

"A menial and a friend; the latter, however, left the convent for Italy, when the noble Genoese determined to remain until this inquiry was over There was something said of heavy affairs which required that some explanations of the delay should be sent to others."

Peterchen again looked steadily at the Prior, smiling, as in pity, of his ignorance.

"Look thou, good Prior, much as I love thee and thy convent, and Melchior von Willading and his daughter, I would have spared myself this journey, but for that same Genoese. Let there be no questions, however, between us: the proper time to speak will come, and God forbid that I should be precipitate! Thou shalt then see in what manner a bailiff of the great canton can acquit himself! At present we will trust to thy prudence. The friend hath gone to Italy in haste, that the delay may not create surprise! Well, each one to his humor on the highway: it is mine to journey in honor and security, though others may have a different taste. Let there be little said, good Michael: not so much as an imprudent look of the eye;--and now, o' Heaven's sake, thy glass of kirschwasser!"

They were at the door of the refectory, and the conversation ceased. On entering, Peterchen found his friend the baron, the Signor Grimaldi, and the châtelain of Sion, a grave ponderous dignitary of justice, of German extraction like himself and the Prior, but whose race, from a long residence on the confines of Italy, had imbibed some peculiarities of the southern character. Sigismund and all the rest of the travellers were precluded from joining the repast, to which it was the intention of the prudent canons to give a semi-official character. The meeting between Peterchen and those who had so lately quitted Vévey was not distinguished by any extraordinary movements of courtesy; but that between the bailiff and the châtelain, who represented the authorities of friendly and adjoining states, was marked by a profusion of politic and diplomatic civilities. Various personal and public inquiries were exchanged, each appearing to strive to outdo the other in manifesting interest in the smallest details on those points in which it was proper for a stranger to feel an interest. Though the distance between the two capitals was fully fifteen leagues, every foot of the ground was travelled over by one or the other of the parties, either in commendation of its beauties, or in questions that touched its interests.

"We come equally of Teutonic fathers, Herr Châtelain," concluded the bailiff, as the whole party placed themselves at table, after the reverences and homages were thoroughly exhausted, "though Providence has cast our fortunes in different countries. I swear to thee, that the sound of thy German is music to my ears! Thou hast wonderfully escaped corruptions, though compelled to consort so much with the bastards of Romans, Celts, and Burgundians, of whom thou hast so many in this portion of thy states. It is curious to observe,"--for Peterchen had a little of an antiquarian flavor among the other crude elements of his character--"that whenever a much-trodden path traverses a country, its people catch the blood as well as the opinions of those who travel it, after the manner that tares are scattered and sown by the passing winds. Here has the St. Bernard been a thoroughfare since the time of the Romans, and thou wilt find as many races among those who dwell on the way-side as there are villages between the convent and Vévey. It is not so with you of the Upper Valais, Herr Châtelain; there the pure race exists as it came from the other side of the Rhine, and honored and preserved may it continue for another thousand years!"

There are few people so debased in their own opinion as, not to be proud of their peculiar origin and character. The habit of always viewing ourselves, our motives, and even our conduct, on the favorable side, is the parent of self-esteem; and this weakness, carried into communities, commonly gets to be the cause of a somewhat fallacious gauge of merit among the population of entire countries. The châtelain, Melchior de Willading, and the Prior, all of whom came from the same Teutonic root, received the remark complacently; for each felt it an honor to be descended from, such ancestors; while the more polished and artificial Italian succeeded in concealing the smile that, on such an occasion, would be apt to play about the mouth of a man whose parentage ran, through a long line of sophisticated and politic nobles, into the consuls and patricians of Rome, and most probably, through these again into the wily and ingenious Greek, a root distinguished for civilization when these patriarchs of the north lay buried in the depths of barbarism.

This little display of national vanity ended, the discourse took a more general turn. Nothing occurred during the entertainment, however, to denote that any of the company bethought him of the business on which they had met. But, just as twilight foiled, and the repast was ended, the Prior invited his guests to lend their attention to the matter in hand, recalling them from their friendly attacks, their time-worn jokes, and their attenuated logic, in all of which Peterchen, Melchior, and the châtelain had indulged with some freedom, to a question involving the life or death of at least one of their fellow-creatures.

The subordinates of the convent were occupied during the supper with the arrangements that had been previously commanded; and when Father Michael arose and intimated to his companions that their presence was now expected elsewhere, he led them to a place that had been completely prepared for their reception.

Chapter XXVII

> Was ever tale
> With such a gallant modesty rehearsed?
>
> Home.

Purposes of convenience, as well as others that were naturally connected with the religious opinions, not to say the superstitions, of most of the prisoners, had induced the monks to select the chapel of the convent for the judgment-hall. This consecrated part of the edifice was of sufficient size to contain all who were accustomed to assemble within its walls. It was decorated in the manner that is usual to churches of the Romish persuasion, having its master-altar, and two of smaller size that were dedicated to esteemed saints. A large lamp illuminated the place, though the great altar lay in doubtful light, leaving play for the imagination to people and adorn that part of the chapel. Within the railing of the choir there stood a table: it held some object that was concealed from view by a sweeping pall. Immediately beneath the lamp was placed another, which served the purposes of the clavier, who acted as a clerk on this occasion. They who were to fill the offices of judges took their stations near. A knot of females were clustered within the shadows of one of the side-altars, hovering around each other in the way that their sensitive sex is known to interpose between the exhibition of its peculiar weaknesses and the rude observations of the world. Stifled sobs and convulsive movements occasionally escaped this little group of acutely feeling and warm-hearted beings, betraying the strength of the emotions they would fain conceal. The canons and novices were ranged on one side, the guides and muleteers formed a back-ground to the whole, while the fine form of Sigismund stood, stern and motionless as a statue, on the steps of the altar which was opposite to the females. He watched the minutest proceeding of the investigation with a steadiness that was the result of severe practice in self-command, and a jealous determination to suffer no new wrong to be accumulated on the head of his father.

When the little confusion produced by the entrance of the party from the refectory had subsided, the Prior made a signal to one of the officers of justice. The man disappeared, and shortly returned with one of the prisoners, the investigation being intended to embrace the cases of all who had been detained by the prudence of the monks. Balthazar (for it was he) approached the table in his usual meek manner. His limbs were unbound, and his exterior calm, though the quick unquiet movements of his eye, and the workings of his pale features, whenever a suppressed sob from among the females reached his ear, betrayed the inward struggle he had to maintain, in order to preserve appearances. When he was confronted with his examiners, Father Michael bowed to the châtelain; for, though the others were admitted by courtesy to participate in the investigations, the right to proceed in an affair of this nature within the limits of the Valais, belonged to this functionary alone.

"Thou art called Balthazar?" abruptly commenced the judge, glancing at his notes.

The answer was a simple inclination of the body.

"And thou art the headsman of the canton of Berne?"

A similar silent reply was given.

"The office is hereditary in thy family; it has been so for ages?"

Balthazar erected his frame, breathing heavily, like one oppressed at the heart, but who would bear down his feelings before he answered.

"Herr Châtelain," he said with energy, "by the judgment of God it has been so."

"Honest Balthazar, thou throwest too much emphasis into thy words," interposed the bailiff. "All that belongs to authority is honorable, and is not to be treated as an evil. Hereditary claims, when venerable by time and use, have a double estimation with the world, since it brings the merit of the ancestor to sustain that of the descendant. We have our rights of the bürgerschaft, and thou thy rights of execution. The time has been when thy fathers were well content with their privilege."

Balthazar bowed in submission; but he seemed to think any other reply unnecessary. The fingers of Sigismund writhed on the hilt of his sword, and a groan, which the young man well knew had been wrested from the bosom of his mother, came from the women.

"The remark of the worthy and honorable bailiff is just," resumed the Valaisan; "all that is of the state is for the good of the state, and all that is for the comfort and security of man is honorable. Be not ashamed, therefore, of thy office, Balthazar, which, being necessary, is not to be idly condemned; but answer faithfully and with truth to the questions I am about to put.-- Thou hast a daughter?"

"In that much, at least, have I been blessed!"

The energy with which he spoke caused a sudden movement in the judges. They looked at each other in surprise, for it was apparent they did not expect these touches of human feeling in a man who lived, as it were, in constant warfare with his fellow-creatures.

"Thou hast reason," returned the châtelain, recovering his gravity; "for she is said to be both dutiful and comely. Thou wert about to marry this daughter?"

Balthazar acknowledged the truth of this by another inclination.

"Didst thou ever know a Vévaisan of the name of Jacques Colis?"

"Mein Herr, I did. He was to have become my son."

The châtelain was again surprised; for the steadiness of the reply denoted innocence, and he studied the countenance of the prisoner intently. He found apparent frankness where he had expected to meet with subterfuge, and, like all who have great acquaintance with crime, his distrust increased. The simplicity of one who really had nothing to conceal, unlike that appearance of firmness, which is assumed to affect innocence, set his shrewdness at fault, though familiar with most of he expedients of the guilty.

"This Jacques Colis was to have wived thy daughter?" continued the châtelain, growing more wary as he thought he detected greater evidence of art in the accused.

"It was so understood between us."

"Did he love thy child?"

The muscles of Balthazar's mouth played convulsively, the twitching of the lip seeming to threaten a loss of self-command.

"Mein Herr, I believed it."

"Yet he refused to fulfil the engagement?"

"He did."

Even Marguerite was alarmed at the deep emphasis with which this answer was given, and, for the first time in her life, she trembled lest the accumulating load of obloquy had indeed been too strong for her husband's principles.

"Thou felt anger at his conduct, and at the public manner in which he disgraced thee and thine?"

"Herr Châtelain, I am human. When Jacques Colis repudiated my daughter, he bruised a tender plant in the girl, and he caused bitterness in a father's heart."

"Thou hast received instruction superior to thy condition, Balthazar!"

"We are a race of executioners, but we are not the unnurtured herd that people fancy. 'Tis the will of Berne that made me what I am, and no desire nor wants of my own."

"The charge is honorable, as are all that come of the state," repeated the other, with the formal readiness in which set phrases are uttered; "the charge is honorable for one of thy birth. God assigns to each his station on earth, and he has fixed thy duties. When Jacques Colis refused thy daughter he left his country to escape thy revenge?"

"Were Jacques Colis living, he would not utter so foul a lie!"

"I knew his honest and upright nature!" exclaimed Marguerite with energy! "God pardon me that I ever doubted it!"

The judges turned inquisitive glances towards indistinct cluster of females, but the examination did not the less proceed.

"Thou knowest, then, that Jacques Colis is dead?"

"How can I doubt it, mein Herr, when I saw his bleeding body?"

"Balthazar, thou seemest disposed to aid the examination, though with what views is better known to Him who sees the inmost heart, than to me. I will come at once, therefore, to the most essential facts. Thou art a native and a resident of Berne; the headsman of the canton--a creditable office in itself, though the ignorance and prejudices of man are not apt so to consider it. Thou wouldst have married thy daughter with a substantial peasant of Vaud. The intended bridegroom repudiated thy child, in face of the thousands who came to Vévey to witness the festivities of the Abbaye; he departed on a journey to avoid thee, or his own feelings, or rumor, or what thou wilt; he met his death by murder on this mountain; his body was discovered with the knife in the recent wound, and thou, who shouldst have been on thy path homeward, wert found passing the night near the murdered man. Thine own reason will show thee the connexion which we are led to form between these several events, and thou art now required to explain that which to us seems so suspicious, but which to thyself may be clear. Speak freely, but speak truth, as thou reverest God, and in thine own interest."

Balthazar hesitated and appeared to collect his thoughts. His head was lowered in a thoughtful attitude, and then, looking his examiner steadily in the face, he replied. His manner was calm, and the tone in which he spoke, if not that of one innocent in fact, was that of one who well knew how to assume the exterior of that character.

"Herr Châtelain," he said, "I have foreseen the suspicions that would be apt to fasten on me in these unhappy circumstances, but, used to trust in Providence, I shall speak the truth without fear. Of the intention of Jacques Colis to depart I knew nothing. He went his way privately, and if you will do me the justice to reflect a little, it will be seen that I was the last man to whom he would have been likely to let his intention be known. I came up the St. Bernard, drawn by a chain that your own heart will own is difficult to break if you are a father. My daughter was on the road to Italy with kind and true friends, who were not ashamed to feel for a headsman's child, and who took her in order to heal the wound that had been so unfeelingly inflicted."

"This is true!" exclaimed the Baron de Willading; "Balthazar surely says naught but truth here!"

"This is known and allowed; crime is not always the result of cool determination, but it comes of terror, of sudden thought, the angry mood, the dire temptation, and a fair occasion. Though thou left'st Vévey ignorant of Jacques Colis' departure, didst thou hear nothing of his movements by the way?"

Balthazar changed color. There was evidently a struggle in his bosom, as if he shrunk from making an acknowledgment that might militate against his interests; but, glancing an eye at the guides, he recovered his proper tone of mind, and answered firmly:

"I did. Pierre Dumont had heard the tale of my child's disgrace, and, ignorant that I was the injured parent, he told me of the manner in which the unhappy man had retreated from the mockery of his companions. I knew, therefore, that we were on the same path."

"And yet thou perseveredst?"

"In what, Herr Châtelain? Was I to desert my daughter, because one who had already proved false to her stood in my way?"

"Thou hast well answered, Balthazar," interrupted Marguerite. "Thou hast answered as became thee! We are few, and we are all to each other. Thou wert not to forget our child because it pleased others to despise her."

The Signor Grimaldi bent towards the Valaisan, and whispered near his ear.

"This hath the air of nature." he observed; "and does it not account for the appearance of the father on the road taken by the murdered man?"

"We do not question the probability or justness of such a motive, Signore; but revenge may have suddenly mounted to the height of ferocity in some wrangle: one accustomed to blood yields easily to his passions and his habits."

The truth of these suggestions was plausible, and the noble Genoese drew back in cold disappointment. The châtelain consulted with those about him, and then desired the wife to come forth in order to be confronted with her husband. Marguerite obeyed. Her movement was slow, and her whole manner that of one who yielded to a stern necessity.

"Thou art the headsman's wife?"

"And a headsman's daughter."

"Marguerite is a well-disposed and a sensible woman," put in Peterchen; "she understands that an office under the state can never bring disgrace in the eyes of reason, and wishes no part of her history or origin to be concealed."

The glance that flashed from the eye of Balthazar's wife was withering; but the dogmatic bailiff was by far too well satisfied with his own wisdom to be conscious of its effects.

"And a headsman's daughter," continued the examining judge; "why art thou here?"

"Because I am a wife and a mother. As the latter I came upon the mountain, and as a wife I have mounted to the convent to be present at this examination. They will have it that there is blood upon the hands of Balthazar, and I am here to repel the lie."

"And yet thou hast not been slow to confess thy connexion with a race of executioners!--They who are accustomed to see their fellows die might have less warmth in meeting a plain inquiry of justice!"

"Herr Châtelain, thy meaning is understood. We have been weighed upon heavily by Providence, but, until now, they whom we have been made to serve have had the policy to treat us with fair words! Thou hast spoken of blood; that which has been shed by Balthazar, by his, and by mine, lies on the consciences of those who commanded it to be spilt. The unwilling instruments of thy justice are innocent before God."

"This is strange language for people of thy employment! Dost thou, too, Balthazar, speak and think with thy consort in this matter?"

"Nature has given us men sterner feelings, mein Herr. I was born to the office I hold, taught to believe it right, if not honorable, and I have struggled hard to do its duties without murmuring. The case is different with poor Marguerite. She is a mother, and lives in her children; she has seen one that is near her heart publicly scorned, and she feels like a mother."

"And thou, who art a father, what has been thy manner of thinking under this insult?"

Balthazar was meek by nature, and, as he had just said, he had been trained to the exercise of his functions; but he was capable of profound affections. The question touched him in a sensitive spot, and he writhed under his feelings; but, accustomed to command himself before the public eye, and alive to the pride of manhood, his mighty effort to suppress the agony that loaded his heart was rewarded with success.

"Sorrow for my unoffending child; sorrow for him who had forgotten his faith; and sorrow for them who have been at the root of this bitter wrong," was the answer.

"This man has been accustomed to hear forgiveness preached to the criminal, and he turns his schooling to good account," whispered the wary judge to those near him. "We must try his guilt by other means. He may be readier in reply than steady in his nerves."

Signing to the assistants, the Valaisan now quietly awaited the effect of a new experiment. The pall was removed, and the body of Jacques Colis exposed. He was seated as in life, on the table in front of the grand altar.

"The innocent have no dread of those whose spirits have deserted the flesh," continued the châtelain, "but God often sorely pricks the consciences of the guilty, when they are made to see the works of their own cruel hands. Approach and look upon the dead, Balthazar; thou and thy wife, that we may judge of the manner in which ye face the murdered and wronged man."

A more fruitless experiment could not well have been attempted with one of the headsman's office; for long familiarity with such sights had taken off that edge of horror which the less accustomed would be apt to feel. Whether it were owing to this circumstance, or to his innocence, Balthazar walked to the side of the body unshaken, and stood long regarding the bloodless features with unmoved tranquillity. His habits were quiet and meek, and little given to display. The feelings which crowded his mind, therefore, did not escape him in words, though a gleam of something like regret crossed his face. Not so with his companion. Marguerite took the hand of the dead man, and hot tears began to follow each other down her cheeks, as she gazed at his shrunken and altered lineaments.

"Poor Jacques Colis!" she said in a manner to be heard by all present; "thou hadst thy faults, like all born of woman; but thou didst not merit this! Little did the mother that bore thee, and who lived in thy infant smile--she who fondled thee on her knee, and cherished thee in her bosom, foresee thy fearful and sudden end! It was happy for her that she never knew the fruit of all her love, and pains, and care, else bitterly would she have mourned over what was then her joy, and in sorrow would she have witnessed thy pleasantest smile. We live in a fearful world, Balthazar; a world in which the wicked triumph! Thy hand, that would not willingly harm the meanest creature which has been fashioned by the will of God, is made to take life, and thy heart--thy excellent heart--is slowly hardening in the execution of this accursed office! The judgment seat hath fallen to the lot of the corrupt and designing; mercy hath become the laughing-stock of the ruthless, and death is inflicted by the hand of him who would live in peace with his kind. This cometh of thwarting God's intentions with the selfishness and designs of men! We would be wiser than he who made the universe, and we betray the weakness of fools! Go to--go to, ye proud and great of the earth--if we have taken life, it hath been at your bidding; but we have naught of this on our consciences. The deed hath been the work of the rapacious and violent--it is no deed of revenge."

"In what manner are we to know that what thou sayest is true?" asked the châtelain, who had advanced near the altar, in order to watch the effects of the trial to which he had put Balthazar and his wife.

"I am not surprised at thy question, Herr Châtelain, for nothing comes quicker to the minds of the honored and happy than the thought of resenting an evil turn. It is not so with the despised. Revenge would be an idle remedy for us. Would it raise us in men's esteem? should we forget our own degraded condition? should we be a whit nearer respect after the deed was done than we were before?"

"This may be true, but the angered do not reason. Thou art not suspected, Marguerite, except as having heard the truth from thy husband since the deed has been committed, but thine own discernment will show that naught is more probable than that a hot contention about the past may have led Balthazar, who is accustomed to see blood, into the commission of this act?"

"Here is thy boasted justice! Thine own laws are brought in support of thine own oppression. Didst thou know how much pains his father had in teaching Balthazar to strike, how many long and anxious visits were paid between his parent and mine in order to bring up the youth in the way of his dreadful calling, thou wouldst not think him so apt! God unfitted him for his office, as he has unfitted many of higher and different pretensions for duties that have been cast upon them in virtue of their birthrights. Had it been I, châtelain, thy suspicions would have a better show of reason. I am formed with strong and quick feelings, and reason has often proved too weak for passion, though the rebuke that has been daily received throughout a life hath long since tamed all of pride that ever dwelt in me."

"Thou hast a daughter present?"

Marguerite pointed to the group which held her child.

"The trial is severe," said the judge, who began to feel compunctions that were rare to one of his habits, "but it is as necessary to your own future peace, as it is to justice itself, that the truth should be known. I am compelled to order thy daughter to advance to the body."

Marguerite received this unexpected command with cold womanly reserve. Too much wounded to complain, but trembling for the conduct of her child, she went to the cluster of females, pressed Christine to her heart, and led her silently forward. She presented her to the châtelain, with a dignity so calm and quiet, that the latter found it oppressive!

"This is Balthazar's child," she said. Then folding her arms, she retired herself a step, an attentive observer of what passed.

The judge regarded the sweet pallid face of the trembling girl with an interest he had seldom felt for any who had come before him in the discharge of his unbending duties. He spoke to her kindly, and even encouragingly, placing himself intentionally between her and the dead, momentarily hiding the appalling spectacle from her view, that she might have time to summon her courage. Marguerite blessed him in her heart for this small grace, and was better satisfied.

"Thou wert betrothed to Jacques Colis?" demanded the châtelain, using a gentleness of voice that was singularly in contrast with his former stern interrogatories.

The utmost that Christine could reply was to bow her head.

"Thy nuptials were to take place at the late meeting of the Abbaye des Vignerons--it is our unpleasant duty to wound where we could wish to heal--but thy betrothed refused to redeem his pledge?"

"The heart is weak, and sometimes shrinks from its own good purposes," murmured Christine. "He was but human, and he could not withstand the sneers of all about him."

The châtelain was so entranced by her gentle and sweet manner that he leaned forward to listen, lest a syllable of what she whispered might escape his ears.

"Thou acquittest, then, Jacques Colis of any false intention?"

"He was less strong than he believed himself, mein Herr; he was not equal to sharing our disgrace, which was put rudely and too strongly before him."

"Thou hadst consented freely to the marriage thyself, and wert well disposed to become his wife?"

The imploring look and heaving respiration of Christine were lost on the blunted sensibilities of a criminal judge.

"Was the youth dear to thee?" he repeated, without perceiving the wound he was inflicting on female reserve.

Christine shuddered. She was not accustomed to have affections which she considered the most sacred of her short and innocent existence so rudely probed; but, believing that the safety of her father depended on her frankness and sincerity, by an effort that was nearly superhuman, she was enabled to reply. The bright glow that suffused her face, however, proclaimed the power of that sentiment which becomes instinctive to her sex, arraying her features in the lustre of maiden shame.

"I was little used to hear words of praise, Herr Châtelain,--and they are so soothing to the ears of the despised! I felt as a girl acknowledges the preference of a youth who is not disagreeable to her. I thought he loved me--and--what would you more, mein Herr?"

"None could hate thee, innocent and abused child!" murmured the Signor Grimaldi.

"You forget that I am Balthazar's daughter, mein Herr; none of our race are viewed with favor."

"Thou, at least, must be an exception!"

"Leaving this aside," continued the châtelain, "I would know if thy parents showed resentment at the misconduct of thy betrothed; whether aught was said in thy presence, that can throw light on this unhappy affair?"

The officer of the Valais turned his head aside; for he met the surprised and displeased glance of the Genoese, whose eye expressed a gentleman's opinion at hearing a child thus questioned in a matter that so nearly touched her father's life. But the look and the improper character of the examination escaped the notice of Christine. She relied with filial confidence on the innocence of the author of her being, and, so far from being shocked, she rejoiced with the simplicity and confidence of the undesigning at being permitted to say anything that might vindicate him in the eyes of his judges.

"Herr Châtelain," she answered eagerly, the blood that had mounted to her cheeks from female weakness, deepening to, and warming, her very temples with a holier sentiment: "Herr Châtelain, we wept together when alone; we prayed for our enemies as for ourselves, but naught was said to the prejudice of poor Jacques--no, not a whisper."

"Wept and prayed!" repeated the judge, looking from the child to the father, in the manner of a man that fancied he did not hear aright.

"I said both, mein Herr; if the former was a weakness, the latter was a duty."

"This is strange language in the mouth of a Leadsman's child!"

Christine appeared at a loss, for a moment, to comprehend his meaning; but, passing a hand across her fair brow she continued:

"I think I understand what you would say, mein Herr," she said; "the world believes us to be without feeling and without hope. We are what we seem in the eyes of others because the law makes it so, but we are in our hearts like all around us, Herr Châtelain--with this difference, that, feeling our abasement among men, we lean more closely and more affectionately on God. You may condemn us to do your offices and to bear your dislike, but you cannot rob us of our trust in the justice of heaven. In that, at least, we are the equals of the proudest baron in the cantons!"

"The examination had better rest here," said the prior, advancing with glistening eyes to interpose between the maiden and her interrogator. "Thou knowest, Herr Bourrit, that we have, other prisoners."

The châtelain, who felt his own practised obduracy of feeling strangely giving way before the innocent and guileless faith of Christine, was not unwilling himself to change the direction of the inquiries. The family of Balthazar was directed to retire, and the attendants were commanded to bring forward Pippo and Conrad.

Chapter XXVIII

> And when thou thus
> Shalt stand impleaded at the high tribunal
> Of hoodwink'd Justice, who shall tell thy audit!
>
> Cotton.

The buffoon and the pilgrim, though of a general appearance likely to excite distrust, presented themselves with the confidence and composure of innocence. Their examination was short, for the account they gave of their movements was clear and connected. Circumstances that were known to the monks, too, greatly aided in producing a conviction that they could have had no agency in the murder. They had left the valley below some hours before the arrival of Jacques Colis, and they reached the convent, weary and foot-sore, as was usual with all who ascended that long and toilsome path, shortly after the commencement of the storm. Measures had been taken by the local authorities, during the time lost in waiting the arrival of the bailiff and the châtelain, to ascertain all the minute facts which it was supposed would be useful in ferreting out the truth; and the results of these inquiries had also been favorable to these itinerants, whose habits of vagabondism might otherwise very justly have brought them within the pale of suspicion.

The flippant Pippo was the principal speaker in the short investigation, and his answers were given with a ready frankness, that, under the circumstances, did him and his companion infinite service. The buffoon, though accustomed to deception and frauds, had sufficient mother-wit to comprehend the critical position in which he was now placed, and that it was wiser to be sincere, than to attempt effecting his ends by any of the usual means of prevarication. He answered the judge, therefore, with a simplicity which his ordinary pursuits would not have given reason to expect, and apparently with some touches of feeling that did credit to his heart.

"This frankness is thy friend," added the châtelain, after he had nearly exhausted his questions, the answers having convinced him that there was no ground of suspicion, beyond the adventitious circumstance of their having been travellers on the same road as the deceased; "it has done much towards convincing me of thy innocence, and it is in general the best shield for those who have committed no crime. I only marvel that one of thy habits should have had the sense to discover it!"

"Suffer me to tell you, Signor Castellano, or Podestà, whichever may be your eccellenza's proper title, that you have not given Pippo credit for the wit he really hath. It is true I live by throwing dust into men's eyes, and by making others think the wrong is the right: but mother Nature has given us all an insight into our own interests, and mine is quite clear enough to let me know when the true is better than the false."

"Happy would it be if all had the same faculty and the same disposition to put it in use."

"I shall not presume to teach one as wise and as experienced as yourself, eccellenza, but if an humble man might speak freely in this honorable presence, he would say that it is not common to meet with a fact without finding it a very near neighbor to a lie. They pass for the wisest and the most virtuous who best know how to mix the two so artfully together, that, like the sweets we put upon healing bitters, the palatable may make the useful go down. Such at least is the opinion of a poor street buffoon, who has no better claim to merit than having learned his art on the Mole and in the Toledo of Bellissima Napoli, which, as everybody knows, is a bit of heaven fallen upon earth!"

The fervor with which Pippo uttered the customary eulogium on the site of the ancient Parthenope was so natural and characteristic as to excite a smile in the judge, in spite of the solemn duty in which he was engaged, and it was believed to be an additional proof of the speaker's innocence. The châtelain then slowly recapitulated the history of the buffoon and the pilgrim to his companions, the purport of which was as follows.

Pippo naively admitted the debauch at Vévey, implicating the festivities of the day and the known frailty of the flesh as the two influencing causes. Conrad, however, stood upon the purity of his life and the sacred character of his calling, justifying the company he kept on the respectable plea of necessity, and on that of the mortifications to which a pilgrimage should, of right, subject him who undertakes it. They had quitted Vaud together as early as the evening of the day of the abbaye's ceremonies, and, from that time to the moment of their arrival at the convent, had made a diligent use of their legs, in order to cross the Col before the snows should set in and render the passage dangerous. They had been seen at Martigny, at Liddes, and St. Pierre, alone and at proper hours, making the best of their way towards the hospice; and, though of necessity their progress and actions, for several hours after quitting the latter place, were not brought within the observation of any but of that all-seeing eye which commands a view of the recesses of the Alps equally with those of more frequented spots, their arrival at the abode of the monks was sufficiently seasonable to give reason to believe that no portion of the intervening time had been wasted by the way. Thus far their account of themselves and their movements was distinct, while, on the other hand, there was not a single fact to implicate either, beyond the suspicion that was more or less common to all who happened to be on the mountain at the moment the crime was committed.

"The innocence of these two men would seem so clear, and their readiness to appear and answer to our questions is so much in their favor," observed the experienced châtelain, "that I do not deem it just to detain them longer. The pilgrim, in particular, has a heavy trust; I understand he performs his penance as much for others as for himself, and it is scarce decent in us, who are believers and servants of the church, to place obstacles in his path. I will suggest the expediency, therefore, of giving him at least permission to depart."

"As we are near the end of the inquiries," interrupted the Signor Grimaldi, gravely, "I would suggest, with due deference to a better opinion and more experience, the propriety that all should remain, ourselves included, until we have come to a better understanding of the truth."

Both Pippo and the pilgrim met this suggestion with ready declarations of their willingness to continue at the convent until the following morning. This little concession, however, had no great merit, for the lateness of the hour rendered it imprudent to depart immediately; and the; affair was finally settled by ordering them to retire, it being understood that, unless previously called for, they might depart with the reappearance of the dawn. Maso was the next and the last to be examined.

Il Maledetto presented himself with perfect steadiness of nerve. He was accompanied by Nettuno, the mastiffs of the convent having been kennelled for the night. It had been the habit of the dog of late to stray among the rocks by day, and to return to the convent in the evening in quest of food, the sterile St. Bernard possessing nothing whatever for the support of man or beast except that which came from the liberality of the monks, every animal but the chamois and the lämmergeyer refusing to ascend so near the region of eternal snows. In his master, however, Nettuno found a steady friend, never failing to receive all that was necessary to his wants from the portion of Maso himself; for the faithful beast was admitted at his periodical visits to the temporary prison in which the latter was confined.

The châtelain waited; a moment for the little stir occasioned by the entrance of the prisoner to subside, when he pursued the inquiry.

"Thou art a Genoese of the name of Thomaso Santi?" he asked, consulting his notes.

"By this name, Signore, am I generally known."

"Thou art a mariner, and it is said one of courage and skill. Why hast thou given thyself the ungracious appellation of Il Maledetto?"

"Men call me thus. It is a misfortune, but not a crime, to be accursed."

"He that is so ready to abuse his own fortunes should not be surprised if others are led to think he merits his fate. We have some accounts of thee in Valais; 'tis said thou art a free-trader?"

"The fact can little concern Valais or her government, since all come and go unquestioned in this free land."

"It is true, we do not imitate our neighbors in all their policy; neither do we like to see so often those who set at naught the laws of friendly states. Why art thou journeying on this road?"

"Signore, if I am what you say, the reason of my being here is sufficiently plain. It is probably because the Lombard and Piedmontese are more exacting of the stranger than you of the mountains."

"Your effects have been examined, and they offer nothing to support the suspicion. By all appearances, Maso, thou hast not much of the goods of life to boast of; but, in spite of this, thy reputation clings to thee."

"Ay, Signore, this is much after the world's humor. Let it fancy any quality in a man, and he is sure to get more than his share of the same, whether it be for or against his interest. The rich man's florin is quickly coined into a sequin by vulgar tongues, while the poor man is lucky if he can get the change of a silver mark for an ounce of the better metal. Even poor Nettuno finds it difficult to get a living here at the convent, because some difference in coat and instinct has given him a bad name among the dogs of St. Bernard!"

"Thy answer agrees with thy character; thou art said to have more wit than honesty, Maso, and thou art described as one that can form a desperate resolution and act up to its decision at need?"

"I am as Heaven willed at the birth, Signor Castellano, and as the chances of a pretty busy life have served to give the work its finish. That I am not wanting in manly qualities on occasion, perhaps these noble travellers will be willing to testify, in consideration of some activity that I may have shown on the Leman, during their late passage of that treacherous water."

Though this was said carelessly, the appeal to the recollection and gratitude of those he had served was too direct to be overlooked. Melchior de Willading, the pious clavier, and the Signor Grimaldi all testified in behalf of the prisoner, freely admitting that, without his coolness and skill, the Winkelried and all she held would irretrievably have been lost. Sigismund was not content with so cold a demonstration of his feelings. He owed not only the lives of his father and him self to the courage of Maso, but that of one dearer than all; one whose preservation, to his youthful imagination, seemed a service that might nearly atone for any crime, and his gratitude was in proportion.

"I will testify more strongly to thy merit, Maso, in face of this or any tribunal;" he said, grasping the hand of the Italian. "One who showed so much bravery and so strong love for his fellows, would be little likely to take life clandestinely and like a coward. Thou mayest count on my testimony in this strait--if thou art guilty of this crime, who can hope to be innocent?"

Maso returned the friendly grasp till their fingers seemed to grow into each other. His eye, too, showed he was not without wholesome native sympathies, though education and his habits might have warped them from their true direction. A tear, in spite of his effort to suppress the weakness started from its fountain, rolling down his sunburnt cheek like a solitary rivulet trickling through a barren and rugged waste.

"This is frank, and as becomes a soldier, Signore," he said, "and I receive it as it is given, in kindness and love. But we will not lay more stress upon the affair of the lake than it deserves. This keen-sighted châtelain need not be told that I could not be of use in saving your lives, without saving my own; and, unless I much mistake the meaning of his eye, he is about to say that we are fashioned like this wild country in which chance has brought us together, with our spots of generous fertility mingled with much unfruitful rock, and that he who does a good act to-day may forget himself by doing an evil turn to-morrow."

"Thou givest reason to all who hear thee to mourn that thy career has not been more profitable to thyself and the public," answered the judge; "one who can reason so-well, and who hath this clear insight into his own disposition, must err less from ignorance than wantonness!"

"There you do me injustice, Signor Castellano, and the laws more credit than they deserve. I shall not deny that justice--or what is called justice--and I have some acquaintance. I have been the tenant of many prisons before this which has been furnished by the holy canons, and I have seen every stage of the rogue's progress, from him who is still startled by his first crime, dreaming heavy dreams, and fancying each stone of his cell has an eye to reproach him, to him who no sooner does a wrong than it is forgotten in the wish to find the means of committing another; and I call Heaven as a witness, that more is done to help along the scholar in his study of vice, by those who are styled the ministers of justice, than by his own natural frailties, the wants of his habits, or the strength of his passions. Let the judge feel a father's mildness, the laws possess that pure justice which is of things that are not perverted, and society become what it claims to be, a community of mutual support, and, my life on it, châtelain, thy functions will be lessened of most of their weight and of all their oppression."

"This language is bold, and without an object. Explain the manner of thy quitting Vévey, Maso, the road thou hast travelled, the hours of thy passages by the different villages, and the reason why thou wert discovered near the Refuge, alone, and why thou quittedst the companions with whom thou hadst passed the night so early and so clandestinely?"

The Italian listened attentively to these several interrogatories; when they were all put, he gravely and calmly set about furnishing his answers. The history of his departure from Vévey, his appearance at St. Maurice, Martigny, Liddes, and St. Pierre, was distinctly given, and it was in perfect accordance with the private information that had been gleaned by the authorities. He had passed the last habitation on the mountain, on foot and alone, about an hour before the solitary horseman, who was now known to be Jacques Colis, was seen to proceed in the same direction; and he admitted that he was overtaken by the latter, just as he reached the upper extremity of the plain beneath Vélan, where they were seen in company, though at a considerable distance, and by a doubtful light, by the travellers who were conducted by Pierre.

Thus far the account given of himself by Maso was in perfect conformity with what was already known to the châtelain; but, after turning the rock already mentioned in a previous chapter, all was buried in mystery, with the exception of the incidents that have been regularly related in the narrative. The Italian, in his further explanations, added that he soon parted with his companion, who, impatient of delay, and desirous of reaching the convent before night, had urged his beast to greater speed, while he himself had turned a little aside from the path to rest himself, and to make a few preparations that he had deemed necessary before going directly to the convent.

The whole of this short history was delivered with a composure as great as that which had just been displayed by Pippo and the pilgrim; and it was impossible for any present to detect the slightest improbability or contradiction in the tale. The meeting with the other travellers in the storm

Maso ascribed to the fact of their having passed him while he was stationary, and to his greater speed when in motion; two circumstances that were quite as likely to be true as all the rest of the account. He had left the Refuge at the first glimpse of dawn, because he was behind his time, and it had been his intention to descend to Aoste that night, an exertion that was necessary in order to repair the loss.

"This may be true," resumed the judge; "but how dost thou account for thy poverty? In searching thy effects, thou art found to be in a condition little better than that of a mendicant. Even thy purse is empty, though known to be a successful and desperate trifler with the revenue, in all those states where the entrance duty is enforced."

"He that plays deepest, Signore, is most likely to be stripped of his means. What is there new or unlooked for in the fact that a dealer in the contraband should lose his venture?"

"This is more plausible than convincing. Thou art signalled as being accustomed to transport articles of the jewellers from Geneva into the adjoining states, and thou art known to come from the head-quarters of these artisans. Thy losses must have been unusual, to have left thee so naked. I much fear that a bootless speculation in thy usual trade has driven thee to repair the loss by the murder of this unhappy man, who left his home well supplied with gold, and, as it would seem, with a valuable store of jewelry, too. The particulars are especially mentioned in this written account of his effects, which the honorable bailiff bringeth from his friends."

Maso mused silently, and in deep abstraction. He then desired that the chapel might be cleared of all but the travellers of condition, the monks, and his judges. The request was granted, for it was expected that he was about to make an important confession, as indeed, in a certain degree, proved to be the fact.

"Should I clear myself of the charge of poverty, Signor Castellano," he demanded, when all the inferiors had left the place, "shall I stand acquitted in your eyes of the charge of murder?"

"Surely not: still thou wilt have removed one of the principal grounds of temptation, and in that thou wilt be greatly the gainer, for we know that Jacques Colis hath been robbed as well as slain."

Maso appeared to deliberate again, as a man is apt to pause before he takes a step that may materially affect his interests. But suddenly deciding, like a man of prompt opinions, he called to Nettuno, and, seating himself on the steps of one of the side-altars, he proceeded to make his revelation with great method and coolness. Removing some of the long shaggy hair of the dog, Il Maledetto showed the attentive and curious spectators that a belt of leather had been ingeniously placed about the body of the animal, next its skin. It was so concealed as to be quite hid from the view of those who did not make particular search, a process that Nettuno, judging by the scowling looks he threw at most present, and the manner in which he showed his teeth, would not be likely to permit to a stranger. The belt was opened, and Maso laid a glittering necklace of precious stones, in which rubies and emeralds vied with other gems of price, with some of a dealer's coquetry, under the strong light of the lamp.

"There you see the fruits of a life of hazards and hardships, Signor Châtelain," he said; "if my purse is empty, it is because the Jewish Calvinists of Geneva have taken the last liard in payment of the jewels."

"This is an ornament of rare beauty and exceeding value, to be seen in the possession of one of thy appearance and habits, Maso!" exclaimed the frugal Valaisan.

"Signore, its cost was a hundred doppie of pure gold and full weight, and it is contracted for with a young noble of Milano, who hopes to win his mistress by the present, for a profit of fifty. Affairs were getting low with me in consequence of sundry seizures and a total wreck, and I took the adventure with the hope of sudden and great gain. As there is nothing against the laws of Valais in the matter, I trust to stand acquitted, châtelain, for my frankness. One who was master of this would be little likely to shed blood for the trifle that would be found on the person of Jacques Colis."

"Thou hast more," observed the judge, signing with his hand as he spoke; "let us see all thou hast."

"Not a brooch, or so much as a worthless garnet."

"Nay, I see the belt which contains them among the hairs of the dog."

Maso either felt or feigned a well-acted surprise. Nettuno had been placed in a convenient attitude for his master to unloosen the belt, and, as it was the intention of the latter to replace it, the animal still lay quietly in the same position, a circumstance which displaced his shaggy coat, and allowed the châtelain to detect the object to which he had just alluded.

"Signore," said the smuggler, changing color but endeavoring to speak lightly of a discovery which all the others present evidently considered to be grave, "it would seem that the dog, accustomed to do these little offices in behalf of his master, has been tempted by success to undertake a speculation on his own account. By my patron saint and the Virgin! I know nothing of this second adventure."

"Trifle not, but undo the belt, lest I have the beast muzzled that it may be performed by others." sternly commanded the châtelain.

The Italian complied, though with an ill grace that was much too apparent for his own interest. Having loosened the fastenings, he reluctantly gave the envelope to the Valaisan. The latter cut the cloth, and laid some ten or fifteen different pieces of jewelry on the table. The spectators crowded about the spot in curiosity, while the judge eagerly referred to the written description of the effects of the murdered man.

"A ring of brilliants, with an emerald of price, the setting chased and heavy," read the Valaisan.

"Thank God, it is not here!" exclaimed the Signor Grimaldi. "One could wish to find so true a mariner innocent of this bloody deed!"

The châtelain believed he was on the scent of a secret that had begun to perplex him, and as few are so inherently humane as to prefer the advantage of another to their own success, he heard both the announcement and the declaration of the noble Genoese with a frown.

"A cross of turquoise of the length of two inches, with pearls of no great value intermixed," continued the judge.

Sigismund groaned and turned away from the table.

"Unhappily, here is that which too well answers to the description!" slowly and with evident reluctance, escaped from the Signor Grimaldi.

"Let it be measured," demanded the prisoner.

The experiment was made, and the agreement was found to be perfect

"Bracelets of rubies, the stones set in foil, and six in number," continued the methodical châtelain, whose eye now lighted with the triumph of victory.

"These are wanting!" cried Melchior de Willading, who, in common with all whom he had served, took a lively interest in the fate of Maso. "There are no jewels of this description here!"

"Come to the next, Herr Châtelain," put in Peterchen, leaning to the side of the law's triumph; "let us have the next, o' God's name!"

"A brooch of amethyst, the stone of our own mountains, set in foil, and the size of one-eighth of an inch; form oval."

It was lying on the table, beyond all possibility of dispute. All the remaining articles, which were chiefly rings of the less prized stones, such as jasper, granite, topaz, and turquoise, were also identified, answering perfectly to the description furnished by the jeweller, who had sold them to Jacques Colis the night of the fête, when, with Swiss thrift, he had laid in this small stock in trade, with a view to diminish the cost of his intended journey.

"It is a principle of law, unfortunate man," remarked the châtelain, removing the spectacles he had mounted in order to read the list, "that effects wrongly taken from one robbed criminate him in whose possession they are found, unless he can render a clear account of the transfer. What hast thou to say on this head?"

"Not a syllable, Signore; I must refer you and all others to the dog, who alone can furnish the history of these baubles. It is clear that I am little known in the Valais, for Maso never deals in trifles insignificant as these."

"The pretext will not serve thee, Maso; thou triflest in an affair of life and death. Wilt thou confess thy crime, ere we proceed to extremities?"

"That I have been long at open variance with the law, Signor Castellano, is true, if you will have it so; but I am as innocent of this man's death as the noble Baron de Willading here. That the Genoese authorities were looking for me, on account of some secret understanding that the republic has with its old enemies, the Savoyards, I frankly allow too; but it was a matter of gain, and not of blood. I have taken life in my time, Signore, but it has been in fair combat, whether the cause was just or not."

"Enough has been proved against thee already to justify the use of the torture in order to have the rest."

"Nay; I do not see the necessity of this appeal," remarked the bailiff. "There lies the dead, here is his property, and yonder stands the criminal. It is an affair that only wants the forms, methinks, to be committed presently to the axe."

"Of all the foul offences against God and man," resumed the Valaisan, in the manner of one that is about to sentence, "that which hastens a living soul, unshrived, unconfessed, unprepared, and with all its sins upon it, into another state of being and into the dread presence of his Almighty Judge, is the heaviest, and the last to be overlooked by the law. There is less excuse for thee, Thomaso Santi, for thy education has been far superior to thy fortunes, and thou hast passed a life of vice and violence in opposition to thy reason and what was taught thee in youth. Thou hast, therefore, little ground for hope, since the state I serve loves justice in its purity above all other qualities."

"Nobly spoken! Herr Châtelain," cried the bailiff, "and in a manner to send repentance like a dagger into the criminal's soul. What is thought and said in Valais we echo in Vaud, and I would not that any I love stood in thy shoes, Maso, for the honors of the emperor!"

"Signori, you have both spoken, and it is as men whom fortune hath favored since childhood. It is easy for those who are in prosperity to be upright in all that touches money, though by the light of the blessed Maria's countenance I do think there is more coveted by those who have much than by the hardy and industrious poor. I am no stranger, to that which men call justice, and know how to honor and respect its decrees as they deserve. Justice, Signori, is the weak man's scourge and the strong man's sword: it is a breast-plate and back-plate to the one and a weapon to be parried by the other. In short, it is a word of fair import, on the tongue, but of most unequal application in the deed."

"We overlook thy language in consideration of the pass to which thy crimes have reduced thee, unhappy man, though it is an aggravation of thy offences, since it proves thou hast sinned equally against thyself and us. This affair need go no farther; the headsman and the other travellers may be dismissed: we commit the Italian to the irons."

Maso heard the order without alarm, though he appeared to be maintaining a violent struggle with himself. He paced the chapel rapidly, and muttered much between his teeth. His words were not intelligible, though they were evidently of strong, if not violent, import. At length he stopped short, in the manner of one who had decided.

"This-matter grows serious," he said: "it will admit of no farther hesitation. Signor Grimaldi, command all to leave the chapel in whose discretion you have not the most perfect confidence."

"I see none to be distrusted," answered the surprised Genoese.

"Then will I speak."

Chapter XXIX

Thy voice to us is wind among still woods.

Shelley.

Notwithstanding the gravity of the facts which were accumulating against him, Maso had maintained throughout the foregoing scene much of that steady self-possession and discernment which were the fruits of adventure in scenes of danger, long exposure, and multiplied hazards. To these causes of coolness, might be added the iron-like nerves inherited from nature. The latter were not easily disturbed, however critical the state to which he was reduced. Still he had changed color, and his manner had that thoughtful and unsettled air which denote the consciousness of being in circumstances that require uncommon wariness and judgment. But his final opinion appeared to be formed when he made the appeal mentioned in the close of the last chapter, and he now only waited for the two or three officials who were present to retire, before he pursued his purpose. When the door was closed, leaving none but his examiners, Sigismund Balthazar, and the group of females in the side-chapel, he turned, with singular respect of manner, and addressed himself exclusively to the Signor Grimaldi, as if the judgment which was to decide his fate depended solely on his will.

"Signore," he said, "there has been much secret allusion between us, and I suppose that it is unnecessary for me to say, that you are known to me.'

"I have already recognized thee for a country man," coldly returned the Genoese; "it is vain however, to imagine the circumstance can avail a murderer. If any consideration could induce me to forget the claims of justice, the recollection of thy good service on the Leman would prove thy best friend. As it is, I fear thou hast naught to expect from me."

Maso was silent. He looked the other steadily in the face, as if he would study his character, though he guardedly prevented his manner from losing its appearance of profound respect.

"Signore, the chances of life were greatly with you at the birth. You were born the heir of a powerful house, in which gold is more plenty than woes in a poor man's cabin, and you have not been made to learn by experience how hard it is to keep down the longings for those pleasures which the base metal will purchase, when we see others rolling in its luxuries."

"This plea will not avail thee, unfortunate man; else were there an end of human institutions. The difference of which thou speakest is a simple consequence of the rights of property; and even the barbarian admits the sacred duty of respecting that which is another's."

"A word from one like you, illustrious Signore, would open for me the road to Piedmont," continued Maso, unmoved: "once across the frontiers, it shall be my care never to molest the rocks of Valais again. I ask only what I have been the means of saving, eccellenza,--life."

The Signor Grimaldi shook his head, though it was very evident that he declined the required intercession with much reluctance. He and old Melchior de Willading exchanged glances; and all who noted this silent intercourse understood it to say, that each considered duty to God a higher obligation than gratitude for a service rendered to themselves.

"Ask gold, or what thou wilt else, but do not ask me to aid in defeating justice. Gladly would I have given for the asking, twenty times the value of those miserable baubles for whose possession, Maso, thou hast rashly taken life; but I cannot become a sharer of thy crime, by refusing atonement to his friends. It is too late: I cannot befriend thee now, if I would."

"Thou nearest the answer of this noble gentleman," interposed the châtelain; "it is wise and seemly, and thou greatly overratest his influence or that of any present, if thou fanciest the laws can be set aside at pleasure. Wert thou a noble thyself, or the son of a prince, judgment would have its way in the Valais!"

Maso smiled wildly; and yet the expression of his glittering eye was so ironical as to cause uneasiness in his judge. The Signor Grimaldi, too, observed the audacious confidence of his air with distrust, for his spirit had taken secret alarm on a subject that was rarely long absent from his thoughts.

"If thou meanest more than has been said," exclaimed the latter, "for the sake of the blessed Maria be explicit!"

"Signor Melchior," continued Maso, turning to the baron, "I did you and your daughter fair service on the lake!"

"That thou didst, Maso, we are both willing to admit, and were it in Berne,--but the laws are made equally for all, the great and the humble they who have friends, and they who have none,"

"I have heard of this act on the lake," put in Peterchen; "and unless fame lieth--which. Heaven knows, fame is apt enough to do, except in giving their just dues to those who are in high trusts,--thou didst conduct thyself in that affair, Maso, like a loyal and well-taught mariner: but the honorable châtelain has well remarked, that holy justice must have way before all other things. Justice is represented as blind, in order that it may be seen she is no respecter of persons: and wert thou an Avoyer, the decree must come. Reflect maturely, therefore, on all the facts, and thou wilt come, in time, to see the impossibility of thine own innocence. First, thou left the path, being ahead of Jacques Colis, to enter it at a moment suited to thy purposes: then thou took'st his life for gold--"

"But this is believing that to be true, Signor Bailiff, which is only yet supposed," interrupted Il Maledetto; "I left the path to give Nettuno his charge apart from curious eyes; and, as for the gold of which you speak, would the owner of a necklace of that price be apt to barter his soul against a booty like this which comes of Jacques Colis!"

Maso spoke with a contempt which did not serve his cause; for it left the impression among the auditors, that he weighed the morality and immorality of his acts simply by their result.

"It is time to bring this to an end," said the Signor Grimaldi, who had been thoughtful and melancholy while the others spoke: "thou hast something to address particularly to me, Maso; but if thy claim is no better than that of our common country, I grieve to say, it cannot be admitted."

"Signore, the voice of a Doge of Genoa is not often raised in vain, when he would use it in behalf of another!"

At this sudden announcement of the traveller's rank, the monks and the châtelain started in surprise, and a low murmur of wonder was heard in the chapel. The smile of Peterchen, and the composure of the Baron de Willading, however, showed that they, at least, learned nothing new. The bailiff whispered the prior significantly, and from that moment his deportment towards the Genoese took still more of the character of formal and official respect. On the other hand, the Signor Grimaldi remained composed, like one accustomed to receive deference, though his manner lost the slight degree of restraint that had been imposed by the observance of the temporary character he had assumed.

"The voice of a Doge of Genoa should not be used in intercession, unless in behalf of the innocent," he replied, keeping his severe eye fastened on the countenance of the accused.

Again Il Maledetto seemed laboring with some secret that struggled on his tongue.

"Speak," continued the Prince of Genoa; for it was, in truth, that high functionary, who had journeyed incognito, in the hope of meeting his ancient friend at the sports of Vévey, "Speak, Maso, if thou hast aught serious to urge in favor of thyself; time presses, and the sight of one to whom I owe so much in this great jeopardy, without the power to aid him, grows painful."

"Signor Doge, though deaf to pity, you cannot be deaf to nature."

The countenance of the Doge became livid; his lips trembled even to the appearance of convulsions.

"Deal no longer in mystery, man of blood!" he said with energy. "What is thy meaning?"

"I entreat your eccellenza to be calm. Necessity forces me to speak; for, as you see, I stand between this revelation and the block--I am Bartolo Contini!"

The groan that escaped the compressed lips of, the Doge, the manner in which he sank into a seat, and the hue of death that settled over his aged countenance, until it was more ghastly even than that of the unhappy victim of violence, drew all present, in wonder and alarm, around his chair. Signing for those who pressed upon him to give way, the Prince sat gazing at Maso, with eyes that appeared ready to burst from their sockets.

"Thou Bartolomeo!" he uttered huskily, as if horror had frozen his voice.

"I am Bartolo, Signore, and no other. He who goes through many scenes hath occasion for many names. Even your Highness travels at times under a cloud."

The Doge continued to stare on the speaker with the fixedness of regard that one might be supposed to fasten on a creature of unearthly existence.

"Melchior," he said slowly, turning his eyes from one to the other of the forms that filled them, for Sigismund had advanced to the side of Maso, in kind concern for the old man's condition,--"Melchior, we are but feeble and miserable creatures in the hand of one who looks upon the proudest and happiest of us, as we look upon the worm that crawls the earth! What are hope, and honor, and our fondest love, in the great train of events that time heaves from its womb, bringing forth to our confusion? Are we proud? fortune revenges itself for our want of humility by its scorn. Are we happy? it is but the calm that precedes the storm. Are we great? it is but to lead us into abuses that will justify our fall. Are we honored stains tarnish our good names, in spite of all our care!"

"He who puts his trust in the Son of Maria need never despair!" whispered the worthy clavier touched nearly to tears by the sudden distress of one whom he had learned to respect. "Let the fortunes of the world pass away, or change as they will, his chastening love outliveth time!"

The Signor Grimaldi, for, though the elected of Genoa, such was in truth the family name of the Doge, turned his vacant gaze for an instant on the Augustine, but it soon reverted to the forms and faces of Maso and Sigismund, who still stood before him, filling his thoughts even more than his sight.

"Yes, there is a power--" he resumed, "a great and beneficent Being to equalize our fortunes here, and when we pass into another state of being, loaded with the wrongs of this, we shall have justice! Tell me, Melchior, thou who knew my youth, who read my heart when it was open as day, what was there in it to deserve this punishment? Here is Balthazar, come of a race of executioners--a man condemned of opinion--that prejudice besets with a hedge of hatred--that men point at with their fingers, and whom the dogs are ready to bay--this Balthazar is the father of that gallant youth, whose form is so perfect, whose spirit is so noble, and whose life so pure; while I, the last of a line that is lost in the obscurity of time, the wealthiest of my land, and the chosen of my peers, am accursed with an outcast, a common brigand, a murderer, for the sole prop of my decaying house--with this Il Maledetto--this man accursed--for a son!"

A movement of astonishment escaped the listeners, even the Baron de Willading not suspecting the real cause of his friend's distress. Maso alone was unmoved; for while the aged father betrayed the keenness of his anguish, the son discovered none of that sympathy of which even a life like his might be supposed to have left some remains in the heart of a child. He was cold, collected, observant, and master of his smallest action.

"I will not believe this," exclaimed the Doge, whose very soul revolted at this unfeeling apathy, even more than at the disgrace of being the father of such a child; "thou art not he thou pretendest to be; this foul lie is uttered that my natural feelings may interpose between thee and the block! Prove thy truth, or I abandon thee to thy fate."

"Signore, I would have saved this unhappy exhibition, but you would not. That I am Bartolo this signet, your own gift sent to be my protection in a strait like this, will show. It is, moreover, easy for me to prove what I say, by a hundred witnesses who are living in Genoa."

The Signor Grimaldi stretched forth a hand that trembled like an aspen to receive the ring, a jewel of little price, but a signet that he had, in truth, sent to be an instrument of recognition between him and his child, in the event of any sudden calamity befalling the latter. He groaned as he gazed at its well-remembered emblems, for its identity was only too plain.

"Maso--Bartolo--Gaetano--for such, miserable boy, is thy real appellation--thou canst not know how bitter is the pang that an unworthy child brings to the parent, else would thy life have been different. Oh! Gaetano! Gaetano! what a foundation art thou for a father's hopes! What a subject for a father's love! I saw thee last a smiling innocent cherub, in thy nurse's arms, and I find thee with a blighted sod, the pure fountain of thy mind corrupted, a form sealed with the stamp of vice, and with hands dyed in blood; prematurely old in body, and with a spirit that hath already the hellish taint of the damned!

"Signore, you find me as the chances of a wild life have willed. The world and I have been at loggerheads this many a year, and in trifling with its laws, I take my revenge of its abuse--" warmly returned Il Maledetto, for his spirit began to be aroused. "Thou bear'st hard upon me, Doge--father-- or what thou wilt--and I should be little worthy of my lineage, did I not meet thy charges as they are made. Compare thine own career with mine, and let it be proclaimed by sound of trumpet if thou wilt, which hath most reason to be proud, and which to exult. Thou wert reared in the hopes and honors of our name; thou passed thy youth in the pursuit of arms according to thy fancy, and when tired of change, and willing to narrow thy pleasures, thou looked about thee for a maiden to become the mother of thy successor; thou turned a wishing eye on one young, fair, and noble, but whose affections, as her faith, were solemnly, irretrievably plighted to another."

The Doge shuddered and veiled his eye; but he eagerly interrupted Maso.

"Her kinsman was unworthy of her love," he cried; "he was an outcast, and little better than thyself, unhappy boy, except in the chances of condition."

"It matters not, Signore; God had not made you the arbiter of her fate. In tempting her family by your greater riches, you crushed two hearts, and destroyed the hopes of your fellow-creatures. In her was sacrificed an angel, mild and pure as this fair creature who is now listening so breathlessly to my words; in him a fierce untamed spirit, that had only the greater need of management, since it was as likely to go wrong as right. Before your son was born, this unhappy rival, poor in hopes as in wealth, had become desperate; and the mother of your child sank a victim to her ceaseless regrets, at her own want of faith as much as for his follies."

"Thy mother was deluded, Gaetano; she never knew the real qualities of her cousin, or a soul like hers would have lothed the wretch."

"Signore, it matters not," continued Il Maledetto, with a ruthless perseverance of intention, and a coolness of manner that would seem to merit the description which had just been given his spirit, that of possessing a hellish taint; "she loved him with a woman's heart; and with a woman's ingenuity and confidence, she ascribed his fall to despair for her loss."

"Oh, Melchior! Melchior! this is fearfully true!" groaned the Doge.

"It is so true, Signore, that it should be written on my mother's tomb. We are children of a fiery climate; the passions burn in our Italy like the hot sun that glows there. When despair drove the disappointed lover to acts that rendered him an outlaw, the passage to revenge was short. Your child was stolen, hid from your view, and cast upon the world under circumstances that left little doubt of his living in bitterness, and dying under the contempt, if not the curses, of his fellows. All this, Signor Grimaldi, is the fruit of your own errors. Had you respected the affections of an innocent girl, the sad consequences to yourself and me might have been avoided."

"Is this man's history to be believed, Gaetano?" demanded the baron, who had more than once betrayed a wish to check the rude tongue of the speaker.

"I do not--I cannot deny it; I never saw my own conduct in this criminal light before, and yet now it all seems frightfully true!"

Il Maledetto laughed. Those around him thought his untimely merriment resembled the mockery of a devil.

"This is the manner in which men continue to sin, while they lay claim to the merit of innocence!" he added. "Let the great of the earth give but half the care to prevent, that they show to punish, offences against themselves, and what is now called justice will no longer be a stalking-horse to enable a few to live at the cost of the rest. As for me, I am proof of what noble blood and illustrious ancestry can do for themselves! Stolen when a child, Nature has had fair play in my temperament, which I own is more disposed to wild adventure and manly risks than to the pleasures of marble halls. Noble father of mine, were this spirit dressed up in the guise of a senator, or a doge, it might fare badly with Genoa!"

"Unfortunate man," exclaimed the indignant prior, "is this language for a child to use to his father? Dost thou forget that the blood of Jacques Colis is on thy soul?"

"Holy Augustine, the candor with which my general frailties are allowed, should gain me credit when I speak of particular accusations. By the hopes and piety of the reverend canon of Aoste, thy patron saint and founder! I am guiltless of this crime. Question Nettuno as you will, or turn the affair in every way that usage warrants, and let appearances take what shape they may, I swear to you my innocence. If ye think that fear of punishment tempts me to utter a lie, under these holy appeals, (he crossed himself with reverence,) ye do injustice both to my courage and to my love of the saints. The only son of the reigning Doge of Genoa hath little to fear from the headsman's blow!"

Again Maso laughed. It was the confidence of one who knew the world and who was too audacious even to consult appearances unless it suited his humor, breaking out in very wantonness. A man who had led his life, was not to learn at this late day, that the want of eyes in Justice oftener means blindness to the faults of the privileged, than the impartiality that is assumed by the pretending emblem. The châtelain, the prior, the bailiff, the clavier, and the Baron de Willading, looked at each other like men bewildered. The mental agony of the Doge formed a contrast so frightful with the heartless and cruel insensibility of the son, that the sight chilled their blood. The sentiment was only the more common, from the silent but general conviction, that the unfeeling criminal must be permitted to escape. There was, indeed, no precedent for leading the child of a prince to the block, unless it were for an offence which touched the preservation of the father's interests. Much was said in maxims and apophthegms of the purity and necessity of rigid impartiality in administering the affairs of life, but neither had attained his years and experience without obtaining glimpses of practical things, that taught them to foresee the impunity of Maso. Too much violence would be done to a factitous and tottering edifice, were it known that a prince's son was no better than one of the vilest, and the lingering feelings of paternity were certain at last to cast a shield before the offender.

The embarrassment and doubt attending such a state of things was happily, but quite unexpectedly, relieved by the interference of Balthazar. The headsman, until this moment, had been a silent and attentive listener to all that passed; but now he pressed himself into the circle, and looking, in his quiet manner, from one to the other, he spoke with the assurance that the certainty of having important intelligence to impart, is apt to give even to the meekest, in the presence of those whom they habitually respect.

"This broken tale of Maso," he said, "is removing a cloud that has lain, for near thirty years before my eyes. Is it true, illustrious Doge, for such it appears is your princely state, that a son of your noble stock was stolen and kept in from your love, through the vindictive enmity of a rival?"

"True!--alas, too true! Would it had pleased the blessed Maria, who so cherished his mother, to call his spirit to Heaven, ere the curse befell him and me!"

"Your pardon, great Prince, if I press you with questions at a moment so painful. But it is in your own interest. Suffer that I ask in what year this calamity befell your family?"

The Signor Grimaldi signed for his friend to assume the office of answering these extraordinary interrogatories, while he buried his own venerable face in his cloak, to conceal his anguish from curious eyes. Melchior de Willading regarded the headsman in surprise, and for an instant he was disposed to repel questions that seemed importunate; but the earnest countenance and mild, decent demeanor of Balthazar, overcame his repugnance to pursue the subject.

"The child was seized in the autumn of the year 1693," he answered, his previous conferences with his friend having put him in possession of all the leading facts of the history.

"And his age?"

"Was near a twelvemonth."

"Can you inform me what became of the profligate noble who committed this for robbery?"

"The fate of the Signore Pantaleone Serrani has never been truly known; though there is a dark rumor that he died in a brawl in our own Switzerland. That he is dead, there is no cause to doubt."

"And his person, noble Freiherr--a description of his person is now only wanting to throw the light of a noon-day sun, on what has so long been night!"

"I knew the unlucky Signore Pantaleone in early youth. At the time mentioned his years might have been thirty, his form was seemly and of middle height, his features bore the Italian outline, with the dark eye, swarthy skin and glossy hair of the climate. More than this, with the exception of a finger lost in one of our affairs in Lombardy, I cannot say."

"This is enough," returned the attentive Balthazar. "Dismiss your grief, princely Doge, and prepare your heart for a new-found joy. Instead of being the parent of this reckless freebooter, God at length pities and returns your real son in Sigismund, a child that might gladden the heart of any parent, though he were an emperor!"

This extraordinary declaration was made to stunned and confounded listeners. A cry of alarm bust from the lips of Marguerite, who approached the group in the centre of the chapel, trembling and anxious as if the grave were about to rob her of a treasure.

"What is this I hear!" exclaimed the mother, whose sensitiveness was the first to take alarm. "Are my half-formed suspicions then too true, Balthazar? Am I, indeed, without a son? I know thou wouldst not trifle with a mother, or mislead this stricken noble in a thing like this! Speak, again, that I may know the truth--Sigismund!--"

"Is not our child," answered the headsman, with an impress of truth in his manner that went far to bring conviction; "our own boy died in the blessed state of infancy, and, to save thy feelings, this youth was substituted in his place by me without thy knowledge."

Marguerite moved nearer to the young man. She gazed wistfully at his flushed, excited features, in which pain at being so unexpectedly torn from the bosom of a family he had always deemed his own, was fearfully struggling with a wild and indefinite delight at finding himself suddenly relieved from a load he had long found so grievous to be borne. Interpreting the latter expression with jealous affection, she bent her face to her bosom, and retreated in silence among her companions lo weep.

In the mean time a sudden and tumultuous surprise took possession of the different listeners, which was modified and exhibited according to their respective characters, or to the amount of interest that each had in the truth or falsehood of what had just been announced. The Doge clung to the hope, improbable as it seemed, with a tenacity proportioned to his recent anguish, while Sigismund stood like one beside himself. His eye wandered from the simple and benevolent, but degraded, man, whom he had believed to be his father, to the venerable and imposing-looking noble who was now so unexpectedly presented in that sacred character. The sobs of Marguerite reached his ears, and first recalled him to recollection. They came blended with the fresh grief of Christine, who felt as if ruthless death had now robbed her of a brother. There was also the struggling emotion of one whose interest in him had a still more tender and engrossing claim.

"This is so wonderful!" said the trembling Doge, who dreaded lest the next syllable that was uttered might destroy the blessed illusion, "so wildly improbable, that, though my soul yearns to believe it, my reason refuses credence. It is not enough to utter this sudden intelligence, Balthazar; it must be proved. Furnish but a moiety of the evidence that is necessary to establish a legal fact, and I will render thee the richest of thy class in Christendom! And thou, Sigismund, come close to my heart, noble boy," he added, with outstretched arms, "that I may bless thee, while there is hope--that I may feel one beat of a father's pulses--one instant of a father's joy!"

Sigismund knelt at the venerable Prince's feet, and receiving his head on his shoulder, their tears mingled. But even at that previous moment both felt a sense of insecurity, as if the exquisite pleasure of so pure a happiness were too intense to last. Maso looked upon this scene with cold displeasure. His averted face denoting a stronger feeling than disappointment, though the power of natural sympathy was so strong as to draw evidences of its force from the eyes of all the others present.

"Bless thee, bless thee, my child, my dearly beloved son!" murmured the Doge, lending himself to the improbable tale of Balthazar for a delicious instant, and kissing the cheeks of Sigismund as one would embrace a smiling infant; "may the God of heaven and earth, his only Son, and the holy Virgin undefiled, unite to bless thee, here and hereafter, be thou whom thou mayest! I owe thee one precious instant of happiness, such as I have never tasted before. To find a child would not be enough to give it birth; but to believe thee to be that son touches on the joys of paradise!"

Sigismund fervently kissed the hand that had rested affectionately on his head during this diction; then, feeling the necessity of having some guarantee for the existence of emotions so sweet, he arose and made a warm and strong appeal to him who had so long passed for his father to be more explicit, and to justify his new-born hopes by some evidence better than; his simple asseveration; for solemnly as the latter had been made, and profound as he knew to be the reverence for truth which the despised headsman not only entertained himself but inculcated in all in whom he had any interest, the revelation he had just made seemed too improbable to resist the doubts of one who knew his happiness to be the fruit or the forfeiture of its veracity.

Chapter XXX

> We rest--a dream has power to poison sleep;
> We rise--one wandering thought pollutes the day;
> We feel, conceive or reason, laugh or weep;
> Embrace fond woe, or cast our cares away.
>
> Shelley.

The tale of Balthazar was simple but eloquent His union with Marguerite, in spite of the world's obloquy and injustice, had been blest by the wise and merciful Being who knew how to temper the wind to the shorn lamb.

"We knew we were all to each other," he continued, after briefly alluding to the early history of their births and love; "and we felt the necessity of living for ourselves. Ye that are born to honors, who meet with smiles and respectful looks in all ye meet, can know little of the feeling which binds together the unhappy. When God gave us our first-born, as he lay a smiling babe in her lap, looking up into her eye with the innocence that most likens man to angels, Marguerite shed bitter tears at the thought of such a creature's being condemned by the laws to shed the blood of men. The reflection that he was to live for ever an outcast from his kind was bitter to a mother's heart. We had made many offers to the canton to be released ourselves, from this charge; we had prayed them--Herr Melchior, you should know how earnestly we have prayed the council, to be suffered to live like others, and without this accursed doom--but they would not. They said the usage was ancient, that change was dangerous, and that what God willed must come to pass. We could not bear that the burthen we found so hard to endure ourselves should go down for ever as a curse upon our descendants, Herr Doge," he continued, raising his meek face in the pride of honesty; "it is well for those who are the possessors of honors to be proud of their privileges; but when the inheritance is one of wrongs and scorn, when the evil eyes of our fellows are upon us, the heart sickens. Such was our feeling when we looked upon our first-born. The wish to save him from our own disgrace was uppermost, and we bethought us of the means."

"Ay!" sternly interrupted Marguerite, "I parted with my child, and silenced a mother's longings, proud nobles, that he might not become the tool of your ruthless policy; I gave up a mother's joy in nourishing and in cherishing her young, that the little innocent might live among his fellows, as God had created him, their equal and not their victim!"

Balthazar paused, as was usual with him when ever his energetic wife manifested any of her strong and masculine qualities, and then, when deep silence had followed her remark, he proceeded.

"We wanted not for wealth; all we asked was to be like others in the world's respect. With our money it was very easy to find those in another canton, who were willing to take the little Sigismund into their keeping. After which, a feigned death, and a private burial, did the rest. The deceit was easily practised, for as few cared for the griefs as for the happiness of the headsman's family The child had drawn near the end of its first year, when I was called upon to execute my office on a stranger. The criminal had taken life in a drunken brawl in one of the towns of the canton, and he was said to be a man that had trifled with the precious gifts of birth, it being suspected that he was noble. I went with a heavy heart, for never did I strike a blow without praying God it might be the last; but it was heavier when I reached the place where the culprit awaited his fate. The tidings of my poor son's death reached me as I put foot on the threshold of the desolate prison, and I turned aside to weep for my own woes, before I entered to see my victim. The condemned man had great unwillingness to die; he had sent for me many hours before the fatal moment, to make acquaintance, as he said, with the hand that was to dispatch him to the presence of his last and eternal judge."

Balthazar paused; he appeared to meditate on a scene that had probably left indelible impressions on his mind. Shuddering involuntarily, he raised his eyes from the pavement of the chapel, and continued the recital, always in the same subdued and tranquil manner.

"I have been the unwilling instrument of many a violent death--I have seen the most reckless sinners in the agonies of sudden and compelled repentance, but never have I witnessed so wild and fearful a struggle between earth and heaven--the world and the grave--passion and the rebuke of Providence--as attended the last hours of that unhappy man! There were moments in which the mild spirit of Christ won upon his evil mood 'tis true; but the picture was, in general, that of revenge so fierce, that the powers of hell alone could give it birth in a human heart. He had with him an infant of an age just, fitted to be taken from the breast. This child appeared to awaken the fiercest conflicting feelings; he both yearned over it and detested its sight, though hatred seemed most to prevail."

"This was horrible!" murmured the Doge.

"It was the more horrible, Herr Doge, that it should come from one who was justly condemned to the axe. He rejected the priests; he would have naught of any but me. My soul lothed the wretch--yet so few ever showed an interest in us--and it would have been cruel to desert a dying man! At the end, he placed the child in my care, furnishing more gold than was sufficient to rear it frugally to the age of manhood, and leaving other valuables which I have kept as proofs that might some day be useful. All I could learn of the infant's origin was simply this. It came from Italy, and of Italian parents; its mother died soon after its birth,"--a groan escaped the Doge--"its father still lived, and was the object of the criminal's implacable hatred, as its mother had been of his ardent love; its birth was noble, and it had been baptized in the bosom of the church by the name of Gaetano."

"It must be he!--it is--it must be my beloved son!--" exclaimed the Doge, unable to control himself any longer. He spread wide his arms, and Sigismund threw himself upon his bosom, though there still remained fearful apprehensions that all he heard was a dream. "Go on--go on--excellent Balthazar," added the Signor Grimaldi, drying his eyes, and struggling to command himself. "I shall have no peace until all is revealed to the last syllable of thy wonderful, thy glorious tale!"

"There remains but little more to say, Herr Doge. The fatal hour arrived, and the criminal was transported to the place where he was to give up his life. While seated in the chair in which he received the fatal blow, his spirit underwent infernal torments. I have reason to think that there were moments when he would gladly have made his peace with God. But the demons prevailed; he died in his sins! From the hour when he committed the little Gaetano to my keeping, I did not cease to entreat to be put in possession of the secret of the child's birth, but the sole answer I received was an order to appropriate the gold to my own uses, and to adopt the boy as my own. The sword was in my hand, and the signal to strike was given, when, for the last time, I asked the name of the infant's family and country, as a duty I could not neglect. 'He is thine--he is thine--' was the answer; 'tell me, Balthazar, is thy office hereditary, as is wont in these regions?' I was compelled, as ye know, to say it was. 'Then adopt the urchin; rear him to fatten on the blood of his fellows!' It was mockery to trifle with such a spirit. When his head fell, if still bad on its fierce features traces of the infernal triumph with which his spirit departed!"

"The monster was a just sacrifice to the laws of the canton!" exclaimed the single-minded bailiff. "Thou seest, Herr Melchior, that we do well in arming the hand of the executioner, in spite of all the sentiment of the weak-minded. Such a wretch was surely unworthy to live."

This burst of official felicitation from Peterchen, who rarely neglected an occasion to draw a conclusion favorable to the existing order of things, like most of those who reap their exclusive advantage, and to the prejudice of innovation, produced little attention; all present were too much absorbed in the facts related by Balthazar, to turn aside; to speak, or think, of other matters.

"What became of the boy?" demanded the worthy clavier, who had taken as deep an interest as the rest, in the progress of the narrative.

"I could not desert him, father; nor did I wish to. He came into my guardianship at a moment when God, to reprove our repinings at a lot that he had chosen to impose, had taken our own little Sigismund to heaven. I filled the place of the dead infant with my living charge; I gave to him the name of my own son, and I can say confidently, that I transferred to him the love I had borne my own issue; though time, and use, and a knowledge of the child's character, were perhaps necessary to complete the last. Marguerite never knew the deception, though a mother's instinct and tenderness took the alarm and raised suspicions. We have never spoken freely on this together, and like you, she now heareth the truth for the first time."

"'Twas a fearful mystery between God and my own heart!" murmured the woman; "I forbore to trouble it--Sigismund, or Gaetano, or whatever you will have his name, filled my affections, and I strove to be satisfied. The boy is dear to me, and ever will be, though you seat him on a throne; but Christine--the poor stricken Christine--is truly the child of my bosom!"

Sigismund went and knelt at the feet of her whom he had ever believed his mother, and earnestly begged her blessing and continued affection. The tears streamed from Marguerite's eyes, as she willingly bestowed the first, and promised never to withhold the last.

"Hast thou any of the trinkets or garments that were given thee with the child, or canst render an account of the place where they are still to be found?" demanded the Doge, whose whole mind was too deeply set on appeasing his doubts to listen to aught else.

"They are all here in the convent. The gold has been fairly committed to Sigismund, to form his equipment as a soldier. The child was kept apart, receiving such education as a learned priest could give till of an age to serve, and then I sent him to bear arms in Italy, which I knew to be the country of his birth, though I never knew to what Prince his allegiance was due. The time had now come when I thought it due to the youth to let him know the real nature of the tie between us; but I shrank from paining Marguerite and myself, and I even did his heart the credit to believe that he would rather belong to us, humble and despised though we be, than find himself a nameless outcast, without home, country, or parentage. It was necessary, however, to speak, and it was my purpose to reveal the truth, here at the convent, in the presence of Christine. For this reason, and to enable Sigismund to make inquiries for his family, the effects received from the unhappy criminal with the child were placed among his baggage secretly. They are, at this moment, on the mountain."

The venerable old prince trembled violently; for, with the intense feeling of one who dreaded that his dearest hopes might yet be disappointed, he feared, while he most wished, to consult these mute but veracious witnesses.

"Let them be produced!--let them be instantly produced and examined!" he whispered eagerly to those around him. Then turning slowly to the immovable Maso, he demanded--"And thou, man of falsehood and of blood! what dost thou reply to this clear and probable tale?"

Il Maledetto smiled, as if superior to a weakness that had blinded the others. The expression of his countenance was filled with that look of calm superiority which certainty gives to the well-informed over the doubting and deceived."

"I have to reply, Signore, and honored father," he coolly answered, "that Balthazar hath right cleverly related a tale that hath been ingeniously devised. That I am Bartolo, I repeat to thee, can be proved by a hundred living tongues in Italy.--Thou best knowest who Bartolo Contini is, Doge of Genoa.'

"He speaks the truth," returned the prince, dropping his head in disappointment. "Oh! Melchior, I have had but too sure proofs of what he intimates! I have long been certain that this wretched Bartolo is my son, though never before have I been cursed with his presence. Bad as I was taught to think him, my worst fears had not painted him as I now find the truth would warrant."

"Has there not been some fraud--art thou not the dupe of some conspiracy of which money has been the object?"

The Doge shook his head, in a way to prove that he could not possibly flatter himself with such a hope.

"Never: my offers of money have always been rejected."

"Why should I take the gold of my father?" added Il Maledetto; "my own skill and courage more than suffice for my wants."

The nature of the answer, and the composed demeanor of Maso, produced an embarrassing pause.

"Let the two stand forth and be confronted," said the puzzled clavier at length; "nature often reveals the truth when the uttermost powers of man are at fault--if either is the true child of the prince, we should find some resemblance to the father to support his claim."

The test, though of doubtful virtue, was eagerly adopted, for the truth had now become so involved, as to excite a keen interest in all present. The desire to explain the mystery was general, and the slightest means of attaining such an end became of a value proportionate to the difficulty of effecting the object. Sigismund and Maso were placed beneath the lamp, where its light was strongest, and every eye turned eagerly to their countenances, in order to discover, or to fancy it discovered, some of those secret signs by which the mysterious affinities of nature are to be traced. A more puzzling examination could not well have been essayed. There was proof to give the victory to each of the pretenders, if such a term may be used with propriety as it concerns the passive Sigismund, and much to defeat the claims of the latter. In the olive-colored tint, the dark, rich, rolling eye, and in stature, the advantage was altogether with Maso, whose outline of countenance and penetrating expression had also a resemblance to those of the Doge, so marked as to render it quite apparent to any who wished to find it. The habits of the mariner had probably diminished the likeness, but it was too obviously there to escape detection. That hardened and rude appearance, the consequence of exposure, which rendered it difficult to pronounce within ten years of his real age, contributed a little to conceal what might be termed the latent character of his countenance, but the features themselves were undeniably a rude copy of the more polished lineaments of the Prince.

The case was less clear as respects Sigismund. The advantage of ruddy and vigorous youth rendered him such a resemblance of the Doge--in the points where it existed--as we find between the aged and those portraits which have been painted in their younger and happier days. The bold outline was not unlike that of the noble features of the venerable Prince, but neither the eye, the hair, nor the complexion, had the hues of Italy.

"Thou seest," said Maso, tauntingly, when the disappointed clavier admitted the differences in the latter particulars, "This is an imposition that will not pass. I swear to you, as there is faith in man, and hope for the dying Christian, that so far as any know their parentage, I am the child of Gaetano Grimaldi, the present Doge of Genoa, and of no other man! May the saints desert me!--the blessed Mother of God be deaf to my prayers!--and all men hunt me with their curses, if I say aught in this but holy truth!"

The fearful energy with which Maso uttered this solemn appeal, and a certain sincerity that marked his manner, and perhaps we might even say his character, in spite of the dissolute recklessness of his principles, served greatly to weaken the growing opinion in favor of his competitor.

"And this noble youth?" asked the sorrowing Doge--"this generous and elevated boy, whom I have already held next to my heart, with so much of a father's joy--who and what is he?"

"Eccellenza, I wish to say nothing against the Signor Sigismondo. He is a gallant swimmer, and a staunch support in time of need. Be he Swiss, or Genoese, either country may be proud of him, but self-love teaches us all to take care of our own interests before those of another. It Would be far pleasanter to dwell in the Palazzo Grimaldi, on our warm and sunny gulf, honored and esteemed as the heir of a noble name, than to be cutting heads in Berne; and honest Balthazar does but follow his instinct, in seeking preferment for his son!"

Each eye now turned on the headsman, who quailed not under the scrutiny, but maintained the firm front of one conscious that he had done no wrong.

"I have not said that Sigismund is the child of any," he answered in his meek manner, but with a steadiness that won him credit with the listeners. "I have only said that he belongs not to me. No father need wish a worthier son, and heaven knows that I yield my own claims with a sorrow that it would be grievous to bear, did I not hope a better fortune for him than any which can come from a connexion with a race accursed. The likeness which is seen in Maso, and which Sigismund is thought to want, proves little, noble gentlemen and reverend monks; for all who have looked closely into these matters know that resemblances are as often found between the distant branches of the same family, as between those who are more nearly united. Sigismund is not of us, and none can see any trace of either my own or of Marguerite's family in his person or features."

Balthazar paused that there might be an examination of this fact, and, in truth, the most ingenious fancy could not have detected the least affinity in looks, between either of those whom he had so long thought his parents and the young soldier.

"Let the Doge of Genoa question his memory, and look farther than himself. Can he find no sleeping smile, no color of the hair, nor any other common point of appearance, between the youth and some of those whom he once knew and loved?"

The anxious prince turned eagerly towards Sigismund, and a gleam of joy lighted his face again, as he studied the young man's features.

"By San Francesco! Melchior, the honest Balthazar is right. My grandmother was a Venetian, and she had the fair hair of the boy--the eye too, is hers--and--oh!" bending his head aside and veiling his eyes with his hand, "I see the anxious gaze that was so constant in the sainted and injured Angiolina, after my greater wealth and power had tempted her kinsmen to force her to yield an unwilling hand!--Wretch! thou art not Bartolo; thy tale is a wicked deception, invented to shield thee from the punishment due to thy crime!"

"Admitting that I am not Bartolo, eccellenza, does the Signer Sigismondo claim to be he? Have you not assured yourself that a certain Bartolo Contini, a man whose life is passed in open hostility to the laws, is your child? Did you not employ your confidant and secretary to learn the facts? Did he not hear from the dying lips of a holy priest, who knew all the circumstances, that 'Bartolo Contini is the son of Gaetano Grimaldi'? Did not the confederate of your implacable enemy, Cristofero Serrani, swear the same to you? Have you not seen papers that were taken with your child to confirm it all, and did you not send this signet as a gage that Bartolo should not want your aid, in any strait that might occur in his wild manner of living, when you learned that he resolutely preferred remaining what he was, to becoming an image of sickly repentance and newly-assumed nobility, in your gorgeous palace on the Strada Balbi?"

The Doge again bowed his head in dismay, for all this he knew to be true beyond a shadow of hope.

"Here is some sad mistake," he said with bitter regret. "Thou hast received the child of some other bereaved parent, Balthazar; but, though I cannot hope to prove myself the natural father of Sigismund, he shall at least find me one in affection and good offices. If his life be not due to me, I owe him mine; the debt shall form a tie between us little short of that to which nature herself could give birth."

"Herr Doge," returned the earnest headsman, "let us not be too hasty. If there are strong facts in favor of the claims of Maso, there are many circumstances, also, in favor of those of Sigismund. To me, the history of the last is probably more clear than it can be to any other. The time; the country, the age of the child, the name, and the fearful revelations of the criminal, are all strong proofs in Sigismund's behalf, Here are the effects that were given me with the child; it is possible that they, too, may throw weight into his scale."

Balthazar had taken means to procure the package in question from among the luggage of Sigismund, and he now proceeded to expose its contents, while a breathless silence betrayed the interest with which the result was expected. He first laid upon the pavement of the chapel a collection of child's clothing. The articles were rich, and according to the fashions of the times; but they contained no positive proofs that could go to substantiate the origin of the wearer, except as they raised the probability of his having come of an elevated rank in life. As the different objects were placed upon the stones, Adelheid and Christine kneeled beside them, each too intently absorbed with the progress of the inquiry to bethink themselves of those forms which, in common, throw a restraint upon the manners of their sex. The latter appeared to forget her own sorrows, for a moment, in a new-born interest in her brother's fortunes while the ears of the former drank in each syllable that fell from the lips of the different speakers, with an avidity that her strong sympathy with the youth could alone give.

"Here is a case containing trinkets of value," added Balthazar. "The condemned man said they were taken through ignorance, and he was accustomed to suffer the child to amuse himself with them in the prison."

"These were my first offerings to my wife, in return for the gift she had made me of the precious babe," said the Doge, in such a smothered voice as we are apt to use when examining objects that recall the presence of the dead--"Blessed Angiolina! these jewels are so many tokens of thy pale but happy countenance; thou felt a mother's joy at that sacred moment, and could even smile on me!"

"And here is a talisman in sapphire, with many Eastern characters; I was told it had been an heirloom in the family of the child, and was put about his neck at the birth, by the hands of his own father."

"I ask no more--I ask no more! God be praised for this, the last and best of all his mercies!" cried the Prince, clasping his hands with devotion. "This jewel was worn by myself in infancy, and I placed it around the neck of the babe with my own hands, as thou sayest--I ask no more."

"And Bartolo Contini!" uttered Il Maledetto.

"Maso!" exclaimed a voice, which until then had been mute in the chapel. It was Adelheid who had spoken. Her hair had fallen in wild profusion over her shoulders, as she still knelt over the articles on the pavement, and her hands were clasped entreatingly, as if she deprecated the rude interruptions which had so often dashed the cup from their lips, as they were about to yield to the delight of believing Sigismund to be the child of the Prince of Genoa.

"Thou art another of a fond and weak sex, to swell the list of confiding spirits that have been betrayed by the selfishness and falsehood of men," answered the mocking mariner. "Go to, girl!--make thyself a nun; thy Sigismund is an impostor."

Adelheid, by a quick but decided interposition of her hand, prevented an impetuous movement of the young soldier, who would have struck his audacious rival to his feet. Without changing her kneeling attitude, she then spoke, modestly but with a firmness which generous sentiments enable women to assume even more readily than the stronger sex, when extraordinary occasions call for the sacrifice of that reserve in which her feebleness is ordinarily intrenched.

"I know not, Maso, in what manner thou hast learned the tie which connects me with Sigismund," she said; "but I have no longer any wish to conceal it. Be he the son of Balthazar, or be he the son of a prince, he has received my troth with the consent of my honored father, and our fortunes will shortly be one. There might be forwardness in a maiden thus openly avowing her preference for a youth; but here, with none to own him, oppressed with his long-endured wrongs, and assailed in his most sacred affections, Sigismund has a right to my voice. Let him belong to whom else he may, I speak by my venerable father's authority, when I say he belongs to us."

"Melchior, is this true?" cried the Doge.

"The girl's words are but an echo of what my heart feels," answered the baron, looking about him proudly, as if he would browbeat any who should presume to think that he had consented to corrupt the blood of Willading by the measure.

"I have watched thine eye, Maso, as one nearly interested in the truth," continued Adelheid, "and I now appeal to thee, as thou lovest thine own soul, to disburthen thyself! While thou may'st have told some truth, the jealous affection of a woman has revealed to me that thou hast kept back part. Speak, then, and relieve the soul of this venerable prince from torture,"

"And deliver my own body to the wheel! This may be well to the warm imagination of a love-sick girl, but we of the contraband have too much practice in men uselessly to throw away an advantage."

"Thou mayest have confidence in our faith. I have seen much of thee within the last few days, Maso, and I wish not to think thee capable of the bloody deed that hath been committed on the mountain, though I fear thy life is only too ungoverned; still I will not believe that the hero of the Leman can be the assassin of St. Bernard."

"When thy young dreams are over, fair one, and thou seest the world under its true colors, thou wilt know that the hearts of men come partly of Heaven and partly of Hell."

Maso laughed in his most reckless manner as he delivered this opinion.

"'Tis useless to deny that thou hast sympathies," continued the maiden steadily; "thou hast in secret more pleasure in serving than in injuring thy race. Thou canst not have been in such straits in company with the Signor Sigismondo, without imbibing some touch of his noble generosity. You have struggled together for our common good, you come of the same God, have the same manly courage, are equally stout of heart, strong of hand, and willing to do for others. Such a heart must have enough of noble and human impulses to cause you to love justice. Speak, then, and I pledge our sacred word, that thou shalt fare better for thy candor than by taking refuge in thy present fraud. Bethink thee, Maso, that the happiness of this aged man, of Sigismund himself, if thou wilt, for I blush not to say it--of a weak and affectionate girl, is in thy keeping. Give us truth holy; sacred truth, and we pardon the past."

Il Maledetto was moved by the beautiful earnestness of the speaker. Her ingenuous interest in the result, with the solemnity of her appeal shook his purpose.

"Thou know'st not what thou say'st, lady; thou ask'st my life," he answered, after pondering in a way to give a new impulse to the dying hopes of the Doge.

"Though there is no quality more sacred than justice," interposed the châtelain, who alone could speak with authority in the Valais; "it is fairly within the province of her servants to permit her to go unexpiated, in order that greater good may come of the sacrifice. If thou wilt prove aught that is of grave importance to the interests of the Prince of Genoa, Valais owes it to the love it bears his republic to requite the service."

Maso listened, at first, with a cold ear. He felt the distrust of one who had sufficient knowledge of the world to be acquainted with the thousand expedients that were resorted to by men, in order to justify their daily want of faith. He questioned the châtelain closely as to his meaning, nor was it until a late hour, and after long and weary explanations on both sides, that the parties came to an understanding.

On the part of those who, on this occasion, were the representatives of that high attribute of the Deity which among men is termed justice, it was sufficiently apparent that they understood its exercise with certain reservations that might be made at pleasure in favor of their own views; and, on the part of Maso, there was no attempt to conceal the suspicions he entertained to the last, that he might be a sufferer by lessening in any degree the strength of the defences by which he was at present shielded, as the son, real or fancied, of a person so powerful as the Prince of Genoa.

As usually happens when there is a mutual wish to avoid extremities, and when conflicting interests are managed with equal address, the negotiation terminated in a compromise. As the result will be shown in the regular course of the narrative, the reader is referred to the closing chapter for the explanation.

Chapter XXXI

"Speak, oh, speak!
And take me from the rack."

Young.

It will be remembered that three days were passed in the convent in that interval which occurred between the arrival of the travellers and those of the châtelain and the bailiff. The determination of admitting the claims of Sigismund, so frankly announced by Adelheid in the preceding chapter, was taken during this time. Separated from the world, and amid that magnificent solitude where the passions and the vulgar interests of life sank into corresponding insignificance as the majesty of God became hourly more visible, the baron had been gradually won upon to consent. Love for his child, aided by the fine moral and personal qualities of the young man himself, which here stood out in strong relief, like one of the stern piles of those Alps that now appeared to his eyes so much superior, in their eternal beds, to all the vine-clad hills and teeming valleys of the lower world, had been the immediate and efficient agents in producing this decision. It is not pretended that the Bernese made an easy conquest over his prejudices, which was in truth no other than a conquest over himself, he being, morally considered, little other than a collection of the narrow opinions and exclusive doctrines which it was then the fashion to believe necessary to high civilization. On the contrary, the struggle had been severe; nor is it probable that the gentle blandishments of Adelheid, the eloquent but silent appeals to his reason that were constantly made by Sigismund in his deportment, or the arguments of his old comrade, the Signor Grimaldi, who, with a philosophy that is more often made apparent in our friendships than in our own practice, dilated copiously on the wisdom of sacrificing a few worthless and antiquated opinions to the happiness of an only child, would have prevailed, had the Baron been in a situation less abstracted from the ordinary circumstances of his rank and habits, than that in which he had been so accidentally thrown. The pious clavier, too, who had obtained some claims to the confidence of the guests of the convent by his services, and by the risks he had run in their company, came to swell the number of Sigismund's friends. Of humble origin himself, and attached to the young man not only by his general merits, but by his conduct on the lake, he neglected no good occasion to work upon Melchior's mind, after he himself had become acquainted with the nature of the young man's hopes. As they paced the brown and naked rocks together, in the vicinity of the convent, the Augustine discoursed on the perishable nature of human hopes, and on the frailty of human opinions. He dwelt with pious fervor on the usefulness of recalling the thoughts from the turmoil of daily and contracted interests, to a wider view of the truths of existence. Pointing to the wild scene around them, he likened the confused masses of the mountains, their sterility, and their ruthless tempests, to the world with its want of happy fruits, its disorders, and its violence. Then directing the attention of his companion to the azure vault above them, which, seen at that elevation and in that pure atmosphere, resembled a benign canopy of the softest tints and colors, he made glowing appeals to the eternal and holy tranquillity of the state of being to which they were both fast hastening, and which had its type in the mysterious and imposing calm of that tranquil and inimitable void. He drew his moral in favor of a measured enjoyment of our advantages here, as well as of rendering love and justice to all who merited our esteem, and to the disadvantage of those iron prejudices which confine the best sentiments in the fetters of opinions founded in the ordinances and provisions of the violent and selfish.

It was after one of these interesting dialogues that Melchior de Willading, his heart softened and his soul touched with the hopes of heaven, listened with a more indulgent ear to the firm declaration of Adelheid, that unless she became the wife of Sigismund, her self-respect, no less than her affections, must compel her to pass her life unmarried. We shall not say that the maiden herself philosophized on premises as sublime as those of the good monk, for with her the warm impulses of the heart lay at the bottom of her resolution; but even she had the respectable support of reason to sustain her cause. The baron had that innate desire to perpetuate his own existence in that of his descendants, which appears to be a property of nature. Alarmed at a declaration which threatened annihilation to his line, while at the same time he was more than usually under the influence of his better feelings, he promised that if the charge of murder could be removed from Balthazar, he would no longer oppose the union. We should be giving the reader an opinion a little too favorable of the Herr von Willading, were we, to say that he did not repent having made this promise soon after it was uttered. He was in a state of mind that resembled the vanes of his own towers, which changed their direction with every fresh current of air, but he was by far, too honorable to think seriously of violating a faith that he had once fairly plighted. He had moments of unpleasant misgivings as to the wisdom and propriety of his promise, but they were of that species of regret, which is known to attend an unavoidable evil. If he had any expectations of being released from his pledge, they were bottomed on certain vague impressions that Balthazar would be found guilty; though the constant and earnest asseverations of Sigismund in favor of his father had greatly succeeded in shaking his faith on this point. Adelheid had stronger hopes than either; the fears of the young man himself preventing him from fully participating in her confidence, while her father shared her expectations on that tormenting principle, which causes us to dread the worst. When, therefore, the jewelry of Jacques Colis was found in the possession of Maso, and Balthazar was unanimously acquitted, not only from this circumstance, which went so conclusively to criminate another, but from the want of any other evidence against him than the fact of his being found in the bone-house instead of the Refuge, an accident that might well have happened to any other traveller in the storm, the baron resolutely prepared himself to redeem his pledge. It is scarcely necessary to add how much this honorable sentiment was strengthened by the unexpected declaration of the headsman concerning the birth of Sigismund. Notwithstanding the asseveration of Maso that the whole was an invention conceived to fervor the son of Balthazar, it was supported by proofs so substantial and palpable, to say nothing of the natural and veracious manner in which the tale was related, as to create a strong probability in the minds of the witnesses, that it might be true. Although it remained to be discovered who were the real parents of Sigismund, few now believed that he owed his existence to the headsman.

    A short summary of the facts may aid the reader in better understanding, the circumstances on which so much dénouement depends.

    It has been revealed in the course of the narrative that the Signor Grimaldi had wedded a lady younger than himself, whose affections were already in the possession of one that, in moral qualities, was unworthy of her love, but who in other respects was perhaps better suited to become her husband, than the powerful noble to whom her family had given her hand. The birth of their son was soon followed by the death of the mother, and the abduction of the child. Years had passed, when the Signor Grimaldi was first apprized of the existence of the latter. He had received this important information at a moment when the authorities of Genoa were most active in pursuing those who had long and desperately trifled with the laws, and the avowed motive for the revelation was an appeal to his natural affection in behalf of a son, who was likely to become the victim of his practices. The recovery of a child under such circumstances was a blow severer than his loss, and it will readily be supposed that the truth of the pretension of Maso, who then went by the name of Bartolomeo Contini, was admitted with the greatest caution. Reference had been made by the friends of the smuggler to a dying monk, whose character was above suspicion, and who corroborated, with his latest breath, the statement of Maso, by affirming before God and the saints that he knew him, so far as man could know a fact like this, to be the son of the Signer Grimaldi; This grave testimony, given under circumstances of such solemnity, and supported by the production of important papers that had been stolen with the child, removed the suspicions of the Doge. He secretly interposed his interest to save the criminal, though, after a fruitless attempt to effect a reformation of his habits by means of confidential agents, he had never consented to see him.

Such then was the nature of the conflicting statements. While hope and the pure delight of finding himself the father of a son like Sigismund, caused the aged prince to cling to the claims of the young soldier with fond pertinacity, his cooler and more deliberate judgment had already been formed in favor of another. In the long private examination which succeeded the scene in the chapel, Maso had gradually drawn more into himself, becoming vague and mysterious, until he succeeded in exciting a most painful state of doubt and expectation in all who witnessed his deportment. Profiting by this advantage, he suddenly changed his tactics. He promised revelations of importance, on the condition that he should first be placed in security within the frontiers of Piedmont. The prudent châtelain soon saw that the case was getting to be one in which Justice was expected to be blind in the more politic signification of the term. He, therefore, drew off his loquacious coadjutor, the bailiff, in a way to leave the settlement of the affair to the feelings and wishes of the Doge. The latter, by the aid of Melchior and Sigismund, soon effected an understanding, in which the conditions of the mariner were admitted; when the party separated for the night. Il Maledetto, on whom weighed the entire load of Jacques Colis' murder, was again committed to his temporary prison, while Balthazar, Pippo, and Conrad, were permitted to go at large, as having successfully passed the ordeal of examination.

Day dawned upon the Col long ere the shades of night had deserted the valley of the Rhone. All in the convent were in motion before the appearance of the sun, it being generally understood that the event which had so much disturbed the order of its peaceful inmates' lives, was to be brought finally to a close, and that their duties were about to return into the customary channels. Orisons are constantly ascending to heaven from the pass of St. Bernard, but, on the present occasion, the stir in and about the chapel, the manner in which the good canons hurried to and fro through the long corridors, and the general air of excitement, proclaimed that the offices of the matins possessed more than the usual interest of the regular daily devotion.

The hour was still early when all on the pass assembled in the place of worship. The body of Jacques Colis had been removed to a side chapel, where, covered with a pall, it awaited the mass for the dead. Two large church candles stood lighted on the steps of the great altar, and the spectators, including Pierre and the muleteers, the servants of the convent, and others of every rank and age, were drawn up in double files in its front. Among the silent spectators appeared Balthazar and his wife, Maso, in truth a prisoner, but with the air of a liberated man, the pilgrim, and Pippo. The good prior was present in his robes, with all of his community. During the moments of suspense which preceded the rites, he discoursed civilly with the châtelain and the bailiff, both of whom returned his courtesies with interest, and in the manner in which it becomes the dignified and honored to respect appearances in the presence of their inferiors. Still the demeanor of most was feverish and excited, as if the occasion were one of compelled gaiety, into which unwelcome and extraordinary circumstances of alloy had thrust themselves unbidden.

On the opening of the door a little procession entered, headed by the clavier. Melchior de Willading led his daughter, Sigismund came next, followed by Marguerite and Christine, and the venerable Doge brought up the rear. Simple as was this wedding train, it was imposing from the dignity of the principal actors, and from the evidences of deep feeling with which all in it advanced to the altar. Sigismund was firm and self-possessed. Still his carriage was lofty and proud, as if he felt that a cloud still hung over that portion of his history to which the world attached so much importance, and he had fallen back on his character and principles for support. Adelheid had lately been so much the subject of strong emotions, that she presented herself before the priest with less trepidation than was usual for a maiden;

but the fixed regard, the colorless cheek, and an air of profound reverence, announced the depth and solemn character of the feelings with which she was prepared to take the vows.

The marriage rites were celebrated by the good clavier, who, not content with persuading the baron to make this sacrifice of his prejudices, had asked permission to finish the work he had so happily commenced, by pronouncing the nuptial benediction. Melchior de Willading listened to the short ceremony with silent self-approval. He felt disposed at that instant to believe he had wisely sacrificed the interests of the world to the right, a sentiment that was a little quickened by the uncertainty which still hung over the origin of his new son, who might yet prove to be all that he could hope, as well as by the momentary satisfaction he found in manifesting his independence by bestowing the hand of his daughter upon one whose merit was so much better ascertained than his birth. In this manner do the best deceive themselves, yielding frequently to motives that would not support investigation when they believe themselves the strongest in the right. The good-natured clavier had observed the wavering and uncertain character of the baron's decision, and he had been induced to urge his particular request to be the officiating priest by a secret apprehension that, descended again into the scenes of the world, the relenting father might become, like most other parents of these nether regions, more disposed to consult the temporal advancement than the true happiness of his child.

As one of the parties was a Protestant, no mass was said, an omission, however, that in no degree impaired the legal character of the engagement. Adelheid plighted her unvarying love and fidelity with maiden modesty, but with the steadiness of a woman whose affections and principles were superior to the little weaknesses which, on such occasions, are most apt to unsettle those who have the least of either of these great distinctive essentials of the sex. The vows to cherish and protect were uttered by Sigismund in deep manly sincerity, for, at that moment, he felt as if a life of devotion to her happiness would scarcely requite her single-minded, feminine, and unvarying truth.

"May God bless thee, dearest," murmured old Melchior, as, bending over his kneeling child, he struggled to keep down a heart which appeared disposed to mount into his throat, in spite of its master's inclinations; "bless thee--bless thee, love, now and for ever. Providence has dealt sternly with thy brothers and sisters, but in leaving thee it has still left me rich in offspring. Here is our good friend, Gaetano, too--his fortune has been still harder--but we will hope--we will hope. And thou, Sigismund, now that

Balthazar hath disowned thee, thou must accept such a father as Heaven sends. All accidents of early life are forgotten, and Willading, like my old heart, hath gotten a new owner and a new lord!"

The young man exchanged embraces with the baron, whose character he knew to be kind in the main, and for whom he felt the regard which was natural to his present situation. He then turned, with a hesitating eye, to the Signor Grimaldi. The Doge succeeded his friend in paying the compliments of affection to the bride, and had just released Adelheid with a warm paternal kiss.

"I pray Maria and her holy Son in thy behalf!" said the venerable Prince with dignity. "Thou enterest on new and serious duties, child, but the spirit and purity of an angel, a meekness that does not depress, and a character whose force rather relieves than injures the softness of thy sex, can temper the ills of this fickle world, and thou may'st justly hope to see a fair portion of that felicity which thy young imagination pictures in such golden colors. And thou," he added, turning to meet the embrace of Sigismund, "whoever thou art by the first disposition of Providence, thou art now rightfully dear to me. The husband of Melchior de Willading's daughter would ever have a claim upon his most ancient and dearest friend, but we are united by a tie that has the interest of a singular and solemn mystery. My reason tells me that I am punished for much early and wanton pride and wilfulness, in being the parent of a child that few men in any condition of life could wish to claim, while my heart would fain flatter me with being the father of a son of whom an emperor alight be proud! Thou art, and thou art not, of my blood. Without these proofs of Maso's, and the testimony of the dying monk, I should proclaim thee to be the latter without hesitation; but be thou what thou may'st by birth, thou art entirely and without alloy of my love. Be tender of this fragile flower that Providence hath put under thy protection, Sigismund; cherish it as thou valuest thine own soul; the generous and confiding love of a virtuous woman is always a support, frequently a triumphant stay, to the tottering principles of man. Oh! had it pleased God earlier to have given me Angiolina, how different might have been our lives! This dark uncertainty would not now hang over the most precious of human affections, and my closing hour would be blessed. Heaven and its saints preserve ye both, my children, and preserve ye long in your present innocence and affection!"

The venerable Doge ceased. The effort which had enabled him to speak gave way, and he turned aside that he might weep in the decent reserve that became his station and years.

Until now Marguerite had been silent, watching the countenances, and drinking in with avidity the words, of the different speakers. It was now her turn. Sigismund knelt at her feet, pressing her hands to his lips in a manner to show that her high, though stern character, had left deep traces in his recollection. Releasing herself from his convulsed grasp, for just then the young man felt intensely the violence of severing those early ties which, in his case, had perhaps something of wild romance from their secret nature, she parted the curls on his ample brow, and stood gazing long at his face, studying each lineament to its minutest shade.

"No," she said mournfully shaking her head, "truly thou art not of us, and God hath dealt mercifully in taking away the innocent little creature whose place thou hast so long innocently usurped. Thou wert dear to me, Sigismund--very dear--for I thought thee under the curse of my race; do not hate me, if I say my heart is now in the grave of--"

"Mother!" exclaimed the young man reproachfully.

"Well I am still thy mother," answered Marguerite, smiling, though painfully; "thou art a noble boy, and no change of fortune can ever alter thy soul. 'Tis a cruel parting, Balthazar and I know not, after all, that thou didst well to deceive me; for I have had as much grief as joy in the youth--grief, bitter grief, that one like him should be condemned to live under the curse of our race--but it is ended now--he is not of us--no, he is no longer of us!"

This was uttered so plaintively that Sigismund bent his face to his hands and sobbed aloud. "Now that the happy and proud weep, 'tis time that the wretched dried their tears," added the wife of Balthazar, looking about her with a sad mixture of agony and pride struggling in her countenance: for, in spite of her professions, it was plain that she yielded her claim on the noble youth with deep yearnings and an intense agony of spirit. "We have one consolation, at least, Christine--all that are not of our blood will not despise us now! Am I right, Sigismund--thou too wilt not torn upon us with the world, and hate those whom thou once loved?"

"Mother, mother, for the sake of the Holy Virgin, do not harrow my soul!"

"I will not distrust thee, dear; thou didst not drink at my breast, but thou hast taken in too many lessons of the truth from my lips to despise us--and yet thou art not of us; thou mayest possibly prove a Prince's son, and the world so hardens the heart--and they who have been sorely pressed upon become suspicious--"

"For the love of God, cease, mother, or thou wilt break my heart!"

"Come hither, Christine. Sigismund, this maiden goes with thy wife: we have the greatest confidence in the truth and principles of her thou hast wedded, for she has been tried and not found wanting. Be tender to the child; she was once thy sister, and then thou used to love her."

"Mother--thou wilt make me curse the hour I was born!"

Marguerite, while she could not overcome the cold distrust which habit had interwoven with all her opinions, felt that she was cruel, and she said no more. Stooping, she kissed the cold forehead of the young man, gave a warm embrace to her daughter, over whom she prayed fervently for a minute, and then placed the insensible girl into the open arms of Adelheid. The awful workings of nature were subdued by a superhuman will, and she turned slowly towards the silent, respectful crowd, who had scarcely breathed during this exhibition of her noble character.

"Doth any here," she sternly asked, "suspect the innocence of Balthazar?"

"None, good woman, none!" returned the bailiff, wiping his eyes; "go in peace to thy home, o' Heaven's sake, and God be with thee!"

"He stands acquitted before God and man!" added the more dignified châtelain.

Marguerite motioned for Balthazar to precede her, and she prepared to quit the chapel. On the threshold she turned and cast a lingering look at Sigismund and Christine. The two latter were weeping in each other's arms, and the soul of Marguerite yearned to mingle her tears with those she loved so well. But, stern in her resolutions, she stayed the torrent of feeling which would have been so terrible in its violence had it broken loose, and followed her husband, with a dry and glowing eye. They descended the mountain with a vacuum in their hearts which taught even this persecuted pair, that there are griefs in nature that surpass all the artificial woes of life.

The scene just related did not fail to disturb the spectators. Maso dashed his hand across his eyes, and seemed touched with a stronger working of sympathy than it accorded with his present policy to show, while both Conrad and Pippo did credit to their humanity, by fairly shedding tears. The latter, indeed, showed manifestations of a sensibility that is not altogether incompatible with ordinary recklessness and looseness of principle. He even begged leave to kiss the hand of the bride, wishing her joy with fervor, as one who had gone through great danger in her company. The whole party then separated with an exchange of cordial good feeling which proves that, however much men may be disposed to jostle and discompose their fellows in the great highway of life, nature has infused into their composition some great redeeming qualities to make us regret the abuses by which they have been so much perverted.

On quitting the chapel, the whole of the travellers made their dispositions to depart. The bailiff and the châtelain went down towards the Rhone, as well satisfied with themselves as if they had discharged their trust with fidelity by committing Maso to prison, and discoursing as they rode along on the singular chances which had brought a son of the Doge of Genoa before them, in a condition so questionable. The good Augustines helped the travellers who were destined for the other descent into their saddles, and acquitted themselves of the last act of hospitality by following the footsteps of the mules, with wishes for their safe arrival at Aoste.

The path across the Col has been already described. It winds along the margin of the little lake, passing the site of the ancient temple of Jupiter at the distance of a few hundred yards from the convent. Sweeping past the northern extremity of the little basin, where it crosses the frontiers of Piedmont, it cuts the ragged wall of rock, and, after winding *en corniche* for a short distance by the edge of a fearful ravine, it plunges at once towards the plains of Italy.

As there was a desire to have no unnecessary witnesses of Maso's promised revelations, Conrad and Pippo had been advised to quit the mountain before the rest of the party, and the muleteers were requested to keep a little in the rear. At the point where the path leaves the lake, the whole dismounted, Pierre going ahead with the beasts, with a view to make the first precipitous pitch from the Col on foot. Maso now took the lead. When he reached the spot where the convent is last in view, he stopped and turned to gaze at the venerable and storm-beaten pile.

"Thou hesitated," observed the Baron de Willading, who suspected an intention to escape.

"Signore; the look at even a stone is a melancholy office, when it is known to be the last. I have often climbed to the Col, but I shall never dare do it again; for, though the honorable and worthy châtelain, and the most worthy bailiff, are willing to pay their homage to a Doge of Genoa in his own person, they may be less tender of his honor when he is absent. Addio, caro San Bernardo! Like me, thou art solitary and weather-beaten, and like me, though rude of aspect, thou hast thy uses. We are both beacons--thou to tell the traveller where to seek safety, and I to warn him where danger is to be avoided."

There is a dignity in manly suffering, that commands our sympathies. All who heard this apostrophe to the abode of the Augustines were struck with its simplicity and its moral. They followed the speaker in silence, however, to the point where the path makes its first sudden descent. The spot was favorable to the purpose of Il Maledetto. Though still on the level of the lake, the convent, the Col, and all it contained, with the exception of a short line of its stony path, were shut from their view, by the barrier of intervening rock. The ravine lay beneath, ragged, ferruginous, and riven into a hundred faces by the eternal action of the seasons. All above, beneath, and around, was naked, and chaotic as the elements of the globe before they received the order-giving touch of the Creator. The imagination could scarce picture a scene of greater solitude and desolation.

"Signore," said Maso, respectfully raising his cap, and speaking with calmness, "this confusion of nature resembles my own character. Here everything is torn, sterile, and wild; but patience, charity, and generous love, have been able to change even this rocky height into an abode for those who live for the good of others. There is none so worthless that use may not be made of him. We are types of the earth our mother; useless, and savage, or repaying the labor, that we receive, as we are treated like men, or hunted like beasts. If the great, and the powerful, and the honored, would become the friends and monitors of the weak and ignorant, instead of remaining so many watch-dogs to snarl at and bite all that they fear may encroach on their privileges, raising the cry of the wolf each time that they hear the wail of the timid and bleating lamb, the fairest works of God would not be so often defaced. I have lived, and it is probable that I shall die an outlaw; but the severest pangs I ever know come from the the mockery which accuses my nature of abuses that are the fruits of your own injustice. That stone," kicking a bit of rock from the path into the ravine beneath, "is as much master of its direction after my foot has set its mass in motion, as the poor untaught being who is thrown upon the world, despised, unaided, suspected, and condemned even before he has sinned, has the command of his own course. My mother was fain and good. She wanted only the power to withstand the arts of one, who, honored in the opinions of all around her, undermined her virtue. He was great, noble, and powerful; while she hath little beside her beauty and her weakness. Signori,--the odds against toward Aoste. Nettuno was at his heels. It was evident that he endeavored to outstrip Pippo and Conrad, who were trudging ahead by the more beaten road. In a few minutes he turned the brow of a beetling rock, and was lost to view.

This was the last that was known of Il Maledetto. At Genoa, the Doge secretly received the confirmation of all that he had heard, and Sigismund was legally placed in possession of his birth-right. The latter made many generous but useless efforts to discover and to reclaim his brother. With a delicacy that could hardly be expected, the outlaw had withdrawn from a scene which he now felt to be unsuited to his habits, and he never permitted the veil to be withdrawn from the place of his retreat.

The only consolation that his relatives ever obtained, arose from an event which brought Pippo under the condemnation of the law. Before his execution, the buffoon confessed that Jacques Colis fell by the hands of Conrad and himself, and that, ignorant of Maso's expedient on his own account, they had made use of Nettuno to convey the plundered jewelry undetected across the frontiers of Piedmont.

her were too much. I was the punishment of her fault. I came into a world then, in which every man despised me before I had done any act to deserve its scorn,"

"Nay, this is pushing opinions to extremes!" interrupted the Signor Grimaldi, who had scarce breathed, in his eagerness to catch the syllables as they came from the other's tongue.

"We began, Signori, as we have ended; distrustful, and struggling to see which could do the other the most harm. A reverend and holy monk, who knew my history, would have filled a soul with heaven that the wrongs of the world had already driven to, the verge of hell. The experiment failed. Homily and precept," Maso smiled bitterly as he continued, "are but indifferent weapons to fight with against hourly wrongs; instead of becoming a cardinal and the counsellor of the head of the church, I am the man ye see. Signor Grimaldi, the monk who gave me his care was Father Girolamo. He told the truth to thy secretary, for I am the son of poor Annunziata Altieri, who was once thought worthy to attract thy passing notice. The deception of calling myself another of thy children was practised for my own security. The means were offered by an accidental confederacy with one of the instruments of thy formidable enemy and cousin, who furnished the papers that had been taken with the little Gaetano. The truth of what I say shall be delivered to you at Genoa. As for the Signor Sigismondo, it is time we ceased to be rivals. We are brothers, with this difference in our fortunes, that he comes of wedlock, and I of an unexpiated, and almost an unrepented, crime!"

A common cry, in which regret, joy, and surprise were wildly mingled, interrupted the speaker. Adelheid threw herself into her husband's arms, and the pale and conscience-stricken Doge stood with extended arms, an image of contrition, delight, and shame. His friends pressed around him with consolation on their tongues, and the blandishments of affection in their manner, for the regrets of the great rarely pass away unheeded, like the moans of the low.

"Let me have air!" exclaimed the prince; "give me air or I suffocate! Where is the child of Annunziata?--I will at least atone to him for the wrong done his mother!"

It was too late. The victim of another's fault had cast himself over the edge of the precipice with reckless hardihood, and he was already beyond the reach of the voice, in his swift descent, by a shorter but dangerous path,